an ELIXIR for WANDERLUST

an ELIXIR for WANDERLUST

ALISTAIR REEVES

All rights reserved. No part of this publication may be reproduced, stored in a retrieval system, or transmitted in any form or by any means electronic, mechanical, photocopying, recording, or otherwise without prior written permission from Podium Publishing.

This is a work of fiction. Names, characters, places, and incidents are either products of the author's imagination or used fictitiously. Any resemblance to actual events, locales, or persons, living, dead, or undead, is entirely coincidental.

Copyright © 2026 by Alistair Reeves

Cover design by Alistair Reeves

ISBN: 978-1-0394-7595-3

Published in 2026 by Podium Publishing
www.podiumentertainment.com

To all the wanderers

CONTENT WARNING

A particular note for my trans readers: The character of Kessian uses language for his anatomy and participates in sexual acts that others might find dysphoric. I understand this can be difficult, in particular while trans representation remains a small proportion of queer literature. Please take care of yourselves, and may the future hold such a trove of trans representation that avoiding works that trigger our dysphoria no longer feels like choosing between reading or not reading at all.

Beyond this, please find below a list of potentially triggering content contained within *An Elixir for Wanderlust*. Though I've tried my best to include triggers I know, this list may not be exhaustive, so please use your discretion while reading.

This book contains: drowning, multiple cases of family bereavement, references to homophobia, transphobia and ableism, supernatural horror elements, abusive/neglectful family dynamics, and coercion via magical truth serum.

an ELIXIR for WANDERLUST

CHAPTER 1

I said I'd sooner die than go back to Shearwater, but death forced me to return anyway.

It had been nine years since I'd last driven the curving country roads covered in ivy arches and high hedgerows. Old cottages hunkered in their overgrown gardens, kitschy statues of fairies and gnomes peeking out of flower beds. I passed a sign that raised all the hair on my arms.

Shearwater Spring.
Take a magical step through time.

I stopped my caravan, Lunaris, in the church car park. A black canopy of umbrellas loitered on the stairs leading into the funeral service, a queue of people offering condolences and prayers to the family. My family.

I couldn't bring my umbrella. It was designed like a sunflower. I'd look as though I were *cheerful* to attend my grandfather's funeral.

"Right. Just go. Say hi. Pay my respects. Leave. That's it."

As if to soothe me, the seat warmer turned on and the old radio sputtered out an acoustic version of a song Grandad used to play on every trip to the seaside.

There's a place where the sun shines warm all day
and we're together, oh, together
with all the time in the world

I patted the dashboard. Lunaris couldn't quite give me a hug, but this was the next best thing.

Before I left, I opened the cupboard under the sink, dug through the back for a bottle of whiskey, poured myself a generous portion, necked it, then braved the weather.

Rain spattered the suit I'd had fitted for the occasion. Grandad deserved my respects, and of all the passive-aggressive comments I'd receive today, I refused to let my clothes be one. Lunaris waved her windshield wipers to say, *Goodbye and good luck.*

Searching the crowd, I experienced the surreal, temporal crisis of seeing faces both familiar and unrecognizable. I'd come here to say goodbye, but it was saying hello that had me biting my nails.

My cousin Amelia stood a little apart from the others in a serene black suit interrupted by a loudly purple tie. When I'd left, she'd had the oversized hands and feet of an adolescent puppy and ears that earned her the nickname "Fins." She'd grown into both. She was my height, smoking a cigarette on the path leading up to the church.

Back when I'd known her, she'd held that lowly spot in the family hierarchy reserved for the sin of never tolerating anyone's bullshit. Amelia wasn't rude or blunt. (That title was mine.) She just had boundaries. A criminal offense in a family like ours.

As my fellow black sheep, she was the best bridge to my re-introduction.

"Hey."

"Well, you're not the ghost I expected to see here today," she said, letting me under her umbrella.

"Figured I should say goodbye."

"Brave man." She cocked her head, looking me over. "I like the mustache."

"Thanks. I like your tie."

"Aunt Lettie already gave it the look. You know the one." She performed a perfect imitation of our auntie's sneer, complete with the up-and-down eyes that catalogued your every sin and faxed them straight to God.

"Can't wait to hear what she has to say about my mustache, then."

"You know she won't miss an opportunity to imply Grandad might have lasted a few years longer if you'd stuck around."

Grandad and everyone else had only lasted this long because I'd left.

"Cigarette?" She offered me the pack.

"Don't smoke."

"Good boy."

"I'm older than you."

"By what? Six months?" She scoffed.

My mother, accepting condolences from a stooped gentleman, broke eye contact with him to glare across the lawn at me. My sibling, Fae, followed her gaze. Their face registered shock at the sight of me before they gave a tentative wave.

"That's my cue."

Amelia put out her cigarette with a black stiletto. "I'll join you."

"For emotional support?"

"For entertainment."

In my head, I'd practiced a long speech about how much I'd missed them. (I didn't. Not in a malicious way, but I'd been on my own so long, I'd forgotten how to miss anyone.) Compliments I could employ to break the ice. (Not my specialty; even white lies sounded fake in my mouth.) And memories to reminisce over. (Risky if no one else remembered, or if I'd remembered wrong.)

All I could say when faced with my mother was exactly what I'd said to Amelia. "Hey."

Her face split into an over-bright, artificial smile, and she threw her arms around me. "Oh, Tal! You're home. We didn't know if you'd come. It's been so long. How long has it been?"

"Since Laurelie died, so nine years," I said.

She faltered long enough for me to know I'd said something wrong. I did that. I didn't know how to pad my answers in soft half-truths. I forgot we weren't supposed to talk about death directly, even at a funeral, even when it was so long ago. Conversations always felt like minefields in which everyone except me had been given a map of where to step, and where not to.

Fae winced.

Mum recovered. "That long already? Time just flies. You'll come to dinner after the wake, of course?"

"I really shouldn't stay long," I said.

"Oh, but it will only be another hour or two. Surely nothing terrible will happen."

Terrible things followed me and did not offer extensions on curfew, but I said, "Sure, we'll see."

She nodded as if that settled it. "Then go in, go in. Sit at the front with us."

As I passed, Fae grabbed my arm. "Hey. Missed you."

I struggled with a smile. "Missed you, too."

I walked through the church doors, into the cocoon of quiet that made all holy places a little creepy. I waited just inside for Amelia, who hugged my family members before joining me.

"That wasn't so bad," she said.

"She's furious with me," I countered.

I was not terribly good at reading people. It took a while to learn their tells, particularly with people like my mum, who did her best to always be bright and chipper. Even nine years later, her tells were the same.

In front of the altar was the coffin. Closed, mercifully closed, and covered with lilies and alstroemeria. A portrait had been placed in the center, but it was from a long time ago, when Grandad had been around my age, and it occurred to me that I didn't know what he looked like now, before he'd died, which made the closed casket seem less a mercy in spite of my fear of seeing his corpse.

"Ah, my eyes must be going, but Marlowe, isn't that our Taliesin?"

"It's not your eyes, love."

I looked over to see my aunt waving to me. "Oh, Taliesin! Tal! Come sit with your aunt Lettie."

"Notice they didn't invite me, their own daughter, but I'll be coming anyway," said Amelia.

I was grateful. Aunt Lettie was the sort who could never get warm and insisted everyone bake in a house heated several degrees above comfortable, or she'd catch her death. I never knew if she always looked angry because she was, or because she painted her eyebrows that way. Today she wore a black fur coat so large that, with her slim legs sticking out the bottom, she looked like an ostrich.

Uncle Marlowe had adopted the same posture he adopted in the armchair from which he watched nature documentaries, so that he seemed transported into the pew from his sitting room. Slouched back, hands laced around his belly, and a slight pout to his lip.

"How are you keeping now?" he asked.

"Given the circumstances, dreadful," I said.

"Hell, join the club."

"Marlowe!" Aunt Lettie gave his arm a slap for cursing in church. "So you've heard about your grandfather."

"That's why I'm here."

"Such a surprise. Oh, he was old, of course, but he seemed well enough. Your mum has been so busy with the funeral arrangements, bless her heart. I don't know what we'd do without her. In my grief, I was no help, of course. Found him, we did. Collapsed in the house. It would have done her such good if you'd been here. I understand, of course, but would it kill you to visit more?"

Amelia made eye contact as if to say, *I told you so.* I'd always liked Marlowe and tolerated Lettie, who could make you feel guilty for failing to blow out all the candles on your own birthday cake.

Marlowe interrupted Lettie's ramble. "Still have that amulet I gave you?"

I flicked the coin hanging from my left ear. "Of course."

He nodded with gruff satisfaction. "Good."

The pews filled, and eventually a priest took to the pulpit to start the eulogy.

"We are all here today to say goodbye to Edwin Ashborne, but goodbyes even at his age are bittersweet, so let us remember him, first. Edwin was generous, a pillar of kindness within our community who could never be too put upon to help a stranger—but of course, nothing could quite match his devotion to his family."

He began to list the names of those surviving family members, and I had the harrowing thought he might not mention me. After all, I'd been gone for nine years. Did I really count as family any longer?

He mentioned how Grandad loved his games of backgammon with Marlowe, and Amelia made Sunday roasts better than he did. Down the line of grandchildren he went, my heart bracing for the absence of my own name.

The priest said, "And lastly, Taliesin Ashborne, to whom Edwin devoted nine years trying to make this place home again; he hoped one day it would be."

A few people whispered. Some even turned in their seats to search the crowd for the long-estranged grandchild.

I bowed my head and didn't meet their eyes.

Instead of relief that my name had not been forgotten, I felt a bitter ache. I could never call anyplace home. Not for long. And especially not here.

Once the eulogy ended, a few family members gave their own tearful speeches and goodbyes. It ended with a song—the same one Lunaris played to comfort me. As pallbearers rose to carry the casket out to the graveyard, we filed out in a somber procession after them. A cold drizzle wept through my suit.

At the freshly dug grave, the pallbearers set the casket onto the device that would lower it down. It reminded me of a gurney. The priest said a prayer as the casket slowly sank beneath the earth, and that's when everyone began to cry. My family and other mourners dropped flowers and mementos into the hole. I hadn't brought anything, and once again felt the gulf between me and this place, these people, more keenly than I felt any grief.

I wanted to feel sad. I was *theoretically* sad. But none of it felt particularly real, and the more I felt guilty for my inability to shed a single tear, the closer I got to crying out of frustration more than anything. I'd said goodbye a long, long time ago. It had been harder the first time.

While I stood there stiffly, a witch with an osprey familiar came up next to me and laid a heavy hand on my shoulder.

As a general rule, I didn't like being touched. There were exceptions, but this stranger was not one. He had watery blue eyes and the broad build of a rugby player who'd gotten old.

"He talked about you nonstop. He would have been happy you came," he said.

"Do I know you?"

The osprey shuffled to the shoulder closest to me, and I didn't appreciate the proximity to its hooked beak. The man said, "There will be time for introductions later, but I thought I'd give you this to pay your respects."

From his other hand he extended a single white lily. I took it more to disengage from him than out of gratitude.

The open grave had an awful gravity to it. I stood at its edge and wondered what I should say, if anything. There was simultaneously too much, and nothing at all worth saying. He couldn't hear me now, nor take the last nine years back.

I dropped the lily and said the one word I said over and over in my life on the road. "Goodbye."

As I headed back to Lunaris so I could drive to the wake, I caught a flickering shadow out of the corner of my eye, but when I turned to search the trees, there was nothing there.

CHAPTER 2

A shroud of fog skirted the three-story house my grandad had converted into Shearwater Spa.

I'd hoped the wake would be held at a pub or the local community center, but I could never be so lucky. The Victorian manor's steeply pointed lintels and roof ridge decorations gave the impression of teeth, the paired windows like many sets of eyes. Its door was newly painted sage green.

"It used to be cardamon," I said as I parked Lunaris in the farthest bay available, halfway in a hedge.

She unbuckled my seat belt for me in quiet encouragement.

I got out. The rain had inconveniently stopped, so I could hear the spring. Its trickling waters dripped into my ears. A poisonous sound. I hurried inside after a couple of mourners.

The large sitting rooms of the main level had been converted into dining areas for patrons staying the night, and now featured buffet tables laden with crudites and finger sandwiches. Seeing no one I recognized, I went there to gather a plate just to give my hands something to do.

"I'm so glad you're here."

I jumped, turning to find Fae behind me. "You may be the only one who feels that way. Mum wanted to strangle me."

"That's not true. Well, not entirely. It's just . . . hard, you know? No one's fault, just hard."

Mum *definitely* viewed it as my fault. I shrugged it off rather than argue. "How are you holding up?"

"I'm fine. Did you get my letter? I'm going by Fae now. Trying they/them pronouns on for size."

It had been welcome news when I'd heard. Having another queer family member hadn't been on my bingo card. "I did get that one. I'm happy for you."

A frown line appeared between their brows. "You could reply to my letters from time to time, you know?"

I happened to take a bite of a finger sandwich. It had gone soggy, and the texture made me gag. The look of disgust made Fae wince. "Or not."

Before I could find the words to explain, the man with the osprey from earlier leaned in. "Taliesin Ashborne, I was hoping I could have a word."

Fae's expression darkened at the sight of him. "I was just going," they said, but leaned in to whisper in my ear as they passed. "Find me later? There's something else I need to tell you."

I nodded. The man fed a piece of smoked salmon to his osprey familiar. The sound of fish sliding wetly down its gullet made my gorge rise. I gently set my tray of mostly uneaten crudites aside. "Do I know you?"

"No, unfortunately not. You were young when you left Shearwater, so we weren't acquainted. I'm Westley Warwick. I knew your grandfather quite well, you see. We were business partners."

I didn't know my grandfather had any business partners. I recalled him running himself ragged to run the spa on his own. It had not been fruitful back then, the magic all but gone, and with it the tourism keeping our lives afloat.

As if Warwick could read my thoughts, he said, "Yes, it wasn't much of a business back then, but we did restore it to its former glory, as I'm sure you've heard. I wondered if you had any interest in returning more permanently."

I narrowed my eyes. Westley Warwick wore a tailored suit and a watch valued higher than everything I owned. He did not so much ask questions as make open-ended statements for me to fill. The conversation made me feel like a fish herded into the shallows by a sea lion.

"No. I'm only here for the funeral."

"Oh, well, I'm very sorry to hear that. It would be good to have you back, particularly after the loss of Edwin. Shearwater will need another Keeper."

I frowned, about to open my mouth and ask what he meant by that, but he continued, "All the same, I hope you'll pay me a visit before you go." He reached into the inner pocket of his suit jacket and retrieved a business card, matte black with his name in gloss so you could only read it when it was turned to the light. On the reverse were his contact details.

"Give me a call," he said, then turned to mingle with the crowd.

Unfortunately, he wasn't the only shark in the waters of this wake. Gossiping Anne-Marie from down the road interrogated me about my life, then dragged in my uncle Pat, who was not actually my uncle by blood, but a longtime friend of my mum's we'd forever known as an uncle. He asked if I had a girlfriend. I'd been out of the closet since I was thirteen.

When they'd done with me, other residents of Shearwater took their place, all of them following a similar refrain.

"Still living out of your caravan?"

"Lunaris is still with me, yeah."

"What are you doing for a living these days?"

"I'm a ceramic artist."

"Oh . . . any money in that?"

"I've not starved yet."

"What's that on your face?"

"My mustache?"

Some comments were made in jest. Others hid passive-aggressive barbs I tried not to notice, but you only needed the barest touch for a nettle to sting, and I found myself sore and seeking out the bar sooner rather than later.

I pushed spilled salt around with my index finger, making a perfect ring while I waited for the barman to notice me.

Someone else did first. A voice at my ear said, "If I can guess your preferred drink, will you let me buy you one?"

I looked up. The man who'd spoken looked like he'd been assembled in a craft store, or by a fanciful teenage girl with good taste. I realized if

I'd said that out loud, it would sound like an insult, though I'd meant it positively.

He had hair down to his waist in a thick plait, dyed gradient shades of blue to match his eyes, and a spray of freckles across his nose and cheeks like stardust. Some sparkling makeup, perhaps. Though he'd dressed in dark colors for the funeral like everyone, his braces were embroidered with tiny flowers, a colorful reprieve in a dark cloud.

I'd learned over many years alone to take company where I could, but he was so beautiful I blushed. "You don't have to guess right."

"But the game's the fun bit."

"Not the only fun bit, I hope."

He laughed, loud and without self-consciousness. "That should have been my line. Stop distracting me. Gin and tonic?"

I winced.

"Damn. All right. Whiskey sour?"

I tilted my head from side to side. "Close. I wouldn't say no."

"Surely you're not a whiskey-on-the-rocks man?"

"Afraid so."

"Well, three guesses isn't bad. Oi, Travis! Whiskey on the rocks and a gin and tonic over here."

I accepted, heart skipping. "Sorry for insulting your drink."

"So long as your taste in men is better than your taste in booze."

It might have been poor form to hit on a man at my grandfather's wake, but it had been a long, anxious day of reintegrating myself with the estranged family I likely wouldn't see again until the next funeral, and the relief of finding someone with whom conversation flowed easily was too great to check myself. "I have a type. Blue hair. Five three. Cheeky grin."

He bit his lip and leaned in close. "I'm Kessian."

"Tal."

He tilted his head. "Tal . . . Tal. Have we met before?"

He felt familiar, like someone I'd known longer than ten minutes, but— "No. I'd remember you." I hoped the deflection might hint to him that I'd rather not talk about my relation to the deceased.

Kessian seemed to understand. He smiled. It was a secretive thing, dimpled on the right and not the left. He tipped his glass against my own after the barman handed them to us. "Charmer. Cheers."

I asked about his work. He told me he'd been with the Shearwater Spa for a few years. That explained his presence at the wake; I wondered how well he'd known Grandad. When he asked about my own work, I got carried away describing the newest mug I'd made, how I'd been experimenting with glazes and got one that reminded me of the aurora, how I'd enchanted it to keep your drink at the perfect temperature.

"And now I'm trying to design a teapot to do the same thing, but I'm not so sure about the proportions yet, and—" Mid-sentence, I stopped short. I'd been rambling. Something I was unfortunately prone to, and which I'd learned most people found obnoxious, boring, or both. "And none of this is probably very interesting."

Kessian had been leaning on the bar, sucking on the orange slice that garnished his gin and tonic. He said, "Incorrect. The sexiest thing a man can do is yap passionately about his eclectic, hyper-specific interests. Join me outside for a smoke?"

My blissful little bubble popped. I'd really wanted to kiss Kessian just now, but the smell of smoke would invariably put me off. Certain sensory experiences always did. "I don't smoke."

"Join me anyway?" Kessian said.

Good company was still good company. I'd sate my loneliness where I could. We might just have to forgo kissing . . .

I slid off my stool, and he gave the crowd of mourners a once-over before sneaking out the back door.

It was too cold to use the patio and gardens, so none of the furniture had been set out, and nobody else was there.

Instead of reaching into his pocket for a pack of smokes, Kessian grabbed me by my belt loops, dragged me out of sight of the pub windows, and kissed me.

CHAPTER 3

He didn't taste like cigarettes; he tasted like oranges.

It took a moment for my mind to catch up, but my body needed no such reflection period. I pressed him against the wall and kissed him back.

He had a practiced mouth, a talent for applying just the right pressure to make mine open. He tilted my jaw and made sparks shoot down my spine with the stroke of his tongue over my lower lip.

He broke away too soon and said, "I don't smoke either. I just wanted to kiss you."

"I gathered." My voice sounded rougher than usual. It was my grandfather's wake, and perhaps it was disrespectful to get off with a stranger when I ought to be mourning him.

But I felt as though I'd already mourned everybody here; nine years of estrangement will do that to a person. Instead, I found myself mourning an unrealized future. A series of *what-if's* that would never come to pass.

I was never around long enough for anyone to stick, and given what I was running from, that was probably for the best, but loneliness, for all its familiarity, had never gotten easier.

Kessian pulled back, his breath a butterfly's kiss against my lips. I drank in his sea-blue eyes and a mouth shaped perfectly for wrapping around—

Hell. I really needed to get laid more often.

I couldn't recall if it had been two months or three since I'd last been to bed with anyone. If flesh had memory, mine often forgot the warmth of a body lying next to mine. Once upon a time, I'd lived in a big house with many people who hugged me goodnight, patted me on the back for passing exams, punched my arm when I said something insensitive. Incidental, platonic touches that let me know I was not alone.

Now I was an unfortunate contradiction who at once hated touch and craved it. More precisely, I craved connection, no matter how brief, if only to indulge the fantasy of being loved again. Given the abrasive first impressions I gave off, opportunities for those connections were rare.

I kissed him again. He invited me, with a subtle tilt of his head and arch of his back, to press him against the wall. His breath drew short when I did, a little gasp of satisfaction when he felt my cock stiffening against his stomach.

I shouldn't risk sleeping with anyone this close to home, even if home was like a stranger wearing a family member's old clothes. But I wouldn't be staying long. In the morning, I'd be gone.

Kessian drew back. "Want to blow this popsicle stand?"

My frankness didn't always serve me well, but it did now. "I'd rather blow you."

"Ohoho, *love* that, but, er. You should know— Not possible in the *traditional* sense of the word."

"Why?"

"I'm transgender."

Kessian had taken a humorless day and made me laugh. Plus, he looked like a man who liked having his hair pulled.

"Po-tay-to, Po-tah-to. Hole is hole."

I kicked myself. My frankness had gone too far. The only thing getting blown now was this situation. Up. Blown up.

Kessian stared at me for a solid five seconds (I started counting) before, to my surprise, erupting into laughter.

"Well, that's— The first I've heard that one. I like it. Very inclusive."

"Sorry."

"Don't be. It's about a thousand percent sexier than the things most people tell me."

"Really?"

"Oh, you know. 'Have you had the surgery?' Or, 'I'm bi so you're the best of both worlds!' Or my personal favorite, 'You have titties? Show me.' You know, treating me like I'm half a man, an exotic fetish or a circus freak. Now, 'Hole is hole'? Refreshing. Revolutionary. A promising start."

"I haven't fucked you yet. It could be tragic."

"Spoken like someone who's aware of his faults and listens well to instructions."

It was rare to find someone who put me so at ease, made banter feel easy, turned the curse of my bluntness into a blessing.

Playing along, I said, "What are my instructions, Your Highness?"

"Hmm." Kessian tapped his lower lip. He took my chin in his hands, examining me with eyes hungry as the ocean. "Every king needs a throne, and your face looks pretty enough to sit on."

Heat swelled low in my belly. "My place or yours?"

"Mine isn't far. C'mon, I'll drive."

Mine was in the car park, but then I'd have to introduce him to Lunaris, which always invited awkward questions. I followed him.

Normally, a drive of any length between agreeing to hook up and the sex itself would be an agony of social awkwardness, but Kessian's old Volvo had a medley of dashboard decorations for conversation starters, and Kessian himself could hold a conversation on his own.

He pointed to George Carvermory's ramshackle cottage with the bathtub in the garden and nattered about how the man drank a bit too much but played a mean game of backgammon. He regaled me with a misadventure he'd had in the play park when he'd realized his arse had gotten too fat for the children's swings and nearly had to call someone to cut him out of it. He rambled about how good the battered sausage was at the local chippy, Hot Piece of Bass, and joked we could share a conciliatory one if *my* sausage didn't go down so well.

I listened along and did not mention that all these places were familiar to me, because through Kessian's eyes they were all new. I used to see George Carvermory at Mass every Sunday. I'd chipped a tooth on that seesaw next to the swings. I'd eaten fish and chips from Hot Piece of Bass with my family every Friday.

But as we got closer to his home, a stone of dread calcified in my heart.

His was a park home near enough the strid I could hear its water whispering in the trees beyond. If you listened for long enough, the "babble" of a brook lived up to the name, sounding like many voices all clamoring to be heard from the deep. It raised the hair on the back of my neck, memories flooding through me just as its icy water once had.

"You all right?" Kessian asked.

His fingers knotted with mine—a warming counterpoint to the cold memory.

I said, "Is this one your house?"

Usually, if you'd seen one park home, you'd seen them all. Not so with Kessian's.

His had a garden of wildflowers, a sun catcher in every window, and every door painted a different hue. He led me through one the color of baked cherries into a bedroom with so many rich, dark textiles I felt cocooned in his personality.

He turned and untangled our fingers to knot his in my hair instead. The subtle scrape of his nails against my scalp was luxurious, the citrus taste of his kiss exquisite.

His other hand guided mine to his belt. I had to stop kissing to focus on wrenching open the clasp, and his mouth found the precise spot between jaw and ear that sent a cascade of shivers down my back. The heat, which had cooled on our walk, stoked anew.

I'd never been with a trans man, which perhaps should have been something I'd said initially, but my inexperience hadn't occurred to me as an obstacle.

I said, "What are the rules?"

Kessian paused in kissing my neck to throw his head back and sigh as if I'd said something erotic. "Music to my ears."

"I like rules. Structure."

"Pussy's a yes, anal's a no."

"Words like pussy are . . . ?"

"Good. I like pussy. Cunt is best. Rolls off the tongue, has the same oomph as cock, right?" He arched against my hand as I slipped it into the waistband of his boxer briefs. It was gratifying to hear his voice catch. "Never got on with clit, though. That's my cock, now."

I slid two fingers between the wet lips of his cunt and stroked along until he shuddered and bucked into my hand. "Here?"

"Yes!" he gasped, murmuring directions into my ear. "Wait. Wet your fingers."

I took my hand out to suck on them. He watched me, pupils blown wide. I stuck my slick fingers between his legs. He whimpered.

"Better?"

"Yes. That's good— Wait, slow down a bit. Firmer. Try circular motions—fuck! Yeah. Like that."

I was grateful for the direction, otherwise lost as to what I was doing, but far too turned on to feel anxious about it. Kessian moaned with his lips dragging hot breath against my neck, which *very* effectively drowned out the voices in my head and informed me I was doing a good job.

"Still want to sit on my face?" I asked when he seemed warmed up.

He groaned lewdly into my shoulder. "Nope. No. Changed my mind."

With effort, he pulled away, wiggling out of his trousers and boxer briefs, stripping his shirt off, and rifling through his bedside drawer. I only had a second to admire his figure before he turned, took my hand, and slapped a condom into it.

"I take it you don't need instructions for this part," he said as he got onto the bed on all fours.

Both my face and my cock heated to the surface temperature of the sun. Figuratively, not literally.

If not for the fact my clothes made me feel too hot all of a sudden, I wouldn't have been able to resist unzipping, donning the condom, and jumping him right away. As things stood, I had to clumsily wrestle out of everything to ensure the sweaty, sensory nightmare of clothes didn't impede my enjoyment of his body.

Which was a very, very nice body. The heart shape his arse made while bent over was marked at the top by two dimples on either side of his spine, like imprints for my thumbs. I grasped his hips and positioned myself at his entrance. He gave his hips a wiggle until his lips enfolded the head of my cock.

"Stop teasing," he said.

I thrust in. The slap of my hips against him and the pleased cry he let out were both gratifyingly loud, but much as I wanted to hear him make that noise again, I had to pause. I gripped his hips so he couldn't move and I could get a hold of myself, bent over him like I was about to bow down in prayer.

The thought had never occurred to me that pussy would feel different from anal, and the sensation of Kessian wetly engulfing my cock made my mind go blank.

A rare accomplishment, given how prone I was to overthinking.

"You all right back there?"

"You feel *really* good."

Kessian resisted the restraint of my hands, sidling his hips back, taking me deeper. I ground my teeth together to quell the spike of heat in my belly.

"I hear it feels even better when you move," Kessian said. "Do you remember how?"

I let him goad me. I drew my hips back and slammed back in, driving him face-first into the mattress. The noise he made this time came out surprised and delighted, muffled by the bed covers. He looked so good like that, I had to pin him down by the shoulders and keep going.

We made the mattress creak. His long plait had slunk down his back and over his shoulder to pool in a coil on the covers. I could picture winding it around my fist and pulling. Making his back arch and his neck crane so I could see the look on his face while I made him cum.

Hell, I was really pent up, thinking like this.

It would be rude to do without asking first. "Do you like having your hair pulled?" I thrust in hard.

"Mmmffffuuuck!" He nodded feverishly. "Yes. Please."

I planted one hand on the mattress over his shoulder. He did something that nearly unraveled me. He leaned his cheek against my wrist like a cat craving affection, his lips leaving a damp kiss against my hammering pulse.

My free hand swept up his back, rubbing a line with my thumb along the valley of his spine until I came to the base of his neck. I tangled my fingers in his hair, briefly massaging his scalp until he was practically purring.

"And you warned me you might be a tragic lay," he whispered, his voice husky.

I untangled my hand and instead wound his plait around my fist, silky and *right*. "I haven't made you cum yet."

"Didn't anyone ever tell you it's about the journey, not the desti—NAY—tionnghh."

I pulled his hair, forcing him to crane his neck and look at me, his freckled cheeks tinged pink. I started moving again just to see his eyes roll back and his mouth fall open. He looked better than I'd envisioned. *Felt* a lot better.

Leaning down, I indulged in putting my mouth to the vein that stood out on the side of his exposed neck. I could taste his heartbeat, the salt on his skin. I wanted to bite down. Leave a mark. Like a lover's graffiti to say, *I was here*.

I didn't normally have those inclinations. Maybe it was the stress of the day, or the length of time I'd gone without a solitary, passing touch, or maybe it was the proximity of the strid, its waters singing just outside the window.

I didn't care. I'd needed this.

Kessian said, "Yes. Bite me."

If he'd somehow read my mind, I was too turned on to ask. I opened my mouth against the column of his throat and let him feel the graze of my teeth before applying pressure. He shuddered under me, clenching around my cock, and I could tell from the desperate way he threw his hips back, the way he said, "Don't stop," that he was close.

I chased that finish, but by then each of my hedonistic urges had been well-received, and now I only had one more: I wanted his mouth on mine while I brought him to the brink.

I loosened my grip on his hair, palming the back of his head with his plait still looped around my hand. He had to crane his neck and angle his mouth against mine. It should have been awkward. Uncomfortable. But his lips parted for my tongue, and his moans tasted sweet, and his body went buttery under mine as he shuddered with climax.

When he melted into stillness, I said, "Roll over."

He did. His body welcomed me back inside. Both his arms and legs wound around me as I worked up to my own orgasm.

It didn't take long. His eyes were dark with pupil, hooded, and holding my gaze, until I kissed him again and finally, finally let go.

My loud current of thoughts went blissfully quiet, but not for long. Kessian's fingers ran through my hair while we kissed.

Usually, when we'd both gotten what we needed, me and my rare, ill-fated encounters would end.

I needed to roll over. Clean myself up. Get ready to go. I could indulge in hair pulling and neck biting and even kissing while we both came, but I couldn't risk cuddling and pillow talk. Not when *goodbyes* were the universal conclusion to any brief moments of intimacy I could scrape out of the cracked road I'd been running on most of my life.

But he kissed me like he was savoring the taste of something new.

Rain tapped on the window as if to say, *Stay a while.*

I said, "I should go."

In doing so, I'd broken the kiss. Kessian tilted his head, looking at me through his lashes. "I was going to ask how long before you're up for round two."

His tongue dipped between his lips, still tasting me there, and I must have gone mad. I had to be mad. Because I kissed him again. I let him pull me back down, all that sweaty, flushed skin against mine, and I forgot—*idiot, you can't ever forget*—what I was running from.

Then I noticed it. It was admittedly difficult to notice anything but the satin of Kessian's mouth moving against mine, but a frisson of unease worked its way through.

The tapping on the window. It sounded too even, too punctuated, too sharp for rain.

Kessian started kissing my jaw, working his way toward the spot he'd marked. I risked a glance toward the window.

A dark branch of a sapling splintered like black lightning across the upper-right corner. It didn't move with the erratic rhythm of a tree caught in the wind, though. It tapped evenly against the window.

One, two, three.

Then the rest of the darkness resolved, and I saw it was not a branch at all.

It was an antler.

CHAPTER 4

I broke away from Kessian so quickly, he let out a disgruntled noise of surprise.

I said, "Sorry."

"What's wrong?"

"I forgot. There's something I have to— I can't stay."

"Oh." Kessian flopped back against the pillows, managing to look like a painted invitation with his arms thrown over his head, one thigh cocked apart from the other. "I'll just be here. Naked. Getting cold. What a shame."

"Sorry," I said again, but I could feel the shadows watching, and another firm *tap* on the glass had me shoving myself into my pants, yanking on my black funeral attire.

"You all right?" Kessian said.

"Yeah, good. Just forgot—" *I'm being hunted.* "—something at the funeral."

"Mm-hm. Well, all right. I'll walk you to the door."

Kessian threw on a silk robe, tying it loosely shut. It fell off one shoulder. If life were fair, I'd have pushed him up against the wall to kiss him until the tie came undone.

Life wasn't fair.

As we walked down the hall, Kessian walked a little stiffly.

I paused at the door. "Thank you for the sex."

Kessian snorted a laugh. "It was really good sex."

"Really, very good. I hope I wasn't too . . . rough?"

He shook his head. "No, you were perfect. Hip gets stiff sometimes. Don't worry your head over it."

He didn't elaborate further, and it wasn't my business. *Goodbye* was on the tip of my tongue, but I tempted fate by lingering a second too long on the threshold.

"If you're ever in town again, you know where to find me." A flash of something crossed Kessian's face but vanished before I could identify it. "In case you want to take a rain check on round two."

I would never be back, but I could picture it. Slipping a note under his door asking if he'd meet me at the chippy. Buying him the sausage roll he liked and sucking the flakes of pastry off the corner of his mouth. Falling into bed together, and everyone knowing, because it was a small town and Frankie who ran the chippy couldn't resist gossiping. She was more accurate than a tabloid but no less salacious. I'd introduce him to Lunaris, who would put a kettle on to boil before I asked, and we'd take our time with each other while falling fast and hard, pretending not to.

All I had were these idle fantasies, which went away by sunrise as readily as a dream. Every bright, shining connection of mine died before it became anything more.

"I won't be coming back," I said, because I'd never managed the social etiquette of a polite white lie.

He seemed to understand. "Most people don't in Shearwater."

I had the maddening urge to kiss him goodbye, but in the end I couldn't even say the word. I just turned and left.

I rushed back to Lunaris, watching the darkness and the trees for a moving shadow darker than the rest.

I couldn't see one, but knew it was there. It followed me. It had ever since the night I fell into the strid.

Fell wasn't the right word. My recollection of the night had the quality of a rained-on letter whose ink had run too much to read, but there'd been a song. Music both strange and familiar. I'd never heard it before, yet each note seemed to have been plucked from my heartstrings, from an instrument made of my hollowed-out bones, strung with my hair. It had drawn me out of my bed, barefoot into the woods, to the banks of the strid, where the water sang such splendid music to me. The lyrics were, *Please come home.*

Others had come with me, drawn by the same song. We stepped in hand in hand.

The thing about the strid is nobody who falls in comes out alive.

Farther upstream, the river cuts a broad swathe through the countryside, but in Shearwater the rocks choke it to a stream so narrow you could leap from one bank to the other. Except, all that water needs a place to go, so it burrows deep, making a ravine of the rocks. No matter how strong a swimmer you are, the current is stronger. It swallows anything that falls in, and none of the song's listeners who go in come out.

Except me.

For some reason, I floated to the surface of Shearwater Spring like a bit of flotsam caught harmlessly in the current. Every bone in my body ought to have been broken, my lungs like fishbowls. I had no right to be alive, yet I was.

But I wasn't the same. I started seeing that *thing*.

The sight of Lunaris waiting in the spa's car park was a welcome one. I didn't need to fumble for keys; she unlocked her doors for me the moment I touched the handle. She didn't start the engine, though, and when I did find my keys to turn them in the ignition, she stayed stubbornly quiet.

The lights dimmed warmly in welcome, and I heard someone move in the living room. I was not alone.

I maneuvered past the driver's seat to get to the dining area, unafraid because if something meant to harm me, Lunaris would not have let me in.

Fae, tucked into the booth around the dinner table, set down a steaming teacup. "Were you really leaving already?"

"What are you doing here?"

They looked offended. "Lunaris made me tea. I wanted to talk to you."

"We shouldn't."

"I'm getting married."

It stunned me silent. No one had told me. I'd never even met their partner. "Congratulations."

"Thanks."

"Who's the lucky—?"

"You remember Camilla Hofstedder?"

"Your straight best friend you pined over all through high school?"

"Yeah. Turns out, not so straight." They took a sip of tea, collecting themselves. "Lunaris makes a good pot of tea. Just have one cup with me and listen, okay?"

I glanced out the window to search for any shadows, but Lunaris pointedly drew her curtains. If we were still in danger, she wouldn't allow us to sit around nattering over tea.

"All right. Just one cup." I sat, trying to relax, but conversations with my estranged family caused a different sort of anxiety.

Fae waited for me to get another cup for myself, but I waved for them to drink theirs. "I only have the one mug."

At the wake, I'd only had a brief minute to talk to them before they'd been pulled away by other friends and family. This was the first moment I got to really take them in.

They'd grown out their hair. It was the same brunette as mine, with the same untamed waves, but they'd styled half of it up into a knot at the back of their head. Tattoos dotted and formed fern patterns on their thumbs, index, and ring fingers. The left ring finger had a particularly elaborate design, perhaps in place of an engagement ring.

It was otherwise difficult to recognize them or any family resemblance between us. They had a soft, forgiving face. Their eyes were warm brown instead of green. Their smile came more easily than mine.

But we'd been close, once.

"The wedding's in a month. I want— It would be nice if you could come."

"You know I can't."

They glanced at the curtained window. "It's been years. Is it really still out there?"

"I saw it. Tonight."

Fae's jaw firmed, but I couldn't tell if that was from determination or fear, and I needed to convince them to feel the latter. "It's never stopped. I see it on the road from time to time, whenever I pause anywhere for a day or two too many, but it never shows up this fast. I've been here less than a day. It's too risky."

"You can't just live your life on the road forever."

"It's what works."

"Barely." Fae swallowed and spoke with cultivated assertiveness. "I'd really like to have my brother at my wedding."

I didn't think after so long away that my family would hold much power over my heart. It had been nine years, and they were all but strangers to me. But there was something about family, and something about Shearwater, that never failed to jab my tenderest bruises.

We'd been a normal family, once, but after I'd nearly died in the strid, things changed. Nightmares of a shadowy figure with dripping antlers haunted my sleep. Eventually, it followed me into the daylight, too.

Everyone assured me it was normal after a traumatic experience, and with time and healing, the nightmares would go away. I wasn't convinced they *were* nightmares.

Until that nightmare killed my twin sister . . . Then they believed me.

"It's not a good idea," I said.

"You won't even try?"

"After what happened to Laurelie? No."

Fae looked undeterred. They took a measured sip of their tea—making it last, so I couldn't kick them out when they'd finished—and leveled me with their best big-sibling expression.

"There's a new healer in town."

"No healer can fix what's wrong with me. We tried."

"He's not your usual healer. His abilities are . . . particular. Strange. He got them quite suddenly after moving to Shearwater, and I always wondered if he could help you."

"Uncle Marlowe tried."

They raised their voice. "Nine years ago, and he didn't try hard enough!"

Lunaris turned the radio on, playing an acoustic song I hadn't heard since our childhood.

Fae cracked a wistful smile. "Lunaris agrees with me. Won't you try?"

"Fae—"

"For *me*."

I leaned back and picked at my cuticles. Eventually, I had to meet their eyes, though I knew my resolve would crumble.

"Fine."

Fae's expression brightened, but only a little. "Good! Great. I'll make you an appointment with the healer."

"If it doesn't work, I *have* to go."

"Camilla will be so happy you said yes."

"If that thing comes after you—"

"There's a fitting at Witches and Stitches for the groomsmen and bridesmaids in a few days. You'll be in my wedding party, won't you?"

"*Fae.*"

"I hear you!" They set their mug down a bit too aggressively, making the ceramic rattle.

I winced. I really did only have the one cup. I could make another, but I'd grown attached to that one. We'd been through a lot together. I was attached to all my meager possessions like that. The stand-ins for proper, healthy emotional attachments.

Fae said, "Look, I understand the risk. I know she was your twin. She was my sister, too. But there's a way to fix this. There has to be, and running away hasn't fixed anything. So come to the fitting. And we're reading out Grandad's will the day after tomorrow, so come for that, too. I'll book you in with the healer tomorrow. Nine a.m.?"

I shrugged helplessly. "I guess you've got it all figured out."

"I always do. See you tomorrow, then."

They stood up, setting their mug in the sink, which Lunaris had already filled with soapy water.

They grabbed their coat from the hook by the door, and paused before leaving. "I know the others may seem off with you right now, but we're all really happy to see you again. Truly."

That was wishful thinking, but I nodded all the same.

As they departed, I scanned the trees for shadows, and I didn't close my door until Fae got safely into their car and drove away.

When they had, I locked up, went down the tiny hall to my bedroom, and paused.

The door to my bedroom had always been the same color from the day Lunaris had first transformed: a neutral, inoffensive beige.

It was now the color of baked cherries.

* * *

Despite the fact I slept in the spa's car park, I ran late to my appointment with the healer the next morning.

It wasn't deliberate—I'd run out of clean washing. Working from out of a caravan meant my uniform mostly consisted of joggers and hoodies, but I didn't want to show up to this appointment looking unwashed. I feared there might be a physio or massage element, so I was extra thorough in the shower.

All said, I was only ten minutes late, but it was enough that Fae greeted me with a scowl.

"I've filled out your forms for you. Please check them over and make sure I didn't forget anything," they said, shoving the papers into my hands.

I skimmed over them while following Fae past the circular stairs to a hallway of doors for separate treatment rooms. A disconcerting sense of déjà vu overwhelmed me. Each door had been painted a different color. Fae stopped outside one with a ginkgo leaf stenciled on.

"Wait here and I'll get him," they said.

Disappearing inside, I heard them say, "Hey, he's ready for y— Is that a *hickey*? I didn't see that when you came in. Did you get that at the *funeral?*"

A familiar voice replied, "We all grieve in our own ways."

I nearly bolted for the stairs, but there wasn't time. Already, the door opened. Already, Fae led out the new healer to introduce me.

We needed no introduction. We'd already met rather intimately.

Fae said, "Kessian, meet my brother, Taliesin. Tal, meet Kessian."

In unison, Kessian and I looked at one another and said, "Oh, shit."

CHAPTER 5

"Shit? Why shit?" Then Fae zeroed back in on the bite mark I'd left on Kessian's neck. "Oh, *shit*. Please tell me you didn't fuck my brother."

Kessian replied, "Does it make it any better if I say he's the one who fucked me?"

"Ugh! No! And you!" Fae turned on me, jabbing me in the chest with a finger. "At Grandad's wake?"

An incriminating silence was all I could muster.

"I can't believe you. Well, actually, I can believe it of you, Kessian. But Tal?"

I could only repeat what Kessian had said. "We all grieve in our own ways."

Kessian suppressed a snicker. He wasn't helping us. I might have found it funny, too, if this didn't involve my family and some last-ditch effort to save me. Seeing a random healer with unique magic was one thing. Spending more time with a man I'd slept with and fantasized about seemed distinctly riskier.

"It's fine," Kessian soothed. "I'm a professional. We can still move forward with the treatment plan, can't we?"

Fae scowled at me. "Can't you?"

My mortification snuffed out any temptation to argue. I would simply refrain from any kind of intimacy with Kessian. The wraith following me only preyed on people I cared about.

So no more sex. No more fantasies. *Definitely* not romantic ones.

"It'll be fine," I told Fae. "I'll be good."

"Right. Good. I'm going to pretend I don't know anything about this." Fae held up their hands in surrender. "No need for introductions. Bye, bye, have a good time, but not *too* good a time, bye!"

They stomped down the stairs. I could hear them puttering around the reception desk. Probably organizing papers and cleaning. Fae cleaned when they were stressed.

"Well, this is a surprise. Not an unpleasant one, though," Kessian said. "Come in."

I shuffled in after him and temporarily forgot the awkwardness of our introduction.

Kessian's treatment room, from the baseboards to the crown moldings of the ceiling, had been painted a deep, dark turquoise. Soft, colorful textiles like the ones he favored in his own home made a cozy sitting area near a pair of sliding doors at the back, leading out to—

I drew up short. Through the glass, the spring's waters trickled over limestone rocks, a vibrant blue against the creamy stone. A few orange leaves spiraled in the current from its miniature falls.

I studied the deeper shadows around the rocks, the trees, but none of them moved unnaturally.

Kessian handed me one of the spa's white robes. I clutched it to my chest. "Do I get my kit off?"

"I usually leave the room to let my clients change, but I'll let you decide whether that's necessary when I saw it all last night in detail."

I clutched the bathrobe a little tighter, my face hot.

"Aw, suddenly shy? I'll step out and give you some privacy. But for the record"—Kessian paused in the doorway, giving me a cheeky wink—"you're even sweeter on the eyes in the daylight."

He left, shutting the door behind him.

Still with no idea what my treatment entailed, I shuffled out of my clothes and donned the robe. I always had the ridiculous notion that I needed to fold my clothes on the available chair, which I did. The absurdity of my situation sank in while I was tucking my briefs into my jeans so they wouldn't be visible. *I slept with him yesterday to solve my loneliness problem, and now he's supposed to solve a nine-year haunting that kept me from coming home.*

Nothing in my life had ever been that simple. Uncle Marlowe had hired exorcists, curse breakers, spoken to scholars in wild magic, and none had answers. The wraith was not something common or well-documented like a poltergeist. It was unique, a strange blend of wild and witch magic born from the strid. What it wanted, how it had come to be, they didn't know. Without a means to communicate with it, they couldn't find out. Without understanding its nature, they couldn't hope to kill it, either. Most spirits were exorcised by burning the remains of the dead, but the bodies of those taken by the strid never surfaced.

The only things keeping me from fleeing were my promise to Fae and the fact I was no longer dressed for running.

Kessian knocked and, at my assent, came inside.

"So how does this work?" I asked.

"I'll explain it all, but I warn you, my magic is a bit unusual."

"Magic? You're a witch?" He had no familiar. At least, not one I could see. I'd met a witch once whose familiar was a ladybird, but tiny familiars were uncommon. But then, mine was a caravan.

"Ah, not quite. My magic doesn't come from within me. It comes from the spring."

All the hair stood up on the back of my neck. "The spring?"

Kessian's smile brightened, and I could have sworn the glittery freckles on his cheeks winked like real stars. "Let me show you."

He opened the glass doors to the spring outside. Numbly, I followed him barefoot across the stone path. The water chanted, shallow falls rippling the uncanny blue. They had not been so bright on the day Laurelie died.

"Since you grew up here, I probably don't have to explain how the magic of the strid works," Kessian said. "It shows us visions of the future. Possibilities that may come to pass, if we play our cards right. But for me, it works a little differently. I can focus those visions. It shows me—us—paths we can take to solve a particular problem, heal from an old trauma, or to achieve a greater sense of contentment in our lives."

"How?" Though based on my current attire, I could hazard a guess. The notion filled me with cold dread.

"First, you take a dip in the spring. Don't worry, I'll turn my back while you're disrobing. All it takes from there is physical contact. The magic channels through us both."

I stopped, rooted to the spot. Perhaps to anyone else, the spring looked serene, beautiful. To me the sound of its chanting waters and the opaque blue disguising any view of the bottom were sinister. I remembered the way they tasted in my lungs, how the icy cold made it hard to move, how the deadly current meant any movement was wasted energy anyway.

Intellectually, I understood the spring was separate from the strid. The strid's waters fed into underground aquifers, which in turn bled into this spring. There was no deadly current, and so long as the wraith wasn't near, nothing to drown me like Laurelie.

But the magic of the spring came from the strid. They were connected. I'd washed up here, though that should have been impossible. Wild magic often was.

I didn't trust it. Not at all.

Kessian realized I'd stopped halfway up the path. He turned to me. "Everything all right?"

"I'm not getting in there," I said. "I can't."

"What's wrong?"

I'd already turned on my heel. "Nothing. I just have to go yell at Fae." With a muttered apology, I stomped back into the house and to reception, where Fae was on the phone. When they saw my approach, they murmured a swift, "Can I call you back in a few minutes?" before hanging up. They drew me through the door into the reception office, away from any early patrons so we wouldn't disturb their holidays.

"Why didn't you tell me I had to get in the water?"

"If I had, would you have come?"

"No."

"Then there's your answer."

Kessian had caught up with me. "I'm sorry, what happened? Did my flirting make it too awkward, or—?"

"It wasn't you. Fae neglected to tell me I had to bathe in the spring."

Fae threw up their hands. "Because I knew you'd react like this, and the spring isn't dangerous!"

"Laurelie *drowned* in that spring!" I shouted.

They both went quiet.

On a chilly night a couple months after my father drowned and I survived, my sister Laurelie silently left our bedroom, went to the spring, and never came out again.

I'd woken to the sounds of her screams, but when I looked out the window, I couldn't see her, only splashes, and something darker than pitch standing waist-deep in the water.

Its body was composed of shadows. They had density, like the swirling mists of a gas giant with its cataclysmic gravity. The shadows obscured the thing's face except for the blank voids of its eyes. Its darkness bled into the roiling water. It attacked my uncle next, then ran off when I chased it.

All we found of Laurelie were her shoes by the shore, taken off and lined up like she'd gone in voluntarily. Perhaps she'd heard the song. It didn't matter. She was gone.

I left Shearwater soon after.

Kessian's jaw dropped, and to my relief, he rounded on Fae, too. "You didn't tell me that!"

"She didn't drown, she *was drowned*. By the wraith, and I'm hoping Kessian can help free you from it," Fae said.

"You still should have said something," I insisted.

Kessian agreed with me. "I'm trying to heal people, not traumatize them by bathing them in their worst memories. If I'd known that, I wouldn't have gone skipping outside like I was leading him into a world of magic and fairy tales."

"All right, I get it!" Fae crossed their arms, but it looked more defensive than defiant. "Maybe I should have said something. I'm sorry. I didn't think you'd bother trying if I told you. Seems I was right. I didn't mean to be insensitive, I was just—" They chewed their lip, glancing between me and Kessian.

I waited, heart hammering in my throat. I'd come in spoiling for a fight, but now they'd apologized, I didn't know what I wanted.

Fae said, "Kessian, can I talk to Tal alone for a minute?"

Kessian nodded, but he paused to pat my arm and apologize once more before he left.

Neither Fae nor I spoke for an awkward length of time. The tension felt the same as it had standing over my grandfather's grave, wondering what I could say, and there was so much, none of which would make the situation better.

Fae broke the silence. "Do you even want to come back?"

It wasn't the question I expected. "What's that supposed to mean?"

"Means what it says on the tin. Do you even miss us? Miss Shearwater?"

All my anger deflated. "Of course I do . . . I'm just used to it."

There was a hard, flat lump on my ribs where a piece of debris in the strid had lodged when I'd fallen in. The magic of the water had healed the skin over it, and it caused me no pain, so it stayed there. Missing them was like that bit of shrapnel stuck between my ribs. It had been there so long, I forgot the pain of what it had been like when the wound was made.

Fae's expression softened, tinged with sadness. "I don't want you to get used to it. I want things to go back to the way they were."

That was it. The thing I'd been grasping at while wondering why I'd really had a go at Fae. I wanted things to go back to normal, too, but they couldn't, because Dad and Laurelie were gone.

But if there was a chance at something close, shouldn't I take it? I hadn't seen any sign of the wraith this morning. All my encounters had taken place at night. Maybe, if I timed my visits to Shearwater right, I could avoid any more.

"You really think Kessian's magic will work?" I asked.

Fae's posture finally relaxed. They said, "Why don't you ask him?"

CHAPTER 6

Kessian insisted that he could guarantee nothing, that he understood my refusal completely, and that his methods were far from standard, but that he'd also had a great deal of success with other clients.

This reassured me far more than if he'd made grandiose claims about the spring's preternatural abilities to fix me. I'd met many a dodgy salesman of essential oils and healing crystals on my travels, but Kessian was obnoxiously forthright.

Which was how I found myself standing on the bank of the spring, toes curled around the flagstone, every instinct within me rearing back from what I was about to do.

Kessian waited patiently and didn't rush me. I still had my robe on and closed it tightly around me to combat the shivers. It was summer, but the sun had yet to burn the dewy night from the air, and I knew the water would be cold, though it wasn't the cold I feared.

"Would it help if I stepped in with you?" Kessian asked.

"You're fully dressed."

"Are you trying to persuade me to get my kit off?"

"No! No, I wasn't implying that."

"Relax." He was already kicking off his shoes and rolling up the legs of his trousers. "I'll keep the rest on and change later."

Technically, we weren't supposed to go in with clothes on. I'd grown up here. I knew the rules. But I appreciated him breaking them for me, and equally appreciated the sly grin he flashed me when he said, "Though for the record, it wouldn't take much persuasion from you. I do remember offering round two."

I really, really could not entertain that thought. His flirting might put me more at ease, but I couldn't afford to get close to anyone. Especially not in Shearwater.

Flagstones had been built into the banks to form a staircase. Kessian descended the first step, submerged to his ankles, and waited for me. The water glowed where it touched him, and I didn't imagine it this time: the starry freckles on his cheeks glowed, too.

"I thought you were wearing makeup," I said.

He glanced away. He didn't strike me as the bashful type last night, but he looked it now. "They first appeared when the spring blessed me with these abilities."

I wasn't sure whether to feel safer or not, knowing the wild magic had shown him such favor, but I'd come this far.

With a deep breath, I took my first step into the water.

The cold effused through me, my skin erupting in goose bumps, but nothing else happened. None of the shadows deepened or moved, a secret tide didn't pull me under, even the voice of the trickling falls sounded less malicious.

Kessian beamed. "All right?"

"Yeah. All right."

He descended the next few steps. He wore a loose-fitting pair of gray trousers and a thin white poet's shirt, which became transparent as gossamer when wet. His long plait floated on the surface, snaking after him.

He closed his eyes and turned his back to me. "You can take off your robe now, if you want."

I considered keeping it to maintain a layer of propriety between us, but the cloying sensation of the thick, towel-like fabric, soaked and clinging to my skin would be sickening. I untied the robe, wadded it, and threw it onto the bank, grateful for the privacy of the gardens and trees as I waded in up to my chest.

"You can open your eyes."

Kessian turned. "Great. I'm going to sit on this shallow rock. If you could just position yourself between my knees. Back to me. Yes, that's good."

I shivered, though not from cold. The glowing water rippling around him felt warmer than the rest. "What do I do?"

"Sink deeper. Float back just enough so your head's in the water."

Normally this would afford me an unflattering look up Kessian's nostrils, but even from this vantage he was unfairly beautiful. His eyes glimmered with cool reflections of the water's vibrant blue.

He hovered his hands over my shoulders. "Physical contact helps the magic flow between us. May I?"

I nodded and drew a sharp breath when his fingers lightly caressed lines up my neck and into my hair.

At once, my mind flooded with images. Racing to eat my ice cream before it melted while sitting on this very bank with Laurelie beside me. Jumping in off the highest rock to see who could make the largest splash. Lunaris, still a scruffy calico, hissing when she got sprayed.

More images followed. Roast dinners at Grandpa's—he always gave me the oyster from the chicken. Dad teaching me the technique for coning clay on the wheel. A sea of black mourners around coffins with no bodies inside. My sweet calico transforming, magic stretching and twisting her into a caravan. Goodbyes. So many goodbyes.

Then just a blankness. A dark, cold expanse of time that lurched nine years forward. The images became more sensory, more illicit. A kiss tasting like citrus, bumping along in an old Volvo, fingers tangled in bedsheets and blue hair, breathing hard into the side of his love-bitten neck.

Kessian pulled back, fingers clenching. "Sorry."

"What was that? Could you see all that?"

"Yes. That wasn't me controlling it, though. It's the spring. It's almost like it wanted to reacquaint itself and got a little . . . greedy." He let out a forced laugh. "I guess it missed you. It's never been that thorough."

I flushed with embarrassment, which was ridiculous. The last few visions weren't anything Kessian hadn't seen before. He'd *been* there. The earlier images, my life in Shearwater before I left, was nothing he hadn't found out after my fight with Fae. Still, I asked, "What's supposed to happen?"

"For locals, it might dive into their history a little before showing us something from the future. Something that will help them navigate their problems, or steer them toward the right path. For visitors and tourists, it can't seem to access their past. I think it can only "see" as far as the boundaries of Shearwater."

It made a strange sort of sense, but I found its attention frightening. Why such particular interest in me? Why had it saved me from drowning and not the countless others?

"Should I keep going?" Kessian asked.

"Yes." We'd already begun. Might as well finish.

"This next part will be strange. Like a dream. Try to relax."

Uncomfortable with the spring as I was, Kessian's fingers in my hair grounded me. As if reading my mind, he kneaded behind my ears and tugged gently on a few strands, sending pleasant shivers through me.

"Seems I'm not the only one who likes having his hair pulled," he murmured.

He was incorrigible. I sank low enough my ears were below the water, muffling all noise, until even the soft ripples fell away. Kessian kneaded soothing circles into my temples, and I drifted into a trance like a paper boat rocking in the surf of dreams.

I woke outside a house.

It had once been a handsome house. A rotted porch wrapped all the way around its first floor, with a swing by the door screeching on rusted chains. The garden had overgrown and crawled in through the broken windows. It had the air of an aged starlet, still breathtaking and stage-worthy, if the world hadn't decided to neglect her for the new and youthful.

I recognized it. This was Grandad's house.

"Shall we go inside?"

Kessian appeared at my shoulder like a ghost. I hadn't heard him approach. He was there as if he'd always been.

"This is my grandad's house."

"I know. I used to visit and help him with the gardening."

A stab of envy went through me. Kessian probably knew present-day Edwin Ashborne better than his own grandson did.

"How is coming back here meant to help me?"

"The more you see, the more it might make sense. Come on."

We walked up the steps of the porch, through the door with its two stained-glass panels, into—

It should have been the foyer, and it was, but it was also a forest. The stairway banisters had grown into trees that twisted through the ceiling, branches sprouted from the walls, and the rug runner had a peculiar, cloying feel underfoot.

Worst of all was the sound.

There'd been a grandfather clock in the hallway, which tick-tick-ticked and chimed on the hour. I remembered, in early childhood, finding the noise so intolerable that I'd screamed and screamed whenever we visited. My parents thought I didn't like Grandad, but it had just been the clock. We stopped coming around so often, until one Christmas, when I'd gotten old enough to understand how clocks like that worked, I jammed the pendulum with an old shoehorn to stop it from ticking.

The clock was there now, overgrown with foliage, its pendulum still swinging to and fro, but instead of ticking, the song of the strid issued from it, its tune like wind, percussion like rain.

"Do you hear that?" I murmured.

Kessian nodded. "What is it?"

The words caught in my throat. "That's the song I heard. The one that lured me into the strid."

"Oh." Kessian's expression changed, assessing the song differently. "It takes on a different sort of beauty when you put it like that."

The grandfather clock lurched. We both jumped at the sound of something spraying inside. I expected blood, but the geyser of it began to leak. Black water hemorrhaged from the cracks around the glass-paneled door, gurgling into the hallway.

The clock didn't tick, but my heart did. A heavy, rapidly accelerating drum. I took a step back from the clock, feet squelching in the sodden rug runner.

"I think we need to leave," I said.

"Nothing here can hurt you."

This failed to reassure me when a hand composed of shadows slammed against the inside of the glass. It arrested the swing of the pendulums, splashing through the water rising in the interior. The fingers squeaked against the pane as they slowly closed to make a fist. Then the hand drew back and punched through, glass shattering and frigid water bursting from within.

I backed away. I grabbed Kessian's wrist and tried to pull him back, too, but he said, "It can't hurt you. This is the safest place to confront your fear."

The thing was emerging from the clock. It moved sinuously and with an irregular pace, like a dancer adapting to an off-beat tempo. Its arm came through first, prowling with its claws grasping the muddy floorboards. Then a shoulder jerked out, popping at an odd angle. The antlers rattled the pendulums and phased through like smoke.

I'd backed up to the front door, still grasping Kessian's wrist. *It can't hurt you*, he'd said, but it seemed plenty capable, and I didn't understand how this vision could help me.

The wraith tilted its head, antlers scraping the ceiling, and pointed at the clock, whose hands abruptly spun backward, rewinding through time. The forest shrank away. The wraith vanished. The variety of clocks cluttering the hallway shrank and vanished, the yellowing wallpaper restored to white, until everything appeared just as it had when I was young.

It all melted away, and for a moment I thought I was back in the waking world because I was standing on the banks of the spring, but Kessian wasn't there, and it was night. I watched the water, which bubbled and glowed. Something was emerging from it. I expected the wraith and took a step back.

But it wasn't the wraith. A dark head of hair emerged, a face coughing up water. A young girl.

I leapt in, wading up to my waist to help her, and it was only when she swept her hair from her eyes and lifted her face that I recognized her.

Laurelie.

That . . . that wasn't possible. If the strid meant to show me both the past and possible futures, then this wasn't one. She'd died.

I heard noise behind me and turned to see lights on in the spa house. Voices carried through the garden, torch beams hunting through the reeds and tracking toward us. In their glare, I couldn't see who held them until we were out of the water.

The torch light lowered. It took a moment for my eyes to adjust, but standing before me was Fae. Not Fae of nine years ago, who'd had longer hair and only wore hoodies with band logos. This Fae's hair had been pinned up and studded with pearls. A wedding style.

They said, "Laurelie? Is that Laurelie?"

Before either of us could answer, the vision changed again.

Now I was racing through the woods, heart pounding as powerfully as the strid waters I could hear just ahead. Through gaps in the trees, I could make out a figure striding toward the bank, his plait swaying behind him in the breeze.

Kessian. He was dressed for a wedding, a gold chain woven through his plait and a colorful shirt beneath his waist coat. He walked with a cane painted like it had been touched by frost.

He moved in steady, trancelike steps toward the strid where a tall, dark creature with an antlered head awaited him, holding out its claws.

I knew it was a vision. (A very realistic one.) I knew it wasn't real. (But if it was a vision of the future, could it come true?)

I also knew that I would not make it to the shore in time, and it felt too real in the moment not to terrify me when Kessian walked across the surface of the river like a water strider, turned to face me, and reached out as if I could pull him to safety.

I tried. I sprinted with shin splints and burning lungs. I held out my hand. Our fingers clasped.

The wraith had no mouth, but I felt it smile as it dragged Kessian down, and me with him.

I shot awake.

CHAPTER 7

I opened my eyes to the spring's chattering falls and the burgeoning need to be sick. I splashed upright, retching. Kessian put an alarmed hand on my back, but I feared the magic would drown me in more visions and shied away.

It was just a vision. It wasn't real. Yet I felt like I was seventeen again, freshly pulled from the spring by my mother, half drowned and painting the rocks in dark colors as I emptied my lungs onto them.

I didn't know what to make of it. The haunted version of my grandfather's house. Laurelie resurrected from the spring, only for Kessian to drown after.

Kessian said, "Are you all right? Can I get you anything?"

I tried to say no, but it came out in a coughing fit. "No, I'm fine, now."

"I'm sorry. The visions aren't usually that . . ."

"Horrific?"

"I was going to say deadly."

"Don't I feel special?" I made a rueful noise. "It figures that to get my sister back, I'd have to sacrifice the both of us. The strid never did play fair."

No matter how Laurelie's death hung over me, turning Kessian into a sacrificial lamb wouldn't help, only give me something else to feel guilty for from beyond the grave.

I shivered at the memory of his retreating back in the woods, the wraith's claws curling around his shoulders. That image would plague my nightmares unless I left as soon as possible.

Kessian looked both shaken and far away, gazing into the water.

I said, "That settles my debate with Fae. I have to go."

"With no clothes on?" Kessian had moved toward the stairs leading out of the spring, blocking my path. My robe was on the bank within his reach, but he made no move to pass it to me.

"Are you going to stop me?" I didn't see why he'd want to keep me around after what we'd seen.

"No . . . No, I won't stop you, but I think I should at least clarify one thing first."

"What's that?"

"Those visions aren't necessarily mutually inclusive. In order for one to be true, the rest don't have to be."

I was aware of how the spring's magic normally worked. It showed visions of the future, but the future was malleable, ever changing, not set in stone. Like the river. To stand with one foot in the water was to feel time and history rush past while the rest of you stood still.

Some of its visions came true while others didn't, but that had been before two dozen people went to their deaths in Shearwater. Kessian's magic seemed slightly different. The spring usually showed one vision. Kessian's had shown me three.

"You're saying that I could save my sister without the both of us dying in her place?" I said.

"Essentially."

"Would you risk that?"

"No, probably not. But I feel obliged to give you all the information. These visions have a way of coming true the harder you try to avoid them."

"I bet you wish you'd said as much before dunking me in here."

He chuckled, but while he didn't necessarily seem flippant about the possibility of his own demise, he didn't seem surprised, either.

"Has it shown you something like that before?"

"Ah, let's just say it isn't the first time I've had to stare my own mortality in the face."

"And it doesn't worry you?"

"You seem pretty determined to leave, so what do I have to worry about?"

That was true. I'd been present in the vision where the wraith drowned us. If I left Shearwater, it couldn't happen. Not like that, at least.

Whatever the reason for Kessian's attitude toward death, he didn't volunteer more, and I would be a fool to stick around to sate my curiosity.

Now I had to break the news to Fae . . .

Kessian left me to change. I didn't see him on my way out of the treatment room, and told myself it was for the best when I already had a litany of goodbyes ahead. I didn't need one more.

At reception, Fae linked elbows with me, handed a fastidiously written note of tasks and reminders over to the teenager with red-rimmed eyes taking over the shift, and at once dragged me toward the doors.

"We're running late for the reading of the will. Mum's not going to be happy, but hopefully she'll be pleased you're staying longer."

"About that—"

"Oh, my car keys. Where did I put them?"

"We can take Lunaris."

"Found them!" They held up a comically large keyring with so many charms it was a wonder how it could be difficult to find. "Sorry, I'm a mess. I still haven't sat down and processed Grandad. With wedding planning and work and helping Mum with the funeral, who has the time?"

My gut pinched with guilt. All things I hadn't been around to lend a hand with, and wouldn't be.

I got in the car. Fae continued to ramble while starting the ignition and pulling out of the spa. "I did tell Grandad we ought to hire more permanent staff, since business hasn't been too bad, but he never got around to it."

"Yeah."

"Now the spa's probably passed to Marlowe, he might be more proactive."

"Fae, about that—"

"And with you back, we wouldn't even need to train you."

"Fae, I can't stay!"

I thought they'd be shocked, but they shouted, "Why not?" So I was the one shocked into silence. Fae's manic rambling made more sense now. They'd been trying to deflect from having this conversation. Probably knew the second they got a look at my face coming out of Kessian's treatment room.

I finally managed an eloquent explanation. "The visions were bad."

"How bad?"

"Deadly bad. For me and for Kessian."

Fae's shoulders sagged. "Really?"

"Really." Blunt as I normally was, even I did not see the point in telling them about Laurelie's resurrection. It would just add salt to the wound. "It's dangerous for me to stay. Shearwater doesn't want me here."

Fae's lip wobbled. "Oh . . ."

The tremor in their voice made my own eyes sting. An ungracious part of me resented my sibling for pushing so hard, opening us up to hope. "I'm sorry. Really."

"I have to pull over and cry now."

"Oh no."

The car crunched over the pavement, Fae put it in park, then they folded over the steering wheel and sobbed.

I was at a loss. We'd barely spoken in nine years, and I didn't know what sort of comfort Fae preferred. Should I sit silently with them? Should I search the glove box for tissues? Should I offer to get out and buy some if there weren't any? Should I try and hug them? Should I try and summon tears, too, so they didn't feel alone? I had felt a little weepy a second ago, but now I just felt awkward.

People should come with instruction manuals, especially for socially isolated weirdos like me.

Fae spared me by talking through their tears. "I thought, even if Grandpa's gone . . . He was old, you know? It was sudden, but not a total surprise. Heart attacks happen to younger men than him. And he was working so hard all the time. So, so hard to find a way to make Shearwater safe for you. So I thought if we lost him but got you back, he'd have liked that. That was something. You know?"

"Yeah," I said.

"I hate it here. I mean, I love it because it's the only home I've ever had and everybody I know lives here, but I hate it. It's not the same. It never has been. Not since . . ."

"Yeah," I said again, only this time with more feeling. "I know. I get it. Trust me, I get it."

"I'm sorry. This is hardest on you, and I'm the one blubbering."

"It's hard on everyone," I conceded. *But yes, it is hardest on me. You all have each other. My familiar turns on the seat warmers when I need a hug.*

I could offer one now. A hug. But it didn't feel right when we both needed more comfort than we had to give.

I opened the glove box, and mercifully there were tissues. I offered Fae one and they mopped their face with it. Checking the rearview mirror, they made a wet noise of derision. "I look like I've been smoking weed with the new receptionist rather than training him."

I didn't know them well anymore, but they hadn't changed *that* much. "Trust me, Fae. No one is ever going to wonder if you dabble in drugs."

They laughed, and the combination of congestion and snot turned it into a snort, which made them laugh harder. I smiled, too. It was a relief, in a way, to have Fae's feelings out in the open.

Even though Kessian couldn't help me, it helped to know someone here would miss me.

It felt strange stepping into Grandad's front foyer, when I'd just been there in the spring's visions. Albeit, a nightmarish version.

Mum had decided it was the best place for the reading of the will. All the furniture was arranged the same, and the grandfather clock still haunted the front hall—thankfully it wasn't leaking or birthing shadow monsters—but it seemed every spare surface, shelf, and storage area overflowed with clocks. Hundreds of clocks.

Grandad had been a horologist. He liked making clocks. He liked fixing them even more. He liked knowing what made them tick and made them die. There'd always been a number of them scattered through the house, but now they were everywhere, and stranger still, many of them no longer worked.

Enough of them did work, though, and the chorus of ticking was the psychological equivalent of an ice pick lobotomy.

The collections gave the place an archival smell, woodsy and old, when in my memories the house always smelled like Sunday roasts and Christmas dinner, because those were the times we visited.

Had those traditions held in my absence? Given how comfortably everyone descended upon the furniture, I assumed so. Mum claimed the wing-backed chair, Fae curled up on the love seat, Uncle Marlowe and Aunt Lettie spread out on the sofa, leaving just enough room for Amelia to squeeze in between them.

The only empty spot was the squashy armchair Grandad favored, still sunken with the impression of him, as if his ghost still weighed it down.

Nobody sat in it, and I didn't feel comfortable doing so. I didn't like the way everything here reminded me of the things I'd missed out on. The house had grown out of whatever meager impression I'd left in it, so I no longer fit anywhere.

I took a seat on the throw rug in front of the fireplace.

"Pull up a dining chair," said Mum.

"It's fine." I just wanted this over with as soon as possible.

Mum sighed. "Should we light a candle?"

"That's a nice idea," Fae said, getting up to search out matches.

"It will take the rest of my lifetime to find anything in this old house, dear, and I have tea with Fern this afternoon," Aunt Lettie said. "Shouldn't we get a wriggle on?"

"There's a candle just there on the mantle, Mum," Amelia said.

"And the matches?" Lettie gestured to all the old, dusty clocks, many of them made of wood. "Let's not burn the place down."

"It was just a thought," Mum said, stern except for the wobble in her chin. "To honor him and show he was loved."

"Oh, Jean, you know I meant nothing bad by it," Lettie said.

"Mum, seriously," Amelia chided. She'd risen with difficulty from the quicksand of the middle crack in the sofa, pulling her cigarette lighter from her pocket. "This'll only take a second."

Lettie huffed. Amelia lit the candle on the mantle, and Mum said, "Thank you, darling."

She took a thick envelope from her handbag and laid it across her knees. With neat precision, she slit it open with a nail file, unfolded the papers, and laid them flat in her lap. She did not immediately read out loud, eyes scanning ahead and lips moving to the words. Lettie's knee jiggled impatiently. Marlowe put his hand on it to still her.

"To my daughter, Jean Ashborne, my son Marlowe Ashborne, and my three grandchildren, Taliesin, Fae, and Amelia, I leave each the sum of one thousand pounds."

Lettie whispered, "Well, that isn't very much."

"Mum. Shut up," Amelia said.

Lettie looked deeply offended, but Marlowe squeezed her knee, and she subsided. Though Lettie's sentiment was rude, it was curious that Grandad, after the spring's surge of magic, hadn't amassed any savings.

My mum took a deep breath and continued.

"To Amelia, I leave my Volkswagen Golf four."

Amelia said a quietly triumphant "yes" under her breath.

"To Fae, I leave all my kitchen supplies and Grandma's cookbook."

Fae's eyes welled up again.

"To Taliesin, I leave . . ." Mum paused. "My entire archive of clocks. May he make sense of them as I never could."

I'd never had the most expressive of faces, but perhaps even I looked shocked. Everyone stared at me, as if hoping I could illuminate what he meant. I didn't have the faintest clue. Though I didn't want to look ungracious, I couldn't think of anything I'd want less than a collection of aggressively ticking clocks.

I only listened with half an ear as Mum continued listing the possessions and whom they'd been left to. A tension had begun to mount in the room, awaiting the declaration of who'd been left the most, perhaps the only, valuable possessions Grandad had.

This house and the spa.

Mum flipped to the final page of the will, reading aloud. "Finally, I leave the property of 37 Culpepper Avenue to—" My mother's expression spasmed, her voice breaking, though I couldn't name the emotion until she'd finished. "To my grandson, Taliesin, so that he'll always have a home in Shearwater."

CHAPTER 8

A stunned silence followed, and then everyone started speaking at once, which was overwhelming and difficult to follow.

"This is ridiculous, Dad," my mum said as though Grandad were still in the room to hear her.

"To Taliesin?" Lettie said. "*Only* to Taliesin?"

"Let it not be said he didn't play favorites." Marlowe chuckled, as though he found this darkly amusing.

"The toilet screams when you flush it," Amelia warned me. "Pretty sure it's haunted."

"Wait," I said. "What about the spa?"

"He shouldn't have it all to himself, surely," Lettie said, ignoring me.

But Marlowe didn't. "Nobody's told you?" When I shook my head, his amusement shriveled up. "He sold it years ago."

"To who?"

"Westley Warwick."

I didn't have time to process the strangeness of that or ask why before Lettie returned to the issue of the house.

"It's ridiculous. No offense meant, Tal, but you don't even live in Shearwater."

"He can't," my mum agreed.

"Then he sells it and we get nothing?"

I didn't want it. Not the clocks, not the house. I did want a home, but a home was more than four walls, brick and mortar. Homes were built by love, and I wouldn't find enough here for the foundations.

When Laurelie and I were small—no older than seven—my mum had been going through her old jewelry box, showing us heirlooms and trinkets and gifts from Dad, passed down from family. Laurelie had asked if she could have the engagement ring passed down from Grandma to our dad when he'd proposed.

Mum had said, "Sorry, dear, that will be for Tal when he proposes to his future wife."

I had said, "I don't want it because I'll have a husband. Give it to Laurelie."

I'd been the favorite, but I didn't realize it until I wasn't anymore. After that, Laurelie got to go on special trips for ice cream instead of me, had her artwork hung over top of mine on the refrigerator, was enrolled in competitive gymnastics while Fae and I made our own games in the garden and the woods.

It wasn't that Mum was homophobic. We had lesbian neighbors whom she'd invited over for tea and sent Christmas cards to. She didn't have a problem with Fae being non-binary and Sapphic, or me being gay. I'd slighted her somehow by saying I didn't want the engagement ring.

I'd always wondered why it mattered so much. Turned over the various reasons Mum might hold something so small against a seven-year-old. I never came up with a reasonable answer, and privately knew that none would be good enough.

The shouting and bickering was too much. Grandad was dead, and instead of grieving him like normal, we were fighting over inheritances.

I got up. Everyone quieted down except Lettie, whom Marlowe hushed.

I said, "I don't want the house. I'll just sell it and we can split the money if it matters so much. In the meantime, I thought you should know I saw the healer at the spa today, but he can't help me, so I'll be going. See you all at the next funeral."

I hadn't meant for that last part to sound so ominous, but the ticking clocks and their stunned expressions were making my skin feel too tight, so I left without another word.

I took a big gulp of the summer air once the door to 37 Culpepper Avenue slammed shut behind me, but the quiet was interrupted at once by Amelia catching up.

She didn't say anything at first. She sat on the front porch step, lit a cigarette, and mumbled with it between her lips. "Family, huh?"

"How am I supposed to fit a decade's worth of dead clocks in a camper van?" It was somehow the first thing out of my mouth, the absurdity of the situation more glaring in the light of a summer's day.

She snorted. "That's the part you're bothered about?"

"Not the only part. Why did he sell the spa to Warwick?" It had been in our family for generations. He'd devoted so much of his time and energy to it. I couldn't fathom why he'd sell it, particularly since the spring's magic had returned.

"Because he's a bad judge of character?"

"You don't like Warwick?"

"Nobody in Shearwater with a copper's worth of sense likes him."

I hadn't gotten the best impression either, but still asked, "Why?"

"The way my dad tells it, at the time Warwick came to Shearwater, the spring was in a bad way. Not much magic left in it, which meant not many tourists. It was looking like Grandad would have to declare bankruptcy. So Warwick swoops in and offers to buy the spa off him, keeping us all on as employees and giving Grandad some meaningless chair on the board of directors.

"Then, after the strid . . . Well, you know. People moved away, even people who'd been here a few generations. Afraid they'd be next, or they lost someone and didn't want the reminder. Can't blame 'em, but Warwick bought up their places for a rotten steal and flipped all them nice, old houses. Now they're nice on the outside, white boxes on the inside. Conveniently, the spring got its magic back after two dozen people drowned in it, so tourism spiked. Warwick rents all those places he's got as bed-and-breakfasts for evil prices. At this point he owns half the high street." She shrugged. "Tale as old as time, right?"

"When did Grandad sell it?"

"Barely a year before you left? He didn't tell any of us. My dad found out years later. He was proper devastated. Always fancied carrying on the family tradition, sprucing the place up."

"And the fact the strid happened to devour two dozen people, and the spring got its magic back after, is just a coincidence?"

Amelia's lips twisted, making the cigarette's ember bob. "You're not saying anything we didn't think ourselves, but there's no proof Warwick did something as malicious as playing the Pied Piper and drowning twenty-four people just to make the spa profitable again."

"No proof. But you think he might have?"

She shrugged.

The timing of it all gave me pause. Perhaps it was overly convenient to pin the greatest tragedy of my life on the man who benefited most from it, but it would be nice to have a villain. A person to blame. Someone with a dastardly plan whose defeat would revert my life back to normal.

Amelia rose and stomped out her cigarette butt with her toe. "Anyway. I didn't come out here to whinge about Westley fucking Warwick."

"What did you come out for?"

"Really, Tal? I came to say goodbye."

Before I could protest, she dragged me into a hug. I couldn't remember the last time I'd had a proper hug, and it showed. I moved stiffly, like a robot learning how to love, then tightened my grip.

Amelia didn't comment on it.

She said, "I wish you didn't have to go. It's nice having one more semi-sane person in the family."

I wanted to pull back, then. She hadn't said anything wrong, quite the contrary. She was saying everything right, and it was making it so much harder to leave, to say goodbye for good.

Maybe I'd been wrong about there not being enough love here from which to build a home, but I couldn't afford to find out.

I was so lost in thought that when she did pull away, I forgot to let go. I released her a second too late. She gave me a knowing look and said, "Come on. I'll give you a lift back."

In the spa's car park, Lunaris waited for me. She greeted me by playing a comforting tune on the radio, something you'd only hear at a speakeasy, crooned by a woman with oiled curls and a long-stemmed cigarette in one hand.

I'd come up with a plan on the way. First, shower with a decontamination spell, because the touch of the spring made my skin crawl, and I didn't trust that it hadn't left some trace upon me. Second, stock up on sandwiches and snacks to keep me on my trip. Third, choose a destination many miles away from Shearwater and drive until it got dark.

I only got through the first of my tasks before a knock came at the door. I'd just thrown on my housecoat when Lunaris flung the door open on my behalf.

Kessian, on the other side, jumped.

I hadn't expected to see him yet again, and couldn't fathom what he wanted from me. I doubted it was round two. The deadly visions from the spring were a mood killer.

But when his eyes roamed my body in nothing but a bathrobe, I second-guessed that assessment.

"Hello," he said absently.

"What are you doing here?" I cringed. "Sorry, that came out wrong. I just didn't expect you."

"No, no, that's understandable after the visions this morning. I came to say sorry. For not helping you."

"You don't need to apologize for that."

"I know. But I wanted to catch you before you left, because maybe there's another way I can help."

My hopes didn't stir, too accustomed to disappointment, but my curiosity did. I might have feared remaining in Shearwater any length of time, but in the vision we'd been dressed for Fae's wedding, so I wasn't overly concerned the both of us would drown until then.

That didn't make the invitation without its own dangers. I liked spending time with Kessian, and the longer I did, the more I liked *him*. It wouldn't be good for my heart to linger long.

Lunaris pointedly put the kettle on to boil.

"All right. Come in for a cup of tea."

I prepared to forgo any myself since I only had the one mug, but I opened the cupboard to find a second.

Lunaris's magic was of the wild variety. It wasn't limitless, but it also wasn't fueled by tithes like mine. I might have dismissed her conjuring a cup for Kessian and not Fae by telling myself I'd been feeling too sick to my stomach for tea at the time, having just seen the wraith outside Kessian's bedroom window, but Lunaris had a way of conveying her intentions, and I would only be half correct.

The cup was dainty, blue, with a galaxy of stars painted inside like a smattering of Kessian's freckles. She even fluffed the dining booth's cushions to make him feel more welcome.

Kessian watched all this wide-eyed before accepting the mug floating in front of him. "Er, thank you, Lunaris! What a charming host."

She flicked her curtains at him flirtatiously.

"I did see in your visions that your familiar became your camper van, but I didn't realize she could do all this."

"She's trying to make you feel welcome because I'm bad at it."

"Not bad at it. More, unprepared. You could say I have bad timing." His eyes dropped down to the opening of my house coat, sticking to my chest hair. "Though from where I'm sitting, it's very *good* timing."

I'd managed to flirt back smoothly that first night I'd met him, but then I'd been three whiskeys deep, and I hadn't known him long enough to develop fluttery feelings.

I was having fluttery feelings.

"Let me go get dressed," I said.

"If, and only if, you insist."

I rushed down the short hall, hoping Kessian didn't notice how my bedroom door was painted the same color as his, because I didn't need him to know that night had left such an impression on me that my familiar redecorated because of it.

In my room, Lunaris immediately flung an outfit suggestion onto the bed for me.

It was just a shark-fang necklace I'd gotten at the beach when I'd first left home. I'd bought it because I liked running my finger over the serrated edge.

"Be serious," I said.

She pulled out my gray sweatpants. No underwear.

"Lunaris."

If it was possible for a sentient camper van to throw down an alternate outfit in a huffy manner, Lunaris managed it, but this one at least made me decent.

I emerged in the best-fitting pair of jeans I owned, and an oversized cable-knit cream jumper that could fit both Kessian and I comfortably inside it.

I wasn't trying to look good for the boy in my living room, but I wasn't *not* trying to look good for him. A double negative that irritated my brain, but felt appropriate when Kessian made me feel two brain cells short of a fruit fly.

"That jumper looks so cozy," Kessian said, feet kicked up on the poof Lunaris conjured for him.

"I think it's alpaca wool," I said.

"Neat. So! Speaking of neat, I have a proposition for you."

I hesitated with my tea halfway to my lips.

"Not that sort of proposition. Well, not that I'd say no. Your rain check still stands. But it has more to do with your situation. Not being able to stay anywhere for long. I think I know a place where you could. Stay, I mean. For longer than a few days or a week. Forever."

I couldn't conceive of such a place. Thus far, anywhere I went, the wraith followed, peeking out of the shadows and into my nightmares whenever I lingered long enough to make a connection, whether they be friend or lover.

I didn't cave to hope, but I still had to ask. "Where's that?"

"A place called Coill Darragh."

CHAPTER 9

I'd never heard of Coill Darragh. According to Kessian, it was a little island village, best known for the wild magic of its forest and its powerful wards, which prevented any outsiders from visiting without permission from the alderman. An invasion of witches plundered the forest for its magic nearly twenty years ago, causing it to drain the townsfolk and lay curses on people. That event made the locals wary of strangers. Coill Darragh had only risen to prominence when a couple discovered a curse cure made from a flower that grew exclusively in those woods.

"You've been on the road a while, so I thought, maybe this is a place you could stay. If the wards can keep anything out, they can keep the wraith out, too," Kessian said. "Or maybe the curse cure would get rid of the wraith altogether."

It should have made me hopeful, but if cynicism was a muscle, mine had been exercised well.

I had Lunaris warded against the wraith, but it always managed to break through. I only continued the practice because it afforded me time. My wards couldn't measure up in strength to those cast in wild magic by a forest to protect an entire town, but I still had more questions than I had hope.

"If they're wary of outsiders, why would they accept me?"

"They give tourists temporary passes, and it's a very artsy village. Lots of local artisans. You make pottery. I'm sure they need . . . pots."

"I mostly make tea sets."

"Even better! I never went anywhere without being offered a cuppa. I'll put in a good word for you."

"You know the whole town, do you?"

"Well, no. I don't get around *that* much. But I do know the alderman and his husband. I can introduce you. If you tell them about your wraith troubles, I'm sure they'll let you in, at least temporarily. Maybe extend your stay if you behave yourself."

If the place was so reclusive, it struck me as strange that Kessian knew anyone there, let alone the alderman. "How did you meet?"

"I visited a few years back. I must have made a good impression because they gave me this."

He pulled a bracelet from his pocket and set it down on the table between us. A stone carved with a rune was twined between the leather cords.

"Only the alderman can make these. It conveys protection from the wards to one person."

"Then it won't work for me."

"No, but they trust me, right? I can talk to them on your behalf."

I considered it. My plan otherwise had been to roam until the day I died, so I didn't have much to lose by investigating another option. "All right," I said. "I'll give it a go."

Kessian beamed. "I'll write to them right away."

"Or you could come with?"

"Not that I don't love the sound of a road trip, but I unfortunately must labor and pay taxes."

My imagination ran away with the image of us driving along country roads singing old pop songs, and I'd reach across to put my hand on his thigh, and he'd smile over at me looking more beautiful than any dream destination we could conjure.

I needed a reality check, but reality had checked out a long time ago.

"Lunaris is magic. We don't have to drive," I said.

She blasted a romantic ballad from the driver's cabin while I got up from the table.

"Lunaris manages to have a lot of personality for a person without a face," Kessian said.

She slammed a cupboard at him.

"No offense meant!"

She slammed the cupboard again. Then once more. Then all of them banged open and shut, rattling the crockery inside. Her lights flickered, then turned red. At the same time, I heard the patter of rain against the window. Only one window, and the sky had been blue when we came inside. I turned, tracking the source of the sound.

Something shuffled outside, and a shadow passed by the curtained window, toward the front door. The handle began to turn.

I didn't need to see it to confirm it. I knew from the frigid susurration of water, the murmur of a river we should have been too far from to hear. The wraith had found me.

The door's deadbolt slammed shut, Lunaris locking the wraith out and us in. I dumped our cups in the sink, heading for the driver's cabin.

Kessian, pale-faced, said, "Tal, what is that?"

I followed his gaze to the door. Black ichor trickled in through the lock.

My hand shot to my earring, touching the coin Uncle Marlowe had given me. I could banish the wraith here and now, but the amulet only had a singular charge. If I could get us to safety by other means, I shouldn't waste it.

I took Kessian's hand and tugged him toward the cabin. "Come on. Quick."

We squeezed through and into the seats. Lunaris turned the key in the ignition for me as I buckled up. Seen through my wing mirror, the wraith pressed against the caravan door, its arm shoved through the lock, trying to pour itself inside. My wards bought us time, but they wouldn't hold. They never had before.

I reversed with more momentum than I'd normally employ, hoping to dislodge the wraith. It clung on, a hissing screech like a scavenger bird trailing from the distended shadows of its jaw. I peeled away from the spa, putting as much weight on the gas as I could.

Beside me, Kessian had gone silent, clutching the handle above the window. I didn't have time to scold myself for inviting him inside when I should have just left. I had to focus on the road.

Shearwater was a country town, and I took those narrow roads at a hazardous clip, driving close to the stone walls in hopes of crushing the wraith in between, but it clambered like a spider onto the roof. The sound of its footsteps overhead made my blood pound in my ears.

"There's a bag of bone powder in the glove compartment. Can you get it?"

Kessian broke from his paralysis, lunging forward to retrieve the silk pouch.

I said, "Pour a good amount of that into the cigarette lighter."

"The what?"

Lunaris had chosen a very vintage model caravan for herself. I hadn't known what a cigarette lighter was, either. "This thing," I said, pulling out the metal cylinder.

He followed my instructions. They were unfortunately complicated. A black claw scraped the windscreen. The wraith slid down onto the bonnet, its gaze intent upon me, blocking my view of the road.

I slammed the brakes. The wraith slid, claws raking metal, and the recoil of our truncated momentum sent it sprawling into the road, where it broke apart like a cracked egg, only to re-form.

I reached across Kessian to take a piece of paper from the glove box, muttering, "Sorry, sorry," under my breath as I nearly elbowed him.

"You're always welcome to invade my personal space, but especially now," Kessian squeaked, eyes trained on the creature rising up from the road.

I hurriedly folded the paper into a plane.

"It's coming back," Kessian warned me. "What else do you need to do? Tell me what to do!"

Lunaris rocked as the wraith climbed back onto the bonnet.

"I have to write the name of our destination and some runes on this, slide it into the heating vent, and Lunaris will get us out of here."

I jumped as the wraith's claw slammed against the glass. I'd warded Lunaris, but the wraith treated my wards like guidelines rather than rules. The shimmer of their magic cast reflections across the paper plane as the wraith tested them.

I drew as quickly as I dared. I couldn't risk messing up. One irregular line, an illegible smudge, could render the spell useless.

"How is Coill Darragh spelled?" I asked.

The wraith's claw penetrated the glass, webbed cracks fracturing through the wards.

"I'm dyslexic!" Kessian said. "C-O-I-L— Shit, one L or two? I have to look it up."

Spelling it wrong would ruin the spell. It wouldn't work. Five claws like sickles jutted through the glass of Lunaris's windscreen, incorporeal enough to penetrate without shattering it. They'd feel plenty corporeal cutting our throats.

Kessian tapped rapidly on his phone. The service out here would be terrible; it always was in rural places. I put a hand to my ear. If I had to use the amulet . . .

The blank voids of the wraith's eyes rolled toward Kessian.

"C-O-I-L-L—" Kessian read.

I hurriedly wrote down what he said.

"D-A-R-R-A-G-H."

I finished writing, flattened the plane, and shoved it through Lunaris's heating vent.

At the same time, the wraith lunged, and before the teleportation spell ferried us to safety, inky black claws shattered the wards and sank into Kessian's chest.

CHAPTER 10

Lunaris's engine whirred like helicopter blades, a steady *whomp, whomp, whomp* rattling my teeth. The wraith shook, too, its form flickering like an old television losing signal, its furious screech dying as if we'd changed the channel.

The road, hedgerows, and sprawling rapeseed fields vanished, replaced by a buzzing miasma of magic like a black sky with far too many stars. The teleportation spell sucked us out of Shearwater and spat us out—

Somewhere else, presumably Coill Darragh, but my eyes weren't on the landscape outside, they were on Kessian.

He clutched his chest, breathing hard and staring down at it. No blood leaked from between his fingers, but I still said, "Are you hurt? Let me see."

I pried his shaking hands away, but he looked unharmed, his shirt intact. I thoughtlessly pushed it up to examine his chest and found it completely unblemished. His top surgery scars were the only sign he'd ever had an injury there.

In a shaky voice, Kessian said, "Trying to get me out of my clothes at a time like this?"

"I thought it was going to rip your heart out."

"Assuming I had a heart to begin with?"

"Shut up. This is serious. How do you feel?"

The sweaty look of relief on his face turned inward. Slowly, his gaze strayed out the window to the world beyond. On his passenger side, I could make out a road wending between the hills into a village of thatched roofs and smoking chimney stacks, embraced by the arms of the forest around it. Judging by the stone obelisk on the side of the road, we were just outside Coill Darragh. If I concentrated, I could almost hear the low thrum of the ward magic walling us out.

Kessian gave his head a shake. "I feel . . . fine. Honestly, I'm as surprised as you are."

I absolutely would look that gift horse in the mouth. I didn't believe the wraith had touched him without leaving some kind of mark. I shuffled into the living room in search of my tithe belt and retrieved a few dried yew berries and larkspur leaves. While not the most adept witch, I'd learned the things I needed to survive. I pressed the tithes into Kessian's heart and cast a spell to detect magic, hexes, curses, poisons, anything malicious the wraith might have left.

"Stick out your tongue," I said.

With a quizzical look, Kessian did. There was nothing there. If the wraith had left anything harmful, runes would have appeared on Kessian's tongue.

I slumped back in the driver's seat, less panicked but no less concerned. "Well, you're not in any *imminent* danger, but I still think you should see a doctor," I said.

"We're here for you, remember? Let's worry about one thing at a time."

I let it go for now, earmarked for later interrogation. "I can't get through the wards."

"I can." Kessian waved the wrist that wore the runestone bracelet. "If you give me the keys, I'll drive Lunaris in, convince them to let you through, and be back before sundown."

"The wards won't affect her?"

"She's a creature of wild magic, isn't she? Like the forest. But I don't think the forest is in the habit of hurting animals. Or caravans."

No one had ever driven Lunaris except me. I hesitated.

"If that's all right with you and Lunaris," Kessian amended.

Lunaris rolled down her windows, turned the radio on, and swished her windshield wipers once for yes.

Kessian grinned. "Does that mean she likes me?"

She was definitely driving at a point I was keen to ignore.

I waited on the roadside for an hour, trying to enjoy the fresh air rather than fixate on the near miss with the wraith or the way Kessian seemed to be the one rooting himself in my life rather than me putting them down anywhere.

Between repainting my bedroom door, conjuring a second mug, and letting Kessian drive her, Lunaris was playing matchmaker. She wanted Kessian to stay.

If I put aside my idle fantasies, it was a bad idea. Between my visions in the spring and the fixedness of the wraith on Kessian in particular—I had to remind myself its first appearance in Shearwater had been outside his bedroom window—no good could come of risking an attachment.

Realistically, I shouldn't take him up on "round two." Because of the wraith, and because I'd be lying to myself that it was nothing more than goodbye sex when the longer we spent together, the less I wanted to say goodbye at all.

I'd resolved to keep things friendly but platonic when Kessian drove back up the hill, leaned out the window, and wolf whistled.

"What's a pretty thing like you doing alone when it's getting dark?"

It took a lot more conviction than I anticipated not to reply, *Waiting for you.*

I said, "Did I get their stamp of approval?"

Kessian held up a cord of leather tied to a runestone.

At a cottage with blue shutters surrounded by flowers and clucking chickens, Kessian knocked on the door, and a man who filled the threshold opened it.

He wore a flannel shirt in a tartan pattern and greeted us with all of a dozen words ("Ah, there you are. I'm Rowan. Nice to meet you, Tal. Come in.") and from there on out answered most questions with, "You're grand."

He led us into a conservatory extension where a blond witch with the energy of a hummingbird was bent over a sewing machine, stitching together something with an offensive amount of pink tulle.

Rowan put a hand on his back and said, "Kessian's back, love."

Watching the casual familiarity and affection of that touch, I'd never felt so terminally single.

The blond spun to face us. "Well, that was quick. I'm Briar Wyngrave. Give me a moment. I'm almost done making a tutu for my niece's ballet recital, and I'd rather not face the wrath of a thirteen-year-old."

"I'll make tea," said Rowan.

Briar talked absently between whirs of the sewing machine. "You're both witches. We don't have many in Coill Darragh. Tell me, what's your speciality?"

"I make ceramics," I said. "Teapots that never let the tea go cold. That sort of thing."

"And I'm, eh, not technically a witch," Kessian said.

The magpie perched on Briar's sewing machine squawked.

"Vatii says you're 'some kind of magic whotsit,' so that's witchy enough for me," Briar said, backstitching the final inseam of the waistband and pulling the garment free to fluff it up and spread on his work table.

Rowan returned. "Tea's ready."

"Right. Let's sit and have a proper chat," Briar said.

He started to rise, hands and knees trembling until he took up the cane leaning against the door. They made their way to the sitting room.

"Thank you for inviting us—me," I said. "I don't know how much Kessian told you."

"He said you've been in a bit of trouble with wild magic. The Shearwater strid, was it? He didn't mention how it affects you in particular. Magical drainage? Headaches? Muscle weakness?"

"A wraith follows me everywhere and drowns the people I love in the strid."

Rowan's teacup clattered as he set it down too heavily in surprise.

Briar looked genuinely aggrieved. "I'm so sorry. That's awful."

"It's fine. Up until now, I got around it by moving around a lot. If I'm never in one place too long, and don't form any close connections, it can't quite find me."

"But you must have lost someone, to know what the wraith does," Briar said.

I swallowed. "Laurelie. My twin."

Kessian was sat next to me on the sofa. Wordlessly, he pressed his knee into mine. The sofa wasn't overly large, and there were three of us on it, so the contact was inevitable due to how squished up we were, but the pressure was an unmistakable show of support. It was comforting and uncomfortable. I wanted it, but I didn't think I could have it.

Gruffly, Rowan said, "I'll make something stronger," and reached into a liquor cabinet by the sofa for a bottle of whiskey.

Briar said, "Tell me everything. Start from the beginning."

I recounted it all. The night a song had lured me into the strid, alongside several other residents of Shearwater. How I alone emerged, alive but changed. How the wraith began appearing immediately, and no matter what the healers or sages tried, nothing worked. The first time I saw the wraith, how it took Laurelie, then tried to take Uncle Marlowe, how I then left home for good.

Up until yesterday, when I'd returned for a funeral.

Briar listened intently while Rowan whisked together some hot concoction of potion ingredients and whiskey—the red flowers turning the drink a blushing color. He said in his gruff voice, "And your family let you go?"

"They didn't have much choice," I said.

"Your man Kessian's alive and well. So you've found some way to avoid it, like."

"Oh, we're not—"

"You have an amulet, don't you?" Kessian said. He touched the coin hanging from my ear, all my focus on the brush of his knuckles against my neck and the weight of him against my side. "I saw you reach for it a couple times when the wraith nearly got us."

"It only has a single charge," I explained. "I try to save it for a scenario where I have no other option."

Briar leaned across the coffee table to get a better look. "How was it made?"

"I don't know," I said, embarrassed by how flustered I sounded. "My uncle Marlowe gave it to me when I left home. He's good at tracking down old magical artifacts."

"If it's one of a kind, it makes sense not to use it until absolutely necessary." Briar leaned back in his chair, rubbing the back of his neck.

Rowan slid the drinks he'd been brewing in front of us. While Kessian's was the usual amber color, mine was tinged red.

Briar said, "If what you suffer from is a curse, then this will cure you. I don't want to sound pessimistic, but it sounds like no curse I've ever heard of. I have to ask: Is there no one in Shearwater who safeguards the strid? Its Keeper?"

Keeper. I'd heard that term before. Warwick had mentioned something about it at the wake. "Er . . . not that I know of, but then I don't know what a Keeper is. Generally, we try to safeguard everyone from the strid, not the other way around. Anyone who's lived in Shearwater knows not to go near the banks."

"Mm-hm. Sounds familiar," Briar said, glancing up at Rowan, who'd come to stand at his shoulder and massage his neck. "I defer to my husband on this subject, though I have a hunch we're of one mind."

Rowan said, "I'm the Keeper of the forest in Coill Darragh. Means I'm tasked with safeguarding the wild magic from those who'd do it harm. I sensed something when you both arrived here." He tilted his head and closed his eyes as if listening to a distant song play in another room. "The forest and your strid, they're like brothers. If you're its Keeper—and you could be; it tends to pass down in families—and your grandfather passing away so recently, well . . . Wild magic has a way of drawing us back home."

I didn't know how to absorb that. "My grandfather never said anything about that."

"Could be he didn't have much mentoring, like me," Rowan said.

"How will I know if I am or not?"

Briar tilted his head. "We could be wrong. Maybe you aren't the Keeper of Shearwater. Maybe that's someone else's responsibility, and all this is a curse. It can't hurt to drink the cure. But if you are, the forest will know. We can take you to it, but, ah, I can't tonight or I'll miss Ciara's ballet recital, so tomorrow morning?"

Rowan rumbled an agreement. "The forest is a sight better at getting down to the root of the matter."

Kessian laughed at the pun, but it seemed Rowan hadn't made it intentionally. He looked befuddled by the laughter.

"And if it turns out you're not the Keeper, you're welcome to call Coill Darragh your home," Briar finished.

"I have work tomorrow, but this is important," Kessian said. "I can come with you."

"You don't have to. I could enchant a portal for you to go home," I said.

Kessian traced the rim of his whiskey glass with a finger, studying the contents before meeting my eyes. "I'm connected to the strid's magic, too. I should go."

I didn't object to the idea immediately. While I found all this talk of wild magic and Keepers unsettling, it would be a relief to get some answers. But . . .

It meant Kessian would stay the night.

Lunaris could provide a guest room, but I'd still be in close proximity to a man I'd tried and failed to get out of my head. What's more, every encounter with the wraith thus far had happened around him.

I gave him a questioning look, hoping he'd take the decision out of my hands. "Are you sure?"

He smiled. "Yeah, I'm sure."

I gritted my teeth, took my glass from the table, and knocked it back.

Briar said, "We'll see you in the morning, then."

I used the bathroom before we left. As I emerged, I overheard Briar saying to Kessian, "I know someone who could make you one, too. There's no shame in it."

And Kessian responded, "No, it's fine. I'm fine. Really."

But he didn't sound fine. He sounded annoyed.

For the second time, I wondered how Kessian had come to be so well-acquainted with Briar Wyngrave.

CHAPTER 11

Lunaris greeted us with low lights, lit candles, a faux fireplace on the mini television mounted to the wall, and the smell of spaghetti Bolognese simmering on the hob.

Not terribly subtle. If she'd put rose petals in the guest bedroom, I'd have taken my chances and slept in the woods. I did not need her exposing how much I liked Kessian, for three reasons.

The first, it was embarrassing. Kessian made no attempts to disguise his attraction to me, but he'd given me the impression those feelings were solely sexual. No strings attached. And I really couldn't afford to garrote myself with the strings I'd invariably tie myself up in.

The second reason was, given the wraith, the strid, and the general direction my life always took, I could end up killing him. Not directly, but the visions from the spring weren't terribly subtle.

And third, based on the fragment of conversation I overheard between him and Briar, Kessian was hiding something.

"Cozy," Kessian said, turning a circle in the doorway. "Is there a reason for the romantic atmosphere?"

"Lunaris is a meddler," I said, turning my back to him so I could open the cupboard and make tea. A calming activity that might distract from Lunaris's intentions.

I jumped as Kessian ran a finger down my spine. "That wasn't a complaint."

A big part of me wanted to lean into that touch, but for the aforementioned three reasons, I held back.

Kessian sensed my hesitation and a flicker of rejection crossed his face before he removed his hand. I wanted to catch his wrist, but I was exhausted and overstimulated, oscillating between keeping my distance and getting as close as I dared.

"Sorry," I murmured. "It can take me five to seven business days to process big things. Today has been a lot of big things."

Kessian recovered himself, nodding. "It is late. Should we have dinner and call it a night?"

Lunaris had taken care of supper, so all I had to do was boil pasta. She could generally prepare anything provided the raw ingredients were available, and luckily I kept leftover Bolognese in the freezer for such occasions as these when the day got away from me.

We settled into the dining booth and tucked in. I tried to ignore the candle flickering between us, focusing on that fragment of an overheard conversation.

"So how did you get to know Briar and Rowan?"

Kessian shrugged. "Like I said, I came here on a trip a couple years back. We have a lot in common, so we get on like a house on fire."

That final conversation had sounded terse to me. I decided to quit being tactful and just ask. "I overheard Briar offering to make you something?"

Kessian paused mid-chew, an unreadable expression crossing his face. "Were you eavesdropping?"

"Just coming back from the toilet. Are you hiding something?"

Lunaris thumped my back with the booth cushion, chastising me for being rude.

Kessian's tone was light. "I was admiring some of the fashion designs he had framed on the wall. Told him it's hard to find clothes that fit me right or let me express myself, so I wish I had that skill. He offered to make me something, but I don't want to fall back on 'mate's rates.' He should be paid for his talent, so I'll save up until I can afford it."

I thought back to what Briar had said. *There's no shame in it.* And the brittle way Kessian had said, *No, it's fine. I'm fine.*

A bad habit I'd never quite kicked: I assumed everyone told me the truth. Not only because I was terrible at lying, but because deceiving people seemed like so much effort, and I could never understand the motivation to expend that on a disguise most people would see through.

But I rarely saw through it. I took most things at face value, and then looked the gullible arsehole when the truth came to light.

In spite of all that, I could tell he wasn't being entirely honest.

What reason did Kessian have to lie to me? The optimistic answer was: none. Realistically, he couldn't have anything to do with the wraith or the drowning of two dozen villagers in Shearwater. He'd moved there three years later.

But he was connected to the strid's magic, and he was hiding something.

"All right. You don't have to tell me," I said.

Kessian's shoulders sagged, whether with relief that I didn't press him or disappointment that I'd seen through the lie, I couldn't tell. I twirled the spaghetti around my fork and moved on to the other thing I wanted to ask.

"If we're going to speak with the forest tomorrow, we should lay out everything we already know."

"Not much," Kessian said. "But go ahead."

"Do you know how you got your abilities? Or why?"

"Not the why. As to how, they came to me after my first soak in the spring. I remember floating on my back with the water in my ears, and I heard a voice. It asked . . ." For a moment, he looked nothing like the coy, playful Kessian I knew. He looked guarded bordering on prickly. "It asked if I had a home."

"Didn't you?"

"No. I'd just moved to Shearwater. I didn't know if I was going to stay."

"Where did you live before?"

"A place called Bellgrave. Not the sunniest place, but it had its upsides."

"I visited once. Made a killing selling coffee cups near the university. Why did you leave?"

"Doesn't matter."

I paused mid-bite. "More secrets?"

"Let me keep a few." He winked, reverting to his light, flirtatious tone. "It adds to my mystique, doesn't it?"

Lunaris thumped me again, but I didn't break eye contact. I needed to be rid of the wraith, and I needed to trust the one helping me do it.

Kessian dropped the mask. "It's not some big, dark secret. It's just a memory I'd rather not revisit, all right?"

Oh. I wasn't rooting out treachery, I was being an asshole. I might associate the strid with every malicious horror that had plagued my life, but it was unfair to lump Kessian in with it just because the wild magic had given him a gift.

I uncrossed my arms. "That's fair. Sorry."

"It's fine. I get that it seems strange. We hook up not knowing anything about each other, and it turns out you're cursed by the same wild magic that blessed me. But I'm putting it all together same as you."

"What happened after you heard the voice in the spring?"

His expression turned inward. "I think of it as a quickening. Some part of the strid connected with some part of me. It felt like a chain, with the strid as one link, me as the second, and then a mysterious third. Maybe that's you."

"What makes you say that?"

"Instinct, I suppose. I felt most certain of it when we were in the spring together, in those visions." The candle flame danced in the reflections of his eyes as he gazed off into the distance. "Something about it felt . . . I don't want to say 'like fate,' but almost like we'd done this before."

It unnerved me to hear it spoken out loud because I agreed. When we'd first met, it felt like I'd known him a long time. After clearing up dinner, I said, "We should get ready for bed. I'll show you to the guest room."

"There's a guest room?"

He sounded disappointed. I rapped my knuckles on the bathroom door. A clock on the wall next to it had no numbers around its face. Instead, icons of the different places it led to were painted around the circumference. The hour hand always hung around the twelve, which showed a sun, but could be spun to the other hours for different times of day or weather. Each also had a smaller icon for different sorts of rooms. At present, it was switched to the lavatory.

"What does it do?" Kessian asked.

"I'll show you."

I opened the door to show him the bog.

He raised an eyebrow. "That's the guest bedroom?"

"No." I shut the door and opened the clock face's glass panel, turning the minute hand to the third hour, which had a picture of a bed next to it. This time when I opened the door, the room had changed, a four-poster bed sat in the center, looking out a big window to a sunset vista.

Kessian's jaw dropped. He pointed to the different pictures on the clock. "These all lead to different rooms?"

"Yes."

"What's this one?" He pointed to a painting of a book.

"Reading room."

"And this one?" Kessian's voice took on a tone of awe as he pointed to a painted clay vase.

"My pottery studio."

I wasn't sure if I imagined the brittle look in Kessian's eyes as he said, "Must be nice." Whatever he felt, it vanished quickly. "Can I see it?"

"Go ahead."

He spun the minute hand to the vase and opened the door.

My pottery studio was one of the first rooms Lunaris crafted for me when we went on the road. The skylights in an A-framed roof gave a view of the star-spattered night, and porthos plants hung from ceiling beams. One corner was devoted to my pottery wheel, the other to the kiln, and on the naked brick wall at the back, all of my work was stored in shelving. A long bench with an apothecary cabinet below housed my tithes and magical ingredients for enchantments. One mug lay there, half finished.

Kessian walked past the shelves with stacks of bowls and mugs in different shapes and sizes. He ran his finger over one with a drip glaze in robin's-egg blue.

"Are they all enchanted?"

None of the work had labels, but I didn't need any. I had a map in my head of all the spells and which shelves they belonged to. "Not all. That section hasn't been glazed or fired yet, and this shelf has enchantments I added in the slip, but for these ones, I'm waiting until I fire them to incorporate the spell. I have some runes I activate in the kiln for specific projects. Recently—" I picked up the half-finished mug from my workbench, showing Kessian the potion brewing inside. "I found a way to make a mug that gives the drinker energy to last until bedtime without a caffeine crash. I'd been working on it a while, but the enchantment gave me cold chills, so it needed some perfecting."

I went on a long time, explaining the different spells and tithes I'd discovered for them, how crafting the tithe into the material made the spells last, before realizing I'd rambled for an embarrassingly long duration.

But Kessian seemed . . . genuinely interested?

"Do you think you could teach me to throw?" he asked.

Without consideration for the late hour, I ripped open a sleeve of clay and slapped it onto my workbench. I began by showing him the motion for wedging the clay, folding it over and over in a spiral to get all the bubbles out.

In daily life, I hated getting dirty hands or things under my nails. Normally I couldn't concentrate until I'd scrubbed myself clean. Cooking was a constant war between prepping meat and sauces and running my fingers under the tap.

With pottery, it was different. There was something about the earthy tactility of it that set me free.

As I sped up, showing him how the layers looked like a ram's horn, I noticed him staring, not at the clay, but at my arms and, particularly, my hands. I'd rolled up my sleeves to the elbow, the veins and muscles of my forearms standing out as I kneaded.

"Did you catch all that?" I asked.

He looked up at me. "I think you'll find you have *all* my attention."

"Great. Now it's your turn to try." I passed him the half-wedged lump of clay to practice on.

"You must give killer massages," he said as he mimicked my motions. "This isn't easy."

"Don't turn it to the left quite so much each time. Just a small turn."

"Are you going to deflect every time I flirt?"

"I've never given a massage, so I wouldn't know."

"I can think of someone you can practice on."

"Focus." I said it as much to him as myself. Though my misgivings about his secrets had mostly fallen away, the fear of letting my lonely heart get carried away hadn't. It was a possibility made more likely by the attentive way Kessian listened to me ramble about my favorite hobby. Once the clay was wedged, I set up my wheel for him, sitting him down, helping to pat the clay until it was dead center. I gave him a minute to experiment with the pedal pressure and speed before finally wetting my hands so we could get to the fun bit.

I gave him a demonstration first. He watched, but I couldn't be sure how much he took in. His gaze kept drifting from the wheel to my face, a curious intensity to his eyes. I felt undressed. Not nude, but . . . known. As I went over the coning technique, the body posture, how to position his hands, my love for the craft seemed as much a fascination to him as my forearms had been a second prior.

When I told him he should give it a go, he snapped to attention.

The moment he applied pressure, the cone of clay began to wobble.

I moved my stool behind him and repositioned his arms. "Like this. Elbows tucked against your waist."

He concentrated, stabilizing the cone with my guidance. The slip on my hands left clay fingerprints on his skin, a map of all the places I was touching him. Leaning against his back with my chin over his shoulder, his hair tickled my cheek, and I could smell the citrus tang of his shampoo.

I'd occupied this position before, in a more heated memory than this moment, but a different sort of intimacy charged the air around us.

Kessian sat rigidly, his spine a taut bowstring. It actually helped, allowing him to move mechanically, keeping an even pressure as, together, we shaped a small pot.

Once finished, I showed him how to lift it from the wheel. Though a little wonky, it had the charm of all first projects—made before perfectionism and the burden of knowledge made everything either flawed or a work in progress.

I held it out to him. "After it dries, it'll be ready for glazing, or we could bisque fire it like this."

"Can I drill a hole in the bottom?"

"What for?"

"Drainage. I think I'll use it as a plant pot." He sat back, beholding his work and leaning into me like it was the most natural thing in the world. He turned to look over his shoulder. A few strands of navy hair stuck to a smear of slip on his cheek. It felt as though I'd swallowed my tongue with the effort not to brush it back.

What if the curse cure hadn't worked? What if the wraith came through the wards? What if I wanted more than a one-night stand? What if I wanted the morning after, and date nights to small-town artisan markets, holidays spent massaging each other's sore feet after walking a new city?

My fears far outnumbered my singular desire to kiss him, but the intensity of that desire was a blaze next to a few sparks.

I looked at his arms, where my hands had left a perfect print in clay around his elbows. I wanted to leave the same ones around his ankles, his wrists, his hips.

Kessian met my eyes. "What are you thinking?"

I couldn't lie, and I couldn't answer, but my gaze flicked down to his mouth—the dagger slash of his upper lip, thin and perfect for smirking.

"Thank you for teaching me," he said. "Anything else you care to impart?"

"Maybe I could teach you glazes another day?"

"Not what I meant."

"It's late."

He sighed. "Most would say that's the perfect time, but if you insist, let's get ready for bed."

He got up, wincing as he straightened up, bones cracking. We left my studio behind.

I let him spin the clock's hand once more, this time to the bed icon. He tried to turn the knob, but it wouldn't open. He rattled it.

"Er, it's locked," he said.

"Let me."

I tried, but the knob wouldn't budge. "Lunaris, stop joking around," I chided lightly. To reset it, I spun the minute hand back to my pottery studio and opened the door.

There it was, just as we'd left it.

I closed the door again, turned the hand to the bed. This time, the door opened.

Onto a wall. Made of bricks, no less.

"I think she's trying to tell you something," said Kessian.

"I think she's being a brat." But no matter how many times I opened the door and closed it, the spare bedroom didn't appear.

Kessian said, "It's all right. I can sleep on the sofa—"

A noise like a car boot slamming issued from the living room as the sofa in question folded up into the wall like origami, leaving no soft furnishings in sight for either of us to rest our heads.

My familiar had betrayed me. There was only one bed left, and we'd have to share it.

CHAPTER 12

I led the way to my bedroom door.

"Nice paint color you chose. I wonder where I've seen that before?" Kessian said.

I flushed. "Lunaris picked it. She's trying to make you feel—" *At home.* "—comfortable."

My "bedroom" was more like half a room with a loft bed and storage underneath. I started rooting through my drawers for a spare pair of pajamas. Given I normally slept naked, there wasn't much to choose from. I found one pair of flannel bottoms.

"Will these be all right?" I asked, holding them up.

Kessian, without further ado, started unbuckling his belt.

I whipped around to give him privacy, only to hear a snorting chuckle. "You've seen it all before."

"That was . . . different." I paused. "Wasn't it?"

"Different because we were three drinks deep, or *balls* deep?"

I blushed so hard, I thought I might be having a hot flash. Did cis men get hot flashes?

"Should I turn around while you change, or can I watch?" Kessian teased.

"Turn around! Please."

Kessian shrugged. "All right, all right. Keep your knickers on. For now."

He turned his back, and so did I. My bedroom was silent except for the rustle of clothes hitting the floor and our breathing, and I wondered if I'd inadvertently created a moment more intimate than the one Kessian suggested. Because he was right, I'd seen him naked before, and he'd seen me. I could picture the curves of his back and his spine like a strung violin. Those two dimples right above his—

"All done," he said. "My modesty is preserved. Do you have a preferred side of the bed, or do you sprawl in the middle?"

"The right side, usually."

"Then I'll take the left."

He flipped over the covers and climbed in. Due to the height limitations of the loft, we couldn't sit up. Once he reached his pillow, he curled up on his side facing the middle, the covers bunched up to his chin.

A masochistic part of my brain took a snapshot of the image, to pull out and flip to when feeling nostalgic about the one time a boy curled up in my bed and looked like he belonged there.

Before getting in with him, I took the amulet off and put it on the bedside, where I could easily retrieve it if need be.

I settled in across from him. Above us, the skylight offered a perfect view of the starry sky, for once so clear you could see every pinprick of light.

I preferred the constellations of freckles on Kessian's cheeks.

"Goodnight," I said into the dark.

He said "Goodnight" too, and maybe it was a mirage cast by the witching hour, but I could have sworn it sounded wistful.

I wake in a garden, watching a man with tattoos and his hair in a top knot dig up delphiniums with a spade. Dominic, my boyfriend. (Ex-boyfriend.) He lays the plants out on some newspaper in two equal bundles. His strong hands used to pull knots out of my shoulders. Now they're pulling up the roots of our life together.

I don't know if the plants will survive the new soil in the tiny garden where I'm going or succumb to environmental shock. The soil in Bellgrave is slightly alkaline, but I haven't had the chance to visit the place I'll be renting in Shearwater, let alone test the pH of the dirt. The sound of the roots tearing makes my heart ache.

Dom doesn't look at me hovering. He didn't tell me he was going to split everything we owned right down the middle. It works with material possessions, but not so well with living things.

The last night in our shared bed, he reaches across the gulf of mattress to put a hand on my thigh and says, "One last hurrah to say goodbye?"

My stomach turns. "So I'm worth one last fuck, but I'm not worth keeping?"

"Hey, don't make it like that."

"You're the one who made it like that."

I roll over, as close to the edge of the bed and as far from him as I can be, trying to view my refusal as a victory while a shameful part of me wonders if I could have given him head good enough to convince him he'd made a mistake. (It wouldn't, because the sex hadn't been the problem. The sex had been the point. The problem was me.)

By the time I've packed my old Volvo to the gills with the contents of my life, my hips pop and I ache in muscles I didn't know I had. An engine starts behind me, and I turn to watch as Dom pulls out of our drive (not ours anymore) and he doesn't pause, doesn't even wave. (I guess it's a kind of closure that I wasn't even worth a goodbye.) It still takes thirty minutes to set off because I can't see the road through the tears in my eyes.

I pass a sign that reads: *Shearwater Spring. Take a magical step through time.* (Can it bring me back to the past and leave me there?)

When I arrive outside the park home, the landlord is waiting to meet me. (His name is Westley Warwick, I remind myself. My lease is only for a year. If he's awful, if the town is awful, I won't be tied to the place. I won't have to rip up deep roots again to go somewhere else.)

He puts the key in my hand, and I let myself in to a house of beige carpets, beige walls, and kitchen cabinets that haven't been updated since the '80s, furnished with a bed and armchair and dining table, all trying to be so generically inoffensive that they loop right around to being hideous, but there's a tiny fenced-in garden out back, and the first thing I do is plant the flowers I got to keep.

The delphiniums don't make it. It's autumn, and they don't have the energy outside their growing season to repair from the sudden damage to their root systems. (I don't heal well, either. I think environmental shock doesn't just apply to plants.)

It takes a month for me to venture out much, and when I finally visit the spring and sink beneath the surface, the world goes quiet enough that I hear it singing in my ear.

Do you have a home?

(I did once, but I made a mistake. I made my home a person so the breakup felt like an eviction notice.)

I surface from the spring. I, Tal, surface from the spring and the dream. No, I'm suddenly, viscerally aware it wasn't quite a dream. A memory, but not mine. Kessian's.

I'm not in the spring anymore. I'm in the kitchen of 37 Culpepper Avenue, light beaming through the window, a sun catcher throwing rainbows across the parquet. A calico cat grooms one paw while sat on the counter next to a steaming teapot shaped like a peony. The smell of cinnamon and apples wafts from the oven, a crumble baking within. I pour a cup, and there's a ring on my finger, then warm arms slip around my waist.

It doesn't last. A cloud blots out the sun, and I sink. Through the floor, through the soil, into the underground grave of the Shearwater strid while water fills my lungs.

I woke gasping. I would have jerked upright, but a tight, binding arm around my chest held me down.

Kessian stirred, making mumbling, sleepy noises. He had one arm and a leg thrown over me, the smallest of big spoons. Soft, even breaths tickled the back of my neck. Neither of us had a shirt on, and it was like I had my back to a bonfire, warming me through.

"Bad dream?" he mumbled, only half aware.

I'd frozen, disoriented and unsure what to do. It felt so much like that moment in the dream, standing in the kitchen while someone embraced me from behind. That part had felt like a proper dream, the kind where the real world leaked through, but before that—

That had been too real.

I felt the moment Kessian woke up properly. His body went stiff with the awareness of our proximity.

"Shit. Sorry. I'm like a limpet in my sleep."

"It's all right. I did have a bad dream," I said.

"About the strid?" He extricated himself, the air cool where his skin had been pressed against mine.

I turned to face him. It was invasive to know what I now did. I hadn't asked to, but something had let me see—no, not just see—*experience* the breakup that had precipitated Kessian's move to Shearwater.

I didn't know whether to tell him or not. It was private. When I'd asked, he hadn't volunteered to tell me. He'd said they were memories he'd rather not revisit, and I'd visited them myself. Probably through the same magic that allowed us to visit the future while bathing in the spring.

Withholding it didn't seem right, either. Perhaps his abilities were not limited to the spring, or our connection to the strid had connected us. Either way, we ought to investigate how it had happened.

Hesitantly, I asked, "Did you have any dreams?"

"Maybe. A bit fuzzy, though. I don't really remember. Doesn't mean we can't talk about yours, though."

I stumbled over my words, not sure how to broach the subject. *Sorry for the invasion of privacy, but I may have just eavesdropped on what looked to be an extremely painful breakup.* Then I remembered the second part of the dream and flushed.

"Oh, I see." Kessian smirked, shuffling closer. "You know, kinks and sexual fantasies are all very natural. We all have them. And, frankly, I've seen some things in my clients' heads that would curl your hair. Or your toes, depending on your predilections."

I flushed harder. "It wasn't that."

Unless you counted fantasies about being financially stable and cooking apple crumble with your husband in a mortgage-free house a kink.

I didn't want to marry Kessian—I'd only just met him. But dreams of domestic bliss had been a staple of my imaginary playpen from the moment I'd left Shearwater. Something I did all the time, with whomever caught my attention, wherever I happened to be, in order to soothe the pain of never having that sort of reliable, sturdy love in my life. My chances of it in reality were slim, so imagination was as good as it got.

Kessian read my expression and said, "Oh. Was it particularly vulnerable, then?"

I steeled myself. "Yes . . . but not for me."

He looked confused. I took a deep breath and said, "I don't know how, but I think the dream was more like a memory. Your memory."

Kessian went still. "What sort of memory?"

"A bad one. It was a breakup. Between you and a guy called Dom."

He sucked in a breath and didn't say anything for a long while. Then he said, "Well, that's embarrassing."

"For Dominic, maybe," I muttered.

"How much did you see?"

"Enough to know he was an arsehole."

"No, I mean . . . what did you see? Exactly?"

Was there something in particular he really didn't want me to? "He killed your plants, asked for breakup sex, then drove off without saying goodbye."

Kessian let out a breath of relief.

"I take it those weren't your happiest memories, but they weren't the worst?"

He shrugged. "I've made my peace with it. On my own, I don't have to worry if my partner can make the rent, or if he's going to tell me he loves me, then twenty-four hours later pack up all his things and leave."

"If you want to take a detour tomorrow, we can track him down and see if the wraith's still hungry," I said darkly.

He snorted a laugh. "Really. It's fine. I'd rather be free to fuck who I want without the emotional turmoil attached."

I tried to ignore the way my gut twisted. Well, that settled where we stood. I should have been relieved, but a yearning for true connection still played cat's cradle with my heartstrings.

Kessian propped himself up on an elbow. "Have you ever had your heart broken, Tal?" When I took too long to answer, he said, "Really? Never?"

"My life hasn't left room for long-term relationships."

"I'd have thought a man with a face like yours would have had at least one runaway romance. Maybe in high school."

"A face like mine?" I laughed ruefully.

"You look like the charming lab partner or librarian who's somehow the last to realize everybody fancies him."

He'd skillfully redirected the conversation away from the dream. I might have persisted, if only to question how I'd found myself inside his memories in the first place, but there would be time for that in the morning, and I didn't want to pick at his old wounds any more than I already had.

"I don't know about that. And no. Even my one-night stands were rare. People usually find me abrasive."

"They just haven't gotten to know you."

"Most people don't get the time to."

"What's the longest stay you've ever risked?"

"A week. In the mountains, where there were more sheep than people. I don't know if it counts."

"And you didn't keep in touch with your family?"

"Oh. Er . . ."

"There's no judgment. I can't remember the last time I heard from my mum. I just wondered."

"You and your mum don't talk either?"

"As soon as I turned eighteen, she told me she wanted to travel, so she was selling the house, and I'd better find a job and a place to rent."

My heart felt like a rusted hinge. Like a creaky door opening a crack. "And she didn't keep in touch?"

"We were talking about *you*." He poked me in the chest. "Fae missed you. Why didn't you pop in from time to time?"

The dark felt like a confessional. "I did at first, but it got hard. We all changed, but we still wrote to the old versions of ourselves. Every correspondence was a reminder of how little we knew each other anymore. It made me feel lonelier than I already was."

"You couldn't visit?"

"I didn't want to risk it. Plus, I never found talking to people easy. It would have been even harder, knowing I could never go back for good."

Kessian moved closer, his cheek pillowed against the back of his wrist. I felt like we were kids at a sleepover, confessing who we had a crush on.

You, I'd have to say. *I have a stupid crush on you.*

"I never would have guessed you found talking to people hard," Kessian said.

"Because with you, it's not."

In the dark, I could just make out the shining midnight of his eyes and the curve of one starry cheekbone catching the moonlight. I couldn't see the subtleties of his expression, and between the two of us, he was better at reading people.

But I thought, over the sound of crickets and frogs chirping outside, I heard his breath catch. "Are you saying you think I'm easy?" Kessian said, tone melodic and teasing.

"That's not what I meant at all!"

"Because for you, I can be," Kessian finished.

His hand splayed against my chest, hot as a brand, and he had to feel my heart speed up. I grabbed his wrist. "We shouldn't."

"You know . . . talk like that might give a guy the impression you're no longer interested in that rain check."

"I think you know it's not for lack of interest." My voice came out rougher than intended.

"Then what is it?"

"You know the answer to that, too. The people I get close to get hurt. It's dangerous." And I was afraid of getting hurt, too.

"Maybe I'm a thrill seeker," he said, leaning in close, closer, until the next words might as well have been a kiss. "Maybe I want you more than I fear what might happen."

"Kessian."

The mattress shifted. He put an arm around me, carding his fingers through the hair at the nape of my neck. All I had to do was lean in.

I wanted to. All the early mistrust of the night had molded into something new while throwing that pot in my studio and peeling open our vulnerabilities.

But the visions from the spring still plagued me, the future too mercurial to let myself slip a step further into Kessian's orbit, and he'd said himself that he'd rather be free to fuck who he wanted. I couldn't afford to catch feelings.

Tomorrow I would either be dragged back into the dangers of Shearwater again, or I would stay in Coill Darragh, safe from the wraith but miles away from Kessian, and I had no reassurance that his heart was tripping as quickly as mine.

Yet I still leaned into his hand where it cupped my jaw. Still couldn't bring myself to push him back.

Something curled over his shoulder around his neck. At first I thought it was a lock of his hair, but he'd tied it up in a knot to sleep, and it was *too* dark, like a slice of pitch.

I jerked back in time to see the long, clawed finger retract, and then the darkness seemed bright around the lightless creature. It hunkered behind Kessian, spooning him like a lover, and though its face was only a collection of shadows, I thought it was grinning.

CHAPTER 13

Kessian's eyes widened as he turned to see what had me so spooked, while I reached blindly behind me for the amulet on my bedside.

My fingers tangled around the earring. The wraith shrilled in a voice like a knife sharpening as I drew back and struck, my fist sinking through the shadows.

I'd always thought of them as having density, but I'd never *felt* them. My hand, lodged inside, moved slowly, as though through thick treacle. I yanked it free, the shadows clinging to my knuckles.

The wraith recoiled, freeing Kessian, who scrabbled behind me. The creature writhed, its darkness dissipating, peeling back from its face where I'd struck it.

Before it vanished, I glimpsed one familiar green eye.

My eye.

Then it melted into nothing, leaving the room silent except for our panting breaths.

Kessian said, "It's gone?"

"For now." I didn't know for how long. It had broken through Lunaris's wards. With the amulet's magic expended, I had no more defenses left. "The curse cure didn't work. Neither did Coill Darragh's wards."

Worse, the air still felt damp and cool, like the essence of the wraith still lingered. I got the distinct impression it was trying to pry its way through the bars of whatever cage the amulet had confined it in. Like it was still there, separated from us by a terrifyingly fragile veil.

A snap above my head made me jump. Lunaris had unlatched the skylight. It opened for us.

I exchanged a look with Kessian. Heart hammering, I crawled through, pulling Kessian after me.

At once, I could see why she'd called us out.

We'd parked a quarter mile from Briar and Rowan's cottage in a passing lane on the country road, with a view of the sheep fields and the forest beyond.

The tree canopy roiled like waves on a stormy sea, and something about it reminded me of smoke signals made by castaways calling for help. Or issuing a warning.

Kessian said, "Tal, we have to go."

"What? What's wrong?"

"I—I don't know. I don't think the amulet's done more than buy us time. I think we need help."

I didn't need convincing. We went back inside, navigating to the driver's cabin, but when I sat down and turned the key in the ignition, the engine revved but didn't turn over.

That Lunaris hadn't started it right away should have been my first clue something was truly wrong.

My second was the curling black shadows issuing from beneath her bonnet.

We'd escaped with her once before. The wraith wasn't going to let us go again. No matter how many times I turned the key, the engine wouldn't start.

Lunaris flung open her doors. Her message could not have been more clear. *Run.*

We clambered out onto the roadside, my bare feet hitting cold gravel. We ran. I risked looking over my shoulder once and saw a shadow phasing through Lunaris's walls, struggling as if she held it back.

A knot formed in my throat. The wraith better not hurt her. I didn't know what I'd do if the one constant in my ever-changing life was suddenly taken from me, too.

I risked looking over my shoulder when a bright light blazed, casting my own shadow long in front of me. Squinting, I watched as the antlered figure pulled itself free from Lunaris's grip, the red beam of her taillights illuminating its grisly movements as it limped after us, wounded but dogged in its pursuit.

We turned a bend in the road. I could see the cottage ahead, but not how close the wraith was behind us.

Kessian stumbled. I put out an arm to steady him. "Almost there."

But he tripped again, this time going down. He let out a groan, holding his hip as he tried to right himself, and I skidded to a stop to help him up. I wound an arm around his waist to support him, limping the rest of the way.

We reached the cottage, sweating despite the cold. I couldn't see the wraith yet, but the wind shrieked through the trees in warning. The cobblestones and gravel chewed the soles of my feet, making the whole world feel sharper, too. I aimed to hammer on the cottage door to wake the couple inside, but before I could, Kessian grabbed my hand.

"Wait—"

"We need to get help."

"I know, but . . . Shit, never mind. It doesn't matter."

Kessian had never struck me as the sort of person to faff about in a survival situation, so the fact he was holding back at all alarmed me. "What's wrong?"

"Never mind. It's stupid. I was just thinking that I'm shirtless, and my top surgery scars are still really obvious, and I didn't like the idea of coming out of the closet like this, but we don't have a whole lot of choice right now."

"Yes, we do," I said, and gathered him close to me. He went rigid with surprise as I leaned past him to pound on the door so hard I could hear the exclamations of shock from the men inside. I hugged Kessian so we were chest to chest, as if protecting him from the cold. Or the wraith. "We can ask to borrow clothes."

Kessian, who could flirt and say the sort of lascivious things that'd get you excommunicated, looked more flustered now than I'd ever seen him.

The door opened. Briar, wearing a housecoat and flanked by Rowan in nothing but boxer shorts, did not ask why we were there. He ushered us inside.

"Did the wraith come?"

"Yes. It tried to take Kessian." *It nearly slit his throat*, I couldn't say. *It has my eyes.*

"I'll get you something warmer to wear," Rowan said.

"So much for it being a curse and an easy fix," said Briar. "Well, this establishes one thing for certain. The shadow isn't a curse, and it isn't a completely separate entity from you, either."

My stomach sank. "What do you mean by that?"

Briar pointed to my wrist, wrapped around Kessian's shoulders. The runestone bracelet was still tied around it. "Nothing can get through the wards into Coill Darragh without one of those, or without becoming a part of the local community, whether by marriage or just . . . love, really. If it got through, that means it's a part of you. You granted it access."

Despair hit me square in the chest. "I—I'm sorry. I didn't mean to."

Rowan said, "Don't worry yourself. It's not us it's after."

"Did your amulet not banish it?" Briar asked.

"Only temporarily. Lunaris's engine wouldn't start. She tried to slow it down. I'm afraid it hurt her."

Kessian's arms squeezed around me. I'd never been so grateful for an excuse to hold him. As the reality of what had nearly come to pass washed over me, crushing him against my chest grounded me better than tapping my thumb and ring finger, or counting backward from a thousand.

Rowan appeared with clothes. Briar's would have been too small for me, but Rowan's were huge. Likewise, Briar's were slightly too big for Kessian. I didn't care, so long as he felt more comfortable. Rowan and Briar retreated to give us privacy, and when they were out of sight, I released him so we could get dressed.

He mouthed, *Thank you.*

Briar's voice carried from the kitchen. "Perhaps get a move on. We may need to visit the forest before dawn."

We dressed quickly and found Briar and Rowan both looking out the window over the sink. They backed away to give us both a view of the fields. In the distance, I could see Lunaris. It was hard to tell if she was all right, but a great, ashy stain rose up her back wall as if she'd been burned.

And in between her and the cottage, the wraith shambled over a fence, half walking, half crawling. It twitched fully upright when it seemed to lay eyes on us.

"Out the back door," Rowan said.

Kessian still limped, so I kept an arm around him for support. We emerged into a garden, though not like one I'd ever seen. Alien plants festooned the flower beds and pots, and it had a smell unlike any greenhouse I'd been to—loamy, sure, but eye-watering, too. As if someone had cut many onions. We borrowed their wellies and followed them out through a back gate, across the fields, heading to the forest. To our right, the shadow put on a burst of speed, aiming to cut us off before we reached the tree line. It melted low to the ground and swept forward like a dark fog of spidery limbs and broken antlers.

We all put on a burst of speed. Briar moved more slowly with his cane, and Kessian couldn't run, hobbled by his injury, but we had a head start. Blood thrumming in my ears, we reached the trees before the wraith.

It felt like walking through a portal from one world into another. When I looked back, the shrubs and trees and flora of the woods fanned out, crowding together, forming walls. We couldn't be more than six steps within the tree line, yet I couldn't see the cottage anymore, or Lunaris.

Or the wraith.

"What happened?" Kessian asked. "Did we teleport?"

"No. The forest is protecting you," Rowan said.

Protect the Keepers.

I shivered, the voice simultaneously a breeze through the canopy and a breath on the back of my neck.

Briar shook himself like he'd walked through a cobweb. "Yeah. I never quite got used to that."

Rowan had gone still. "It's willing to talk, if you're willing to hear it."

I exchanged a look with Kessian. Adrenaline wearing off, I scrambled for what questions to ask. "Can you tell us what the wraith is?"

You. Not you. Like you, but other.

That made no sense to me at all. It only opened more questions. Kessian looked equally frustrated.

"What do you mean, it's me but not me?"

A part of you. A piece, severed. The soul of its wild magic twinned to your own witch's heart.

"And what does it want?"

To go home.

"But . . . I thought Shearwater was its home."

It is . . . a tree without roots. A house unoccupied. A place people come and go but never stay.

"Are you talking about the wraith or Shearwater or me?"

Yes.

I scrubbed a hand roughly through my hair, as if I might tear it out. Kessian leaned into me in a subtle show of comfort.

Briar said, "I know. The riddles don't help matters."

"If it's any comfort, this is the forest being quite direct, like," Rowan said.

"But I was back in Shearwater, and the wraith was there. If it means for all of us to be reunited, to go home, we already have been, and it still tried to drag Kessian off to . . ."

I trailed off. The breeze through the trees whispered eagerly like I'd said the right thing.

I didn't want to believe the implication, but the look shared between Rowan and Briar confirmed they were thinking the same. The strid . . . It wanted us to go back to the strid.

The Keeper will find safe passage. Your dreams are the compass. Time is the road you must travel.

I shivered. Dreams? Like Kessian's memory I'd found myself in? Time, like its visions of the past and future?

"What does that mean? How?" Kessian demanded.

But the forest no longer seemed to listen, its words rushing together, whistling intensely through the trees.

In times of old, its waters ran through the veins of all who drank from its well, and they were it, and it was them, and they were Shearwater. But now it is a poisoned well. The blood of its heart leaks far from its shore, so now the water is not blood, but tears. It cries, "Come home," but no one hears it, and the poison makes it bitter and sour. It ensnares the blood to sleep forever in the depths, but you—you escaped. You, a grave awaiting burial, and your Keeper the spade.

"The Keeper? Who is the Keeper?" I asked.

"The one with whom you share dreams."

The voice rattled my teeth in my skull, made my bones ache, but that last phrase drove a splinter of fear through my heart.

Kessian said, "Does that mean . . . ? Am *I* the Keeper? Am I a danger to him and not the other way around?"

Whether you are each other's salvation or each other's doom rests on the flip of a coin.

It didn't reassure me. Lady Luck had never favored me, and I hated the idea of being anyone else's doom. Especially after Laurelie. I shook my head. "Then I will run like I always do. I'm not risking anyone else's life."

It is too late to run. Running will not save your Keeper. The poison is upon him, too.

The horror took its time settling upon me. I did not quite believe it, yet. Running had always worked. I'd been running for years, and it hadn't quite caught up.

I looked at Kessian. My voice didn't come so I ended up mouthing the words, *I'm sorry.*

He shook his head. He had a determined look, like none of this particularly surprised him. Not calm, but far more accepting than me.

A tremulous quiet followed. The wind died down. The canopy ceased to hiss. The forest seemed to teeter uncertainly upon the edge of what to say.

The one who kept the strid before holds more answers than I. Speak with him, your father's father, and cleanse the poison, or it will take root in the soil wherever you set foot.

CHAPTER 14

The forest released us once the wraith weakened from its pursuit and dissolved into morning mist.

In dawn's peach glow, we returned to Lunaris. While Rowan rooted under the hood for the cause of her engine troubles, Briar and I worked together to re-enchant the broken wards.

They would be stronger with the magic of two witches behind them, but not strong enough. If the wraith was a part of me, no ward that permitted me passage wouldn't grant it the same.

We volleyed back and forth about the revelations of the night. Somehow, the strid had been poisoned, and Kessian had become Keeper, and we would either save or kill each other, and talking to my dead grandfather, who'd been the Keeper before—which was news to me—would help us solve the whole tangled mess.

Or Kessian and I would both die in the attempt.

Lovely.

"It would have been nice to know we needed to speak to your grandad a week ago," Kessian said. His leg was still bothering him after the fall last night, so he sat in the passenger side with the window rolled down, leaning against its edge.

"Actually, I might know someone who can help with that," I said while inscribing a rune on Lunaris's wing mirror. "A necromancer I once met in Belgrave."

Kessian grimaced. "We're not going to dig up Edwin, are we?"

"Er, I hope it won't come to that. I was thinking more like a spirit summoning."

"That could work," Briar piped up, coming around to our side, dusting charcoal from his hands and flicking down his sleeves. It had been a shock when he'd rolled them up, one arm and most of the second covered in runes from countless flesh tithes. I wasn't one to judge, but I'd rarely seen people use them. He continued, "Spirits are notoriously difficult to get straight answers out of, but it's worth a try."

"I'll give the necromancer a call after we cast these wards."

"Ready when you are," Briar said.

Magic surged between us as I pressed my palm over the rune on the wing mirror, the enchantment running between Briar and I like we were two filaments in a bulb. A golden carapace of wards encased Lunaris entirely, then faded to invisibility.

"That'll do," Rowan remarked. "I suppose you won't be lingering long enough for lunch?"

I exchanged a worried look with Kessian. The wraith had already found us here. It wasn't a good idea to tarry any longer. "I think it's best we get a wriggle on. But thank you. For everything, not just the lunch offer."

"Not a bother," Rowan said.

Briar, looking a little too wise for someone with tutu sequins still stuck in his hair, said, "You know who to call if you need any more help with your strid, but I suspect you have what you need in each other already."

They waved and turned to go, leaving me to wonder what he meant by that exactly, when I noticed his cane leaning against Lunaris's bumper.

I snatched it up and jogged after them. "Wait, you forgot this."

Briar turned and feigned surprise. "Ah, silly of me, but you keep it. You never know when it might come in handy. I can have another made." Eyes glimmering, he turned to Rowan. "Dear husband, carry me, please."

Rowan looked fondly at him as he scooped Briar up, whisking him off up the road.

The familiarity of the frost pattern curling up the cane's surface only struck me as I turned back to Kessian. In our shared vision, he'd been using a cane. This cane. I carried it back to him, but he looked at it like it might bite.

I know someone who can make you one, too. There's no shame in it, Briar had said.

I thought Kessian had injured himself last night, but there'd been other instances of Kessian moving stiffly, looking as though he was in pain and dismissing it. He folded his arms across Lunaris's window frame, casting me a wary look. "You've figured it out, haven't you?"

"Are you ill?"

"No. Yes. It's complicated. I didn't want to bother you with it."

"It can't be any more complicated than the mess I've dragged you into. I'd be thrilled if you evened the playing field a bit."

His mouth twitched but didn't quite smile. I waited patiently, twirling the cane between my palms. It was pretty, sturdy yet delicately painted.

"I was cursed with Bowen's Wane. That's how I know Briar. He had it, too, and he developed the cure."

I stopped twirling the cane. I'd heard a bit about Bowen's Wane, a curse that had cropped up sporadically a decade ago, draining a witch's magic. It was fatal. Or it had been.

I could only imagine how it might have wreaked havoc on Kessian's life. "I didn't know non-witches could get it."

"Briar thinks I may have been a witch, but I got Bowen's Wane young enough it stunted my magical growth. No magic pool to draw from, no familiar, but no way to know for sure. It would have killed me if not for Briar. It left me with a few souvenirs. Tin-man hips and knees, chronic pain, fatigue. Some days, I feel fine. Other times, if you put a backpack on me I'd probably fall over backwards. Lately . . ."

"I've put you through the ringer," I realized.

He cringed. "That's why I didn't tell you. I'm not very good at knowing my limits, but I don't like having to sit something out. Don't like being treated like I'm fragile, either."

"I've been told I'm subtle as a sledgehammer." I met his eyes and looked pointedly up at his fringe. "You've had leaves stuck in your hair all morning."

He sat straighter to look in the wing mirror, plucking at the offending memento courtesy of the forest. I leaned in and helped, picking the leaves out and smoothing a few wispy strands. He froze, gaze locking with mine, trepidation in his eyes.

I swallowed, aware of his breath fanning the heavy pulse in my wrist. Seized by the memory of winding his hair around my palm, I had to forcibly shove my hands in my pockets.

"The whole reason I'm doing all this—going back, figuring out how to fix things in Shearwater—is because I don't want anyone else to get hurt," I said. "If you can't do something, I'd rather you tell me."

I held out the cane to him. He looked disappointed, and I didn't know if it was because of what I'd said or because I'd taken a step away rather than leaning in, but he took the cane.

He said, "I'm not good at asking for help."

"Then I'll offer more. If there's something I can do. I don't know what, to tell the truth. A glass of water, a piggyback ride, rub your shoulders."

"You can rub *something*."

"I didn't mean—" At the sight of his teasing smile, my protests died. If he found it easier to deflect from uncomfortable topics with humor and flirting . . . I wouldn't complain, even if it was becoming increasingly difficult not to steal that kiss I'd forgone last night. As he traced the frost pattern with a finger, I said, "Think of it this way: It will be fun to whack people with it if they annoy you."

Kessian smiled appreciatively. "Now you understand me. Enough about the cane, though. Tell me about this necromancer."

I'd first crossed paths with Emery Vale when I'd traveled to Belgrave for a day.

Lunaris and I had set up shop near the university, fully aware it would be the most caffeinated populace, and thus the most likely to buy my hand-thrown mugs. I'd glazed them with colors like the milky way and enchanted the stars to glimmer. Most people liked my staple enchantment, which kept hot drinks at perfect temperature, but one man had an odd request.

"Can you enchant it to make all coffee mocha flavored?"

"I . . . could? But why not just make a mocha?"

"I've discovered I'm lactose intolerant, and I refuse to entertain the soy- and nut-milk varieties."

He'd looked world-weary, and in spite of his tithe belt and other indications of magical aptitude, his familiar was conspicuously absent. I wondered if his had, like Lunaris, given up its form for some alternate purpose, though I'd never met one who had. It was hard not to see myself in the rings of insomnia under his eyes, or the premature graying of his hair.

It meant staying longer than intended, but I couldn't deny his request and stayed an extra two days to fulfil it.

When he returned to collect, he said, "Ignore me if this is all a trade secret, but how do you enchant the mugs so that their charms last?"

I'd explained how I incorporated the tithes into their making, cast the spells while I threw the clay, put potions into the glaze. I joked that perhaps a little love went into them, too, and maybe that helped. All the while, I kept looking over his shoulder. And mine. Feeling watched and hunted.

I'd parked Lunaris on the campus green, within sight of a bridge crossing a river, a weeping willow on its bank. Between the swaying reeds I'd glimpsed movement. After years, I'd come to recognize when the quality of a shadow seemed darker than usual, or when something moved with a particular gait.

The strid wraith was under that bridge. I could tell, and needed to hurry this conversation along, so I could pack up and move once more.

"I should really get going," I'd said.

That's when he'd written something on a napkin, folded it, and handed it to me.

I'd only had the presence of mind to open it once Lunaris and I were far from Belgrave, speeding along the motorway northward to whatever temporary home would have us.

The napkin contained his name, contact details, and a short note.

If you're ever in need of a necromancer.

The address was unlike any other I'd seen and came with instructions for correspondence using a unique spell. I had written to ask about my problem. I wasn't shy about it, and someone who called themselves a necromancer could be trusted with discretion. That he'd seen how jumpy I was and offered to help mattered more to me than the fact his magic was on the edge of taboo. If it could rid me of the strid wraith, I didn't care.

His spells hadn't worked, but hope was a rare indulgence. One I couldn't help but savor whenever it arose.

Now, as I charmed a letter to be delivered to *The Ruined Chapel in the Bog*, I hoped Emery could help me speak to my grandfather.

By the time we'd teleported back to Shearwater, he'd already sent a response. He would come at once.

CHAPTER 15

Emery Vale arrived that rainy afternoon, and he didn't come alone.

The man with him was a walking conundrum. He cut an intimidating figure, muscular and eerie with his white hair and black collar of runes tithed around his neck, yet he had a cheerful disposition, beaming sunnily as he introduced himself.

"Ambrose. Nice to meet you."

"He's my partner," Emery said, and I looked between them again.

Business partner or—

Partner partner?

I bitterly hoped for the former. My time with Briar and Rowan had already given me one too many reminders of my permanent bachelor status, and I didn't need more, but as I donned my waterproof and wellies and marched out with them into the rain, Ambrose put a hand to the small of Emery's back.

Definitely not business partners.

Kessian leaned in to whisper, "Aww, see? The gays can be happy." He used his cane to get down Lunaris's steps, wincing as he got used to the new rhythm.

He'd asked whether he could come. I'd hesitated, not because I didn't want him there, but because he'd already overextended himself helping me. There'd been much back and forth as we danced around propriety.

I'd said, "If you'd rather rest, I don't mind."

"No, I'd like to come, but he's your grandfather, and I'd understand if it would be awkward."

"Because we had sex?"

"No! I mean, if that's awkward to you, then yes, but I mean because you haven't spoken in so long, and I don't want to intrude."

"You're not. You knew him, too. If you want to come, you can."

He'd settled on joining me in the end. Secretly, I was glad of it. The idea of speaking to my grandfather again was nerve-wracking. I hadn't known what to say at his funeral. Kessian didn't struggle for words like I did.

The graveyard where they'd laid my grandfather to rest was a modest plot next to the church I'd attended as a child. It was in the farthest row, under a horse-chestnut tree, which shed a confetti of conkers over the ground.

"We'll prepare everything," Emery said. "But first, a word of warning. Spirits of the deceased aren't always coherent, nor are their memories complete. Murder investigations don't accept the testimony of ghosts for a reason. Too often, their recollections prove faulty. His spirit might offer you leads or clues, but it will be up to you to recover any true evidence."

"You told me this already in your letter," I said.

Emery smiled. "Most people need things repeated, but I'll get on with it."

He opened a pouch and went to place something from it on the headstone but paused. With one finger, he stroked a line over the stone, pausing to rub some indentation or flaw. I stepped closer but couldn't see anything.

"Someone's placed a seal over his grave," Emery said darkly.

"A seal?"

"To prevent you from doing exactly what we've set out to. The seal traps spirits, preventing their summoning."

Frustrated, I said, "Can you figure out who placed it?"

"If we had a drop of blood, strand of hair, or sentimental object from every witch we might suspect, sure. Otherwise, no. We could try to break it, but . . ." His finger worried the spot on the stone, though I could see nothing there. "It will take something powerful to break an enchantment like this."

My heart sank. "I never had a formal education in magic. I'm capable of small spells, charms, nothing grandiose. If you can't break this, I certainly can't."

"Don't sell yourself short," Ambrose said. "The magic on the mug you sold would be no small challenge even for great witches."

Emery agreed. "None of us would be able to do this, except we happen to have an artifact that can."

Ambrose slouched the canvas rucksack off his shoulder, undid its leather straps, and opened it.

It appeared empty, but as he reached in, his arm delved deeper than should have been physically possible, then emerged holding the haft of some great weapon. Opening the mouth of the rucksack wide, he retrieved a war axe, elaborately engraved and glimmering with an enchantment like firelight along its edge.

"You've got stuff like that just lying around?" Kessian said, putting voice to my thoughts exactly.

"The story behind it's a long one," Ambrose said.

"And rather grisly. A bit of an overshare for first meetings," Emery agreed.

"But perhaps we'll tell each other tales over drinks one day when all this is over." Ambrose grinned at Kessian and I. "It could be a—what do you call these things again?"

"A double date," Emery supplied.

I colored. Kessian, wiggling his eyebrows at me, said, "We'd be delighted."

I was pretty sure he was only teasing me, but the way the rain had plastered some of his hair to his cheeks like sweat had done on the night we met, I foolishly hoped he meant it.

The axe looked weighty, but Ambrose swung it in a circle with a deft movement of the wrist that made it appear light as a fairy wand. Raising it above his head, he brought it down as if the tombstone were a stump he could split in half.

Steel rang against stone but didn't sunder it. Something else shattered, though. It rang like a wind chime. The axe's enchanted light flared, and when my eyes adjusted, I saw what looked like shattered glass over the gravestone and in the grass.

"There!" Emery said as though Ambrose hadn't just performed an impossibly miraculous spell. "Now we can begin."

On top of the grave, he placed a candle, enchanted to stay lit in the rain, and a parcel of leaves tied together with string. With an incantation and a tithe of igneous rock, he lit this last on fire as well. It smelled strongly of herbs, rosemary and sage among them. As it burnt, Emery clenched a hand, as if trying to dig his fingers into the grave soil and wrench my grandfather's spirit up.

My heart thumped like a rabbit kicking the ground to warn its warren. I'd called Emery here with a purpose in mind, but it had all been abstract until now.

Icy mist and light formed in the air, my breath clouding in front of me. A tremor went through Emery, and Ambrose silently put a hand to his shoulder and squeezed.

It was a quiet show of comfort he performed unasked, and my heart gave an unexpected twist.

Before Kessian, when was the last time someone had done that for me?

Lunaris tried. She could tuck the blankets around me tighter in bed. She could put the kettle on for a hot cup of tea. But the warmth of another's arms—

The last time had been the day I left Shearwater, and Grandad had hugged me for what felt like an age. At the time, I'd tried to pull back, but he held on. I'd never been very touchy as a boy. Hugs sometimes felt forced or coerced. *Go give your grandparents a hug*, they'd tell me, and I'd try to get it over with, not because I didn't love them, but because touch sometimes felt like too much. Cats got to slap you if you kept stroking them when they'd had enough, but not me.

Nine years spent alone had reversed that. If I'd known, I might have held on to Grandad a little longer.

The mist coalesced into the vague shape of a man. The light swirled like an oil spill until it formed a mirage of my grandfather's face. It didn't open its eyes or speak, and I wondered if I could, my throat closing around a knot of—something. An emotion I was too overwhelmed to name.

Beside me, Kessian met my eyes.

He mouthed, *You okay?*

No, I thought. *This is the first time I'll speak to my grandfather in nine years, and he's dead. He probably won't even recognize me.*

But the first thing that came out of my grandfather's mouth was my name.

"Taliesin?"

His voice sounded like a scratched record.

"Grandad?"

"My boy . . . missed you."

I choked on my words. "I'm sorry. I was afraid if I came back . . . And now you're gone anyway."

"Gone . . . but still love you." His spirit flickered like a television tuned to a dead channel.

"Keeping spirits this side of the veil is difficult. Your time is limited. I suggest you be quick." From the strain in his voice, Emery was struggling to maintain the spell.

I had to gather myself quickly. "Grandad, listen. The strid. We think it's poisoned, and Kessian's Keeper now. We need to cure it or people will keep dying. Do you know how we can do that? Cleanse the poison?"

His words were grated cheese, raw and crumbling. "The strid still has you."

That wasn't an answer. "I—I know that, but what about the poison? Is there an antidote?"

"Tried to find a way to bring you back. All my research—for you."

"Research? What research?"

He kept going, wheezing like a car's dying exhaust. "You . . . you were half the equation. Needed the other half to solve."

His mouth opened wide, a sound like a dying breath and the rush of water chilling me to the bone. Rain dripped into my mouth, tasting like the strid.

Emery had to shout to be heard over the noise, his voice strained. "You don't have much longer."

"Grandad, I don't know what you're talking about. Where do we find your research? How do we cleanse the poison?"

His voice was a gale. "You swam the strid! You drank its water! The blood of Shearwater runs through you. Is tied to you."

I took a step back, the sudden clarity and meaning of his words an arrow through the heart. "What?"

"The wraith is a part of you and a part of the strid. A manifestation of the strid's rage and your grief. It is the poison, but not the poisoner. It must be healed, or it will get sicker and sicker, a place of houses and no homes, unless you—"

"Unless I what?"

"Hurry," Emery growled through gritted teeth.

The spectral mist, musically composed into a body, shifted and burst apart, coming together again by the force of Emery's will. My grandfather's stricken ghost wailed the final verse of his song.

"You must find the one who poisoned Shearwater, and discover the truth behind the wraith." His voice warped, inhuman and shrill. "The true face of the one who killed me!"

The magic keeping him there collapsed like a miniature dying star. The vacuum of its waning power tugged on my insides. The rain poured like it grieved my grandfather's last words as much as I did.

It poured, but I wasn't as soaked as I should be.

I looked up at the umbrella over my head, then over my shoulder at the man holding it.

Kessian opened his mouth to speak, but no words came. Silently, he touched my arm, a question and comfort in the gesture. It confirmed for me what I couldn't quite grasp, even after hearing it from my grandfather's own mouth.

He'd been murdered.

CHAPTER 16

It was not the sort of revelation I could come to terms with in the rain or without something to drink.

We all crammed into Lunaris's narrow cabin. She brewed us tea while Emery and I cast enchantments to dry everyone's clothes, and Kessian tapped on his phone to order us a Chinese takeaway. It was all quietly done, with nothing but the sound of rain on the roof and teaspoons chiming as we stirred our cups. Lunaris had conjured two generic ones for Emery and Ambrose. The starry one she'd made Kessian had never vanished from the cabinet.

Into the silence, Emery said, "I'm sorry. I imagine that was the last thing you expected to hear."

Not the last, but far from the first. Not much surprised me anymore in Shearwater. I didn't know how to parse my feelings. I supposed sadness was amongst them, but something far more familiar cloaked it. Guilt. A sense of responsibility. I'd stayed out of Shearwater to keep my family safe from the wraith, but Grandad had fallen prey to a different sort of danger anyway. Beside me, Kessian hunched in the booth, holding his cup like it was the only thing keeping him warm. I wasn't the only one so affected.

"I don't know how I'm going to tell my family," I said. "Or if I should."

"Have you considered whether to involve the police?" Emery said.

Practically speaking, we'd need to if we wanted to order an autopsy report, but if my grandfather's death hadn't aroused any suspicion, the murder weapon had most likely been magic or medicinal, something to mimic natural causes that left no visible trace behind. In a small town like Shearwater, news of a recently buried local getting dug up for an autopsy would spread easily and make it back to the killer, giving him time to cover his tracks.

It would also make it back to my family, and I didn't want to think of how it might darken Fae's wedding day, or how Mum might twist it all to be my fault.

"Let's keep it between us for now. I may have to involve someone if we need to examine the body." Once out of my mouth, I realized how clinical that sounded. "Sorry."

"It's a strange situation you find yourselves in," Emery said.

"Is there anyone you might suspect?" Ambrose asked.

I'd played over the question on our walk back to Lunaris, the cold rain reminding me of a broad hand passing me a lily for Grandpa's grave. Silently, I rose and went to my bedroom, coming out with the trousers I'd worn to the funeral retrieved from my laundry hamper. I turned the pockets out and a card fluttered to the floor. I picked it up and set it on the table between us all.

Kessian leaned over and tilted it so the light flashed across the glossy name. Something sharp flashed through his eyes, too. "Westley Warwick?"

"He approached me at the wake to give me this. Asked if I'd be staying in Shearwater long, invited me to come by and chat. He called Grandad his business partner, but at the reading of the will, my sibling told me he bought the spa outright. Maybe he's involved. Or maybe he knows something."

Emery hummed. "It doesn't present him with much motive. What reason would he have to kill his partner if the business was his regardless?"

I recalled what Fae had told me. "The spa was failing at the time Warwick bought it. The magic had gone. Not long after my grandad signed it over, the strid called me and two dozen others to our deaths, and the magic returned. Very convenient for Warwick. If he had something to do with it, and Grandad found out . . ." I sighed. I didn't have any evidence Warwick was involved in all those people who drowned, let alone Grandad's death. "Now I say it out loud, it sounds like a long shot."

"No," Kessian said, surprisingly firm. "It's a shot, but not a long one."

"Why do you say that?"

"He's my landlord. The garden-variety greedy sort, raising rent each year while dragging his heels on basic repairs. I didn't have a working shower for six months. Not saying that makes him a murderer, but he lacks enough empathy that I wouldn't put it past him."

He looked at the card rather than meeting our eyes, and I got the sense—as I often did with Kessian—that he was only giving me part of the story.

The conversation made me recall the dream I'd had. Or shared? It had been Kessian's memory, and Warwick had indeed been the landlord to hand over the keys to his park home. Kessian didn't share much of himself easily. He'd only divulged as much because the dream had revealed it, only told me about his recovery from Bowen's Wane because Briar's actions had prompted him to. I didn't suspect him of involvement in all this dark business, but I wondered what else he hid and why.

"That reminds me of something else," I said, trying to choose my words carefully so they didn't come across accusatory. "The dream I had. Or *we* had?"

Emery and Ambrose looked between us curiously, while Kessian kept his eyes averted.

"Right, I forgot. That's never happened to me before."

"Do you know how it happened, or why?"

"Maybe it was an extension of my abilities or a result of the wraith's attack? Hard to say. It could just be a random side effect of our time in the spring."

It hadn't felt that way to me. The dream felt . . . designed. It showed me his memories, yes, but very particular ones. "I think we ought to find out. I don't trust that it isn't the strid messing with us somehow."

"You could attempt a trace spell to see what magic it picks up while you sleep," Emery suggested.

"Another sleepover?" Kessian said, sounding not at all opposed.

It was my turn to avert my eyes. "I don't know if the dreams require close proximity, but it's worth a shot." Ambrose had a knowing look on his face when I next looked up. Clearing my throat, I changed the subject. "Apart from that, I'll need to call Warwick. Though I can't ask him directly whether he's a murderer or happens to know any, so I suppose I should . . . go chat with him and see if I can't find more information in a sneaky fashion?"

Kessian made a face. "I don't mean this as a dig, but you've said yourself that subtlety isn't your strong suit."

"Arrange to see him at his home," Ambrose suggested. "While Tal speaks to Warwick, Kessian could sneak in and search for evidence."

"I don't know what sort of impression I've given, but I'm not a cat burglar," Kessian said.

"No need," Ambrose said, a note of affection hidden in his voice. "Emery is quite good with invisibility spells . . ."

While the three of them watched attentively, I called the number on Warwick's card. I fed him a stilted lie about my hopes of coming back to Shearwater permanently and whether he could help. Luckily, all conversations with me were stilted, so he didn't sound the least bit suspicious. He set aside an hour the following afternoon and provided his address.

His interest in me didn't fill me with confidence. Whether he had anything to do with the deaths in Shearwater had yet to be proven, but whatever he wanted, I could guess it was selfishly motivated.

We all agreed it wouldn't hurt to investigate Grandad's office for any traces of his research as well. He'd left me his clocks and the house. Though legal transfer thereof would probably take a year, bureaucracy being what it was, I didn't imagine my family would object.

With the meeting arranged and night falling, all that remained was to cast the trace spell, get some sleep, and hope we had answers about the strange dreams by morning. Emery provided the tithes for the spell and told me how to cast it. He would come help me extract the results in the morning. While I offered him the guest room, he insisted he could simply teleport home, and it would be more comfortable for them all to sleep in their own beds.

"Except Kessian, of course. But I'm sure he'll be more than comfortable in yours," Emery said.

I tried to hide my flush. I was still determined not to complicate my relationship with Kessian. The wraith might have trapped me in Shearwater for now, and I was committed to cleansing the strid to keep everyone safe, but I didn't know yet whether—given the option—I'd return to Shearwater permanently. There were more ghosts than Grandad's between my family and I, more years of my adulthood spent apart than together. I didn't know whether an exorcism would be worthwhile, or if we'd all grown up too different.

Or maybe I was simply running away again.

I prepared the spell, which involved tithing a plaited vine of willow branches and drawing a rune on Kessian's temple while I tried to ignore how soft the fall of his fringe was against my knuckles, or how sharp the angle of his upper lip was in profile.

He seemed to sense the tension in my silence. "Stop fretting. I do understand the meaning of the word *no*. Aside from the flirting, which unfortunately is how I am with everyone, I won't ask about round two again." That sharp upper lip of his twitched into a smirk. "If you want me, you'll have to come get me."

And I wanted him. Especially then, with the mischief sparking in his eyes. But wanting him and having him were two separate things. I didn't get to keep people, and if I could, it had been so long I'd forgotten the steps. Dating, fucking, how much time needed to elapse before falling in love. I would trip and fall and skip all the steps on the way down.

So I cleared my throat, said "I'll keep that in mind," cast the trace spell with my fingerprint betraying my pulse as it drummed against Kessian's temple, then got ready for bed.

But I couldn't sleep. I lay there, head filled with my grandfather's ghost, the wraith's claws, the forest's cryptic words, but not dreams. I wasn't the only one who was restless. Kessian turned over, the mattress springing. Then a few minutes later, he turned over again.

"Can't get comfortable?" I whispered into the dark.

"Sorry. Am I keeping you up?"

"Not you. Can't seem to shut my brain off."

"Ah. Well, I'm a side sleeper and my hips and legs aren't happy right now unless I'm on my back. I can't imagine the trace spell will work if we don't get at least a couple hours."

"Is there anything I can do to help?"

"It doesn't seem the right time to get up and do stretches, and I can't ask for a massage without going back on my word before, but if you have paracetamol handy, I wouldn't say no."

I went to fetch some and a glass of water, along with something extra, returning to Kessian sat on the edge of the bed, shaking out his legs. Something about the domesticity of finding him like that and placing the pills in his open palms made my heart trip. It seemed like the everyday, mundane occurrence of a couple co-habitating. I'd never had a boyfriend, let alone moved in with one.

The image made it hard not to think of what he'd said before. *If you want me, you'll have to come and get me.* It got me asking dangerous questions like: What if this worked out? What if I found a way to live a normal life? Could I have this? Could I have him? Not for a night, but for as long as our hearts were in it.

A fearful part of me recoiled, not given easily to trust a notion of hope after nine years alone. Particularly not when Kessian could be so cagey about himself, hiding anything vulnerable behind a laughing, gregarious exterior.

He didn't owe me all his secrets, but I wanted something real. I didn't think I could handle it if the first time I opened myself up, it was to find myself in armored arms, cold and a different kind of lonely.

I placed a potion bottle on the nightstand next to him, the contents blue as his eyes. "This might help, too. It's a sleep draft. It'll knock you out for eight hours."

"You're an angel."

As he downed the pills, and I got into bed, the hope crowded out the fear a little.

Come and get me, he'd said.

Take off your armor first, I thought.

CHAPTER 17

That night I dreamed of music.

A familiar tune, it drums into my marrow and plucks a few perilous notes from the lyre made of my veins. I know the song. I've heard it once before, and the fact this is a dream doesn't make me any less afraid.

It's different from the time when the song lured me from my bed and to the banks of the strid. Now, Kessian is by my side, hair damp and tousled, smears of dirt on his cheeks.

We move purposefully through the woods, not in the direction the music pulls me like a wayward child yanking on my hand, but in the direction of the sound itself. The closer I get, the less it sounds like rushing water and percussive heartbeats, the more it sounds like—

A flute. Sort of. There's more resonance, like a flute with multiple chambers. Shrill notes slide into deep, haunting ones, layered over one another, played inexpertly, as if by someone who learned when they were little and has only picked it up on the odd occasion since. A tang of magic tinges each note and makes the air taste like metal.

We venture farther into the woods, Kessian careful to pick his way over a tree root with his cane, until the trees thin and the rush of the strid joins the chorus of the flute. This part of the bank is familiar to me, a rock jutting so far over the water it nearly forms a bridge. Movement disturbs the foliage on the other side, and a man with a thick beard walks out holding the hand of his sixteen-year-old son.

My dad. And me, nine years younger. We sightlessly walk toward the bank, and I don't want to watch us go under, though already it feels as if I swallowed a lungful of water and silt.

Kessian's voice compels me to open my eyes again. "Look."

I follow the point of his finger to a spot in the trees on our side of the bank, in the direction the music's coming from. It takes me a while to pick out the darker shape from the other shadows and trees. A figure—from its size, a man, though I couldn't swear to it. The dark obscures its face, but in silhouette I can see the strange instrument in its hands. My blood runs cold looking at the shape—branching, hollow tines for multiple resonances, its fingers dancing along two. It has the hollow sound of a flute, but it's shaped like an antler.

It's enchanted, music and magic burning through the air, drawing us to our deaths.

I thought it had been the strid's song, but all along someone else had been behind it.

On the crescendo of a shrill note, my father and I splash into the strid. I choke on the memory of how cold it had been. I might have frozen, locked up, but at the sight of this figure—the one responsible for all my misery—I rush toward him.

A branch snaps underfoot. In the nonsensical way of dreams, I didn't think he'd hear me. Then I realize it wasn't Kessian or I who'd made the noise, but someone else. The figure's head snaps 'round, searching the trees. I hope he'll flee toward us, but in a burst of magic, he opens a portal, stepping through and closing it behind him.

Wherever he's gone, it's too dark to see, and with his back to us, I can't see a face illuminated by the spell. The strid's poisoner, my grandfather's murderer, is gone.

I think I hear a ticking clock chime the hour when the scene melts away, dropping me from one world into another, this one softer. It takes me a moment to register my surroundings, and for a second I think I've woken up because I'm in my bed. But it's warmer, and a body shifts against me. Shifts very deliberately, arse grinding back against me, and it's Kessian. I know it before he looks over his shoulder, a scratch across his cheek and his hair come loose from his plait. Not the Kessian I fell asleep beside, because this one is naked and smiling dizzily at me.

I count the freckles on his skin. "They've always reminded me of stars. We should make wishes on yours."

"I wish this night could last forever."

"We made the time we had count."

He kisses me, grinds against my lap, and I clutch his hips and groan in his ear, half aware this is a dream, half confused because he feels so *real*. The warmth of his neck under my lips, the taste of his sweat.

His tone shifts. "When I said 'Come and get me,' this isn't quite what I meant."

We're still tangled up, but in the bedsheets and pajamas and—

The transition between dreaming and wakefulness hit me like a bucket of cold water. I jolted with it, my arm still around Kessian's waist, my palm brazenly splayed against his belly under the T-shirt I loaned him, pulling him back against my—

Oh no. I was hard. I was very hard.

Kessian looked over his shoulder. "Fully awake now, are we?"

I leapt backward, trying to gather the covers to hide myself, for all the good it would do. He'd have been given a stiff poke in the backside with how I'd been spooning him.

"I'm so sorry."

"Don't be embarrassed."

"I'm mortified."

"It was a dream. Perfectly natural response. If it makes you feel any better, I'm just as hot and bothered; I'm just blessed with stealthier tells than you." His eyes flicked down to where I'd bunched the covers over my lap. For a fleeting moment, I thought he would offer to help, but he stuck to what he'd told me, and I had to respect him for it. He was beautiful, experienced, and surely could find somebody else with ninety percent less baggage than me. That plastic bag full of other bags my mum kept under the kitchen sink—that was a decent representation of the infinite layers of my baggage.

He said, "If you need to sort yourself out, I can go."

"No, no, I'll go. Just, give me a minute." I shifted to the edge of the bed, dragging the covers with me. "Maybe avert your eyes."

He covered his eyes like we were about to play hide-and-seek, and I bolted from the bed, hastily fiddling with the clock so I could hide in the bathroom.

I didn't think a cold shower would really help as much as rubbing one out, so with my forehead against the cool tiles and the steam pooling around me, I took my cock in hand and imagined how my morning might have played out if I wasn't so damn terrified. If running away wasn't my default. When I'd finished, toweled off, and emerged once more, I found Kessian making breakfast, a teapot brewing.

"Nice shower?" he asked with a knowing smile.

I pushed aside the thought of shoving him back against the counter as a demonstration of just how inadequate the shower had been but instead—with as much dignity as I could muster—said, "It's free now if you need one as well."

"I think we need to talk about the dream." At my mortified look, he added, "The *other* dream. I had a less sexy one before, and now I'm not sure I was the only one in it."

I paused mid-pour of my tea. "You had the same one?"

"I think so."

"Both of them?"

"One where we saw someone going full Pied Piper on the residents of Shearwater, yourself included. Another where we reenacted the night we first met, yes."

Waking up cuddling him with morning wood was somehow less humiliating than him experiencing the dream with me. It had been emotionally charged, more intimate than our first time by far. "I need to sit down."

"If it helps, let's focus on the first dream."

I scalded my tongue on my tea.

Kessian continued, "The night you went into the strid, do you remember seeing someone in the woods playing the flute?"

"No. Not at all. This whole time, I thought it was the strid calling to us."

"I think it's safe to say the strid had help."

"The same person who murdered my grandfather?"

"Seems likely. If he was trying to find a way to help you, maybe he stumbled across the identity of the man behind it all."

I tapped my thumb and pointer finger together in an agitated stim, head buzzing. The only suspect I had was Warwick. It had looked like a man in the dream. He had to be a witch; he'd used a portal to escape. If he'd lured all those people to their deaths to feed the strid on the tithes of their lives, perhaps my grandfather discovered as much, and Warwick killed him to keep it secret.

"The last time we shared a dream, it was my memory. Something straight out of my past. This time, it was your memory, only not really? We weren't living it as you did, when you went into the strid with your dad. In this dream, we stood on the sidelines, watching the mastermind behind it. So, whose memory were we living?"

"I don't see how it could be anybody else's. I saw you with me."

Kessian's cutlery scraped the plate, making my teeth ache. "How could you have been both in the woods watching the flutist, and on the shore being drawn into the river by the song?"

I finally looked at Kessian after avoiding his eyes all through breakfast. The trace rune on his temple glowed with a silvery light. "Maybe that spell can tell us?"

An hour later, Emery and Ambrose greeted us with a knock at the door.

"Sleep well?" Ambrose asked brightly. When we both cringed and muttered noncommittally, he added, "I'll take that as a no."

"Follow-up question, shall we take a look at the trace spell?" Emery said.

"How exactly does this work?" I asked delicately.

"It will give us an inclination as to how the dreams function. Whether it's letting you share dreams, memories, a window into another realm. Hard to say what it will reveal until I perform the transfer."

"It's not a . . . recreation of the dream, is it?" I asked while Kessian avoided my eye like it'd turn him to stone.

"No, no. That would involve a memory spell. I have done that, but it would be useless in this case. I'd learn no more from it than you have from experiencing the dream. What was it about?"

We told him the non-pornographic half and left the rest out, relieved we weren't about to cause a strange, magical variant of public indecency.

I leaned against the counter, twiddling my thumbs while Emery prepared the second half of the spell. I assumed that's what he was doing, anyway, as he soaked a piece of parchment in a concoction that looked a mix of tea and soup.

When he removed the parchment, it was dry. He held it up in front of Kessian. "Excuse me. This part is a bit awkward."

He flattened the parchment to the rune on Kessian's temple and scrubbed a knuckle over the spot, as if trying to transfer a temporary tattoo. When he pulled the parchment away, the rune had stuck to the parchment and promptly began to disassemble, the ink spreading like ants across the page until it arranged into runic words.

I puzzled over it. I wasn't adept at reading runes quickly, having never been formally educated and making up most of my spells through intuition and experimentation. Emery's eyes glossed over the words before he sat back.

"This ability of yours is not average magic, Kessian. It's far more complicated. According to the trace, you aren't merely visiting Taliesin's dreams or sharing your own. You're tapping into the wild magic of the strid. It's acting through you as a conduit, showing you things deliberately. Both past events and future ones."

A selection of runes I could translate stuck out to me. "It calls him a time walker. Not like—?"

"Time travel," Kessian said, huffing in disbelief. "Through these dreams, I can time travel?"

Emery flexed his fingers. "This is where it gets a little messy. If I'm reading this right, you can't walk through time except from a specific location. A location only referred to here as the Bloodstream."

"Doesn't sound like a pleasant place," Ambrose put in.

I silently agreed. The very notion of time travel set me ill at ease. My life had already gone off the rails when time was a chronological affair; I didn't want to imagine how much worse it could become if I mucked about with the past and future.

But if I was to deal with my wraith problem, I'd have to find out more. Perhaps my Grandad's research could shine a light on it all. He had been obsessed with clocks. Maybe they were related to time travel and this "Bloodstream."

"It doesn't get any more specific about where this Bloodstream is located?" Kessian asked.

"No, but I believe these dreams of yours are like clues. Breadcrumbs you can follow to find answers. This could be why the strid gifted you with the ability in the first place; it meant for you to have it, meant for you to meet and help one another," Emery said.

"That's . . . incredible." There was something the matter with me, because while Kessian sounded delighted by the revelation, my heart sank.

I didn't trust in fate. If the events of my life had happened by design, that only made me hate the strid more. So many of my choices had been taken from me, so I was only left with one: run away.

The past few days, I'd wrestled with my desire to kiss Kessian again, to let him in further than I'd let anyone for the past nine years.

I wish this night would last forever.

Futures were not fixed. Plenty of people who visited the spring saw events that never came to pass.

But plenty of them did.

We only have the one, so make it count.

It appeared my fears were not unfounded. Whatever future I had with Kessian, I would not get to keep it for long.

CHAPTER 18

After saying farewell to Emery and Ambrose, we left to check 37 Culpepper Avenue for Grandad's research, only to find it burning.

A tongue of black smoke issued from a window on the second story to the tune of fire engine sirens. One was already parked up alongside my family's cars. While the firefighters pointed the blast of water from their hoses into the shattered window, my mother caught sight of me, prompting Fae to follow her gaze.

It was difficult to hear over the roar of flames and the hiss of the firehose, but I heard Mum mutter, "I should have known he didn't leave."

Of course this was going to be my fault, too. I nearly turned to go, but Fae was already storming toward me. They took me by the elbow, farther from my mother's scornful gaze.

"I didn't know you'd come back," they said.

"Only yesterday evening. What happened?"

"We don't know yet. One of the neighbors rang us to let us know about the smoke. They'd already called the fire department."

"Which room is that?" I said, pointing to the window the smoke spewed from.

Fae narrowed their eyes, counting the windows. "Grandad's study, I think. Why?"

I ran my hand through my hair in frustration. If any of his research survived, it would be a miracle. Kessian gave a rudimentary overview of what we'd learned in Coill Darragh and why I'd returned, for which I was grateful. I couldn't put my own words together. If someone was already burning evidence, did that mean they knew I'd returned to investigate? Had someone been watching us speak to Grandad's ghost in the graveyard? I hadn't sensed anyone, but that meant nothing if the culprit was a witch. There were plenty of simple spells for stealthily moving about unseen.

Kessian left out the part about Grandad being murdered. I thought that was for the best. They deserved to know, my family, but the last thing we needed was the town in an uproar while we tried to gather what little evidence remained.

"You think someone did this deliberately?" Fae said when Kessian had finished. "To stop you from finding a way to exorcise the wraith?"

"More or less," said Kessian.

"But who? Do you have any ideas?"

Kessian cast me a look. I shook off the miasma of what I felt and turned to face my sibling.

"Warwick."

Westley Warwick lived in an old manor house called Foxbury, located on a ridge overlooking the forested hills where the strid nestled like a snake in the grass.

The manor had been abandoned when I lived in Shearwater, a boarded-up location for teenagers to break in, drink themselves stupid, and tell ghost stories. Now, the handsome facade had been restored and accentuated by a cultivated vine of wisteria, still in bloom despite the summer heat.

Emery had given Kessian an invisibility potion. It had been combined with ingredients to muffle any sound he made, too. The only indication he was still beside me was the rustle of leaves in his wake. We'd also drank half a potion each, which allowed us to communicate telepathically for a short time.

I tested it as we walked the long path up to the manor. *The invisibility will only last an hour, so by 2:15, we need to get out. I'll wind down the conversation earlier. You sneak in with me, and sneak out the same way.* We'd been over it already, but I said it to reassure myself.

Got it. We'll be fine, Kessian reassured me.

As we came to the enormous door—it seemed far too large to knock on, but knock I did—a fizzle of magic went through me. Something in the soil, helping the flowers stay fresh out of season. My nerves buzzed in a similar fashion. The wraith hadn't appeared over a long enough period, so it felt like a stayed execution, but the guillotine's blade still hovered, waiting.

The door opened and a man built like a coat hanger dipped his head. "Taliesin, I presume? Right this way. Mr. Warwick is expecting you."

I didn't know people still had butlers, groundskeepers, that sort of thing. I stepped through the door slowly. A warm pressure at my back told me Kessian had passed behind me. There, then gone. I missed his presence immediately, forced to trust he would be all right, and the rest of the plan would work.

The grandeur of the foyer was intimidating. Old murals on the walls depicted unicorns and mythical creatures amongst florals and filigree, restored from the grime and graffiti tags that used to cover them. The grand staircase was flanked on either side by glass display cases housing strange relics like a museum. An ornate chalice filled with liquid that swallowed the light, a vintage cocktail dress embroidered with glowing thread—but one particular display drew my attention.

A collection of driftwood, moss, and a white horse's skull had been assembled into an eerie statue. From the skull, various branches had been fused together in a configuration resembling antlers, decorated with brass chains. Various holes were drilled into the tines.

It looked so much like the wraith, my blood went cold.

"Recognize it, do you?"

I hadn't heard Warwick's shoes on the marble floor. He stood in an archway leading into a sitting room. Hands behind his back, he walked closer, appraising the strange display.

"I had it made specially to protect this place from the wraith. Superstitious, perhaps. Edwin told me later it only worked because the wraith had no interest in me. Just you."

"That seems to be the case."

"Why do you think that is, I wonder?"

His interest in the topic put me on edge. If I'd been responsible for the drownings or the wraith, I wouldn't be brazen enough to talk about them like this, but perhaps that was part of Warwick's facade.

"I don't know. I always thought it was because I'm the one who survived. Not so sure now."

"I'm sorry. It's probably not your favorite topic. Perhaps one best discussed over tea."

He led me into a conservatory, bright with afternoon sun and providing a luscious view of the gardens outside. Tea had been laid out for us. I'd never got on with fine china, the clinking sound too painfully sharp compared to the less refined ceramics I made. Wanting something to do with my hands won out over my aversion, because Warwick was already stirring a teaspoon of sugar into his cup, his osprey familiar hopping along the broad swathe of his shoulders.

I leaned forward for the sugar, but he waved my hand away and opened a separate cup, also containing sugar. I thought perhaps he was particular about germs, but he said, "That's the salt. I prefer salty tea. Strange, I know."

The very thought made me ill. As I reached for the sugar, though, it flung itself off the table, white granules spilling across the floor as it rolled away.

Warwick raised both eyebrows. "If you don't take sugar, you need only have said."

"That wasn't me," I said, staring at the shattered cup. The lid still rolled on its end, clattering behind a plant pot.

"Hm." Warwick didn't seem to believe me. "Well, Foxbury Manor is quite old. Could be haunted, who knows? Would you prefer something else to drink altogether? I can make us something stronger."

"Tea is fine." I needed a clear head.

Warwick called for his butler to fetch it for me. I dug my fingernail into my palm and focused on the plan. I couldn't ask any direct questions about Grandpa's murder, so Kessian had coached me to ask why Warwick had wanted to speak to me, and see whether I could guide the conversation from there. I could ask about his partnership with my grandfather, how his death affected Warwick, if anything strange had cropped up before it happened, and gauge his responses.

Kessian would have been better at this, but I would have been no more comfortable snooping through Warwick's house.

"So, what was it you wanted to talk to me about?" I asked.

Warwick chuckled. "Straight to the point. I like it. Your grandfather said as much, that you didn't dilly or dally. But I digress. It is a strange thing I called you here for, because I am not entirely sure how much you know about your grandfather's role in Shearwater. As Keeper, I mean."

That Warwick had known about this Keeper business made me feel all the more alienated. Had Grandad's murderer known him better than I had? "He didn't have the opportunity to tell me."

"I know. Quite tragic, that. The role I refer to, and all his work associated with it, was largely pursued in the hopes you could return."

I shifted uncomfortably. The topic of returning never ceased to put me on edge. I didn't know if my aversion came from a genuine dislike of the place or from fear of letting myself want what was out of reach. "He was looking for a way to deal with the wraith, you mean."

"Yes, nasty thing. I'd been trying to help him find a way to trap and banish it, but truth be told, it was quite difficult to research or test when its appearances only coincided with yours. All theoretical, you understand. He had a good head for magical theory, your grandfather."

Kessian's voice filtered into my mind as the butler returned with a replacement sugar. *I think I found his office, but it's locked. Who locks doors in their own house?*

I tensed, covering my silence by stirring sugar into my tea and taking a long sip. *Give me a minute. I'll excuse myself to go to the toilet and find you.*

Third door on your right after coming up the stairs.

"Taliesin?" Warwick asked.

I cleared my throat. "Sorry. It's a lot to take in. No one ever told me about a trap for the wraith. I didn't know that was possible."

"To be clear, we still don't know if it is, but Edwin thought so. I reckon he was quite close to finishing the spell, but alas . . . time got the better of him."

I weighed that coincidence against the one in which Warwick bought the spa and it miraculously regained its profitability soon after. It was very strenuously plausible, but that he spoke openly of it set me off kilter. I was not good at lying, nor at telling when someone else was.

I set my tea down. "I, er, want to know more about this, but I'm bursting for the toilet. Shouldn't have drunk two coffees before coming." This, fortunately, was not a lie.

"Ah, it's the door just past the staircase. Shall I call on Lionel to show you?"

Lionel must have been the butler. Did butlers get assigned names that sounded appropriate for butlers or was that a happy accident?

"I'm sure I can manage. Be right back."

I hurried out, hoping he couldn't sense my blood pressure rising. Making my way back to the foyer, I saw the door he'd indicated, but went up the stairs instead, hoping *Lionel* wasn't lurking anywhere. On the landing, I made my way down the hall to the third door, where I abruptly felt a hand on my elbow.

I'm here.

From my tithe belt, I withdrew the maple seeds and rat's teeth to cast an unlock charm, praying the door wasn't enchanted to resist such spells. The bolt clicked open. I let out a breath of relief as the knob quietly turned in Kessian's invisible hand. The door swung inward to an austere office, diplomas on the walls, a shelf of rugby trophies. Most witches had studies crammed with books.

A series of filing cabinets lined the wall, all locked. Each and every one.

We didn't have time to muddle around looking for a key. I strained the limits of my magic, shattering the teeth and using the smallest amount of each tithe possible.

Then I noticed something dark and shiny under the desk. A safe.

I only had one maple seed and a shard of tooth left. I knew as I pressed it against the dial it wouldn't be enough. The safe's door didn't budge.

Self-derision was one of my greater talents, and I wasted no time in berating myself for not checking here sooner. If anything truly valuable to this investigation existed, it would no doubt be in that safe.

We'd have to return for it. Somehow. Or so I believed, until a soft touch at my wrist drew me back. I couldn't see Kessian, but I felt something stirring around him. It was hard to call it magic, though it could be nothing else. Still, it was no magic like mine. Nor like any other witch's. It murmured like a river, made the air damp and cold.

Kessian started turning the dial on the safe. This way, then that, moving it as if guided by intuition alone.

It clicked open.

How did you know? I asked, but Kessian didn't answer me, and a different sound raised the hair on my arms. So quiet, I might have missed it if we hadn't been so eerily silent in an effort to go unnoticed.

The flutter of wing beats. Warwick's familiar had come looking for me.

I couldn't risk leaving. It would see me, report back on where I'd been. Any second it might fly through the door to investigate why it was open.

I crawled under the desk, the only place I could hide. I didn't know if Kessian had heard it, but a moment later, the throaty chirp of an osprey made its way to my ear, followed by the soft click of its talons hopping across the desk. Right above my head.

I clamped my eyes shut, as if it couldn't see me if I couldn't see it. I'd never been the sort to break the rules or take risks. I had once accidentally stolen a bottle of water. It was in my hand rather than my basket while I did the shopping, and I forgot to scan it at self-checkout. I'd returned to pay for it as soon as I'd realized what I'd done.

The risk now was far more immense, because I was about to be caught red-handed snooping in the office of a man who might have murdered my grandad. The familiar would no doubt hear me hyperventilating any moment n—

I felt something—someone—bump my knees, grasp my jaw, then warm, soft lips pressed against my own. My body recognized the kiss before my mind could register what was happening, but it caught up with the slide of a tongue against mine, tasting tart and vaguely floral. My eyes were already closed. I was tempted to keep them that way. Perhaps this was one of those shared dreams with Kessian. It certainly felt that way.

The kiss broke. I opened my eyes to see Kessian, crammed under the desk with me, the osprey flitting on the windowsill, visible to us but somehow not the other way around.

"Sorry. It was the only way I could think to stop you getting caught," Kessian said.

The invisibility potion. He'd hoped enough trace of it remained on his tongue to make me invisible and silent, too.

Such a trace amount wouldn't last long. I had to rush downstairs if I hoped to avoid the effects wearing off. I would have to ask how he'd known the numbers to the safe later.

"You're brilliant. I hope you know that," I said. Then, overwhelmed with gratitude, I took his face in my hands and kissed him, hard but brief. I didn't think about it. Relief and gratitude overcame my impulse control. For all that it lasted a second, it still blazed through me, because God, I'd wanted to do this nearly every moment since he'd offered a round two. Shock was plain in his eyes when I pulled back. The electric taste of his strange magic tingled on my lips as I fled the office, taking the stairs down two at a time.

I went to the toilet where I was meant to be and waited for the spell to dissipate. It didn't take long. I splashed some water on my face to cool the color in my cheeks, washed up, and returned to the conservatory.

The osprey hadn't come back yet. Warwick said, "Are you feeling all right?"

"Yeah, er, bad stomach. Everything to do with the wraith makes me anxious." I couldn't tell if he believed me. I pressed on. "I wanted to ask you, what happened to my grandpa's research on the trap?"

"Oh, I still have it."

A flicker of alarm went through me. *Because you took it from his study before burning down the rest, or because he gave it to you?* "Can I see it?"

"Of course. Though, I do have a small favor to ask before I do."

I supposed this was how rich people got rich. They never did anything for free. If Grandpa had left me the research rather than the house, I wouldn't have to barter with a possible murderer, but he probably hadn't thought he'd die before the research was complete.

"What would you need from me?"

"As the Keeper, your connection to the strid is quite powerful. I admired your grandfather, I did, but by the end his relationship with the strid was strained, to say the least. Understandably so! He lost two family members to it. I imagine your feelings are no less complicated. But, and I'm sure you've guessed as much by now, the magic of the strid is waning once more."

I blinked. I hadn't guessed as much. It seemed perfectly capable of sharing its visions when I'd swam in it and when I lay my head down to dream. I didn't say as much.

"The magic has been particularly scarce since a young man started harnessing the powers himself. The spring's magic ought to be shared.

I hesitate to say this—I do not want to sound as though I'm blaming Edwin, after all—but to repair the strid, I believe you will need to find a way to . . . forgive it. Work with it, rather than against it."

This conversation required a more delicate touch than I was capable of. How could I reveal that I knew the strid needed cleansing, and that someone had poisoned it, without letting him know I suspected his involvement? I didn't want to discuss Kessian, either, in case my expression gave away that he was currently snooping through Warwick's safe.

I edged around the topic. "I made a trip to Coill Darragh, where the forest is a source of wild magic, too. It told me I need to cleanse the strid, that it'd been poisoned. Maybe the wraith is a manifestation of the poison. If so, my grandfather's research could help. If I could trap it, find a way to communicate with it—"

Warwick dismissed the theory with a wave of his hand. "I don't think it can be reasoned with, and I know you're a man who likes to get to the point, so rather than dissemble further, let me be plain."

His osprey familiar flitted into the room, landing on his shoulder and hissing in his ear. I tensed. Warwick met my eyes.

"Why don't you call out your accomplice, and we'll have ourselves a proper, honest chat?"

CHAPTER 19

Too stunned to speak, I watched as Lionel appeared, escorting a very visible Kessian into the conservatory. He was limping, and Lionel held his cane.

I shot to my feet, and it was very gratifying to see the butler take a fearful step back. He had Kessian's elbow in a pincer-like grip and had clearly made no allowances for Kessian's disability on the way down the stairs. Despite my total lack of history of violent impulses, I had the urge to punch Lionel.

"I'm okay," Kessian soothed.

Lionel still eyed me warily. "I've searched. It isn't hollow, nor is there any sign of transfiguration."

Warwick gave a nod, and Lionel handed the cane back to Kessian, who snatched it. "I expected another Ashborne, but this is much better. Perhaps we can kill several birds with one stone. Lionel, you can leave him with us," said Warwick.

Kessian yanked his elbow free, scowling. "Sorry. I don't know how he found me."

"Don't blame yourselves. A charm on the door alerts me anytime it's opened. I'm quite good at disguising them, and I'd already taken the liberty of collecting Edwin's research, so you wouldn't have found it there." He leaned over to pull a folder from amongst magazines in a rack by his armchair. "Was anything missing, Lionel?"

"A contract, sir." He leaned in to whisper more in Warwick's ear. I couldn't catch what it was he said.

Warwick gave Kessian a disappointed look. "Hand it over."

"I don't have it, whatever it is," Kessian said.

"I'd rather not search you."

"I mean it." Kessian looked to me. "I didn't have time to go through everything in there. There were hundreds of contracts. How would I know which one to take?"

Warwick rolled his eyes. "Have it your way."

I didn't see what he tithed, but a sluice of liquid silver magic coursed over Kessian, into his pockets, through the buttons on his clothes. It dissipated in a sigh, but found nothing.

"That's strange." Warwick pointed the spell at me this time.

The sensation was something I could only compare to finding a tick or some other parasite burrowed beneath my skin. I shuddered with relief when it finally turned to mist, revealing nothing.

Warwick looked cross now. "Did you portal it somewhere safe?"

"No," I said. At the same time, another spell slithered up my throat. I tried not to gag, but it tasted like compost, earthy and rotting. Some sort of truth serum? Powerful magic, not the kind I'd ever performed, but I hadn't seen him cast anything.

Warwick picked up the cup of sugar and held it out to Kessian. "Eat a teaspoon of this, please."

Kessian took a step back.

"That wasn't a request, and if you indeed haven't stolen anything, then you have nothing to fear. It's truth serum. Taliesin has already taken it."

Perhaps the "salt" hadn't really been salt, then. I felt utterly outmatched as a witch. These were spells I'd never cast; I'd never had need of them. Everything I'd learned on the road had been out of necessity.

Kessian still hesitated. Warwick said, "Don't be difficult. The truth will out, one way or another."

With eyes like the bottomless dark of the sea, Kessian wet his finger on his tongue, dipped it in the sugar, and licked it clean.

Warwick said, "I will ask you directly. Did you take the contract?"

Both of us answered "No" in unison.

Warwick grunted, dissatisfied. "Lionel, please double-check the contract is indeed missing. Otherwise, scrape my study for any trace magic they might have used to secret it away. For now, I'm satisfied it's not on their persons, and we have other things to discuss."

Lionel's footsteps echoed off the marble as he left. The sun came through the conservatory at such an angle that I had to squint to look at Warwick, but he seemed relaxed, his concern for the missing document either forgotten or placed on reserve.

"Now that we've dispensed with the secrets, tell me what you were searching for. If not the contract, then what? Because up until a moment ago, you shouldn't have known this spellwork to trap the wraith existed." He tapped my grandfather's folder stuffed with papers.

Kessian sank onto the edge of the sofa next to me. "What spellwork?"

I filled him in on the trap for the wraith, watching his expression darken. Normally so bright-eyed, I'd never seen Kessian like this with anyone. He really hated Warwick, and I got the sense today was not the original source of that hatred. I was coming to feel the same way, but I no longer felt as threatened as when I'd first come in. We needed that research, and Warwick needed me to fix the strid. He cared more about money than anything. Even if he was connected with what happened nearly a decade ago, I doubted he'd risk prison by bringing us to harm now, in broad daylight, within sight of his staff, and without very good reason. We had no evidence he'd killed someone. If we did, I might fear that was reason enough.

So I stopped trying to lie or sneak my way around the conversation, neither of which came naturally, and stated the blunt truth. "My grandad was murdered, and you're the only suspect I have."

Warwick sat up straighter, and the confusion on his face could have been because he hadn't known, or because he had and didn't expect me to find out. "What do you mean, murdered?"

"Does the word 'murdered' mean anything else?"

"I mean this is the first I'm hearing it, and if there'd been a sign of foul play, I'd expect the mortician might have noticed. Who's told you this?"

"His ghost."

Warwick's eyebrows hoisted higher still. "His ghost told you he'd been killed, but not by who?"

"He said to find the truth behind the wraith, and the identity of the poisoner. Then I would find his murderer."

Warwick sat back, blowing out a lungful of air. "That is a lot to take in."

"You had no idea?" Kessian pressed.

"Of course not. I would have reported it to the authorities if I had. Have you?"

"Not yet. I didn't want the killer to hear of it and cover his tracks. I didn't want my family to hear of it, either, but I might have to order an autopsy report. Who knows how long that will take, and how far the killer could have run by the time it turns up anything."

"On that, I might be able to assist." Warwick set the folder on the table, out of my reach, so I understood it was a bargaining chip. "The nice thing about money is you can pull strings, speed things along, and keep it all secret. I don't like the sounds of a murderer in town any more than you, but I would like some assurances from you before I make any calls."

Kessian's lip curled. "You won't do it for the sake of justice? Not even for Edwin?"

Warwick spread his hands. "Yes, I'm sure you think it's quite cut-throat, but I have investments that need protecting. Particularly if tourism in Shearwater takes a downturn, and murderers on the loose are never good for business, nor violent wraiths."

Confusion gripped me. I had no inclination as to what he'd want from me, even less what he'd want from Kessian. Neither of us was wealthy enough to turn the tide of Warwick's fortunes.

Kessian didn't look confused at all, though. He glared and slouched back in his seat, arms crossed.

"What do you want?" I asked warily.

"In exchange for your grandfather's research *and* an expedited autopsy report on your grandfather, kept hush hush so as not to send our culprit into hiding, I'd like to expand my portfolio of property, and I understand that 37 Culpepper Avenue has fallen to you. Agree to sell it to me, and we'll have a deal." He turned his salesman's smile on Kessian. "You already know what I want from you, and frankly, it's been a mercy of me not to demand it sooner."

More secrets? I regarded Kessian with uncertainty. "What's he talking about?"

"I'll tell you later," Kessian muttered. He turned his attention on Warwick. "Yeah. Fine. I'll do it. Not as though I have a choice. But you don't get to demand that from Tal. You already have the spa."

Warwick shrugged. "I wouldn't be where I am today if I did not strike a hard bargain, and I'm not doing this one by half."

I couldn't yet process the feelings rushing through me. 37 Culpepper Avenue hadn't yet felt like mine. I'd been poised to sell it because there was no point in owning a house I couldn't live in. But I'd had that vision in the spring, the one in the kitchen of Culpepper Avenue where warm arms wrapped around me, and I stood in the prismatic light of a sun-catcher at the window while Lunaris—a cat and not a caravan—groomed one paw.

Domestic fantasies were my bread and butter, but I hadn't realized how real it had started to feel. I'd inherited the house, I had a plan to free myself from the wraith. It hadn't seemed *plausible*, but it was no longer impossible, and that made a difference.

Kessian had looked at Warwick with hate, and now I felt much the same. He was ruthless and cared not a whit for the danger my predicament put us in. His money would protect him, as it always did.

I needed that research. If we said no now, there was no way he'd leave it anywhere we could get our hands on it. He'd already caught us today. Even if we managed to steal it, that still left my grandfather's autopsy. The idea of digging him up myself sickened me. I wasn't the spiritual sort, but standing six feet deep in a grave to examine my grandfather's corpse seemed more than bad luck; it was an invitation for the wraith to come and lay me to rest with him.

That wraith still hunted me, and the killer was still free. He could be sitting right across from me, though I couldn't understand why he'd help at all if that were the case. Why not hide the research and deny us any help altogether?

In a way, it seemed the theme of my life, to give up any hope of a home to protect the people I cared about. I knew in my heart Fae and Amelia would understand, but this would become one more thing my mother could blame me for.

Warwick seemed to sense my defeat. "I'll take your agreement in writing. We'll exchange contracts on the house in a week. Kessian, I expect you'll be out in the same time. Lionel!" he called, and the butler appeared in the doorway. "Please could you bring the contracts."

"Of course, sir."

He'd already had them prepared.

CHAPTER 20

I left Foxbury Manor feeling as though I'd made a deal with the devil. The envelope stuffed with my grandfather's research was heavy with what it had cost.

The contract had not included anything for Kessian's part in it. Whatever that was, Warwick hadn't felt the need to get it in writing.

We walked back to Lunaris, parked at the end of Warwick's mile-long drive. The first thing I did inside was fish through the old tithes in my studio for something that could dispel anything Warwick might have cast on us to spy, but none were found, and the truth serum had dissipated.

I got in the driver's seat and turned onto the road, keen to put some distance between myself and Foxbury Manor.

I had so many questions for Kessian. Had he managed to find anything in the study? How had he known the numbers to the safe? Most of all, what had Warwick meant when he said, "You already know what I want from you"?

Then there was the kiss, which, brief as it was, still replayed like a record skipping back to my favorite part. Kessian had kissed me out of necessity, because we'd have been caught otherwise. But I'd kissed him because I'd wanted to. Before I could ask any of my questions, Kessian said, "Could you take me home tonight?"

An unexpected, painful tug in my chest made it hard to breathe, so I only managed a very articulate, "Oh?"

"I'd just like to sleep in my own bed." He looked away, out at the dark world rushing past.

I was worried about the wraith but didn't know how to articulate it without it sounding as though it came from the more selfish desire to keep Kessian close. The change in his demeanor worried me. All the cheer had drained from his eyes. Even the stars on his cheeks seemed dimmer.

I turned down the road toward his place. If the wraith came . . . Lunaris would be there, and she was only marginally more safe than anywhere else.

I parked up outside. "Can I come in so we can talk?"

"'Course."

The memory of standing on this front stoop, imagining a future where I came back, hit me as we walked through the door. Kessian dumped his keys in a bowl by the door, kicked off his shoes, and walked the short distance through his house to the sliding door out back, where there was a small garden crowded with two small patio chairs and a round table with mosaic glass. A hydrangea took up the entire corner, its blooms in various shades of pink, purple, and blue, yellow cone flowers peppered around it, a few dahlias towering out of the bush to one side.

Kessian lit the citronella candle. Dusk was falling and the mosquitos would soon swarm.

"Have a seat. I need to water my plants. They're looking a bit parched."

I sat in one of the chairs, the folder of research in my lap. He moved stiffly as he filled the can from a hose and poured water into one of the hanging baskets, balancing on his cane. I offered to help, but he shook his head.

"It helps calm me. Taking care of something else. Makes up for all the times I can't take care of myself."

It was an opening to ask him more, but I decided to start with the least personal of the questions running through my mind.

"How did you know the numbers to that safe?"

"I didn't know. I can't even remember what they were now."

"But you got it right on the first attempt. How?"

"Do you think that place is haunted?"

The abrupt change in topic caught me off guard. "I went with a friend to a party there once. I never saw anything out of the ordinary, just loads of drunk teenagers." I had been too much of a rule follower to drink. Just trespassing had made me anxious. "Why?"

"Maybe this will sound crazy, but it felt as though someone else's hand guided mine, making me turn the dial to the correct numbers." He paused mid-drizzle of the hydrangea. "Part of me thought maybe . . . maybe it was Edwin's ghost."

My heart thumped hard. It wasn't beyond the realm of possibility, but I hated to think my grandfather had died so restlessly that he'd come back to haunt the living. It was meant to be quite a painful experience for the spirit.

"Did you find something in there?"

He blew his fringe out of his eyes while shaking out the last of the water from the can on some lavender. "I couldn't read through the documents quickly enough to find anything in particular, but some of them didn't look like normal contracts. There were runes on some, and it felt . . . off. A magical signature, but not like yours. More tinny, like the sound your ears make after a concert."

"What's mine like?"

Kessian focused steadily on refilling the watering can. "Smells like burgamot, makes you feel like you're drinking sangria by the sea."

I shouldn't read too much into that, but I'd never been so flattered.

Kessian rushed on to say, "So if we didn't take that contract, who did? Edwin's ghost? Someone else?"

"I don't know." We didn't have any clues to follow on that front. Perhaps my grandfather's autopsy would provide a new direction, but until then, the only lead I had was to talk to my family and go through the research to see what could be used.

Before any of that, I still had another question. The worst one. "Kessian . . . What did Warwick take from you?"

He had his back to me. It went rigid.

"You don't have to tell me. I know you like your secrets." And I was trying not to take that personally. I had no right to them, and I hadn't exactly been consistent about whether I wanted more intimacy from him or less.

But after that kiss, something had changed. I'd spent my life sacrificing my well-being to keep others protected. That was the first time someone had protected me.

"It's not a secret. Not really. It's just—humiliating."

I waited. Eventually, he set the watering can down and slumped into the chair across from me. "When I moved here, I didn't have much. You saw. My whole life fit inside my car. While I was sick with Bowen's Wane, I couldn't work as much, so I couldn't make much money."

"Did you have any family that could step in?"

"Nope. Single child to a single mum, who sold our council house and went backpacking across Europe to live out the youth she couldn't as a teen mother to an extremely high-maintenance queer kid."

"You don't strike me as high-maintenance."

"Maybe not anymore. Back then, I wanted to be in every school activity, try every new hobby, and not only could she not afford to kit me out for whatever latest craft project had taken my fancy, I wanted her involved. I was a stage ten clinger. A bad case of wisteria, and the people I climbed all over couldn't hold me up, so they all left. I can't even really blame them. I'd have probably done the same."

My heart ached with the parallel cut of my own family history, only I'd been the one to leave. Forced out, more like.

"Dom too?" I guessed.

Kessian let out a sad, derisive noise. "Dom liked me that way. Made him feel important to be needed. It was after I got my Bowen's Wane diagnosis that everything fell apart. That was a little *too* needy for him."

I was biased and not given to afford Dom as much grace as Kessian on this. "He was an ass."

"In the end," Kessian agreed. "We weren't married, though we'd talked about it. He hadn't signed up for 'in sickness and in health' yet, and as it turned out, he wasn't ready to be a carer. Maybe if my prognosis wasn't fatal. He said he couldn't watch me waste away, would rather remember the 'real me.' As if I'd become a different person. It's just life, isn't it? Things change. People come and go. They're right for you, then they're wrong."

He said it with a sort of philosophical distance. The kind I often masked with when intellectualizing a painful moment was easier than dealing with the enormity of the feelings it evoked.

"You're probably wondering what any of this has to do with Warwick," Kessian said.

"No. I was thinking how hard it must have been."

Kessian shrugged. "Others have it worse. Anyway, I should tell you. No point hiding it. What's left of my pride is already forfeit, so . . . Warwick evicted me over two months ago."

Anger bubbled up inside of me. "He can't."

"He can. My tenancy was a lease, and he's chosen not to renew. He owns the whole park. You might have noticed it's quiet? I haven't got any neighbors anymore. He's going to tear it all down. Probably build a hotel to fill with tourists. I'd move somewhere else but . . ." This part he looked away for. "Can't afford it, right? I could just about afford this place when I moved, but everything's more expensive now. I've watched every rental that's come up in the past two and a half months. Nothing in my price range. No market for a house share, either. Not many young people stay in Shearwater."

I didn't often see red, but I was starting to. "But you work at the spa. He's the one signing your paychecks. And your abilities are an asset, why would he chase you off?"

"He told you the spring's been less powerful lately, yeah? I think he believes my abilities siphon it more than usual. He'd prefer to charge tourists an extorted rate just for a dip than pay me as an employee to act as an intermediary between visitors and the spring, so their visions are clearer. More useful. In the end, the reason doesn't matter because the result is the same."

"Is there anywhere else near Shearwater that's more affordable?" I asked.

"I'd have to move to the other end of the country, or another country altogether, to find something." He pulled his knee up, resting his chin on it and picking at a fray in his shoelaces. "Besides that, I don't want to leave. Shearwater chose me." He tucked his chin, pressing his forehead against the hole in the knee of his jeans. "Nobody else has."

An alarming answer rose on my tongue. *I would. If I wasn't cursed to always leave and you weren't cursed to be left behind, we'd make a good pair.*

I didn't think he'd believe me.

Kessian sighed. "Listen to me, crying over a broken nail in front of a broken bone. In a week, I'll be living out of my car, but you've lived that way for nine years."

"I had Lunaris."

"Still. I bet it was hard."

"Suffering isn't a competition."

"But if it was, you'd win?"

I let out a breath. "I'm not much good at comfort, but it would help if you didn't deflect. Can I make you tea?"

"I'd take a hug if one's on offer."

Physical affection was not normally my first choice, but I was relieved he asked, because I'd wanted to and didn't know how. We both stood, him leaning on the table a little until I drew him in. He wrapped his arms around my waist and leaned on me instead.

It was nothing like the stiff, awkward hug I'd shared with Amelia a few days ago. There was a type of pottery I'd never gotten to try—kintsugi, where the broken shards were fitted back together, the cracks sealed with gold. The healed pots were made more beautiful by the uniqueness of their scars, but it had never felt the same way for me. My scars made me socially awkward, cowardly, prone to preferring the safety of my imagined fantasies than the risks of more cracks that came from taking chances.

But Kessian fit against me like our broken shards matched, and the way my heart warmed, it could have been molten gold.

I held him close, my nose buried in the citrus tang of his shampoo, and for a second I let myself wonder. What if the visions from the strid were wrong? What if we cleansed the strid, made Shearwater safe? What if we both found a way to stay?

Kessian's arms loosened around my hips, but he didn't step away. "If that's all the questions you have for me, is it all right if I ask you one?"

"Yes."

He looked up at me through his lashes, that rare shyness keeping his voice low. "You kissed me."

"That's not a question."

"Did you mean it?"

The garden was quiet, but my heartbeat was loud. It was a yes or no question, but I felt like I needed better words than a single syllable. I tripped over all the long-winded explanations for how I'd arrived at that moment. My conviction that it would end in goodbye like always, that my heart was full of bubbles and wouldn't survive the kiln if the flame of my affection burned too hot.

Kessian's grip on me loosened. My silence had gone on too long, and he was interpreting it the wrong way.

I didn't let him go. When he met the resistance of my arms, he looked into my eyes again, and this time I didn't fumble for my words or overthink them.

"Yes," I said. "I meant it."

His lips parted in shock, and I leaned in to kiss them.

CHAPTER 21

Kessian briefly startled like a spooked cat, going rigid against me, one hand poised on my arm as if to push me away. Then he softened into the kiss, melted inch by inch closer, until he was flush with my body from hip to shoulder, arching and opening his mouth and taking that wrist he held to loop back around him.

With my fingers knotted in his hair and my tongue parting his lips, I couldn't conceive of why I'd held back before. Why I'd run away rather than risk this entanglement. We were already enmeshed. I could feel it in the way his current of wild magic emulsified with mine, in the slide of his wet tongue like a glaze of slip to glue us both together.

I'd wanted him so badly, and now that I had him rubbing against my hip and gasping against my mouth, I couldn't let go. I swallowed every little sound he made. The shortened breaths, the heady little "mm" when I pushed his legs apart with mine, both so he could take more weight off his leg and so he could grind against my thigh.

"Inside," I said.

"You're sure?"

"You're asking me?"

"In the past you seemed uncertain about round two."

A hidden insecurity undercut the words. "You thought I didn't want you back?"

"The signals were mixed, you must admit."

"I didn't think I could let myself have you." I swallowed thickly around all the explanations I didn't know how to voice. "But I have driven myself half mad with how badly I want you."

He kissed me viciously and tried to claw my shirt off at the same time. We had to part to get it off, which he didn't like, grumbling as I wadded it up and tossed it. He was back in my arms at once. I toed the door shut behind us and bumped the kitchen table on our way past. He was still limping a bit.

"You'll tell me if something hurts, right?" I ran my hand up his leg. "Or if we need to switch positions?"

"I've been trying not to jump you this entire time. I'm not fragile. I'll make it work."

"So you'll tell me?"

"Yes, I'll tell you," he huffed. "Are you going to take me to bed now or keep teasing me?"

In answer, I turned him by the hips against the counter so his back was facing me, the bulge in my trousers fitted firmly against his arse. I held the nape of his neck with one hand and reached around to start unbuttoning his shirt with the other.

"Do we need the bed or can I have you right here?"

"I love how much more confident you are with your clothes off."

"So here's good?"

"You can have me wherever you want me, darling."

He braced against the counter so he could arch his back. The way his body fit flush against mine, the way his hair smelled, it all made me dizzy. All his clothes were made of thin, flowy material. A few buttons down, and his shirt slipped to bare one shoulder. I kissed along that slope, up the column of his neck, nuzzling behind his ear.

He was so responsive to my every touch. Where my lips went, a trail of goose bumps followed. As I slipped a hand into his half-unbuttoned shirt and brushed over a nipple, it hardened to a firm bud. When I finished with the buttons and instead flirted with the hem of his trousers, he didn't seem to know whether to arch his hips forward or back.

I made it so he didn't have to choose, pulling him tight against me. I softly played my fingers through the hair on his belly before ripping off his belt.

Both our breathing came ragged. The anticipation was killing me. I wanted to draw this out, but he was widening his stance and turning his head to breathe against my cheek and kiss it, and he said, "Please don't tease me."

I stuck two of my fingers in my mouth and sucked to wet them. Kessian froze, staring at me with his blue eyes blown black. I didn't know how to make it a show for him rather than a perfunctory action, but it didn't seem to matter. Just seeing me suck on my own fingers did it for him.

After that frozen second, he took my wrist, pulled my hand to his mouth instead, then sucked the same two fingers in between his lips.

My hips jerked against him, a jolt of pleasure going straight to my cock as though *that's* what he was sucking on.

He did make a show of it. Bobbing his head, swirling his tongue, getting my fingers as slick as possible. When he popped his lips free, they were shiny with spit, and I kissed them. Tonguing into his mouth. Letting him know how deranged he was making me while I slipped my hand down his pants.

He stopped moving so much when I ran my slick fingers over the firm bump of his dick. For a second he just froze, then he bent over the counter and shuddered, hips canting for more.

I rubbed him between both fingers, bowing over him to get more leverage, running my fingers lower, between the folds of his pussy. Deeper. Sliding past the first knuckle, and the second, until I could curl them.

He bucked. "Tal!"

I groaned against his neck. "You're *soaked*."

"Tal, *please* will you just finger me." He wiggled his hips, trying to get me to *move*.

And I did. I pressed my fingers in and out. I rocked my hips like I would if my cock was inside him, and one of his hands flew back to try and pull me closer. It landed on my hip, scratching through fabric.

If he wanted me close, I'd give him no room to move. He fit perfectly between my hand knuckles-deep in his cunt and my hips pressed against his arse. His shirt hung off him by one button, and with my chin hooked over his shoulder, I could look down and see where my wrist disappeared into his pants. I couldn't see my fingers inside him, but I could hear them.

Kessian whined, "Tal . . . Tal, I'm close."

"Good. I've got you."

I had my free arm around his chest, my palm against his clavicle. He took that hand and guided it to the back of his head.

"Pull my hair again."

"Oh my God. Okay."

I grabbed a good handful so as not to rip any, pulling so I could kiss his neck, revitalizing the mark I'd left a few days ago. He shuddered when I used my teeth, thighs clamping shut around my hand. The pulse of his orgasm overcame him.

I gave him a moment to come down, panting in his ear. Then I slipped my fingers free, untangled my other hand from his hair, grabbed two glasses from the cabinet above him, and leaned over him to pour water from the sink. I set the first on the counter where he'd collapsed forward onto his folded arms.

His voice sounded parched from panting. "Tal?"

"Mm?"

"Give me a second and I'll get a drink straight from the tap."

"If you prefer that to a glass."

"That was a euphemism for blowing you."

My knees didn't buckle, but it was a close thing with all the blood in my body rushing to one place.

Kessian gulped down the water I'd provided, grabbed me by my belt, and started leading me down the hall to his bedroom, where he chucked a couple pillows on the floor and dropped to his knees upon them.

I tried not to fall to mine as he unbuckled me and opened my fly enough to place a damp, open-mouthed kiss against the head of my exposed dick where it peeked out of the hem of my briefs. I tried to breathe evenly, but every exhale came out ragged, because his eyes were midnight blue and he looked up at me like he really wanted this. Wanted me.

"I know you like to hold back," he said, each word hot and wet where he mouthed my cock through my underwear. "But I don't want you to. Don't hold back."

"I—Kessian!"

"Don't hold back," he said again.

Then he freed me completely from my briefs, put the flat of his tongue against my balls, and licked all the way up. I held my breath. He pursed his lips, sucked on the head, then descended all the way down until he could nuzzle into my pubic hair.

I was going to combust like a teenage boy getting blown for the first time. He seemed to know it, because he pulled off of me, lips shining as they rolled my foreskin back over the head.

"I said *don't* hold back."

"I'm trying not to finish too soon."

"That sounds like holding back to me."

A few strands of hair fell into his face, and I thoughtlessly tucked them behind his ear, cupping his cheek. He leaned into the touch, somehow managing to look coy and innocent even with my cock leaking precum against his cheek.

"Okay," I said. "I'll . . . try."

He smiled and rewarded me with a far more chaste kiss to the tip. One of his hands held my hip, the other arm wound around my waist, trapping me against his mouth as he sucked me down.

Pressure built in my abdomen, pleasure spiking with each bob of his head. He was making wet, lewd noises, moaning like I tasted good, no regard for how sloppy we were getting.

My orgasm curled like a tongue of smoke, low in my belly. He guided my hand to palm the back of his head, and with a few thrusts and the silky knot of his hair in my fist, I knew I couldn't hold out anymore. I stammered out a warning, but Kessian just moaned and relaxed into my hand.

I forgot to breathe so long that I barely made a sound when I came.

He swallowed. I reached for his hand and helped him up, pulling him into my arms so I could kiss him and fall back with him onto the bed.

"Remember when you told me you could be a tragic lay?" Kessian panted. "Never been so glad to call someone a liar."

"Worth the wait?"

He beamed, nuzzling into my shoulder. "Mm. Not to sound like a desperate saddo, but when I woke up this morning getting poked by your erection, and you *still* didn't fuck me, I gave up hope you ever would again."

I covered my face with my hand. "Yes, that was . . ."

"Torture?"

"I was going to say 'stupid,' but 'torture' is more accurate."

He laughed lightly, the bellows of his ribs against mine such a new, unique intimacy.

He softened, got quiet. "Why did you hold back so long?"

"I was . . . afraid."

"Afraid of what?"

I wasn't good with words, but I needed to be now. I needed to express to him why I had such a mental block around developing feelings for him. "Afraid I'd have to leave again. I didn't want to risk a painful goodbye. My life has been so full of them. But . . ." I took his hand and kissed his knuckles. "I'm done with running away. You're worth the risk."

"The risk of what?"

"A broken heart."

He looked at me with round eyes, quiet and searching, like he hadn't expected that answer. His fingers clenched in mine and I squeezed back, leaned in to kiss him, but he spooked away.

His magic flared. I tasted silver. Not on his lips, which broke from the kiss in shock, but in the current between us. The air cooled like a storm coming off the back of a heat wave.

I had to squint to look at him because the stars on his cheeks and in his eyes flared with light.

"What's happening?" he said. "I feel . . . strange."

I was about to say I didn't know, when the flare of magic and the taste in the air changed into something dreadfully familiar.

Damp, the rush of water, a piercing music sharp enough to draw blood.

I should have known too much time had elapsed, that the wraith would not let Kessian and I have this moment for long. Frantically, I searched the room and the window for signs of a shadow, but almost as soon as the wraith's magic had consumed the small bedroom, it dissipated. Kessian's glow dimmed, his own magic dormant once more. We looked at one another, confused. Something buzzed from the floor, making us both jump. Kessian's phone. I got up to fish it out of his trousers. A premonition of dread came over me as I handed it to him, Fae's name flashing across the screen. I could hear their voice though they weren't on speaker.

"Kessian! Have you seen Tal?"

"Uh, yes. He's with me right here. Do you want to talk to him?"

"No. You both need to come right away. Come to the spa."

"What's wrong? What's happened?"

"It's the wraith. The wraith has taken someone again."

My whole body flushed with cold. I'd known. As soon as I'd seen their name on the phone, I'd known.

"Who? Who's it taken?" he asked.

"Amelia. It got Amelia."

CHAPTER 22

We found my family gathered in the reception of the spa. All of them except Amelia. Marlowe sat behind the desk with his head in his hands, face obscured, while Lettie wept and Mum tried to comfort her. Fae sat on the bottom step with Camilla holding them, a picture of a family in grief from which three faces were missing.

And mine, but it always was.

The door chime drew all their attention as I walked in. My mum rounded on me at once, eyes red and a tissue scrunched in her fist.

"You. You've been back a few short days, and now look what's happened."

"Mum, please," Fae pleaded. With their knees tucked and their tear-streaked face, they looked as young as the day I left.

"How did it happen?" I asked through the lump in my throat.

"The same way it's always happened."

"Amelia and I shared a shift today," Fae said. "I was closing up for the day when I heard screaming from the direction of the spring. By the time I got out there, it already had her." Fae shivered, voice breaking. "It dragged her under the water. I tried to go in after her, but it was just like with Laurelie. No body, nothing. Like the spring just . . . absorbed her."

She broke down completely then. Lettie did, too. She wouldn't even look at me. Marlowe barely held it together himself, and I wondered if he hated me, too, now.

"None of it would have happened if you'd left like you were supposed to," Mum said.

"This isn't Tal's fault," Fae argued.

"Then whose is it? Nine years, and nobody else has drowned, but now—" My mother covered her mouth with the back of her hand and looked away, chin wobbling.

Perhaps it was a case of classic dissociation, but rather than rail against the accusation or sink under the weight of my guilt, I found myself envying everyone's ability to express their feelings, raw and out loud, while I probably looked as though I didn't care. A weight crushed the air out of my lungs, my chest was sore with the abusive slam of my heart, but none of it really showed because I wasn't predisposed to tears or raising my voice. I wanted to. I wanted to scream that Amelia was important to me, too, and why didn't I get to grieve her with everyone?

"Do you have anything to say for yourself?" Mum fumed.

"I was trying to fix it," I said quietly.

"Right before Fae's wedding? Did you stop to think how terrible it would be to lose someone so close to the big day?"

"Mum, that isn't fair," Fae protested. "We can put off the wedding."

"We certainly will not. We cannot afford to postpone. This close to the date, we lose our deposit for everything."

"Can we not talk about money right now!" Fae cried.

Mum was looking at me like I should have an answer. All I could think to say was, "I'm sorry."

"Amelia is gone! Don't you get that? Amelia is gone, and Laurelie, and Nathaniel, and none of us will be left if you don't leave," she screamed, taking a step toward me, but she found her path blocked.

Kessian put himself between us. I hadn't noticed him move.

His voice had more gravel in it than when he'd spoken to Warwick. "You're blaming him? You gave up on him when he was *sixteen*, and you've had nine years to sort all this trouble out in the meantime rather than leave the burden to your kids once they'd grown. If you want a scapegoat, look in the mirror."

Stricken silent, my mother did naught but gape at him. When she recovered, she said, "This is a family matter. You don't know the first thing about it."

"I know Tal's sacrificed nine years of his life protecting all the people in this room. I know he's only stuck around this time because the wraith had a lock on me, and if he left I'd probably have been taken next. While you gave up on him, he's been scouring Shearwater for a solution. He may even have found one!"

"Really?" Fae raised their head from their hands. "Are you serious? You found a way to stop it? Can we get Amelia back?"

"Oh, please say you can," Lettie whispered.

"No." I didn't want to get their hopes up. "I mean, I don't know. It's—I haven't had time to read through Grandpa's research yet."

"Research? What research?" Marlowe asked.

I held up the folder. It had a crease in it from where my thumb had gripped too hard.

Mum looked stung. "He never told us about any research. Where did you find that?"

"It's a long story." One I didn't know how to start because it meant revealing Grandpa had been murdered, that I'd spoken to his ghost and raided Warwick's house, bargained with him in hopes of exorcising Shearwater of the wraith before anyone else had to die, and we'd lost Amelia anyway.

Kessian stepped in. "Unfortunately the story comes with more bad news." He gave me a solemn nod of support, and it struck me I'd never had an advocate like this. Someone who helped me find the words and fought in my corner.

It had been a trying day, and it wasn't likely to get easier. I didn't anticipate my family receiving what I had to say well, but I found a silver lining in the unexpected solidarity of Kessian telling the story with me.

We covered everything from the point of my escape to Coill Darragh. They took the news of Grandpa's murder as well as Amelia's "abduction." I wasn't ready to think of her as dead yet. They reacted to Warwick's bargain with equal parts anger and a lack of surprise. Nobody liked him, and after Kessian's chastisement earlier, Mum was only too pleased to latch on to another scapegoat.

It took two rounds of tea and the better part of an hour to cover everything. Marlowe, who'd looked more morose than I'd ever seen him, seemed to take solace in the discovery of Grandpa's research. I laid it out on the desk, and he flipped through it delicately while I read over it with him.

"Warwick told us he'd devised a trap for the wraith. Something to summon and confine it."

"I wonder why he never shared any of this with us," Marlowe said.

"Because he never shared anything with us. We had to find out from Warwick that he'd bought the spa, remember?" my mum said.

"He didn't?" I asked.

Marlowe nodded sadly. "I'm sure you've reached the age now where you realize your parents are not nearly as wise and perfect as you think they are as children."

"Speak for yourself," said Mum.

"Your grandpa was a good grandpa, but . . . he wasn't always the best father," Marlowe finished.

In that moment, time felt folded in two, the past overlaid with the present, drawn in parallel. Yes, I could relate to that, though I wouldn't say so in front of my mother.

Marlowe traced a drawing of a sigil in the notes. There were several versions, altered each time, with a list of tithes that received modifications along the way. "It's incomplete," he said.

"Even this last one?" Kessian asked.

"It's missing a—" I didn't quite know the word for it, the rune and tithe that defined the nature of the creature to be bound.

"A focus," Marlowe said. "It wasn't possible to specify a tithe for the subject to be summoned because we don't really know what the wraith is, nor is it substantial enough to take teeth or hair from. Without a focus, the sigil's just a fancy drawing. It won't work."

"How do you find out what the wraith is without trapping and studying it, though?" Fae asked.

I didn't answer because the thought that came to mind would not win me any more favor amongst my family.

It can break through the wards because it's a part of you.

I thought of falling into the strid with two dozen other people and emerging as the sole survivor. I thought, too, of Kessian's connection to the spring, the way his freckles lit up the moment Amelia was taken by the wraith.

Marlowe caught the look in my eye. "You know how to finish it, don't you?"

"Maybe."

Understanding dawned on Kessian, too. He worried his lip between his teeth, puzzling it out.

Mum grasped Lettie's hand and bounced impatiently. "Well? There's no time to waste. How?"

Marlowe said, "Before we figure out the 'how' we should figure out 'where.' So no one gets hurt this time."

We discussed options and eventually settled on one.

The grounds around the spa and spring hid a number of utility sheds, but one in particular was on the perimeter of the woods, too far to be of use, so it had been abandoned.

The padlock, rusted shut, we broke open with steel cutters. An old spade leaned against the wall, but otherwise the shed's only occupants were spiders, wood lice, and mouse droppings.

I'd driven Lunaris onto the grass as close as I could get her. A rocky ledge was too steep for her to cross, but she'd be near enough in case anything went wrong and we needed to make a quick escape. I hoped it wouldn't come to that.

By the glow of a witch light, I transcribed the runes from my grandfather's notes onto the concrete floor. When I got to the focus, I wrote out two names in runes. Mine and Kessian's.

It made the most sense to me. The wraith was somehow a part of me—that was how it breached Coill Darragh's wards and my own. Kessian was a part of the strid. Its magic flowed through him. If the wraith was a part of me, and a part of the strid, perhaps this would be enough for the trap to work.

What terrified me was we wouldn't know until we tried. If it successfully summoned the wraith but failed to trap it, we'd be in danger with no talisman or recourse except to run.

We pooled our resources for the tithes. The last, the one to represent the wraith, had to come from both of us. I pulled out a strand of my hair. Kessian did the same, taking it from his fringe and handing it to me. We tied them in a knot and soaked them in the spring's waters.

With everything prepared, I turned to face my family. They all looked to one another uncomfortably. Nobody wanted to be this close to the wraith when it appeared.

"It already took Amelia tonight," Marlowe said. "Perhaps we should wait until after the wedding?"

"I'm afraid of it crashing the wedding," I countered. "I'd rather get this over with. None of you have to stay." I cast Kessian a sidelong look. "You as well."

"I don't want to leave you to fight it alone," Fae said.

Kessian said, "He won't be. I'm not leaving."

I was for once glad the depths of my feelings didn't often show on my face, with the way that opened my heart right up.

"We'll stake out a spot nearby. Come to the rescue if anything goes amiss." Marlowe took my hand and shook it. "You're a brave lad, you know that?"

"I don't feel it."

"Well, you are." He pulled me into a hug, which prompted everyone else to join him. Even Mum, though she looked the least comfortable, still sore from Kessian's rebuke earlier.

They left, Fae waving to us nervously as they backed into the night.

"Thank you for staying," I said to Kessian without looking at him. "I'm used to dealing with things alone."

"Me too."

A few hours ago, I'd been kissing him, and now I could hardly look at him. I feared all of this going wrong and what might happen to him. All this time I'd held back from touching him because I didn't want to nurture the feelings that had no chance of taking root in my nomadic life, but those feelings had grown anyway.

I hadn't gotten to grips with what had happened to Amelia, either. Everything had felt very real in Kessian's garden, but not here.

"Might as well rip off the plaster," Kessian said. "I'll be right here."

"It might be easier if you weren't." He looked stung, so I raced to add, "I'm afraid you'll get hurt."

"I survived Bowen's Wane. What's a wraith got on that? And if it drags me off, I don't have to worry about finding a home anymore."

"That's not funny."

"Sorry."

I wasn't good at reading people. That was academic at this point. It wasn't that I didn't notice a change in someone's mood and demeanor, it was that I so rarely could figure out where that change had come from.

I caught a chilliness in Kessian's tone that hadn't been there before, but I must have imagined it, because a moment later he said with his usual confidence, "Let's catch a wraith."

The only thing left to do was cast the spell. As I called upon my magic, drawing deep, Kessian laced his fingers with mine and squeezed.

One rune around the sigil's perimeter lit up, blue as bioluminescent algae. Slowly, one by one, each rune blazed alive. Beside me, Kessian's magic flared, too. A surge of power went through us both, and the slow illumination of the sigil sped up, each rune lighting the others in a domino chain, until the inside of the shed was so bright I had to close my eyes.

I opened them again once the glow died down. The sigil frosted into the ground stayed crisp and poised. All it needed was a prisoner.

But one didn't appear.

"The sigil's alive. The trap worked, didn't it?" Kessian said.

"The trap did. The summoning didn't."

"Maybe it takes a minute?"

We waited with measured breaths, but the shadows didn't stir, the air didn't saturate with cold and damp.

The wraith wasn't coming.

CHAPTER 23

We reported back to my family on our failure. The reception was a mix of disappointment it hadn't worked and relief no one else had been hurt in the attempt.

With nothing left to do but go to sleep, I bid my family goodnight and started toward Lunaris, but Kessian didn't follow.

"Maybe we shouldn't risk sleeping together tonight," he said.

"Why?"

"After Amelia . . . I don't want to have any more of those dreams."

There was more to it, but I couldn't fathom what. I hadn't imagined his chilliness earlier, and it chipped at a chink in my newly donned confidence. I felt like I'd done something wrong.

"I'll see you in the afternoon at the dress fitting?" he said.

"And the morning for the autopsy."

He shivered. "Right. Of course. I'll see you then."

"Goodnight." I leaned in to kiss him, and he turned so my lips brushed his cheek instead.

Definitely hadn't imagined it. He was giving me the cold shoulder. A hairline crack splintered through my heart as I watched him go.

I had run out of anything to eat and had to make a trip to the newsagents, since anything with proper food had long shut. After picking up a handful of granola bars, I found my gaze lingering on the bottles of liquor stocked behind the clerk. In a moment of masochistic optimism, I asked for a bottle of gin based on the barren hope Kessian would join me for a drink next time I asked. If I had the courage to ask again.

Lunaris had two cups of tea waiting when I got in. She seemed just as bewildered as me that Kessian hadn't come. I could understand the reason he gave, but I didn't think it comprised the whole reason, and it hurt more than I dared admit to tuck myself into bed alone, wondering why—right after I'd let him in—he'd let himself out.

It hurt worse when the grief of Amelia's death broke through my denial. She wasn't coming back. No one ever did, except me.

Lunaris pulled the covers tightly around me in a hug, but it wasn't enough. I didn't want to be alone anymore.

The cemetery's morgue smelled more like a hospital than it did of death. The exterior had the look of a giant mausoleum, the interior a wash of cold white paint and fluorescent lighting with the odd religious symbol on the wall. Kessian greeted me outside with a facsimile of his usual warmth, looking as sleepless as I felt. The coroner, Ms. Carlisle, led us down a corridor, sterile tiles clicking cleanly under her heels, her starling familiar whisking after us.

"Normally, I wouldn't allow a family member into the room for this sort of thing. Mr. Warwick insisted I make an exception in your case, but are you sure you're ready?"

No, but I didn't have much choice. Without a means to draw the wraith out, I had one less avenue for investigation into my grandfather's murder.

I didn't like the idea of seeing his body, though. I hadn't wanted to see it at the funeral. It wouldn't look any better a week later.

I said, "I'm ready."

Kessian made no comment. He'd been unusually quiet.

Ms. Carlisle pushed through a door marked *Morgue #5*. "All right, well. This way."

The fluorescent lights gave the room an icy feel as I took in the rows of metal drawers in the wall—a built-in cabinet of corpses—and the singular, thin figure on a table in the center, draped under a cloth. Standing over it was Warwick.

Kessian stiffened at the sight of him. I hadn't expected him to attend either.

"Morning, boys," he said. "Not the brightest way to start the day, digging up an old friend, but we might as well get on with it."

"Do you need to be here?" I'd forgotten my manners, but couldn't bring myself to regret asking. Far as I was concerned, Warwick was still a suspect. I didn't need him sabotaging any evidence. The fact he'd arrived before us already put me in doubt that anything we found here today would represent the truth.

Warwick's expression folded in affront. "I know he was your grandfather, but he was my friend as well. I deserve to know what really happened to him."

Ms. Carlisle cleared her throat, detaching a tablet from a clip under the table. "I can begin by telling you my own findings."

She said it to reassure us that she'd made her own, unbiased report from the autopsy, but I couldn't trust that, either. Warwick had bribed all the authorities necessary to make this happen quickly and quietly. He could do the same thing to uncover only what he wanted uncovered.

Kessian folded his arms. We were of one mind on this.

"Go ahead," I told her. "But if it's all right, I'd like to conduct my own investigation as well."

Ms. Carlisle lifted her chin. "Provided you only use spells approved by the magical morticians' board, then of course."

I'd offended her, but that was an acceptable consequence to trusting Warwick.

She took the sheet and pulled it down to the waist.

I thought the sight of my grandfather's corpse might set me on a downward spiral, but as I took in the sallow, gray features still clouded with makeup and preserved by embalming, I hardly recognized them enough to connect this body with the man I'd known all those years ago. I tried to pick out anything familiar, and on a surface level his face had the same shape. But none of the life was in it.

It made all the difference. I could mentally separate the two. The body from my grandfather.

"During embalming, no signs of injury were present on any part of the body. The initial cause of death was presumed to be natural causes due to his age and general health. My autopsy confirmed the cause of death to be age-related heart failure."

"So he wasn't murdered?" Warwick asked.

"From the physical examination, that would be my conclusion, but I used a spell to detect any magic that might have been used to mimic natural causes. I'll perform the same for you now so you can see the results for yourself."

She directed this statement toward Kessian and me. She'd probably have shown us the findings on that tablet if my doubt in her integrity hadn't prompted her to show us firsthand. I doubly didn't regret offending her. Spells to detect magic were difficult to circumvent. Warwick could have used a spell to cleanse all magical traces, but a lack of any magical residue on a witch would itself be suspicious.

Ms. Carlisle pulled the necessary tithes from drawers in a rolling cart next to her—an oak leaf, poppy seeds, and a jaybird feather. She unfurled her fingers and cast the spell, green smoke sweeping over my grandfather's body, leaving behind various runes, mostly along the wrist of his right hand. I recognized the runes for wakefulness spells, used in place of caffeine, and for hygiene spells, used in place of shower.

All functional spells, except for the signature glowing from his chest, which was such a slew of runes I could hardly read them. They layered over one another like onion skin and seemed to shift the longer I looked at them, but then words started to jump out.

Not words. Names.

Florence Vanderghast

Simon Barkersfield

Nathan Ashborne

Dad. These were the names of everyone who'd died in the strid. Once Once seen, I couldn't stop searching until I found Laurelie's, and once I found it I could see it everywhere, appearing more frequently, like when your mind zeroes in on a single word in a puzzle and becomes blind to all others.

"It's everyone who drowned nine years ago," I said.

"But what does that mean?" Kessian asked. "Did all their ghosts rise up and kill him? Why? Because he was the Keeper and the strid was his responsibility?"

"I had the same thought," Ms. Carlisle said. "But take a step back with me. I think from here you'll see it best."

We followed her a few paces from the table, viewing it from a diagonal.

Up close, the glow of runic names congealed into a formless glow, but from here the runes hovered three-dimensionally over my grandfather's chest, together making an all-too-familiar shape.

It was the wraith's antler, tines pointed downward, some half submerged. As if he'd been gored to death on the wraith's horns.

"That makes no sense," I murmured almost to myself. "The wraith's connected to me. It goes where I go, and I was nowhere *near* Shearwater when Grandad died."

"Are you sure?" Ms. Carlisle said.

I looked between her and Warwick, both looking at me now with uncertainty.

"This wasn't me. It's got to be a trick of some kind. Let me perform the spell. I want to see for myself it wasn't tampered with."

Ms. Carlisle pursed her lips, but she obliged me. She smeared away the remnants of her spell, the green runes and glowing antler drifting away like smoke.

I'd prepared the tithes this morning. Pulling them out, I cast the spell again, my magic less like smoke than sparks. They ignited along the same lines as those that came before, runes in tracery lines like veins, and a glut of them issuing from the spot on Grandad's chest.

"It's not possible," I said again, though I couldn't see any way this could be faked. "I was miles away."

Warwick said, "I'm sorry, lad. It seems to me the wraith murdered him, too."

Four family members. *Four.* Would it only stop once it had us all? Wiped the Ashbornes out of Shearwater?

I ought to tell them all to go, but they wouldn't. They had the wedding, and besides, it had always been easier to make me go instead. Only that clearly hadn't worked. Maybe it never had. I didn't know why the wraith hadn't taken anyone in nine years, but it got Grandad in the end.

Kessian was quiet the entire time. When I looked to him for reassurance, he still squinted searchingly at the glowing antler. He looked terrified.

Warwick noticed, too. "Do you see something else?"

He pulled me by the hand toward the spot where he stood and pointed. "There. Can you read them?"

I squinted, unsure which names he was pointing to at first. My heart stopped when I read the ones he meant.

"I'm not imagining it, am I?" Kessian said. "Those are our names."

CHAPTER 24

The vision from the spring returned to me at the sight of our names burning amongst those who'd already drowned. One fatal premonition was disconcerting but plausibly avoidable. Two was pushing our luck.

I felt powerless. My instincts screamed at me to run, get in Lunaris, drive as far as I could, and take Kessian with me, but it wouldn't help. Running hadn't saved Grandad. It probably wouldn't save us, either. Fleeing to Coill Darragh hadn't gotten us any farther from this mess.

Going from my grandfather's autopsy to a dress fitting felt foolish. Would we fit Amelia's funeral in before or after Fae's wedding?

I was in terrible spirits when I reached the dressmaker's shop. It was sandwiched between a popular pizza chain and a betting shop. The weathered sign read *Witches and Stitches* in a curly, barely legible font. The two sisters who owned it, Ella and Rhia, had probably dressed every bride, groom, and celebrant in Shearwater. Fae was no exception.

Ella's familiar, a turtle dove, cooed a few notes of greeting as I came in. Everyone else had arrived early, chiming in with hellos and waves. I scanned the faces. Fae, Camilla, my mum, and Kessian's were the familiar ones. The empty spot on the sofa was better suited to Amelia, but she wasn't here.

I sat there anyway. "I thought of something while you were out."

"Can we save that chat for later?" Mum interrupted. "Just until after the fitting."

"Right. Of course." I fumbled for something less awkward to talk about and asked Kessian, "Which wedding party are you with? You never said."

He smirked, though still with that reserved calm that put me on edge. "Camilla and Fae fought for me. Fae won."

"Champion of rock paper scissors," Fae said, holding up their fingers. "And I won with scissors. Camilla should have known me better."

The attempt at levity didn't quite catch on, so Rhia took over. "Now everyone's here, would you like to try on your dress?"

As Fae disappeared behind the curtain with Rhia, Ella came and tapped Kessian fondly on the shoulder. When she did, her gaze passed quickly over me, like someone trying not to draw the attention of a feral dog, lest it be provoked.

So news of what had happened to Amelia had spread.

"How are things, Kessian? I heard that damned Westley Warwick wants to put up a hotel where you're living."

Kessian's smile tightened. "Afraid so."

"Ah, and we'll go the same way as Waxy's Candles and Olde Gary's Café, if things keep going as they are."

"He owns this as well?"

"Not him, but another man competing with him. Rent keeps going up. We'll have been here fifty years in January, but Rhia and I aren't as quick as we once were. It's hard, competing with the big chain shops from Pentawynn. Even if all their clothes are tatty garbage."

Their conversation was interrupted as Fae swept back the curtain and spun to show us their dress.

It had been styled to mix feminine and masculine aesthetics. Sheer lace covered their decolletage and arms, with a cream waistcoat and billowing skirt.

Everyone gasped, oohed, and ahhed, except me, who had little practice at making those noises. I also had little experience seeing anyone I loved in a wedding dress, and seeing Fae now, I was struck by just how many things I'd missed out on.

The last time I'd been in Shearwater, they'd been worrying about passing their A levels while begging Mum and Dad for a cat. (They'd been jealous of Lunaris, back before she became a camper van.)

Now, they were getting married.

Fae launched into an explanation about how they wanted to style their hair when someone jostled my shoulder with theirs.

Kessian said under his breath, "Getting a bit emotional seeing your sibling dressed for their wedding?"

"Just a little."

"Hey, hey," Fae said, pointing at us both. "No canoodling in public!"

One of the women I didn't know said, "You should have known better than to invite Kessian, then."

Kessian said, "Don't be jealous, Mel. You had your chance."

In spite of the direction of his jab, it was me getting my hackles up. I had no claim to Kessian. I didn't know where we stood after we'd slept together and he'd been so cool with me afterward, but I still wanted to drape my arm around his shoulders.

"That was before I developed taste," Mel said, kissing the girl next to her on the cheek.

Kessian laughed, unbothered by the slight. "I prefer to think that everybody has a taste for me, I'm just so rich that one bite is enough to satisfy."

I kept my expression neutral, but I caught the implication. Once had been enough, twice too much. I didn't do subtlety or reading between the lines. If I'd overstepped, if he didn't want to take this any further . . .

Actually, I didn't want to think about that right now.

While Rhia pinned Fae's outfit so she could take it in, the rest of us were handed identical suits and dresses to be pinned. I didn't know how one could already have been prepared for me, until Fae patted my arm and said, "I trusted things would work out, and Lunaris let me steal your clothes on that first visit so I'd have your measurements."

I wanted to feel grateful, but Amelia's absence made it difficult to feel as if the trade had been worthwhile.

The changing room was a cramped cupboard. Within, I couldn't spread my arms or even cock my elbows without hitting a wall. The heating was on full blast, turning the claustrophobic space into an oven. As I put the suit jacket on, I prayed I didn't sweat through my shirt.

I hated trying on new clothes, and particularly hated anything with starchy fabrics and layers. Too warm, too textured. They made me feel like bugs were crawling under my skin.

I couldn't stop thinking about that death glow over Grandad. Kessian's name and mine imprinted in the antler of the creature bound to kill us both. What was it all for? A place I hadn't been able to call home for nine years? A family who seemed better off without me?

I could feel myself working up to an overstimulated shutdown. I wanted to flee the place and lie down on Lunaris's cold floor.

When I got to the tie, frustration hit me fully. I hadn't much occasion to wear one and had forgone it at Grandad's funeral. With the length looped around my neck, I thought I'd probably be more successful hanging myself with it than tying it correctly.

A rap of knuckles on the door made me jump, my elbow slamming into the hanger rack installed on the back wall. "Ow."

"Just checking you're all right in there." Kessian's voice.

"Fine." I was not.

"Are you sure?" Kessian lowered his voice. "If you need extra deodorant, I brought some. They always keep it the temperature of hell in here."

"I've forgotten how to tie a tie," I blurted. "And yes, I'm sweating."

"Like a nun in a brothel, yeah. Same. I can help you with the tie."

I opened the door. Instead of letting me out, he let himself in.

"There's not much room."

"Mm-hm, listen." He pitched his voice low so no one could hear. "Fae's putting on a brave face out there, but obviously what happened to Amelia has everyone a bit down. You look like you'd rather be anywhere else."

"Shall I smile and pretend everything's okay?"

"Sometimes people need to pretend. And things will be okay. We'll figure it out."

"After what we saw today, you believe that?"

"I need to pretend sometimes, too."

I felt thoroughly chastised. For the first time, I noticed his hands were shaking. "Sorry."

"Don't be. I know I haven't helped."

It called up memories of his cool cheek, presented in place of a goodnight kiss. "Did I do something wrong?"

"No. Nothing."

"There's something. There's been something since last night. You've been off with me."

"I'm not *off* with you."

"Right. You clam up whenever the topic of sleeping in the same bed comes up, and you swerved my kiss a few hours after we fucked, but it's nothing to do with me." While I tried to hide my hurt, a single exhaled breath caught in my throat, betraying me. "If it was just sex, just say so. I usually only get one night, so I'll just be grateful I got two, yeah?"

Kessian looked as though I'd slapped him, tears springing to his eyes. "Tal, that is *not* how it is."

"Then tell me! I'm not good at reading people. You know this. You know . . . me." Now it was my turn to stare at the lights to keep the tears back.

"I think the wraith taking Amelia was my fault," he blurted.

Stunned, it took me a second to reply. "Unless you played that flute nine years ago, that's bollocks."

"No, listen. When I first came to Shearwater, the spring gave me a vision. I . . . I was the one taken by the wraith in that vision. But there was also a second vision of me living happily ever after in a house where I had a garden and a cat and just . . . just some fucking *stability*, you know? It seemed worth it to see things through for a chance at that. Then the wraith took Amelia. It was after me, and when I'd escaped it, it took her instead. In pursuit of my happy ending, I destroyed hers and made you complicit. And I didn't want to tell you because everyone's been blaming you for this since you were too young to bear the weight of that responsibility, but saving me was a mistake."

Before he could babble any longer, I said, "Do you think the same of me because I survived and no one else has?"

"Of course not, but—"

"None of this is your fault. The way you defended me in front of my mum is how I'm going to defend you now against yourself. You didn't do any of this. The wraith did. Warwick did. If not him, then someone else."

I swallowed thickly. "Look, I understand survivor's guilt, but what does any of that have to do with . . . us?"

He slipped his hands from mine. "We've been in here a while."

"Are you ever going to tell me?"

He glanced up at the light, his eyes misty. Whatever he held back from saying, he didn't want to risk emerging from the changing room red-eyed.

I backed down. "All right, not here."

He looked grateful. "Tonight at yours over a stiff drink?"

"Okay."

He let out a breath and checked the mirror. "Do I look like I've been crying?"

"You haven't been."

"I came close."

I suddenly felt like an arse. Had Kessian's chilliness been a front for more vulnerable feelings this whole time?

"We've been in here so long, they'll just think we've been shagging."

He let out a surprised laugh. "A better cover story than the truth, and I'm sure they'll appreciate making us the butt of their jokes. Help distract them, you know?"

"In that case, here." I reached out a hand and waited to see if he'd accept. When he didn't move, I aggressively mussed his hair, then rubbed a thumb over his lower lip to redden it.

His eyes went suddenly dark, and while I was far from comforted, it brought me a tiny measure of consolation that the fire hadn't gone out, no matter how well he concealed it.

He reached out and popped a few buttons on my shirt, doing them up askew. "For verisimilitude," he said, then reentered the room with a loud "Presenting, Taliesin Ashborne!"

A peal of Camilla's laughter followed, alongside Fae shouting, "Kessian Alore, tell me you did *not* just fuck him in the changing cupboard!"

When I emerged, everyone laughed and shouted all at once, I only caught one comment in every ten.

"You hussy, that's my *brother*."

"How was there any room to *move* in there?"

"You weren't gone, what, five minutes?"

"Aw, let the gays be happy."

Kessian offered an indolent shrug. "It's not my fault he can't resist me."

Our ploy had worked. The mood lightened as darts were placed and garments adjusted. It wasn't as merry an occasion as it should have been, but Kessian had been right that sometimes people needed to pretend.

We left together, the two of us, walking without touching or pretending. At least for the first five minutes.

Then, tentatively, Kessian reached out with a pinky and linked it with mine.

CHAPTER 25

Lunaris had optimistically brewed two cups of tea when we returned, and so must have been disappointed in me when I bypassed them for the liquor under the sink. I pulled out the whiskey and gin.

"G&T?"

"I thought you hated gin," Kessian said.

"I do. You don't."

I'd bought it for him, but I didn't want to say so, particularly after our conversation in the changing rooms. Might scare him off. The extra mug, the color of my bedroom door, gin stocked in the liquor cabinet . . . I'd held off sleeping with him so long, but the signs I'd already let him in were there.

Presenting him with his drink, I sat across from him in the dining booth. A sip of the whiskey warmed me up and gave me the courage to reach out and link our pinkies again.

He smiled weakly. "You're going to think I'm a bag of cats."

"I like cats."

He took a deep drink and, studying the glass rather than me, said, "I never used to drink, 'cause one time my mum came home wasted and told me she liked her life better before she had me."

"God, Kessian."

I didn't know what to say, and it looked like he might not say more, but then he did. Much more.

"It's a pattern. I need a lot of personalized attention or I get neurotic and needy, so she left first chance she got. My first serious girlfriend left me because I was trans, and she wasn't into men. Dom left because I was sick and dying, and he couldn't handle that. And maybe that's life. People come and go, things change, or the world changes and you no longer fit in where you used to, but for me it felt like every time I became more myself or more vulnerable, the people I loved stopped loving me back."

It broke my heart to hear it put that way. My goodbyes had been many but brief. Apart from leaving Shearwater, I'd never had the time to get attached. I didn't know which of us was better off.

"But you . . . you know all those things about me and said I was worth the risk anyway."

"I didn't mean you're a risk because of any of those things."

"I know what you meant. You were risking your heart. And if I'd known you would, I'd never have let you."

"Why?"

"They say it's better to have loved and lost, right? Somewhere along the line, I started to believe no one would choose me for good. So I chose Shearwater. It felt safe. Places can't leave you, but people can."

"Then Warwick evicted you."

He nodded, smiling mirthlessly and taking another drink. "Every time I think I've got something stable going . . . Poof. Gone. We haven't known each other long, but I go one of two ways. I either never fall, or I fall fast and hard, and I knew you'd be the latter, and I couldn't get it out of my head. What if you, after accepting all those vulnerable things about me, found some new reason I wasn't worth keeping? Something else that made me feel even harder to love than being disabled, trans, and more high maintenance than a bonsai tree. 'Cause being rejected by someone who doesn't know me, that's fine. But you . . . I don't think I could take it from you."

I wet my lips. Now came the hard part. I could see where the conversation led, the two of us bound for different destinations. This past week was just the brief slice of time in which our paths intersected.

"I said I'd risk a broken heart. You're saying you can't."

Tears sprang to his eyes again. This time, he didn't stymie them. "If we survive this, I can't afford to stay in Shearwater."

"You could come with me and Lunaris—"

"*No*, I can't. I need my independence, Tal. I was completely dependent on Dom, and it left me in a terrible place when he left. I had friends in that city, but it's hard to keep them when you only see each other once in a blue moon. I don't want to feel like my entire life dissolves every time I have a breakup or have to move house. I want to find something with just a *shred* of plausible permanency. And I can't ask that of you after a week, and you can't promise it to me, either, so . . ."

His home had to be a place. I wanted mine to be a person. The Venn diagram of our needs was two circles.

"Oh." Pain sliced through me, sharper than it had any right to be. We'd only known each other a short time, but it hurt like I'd known him much longer. "I . . . get it. I think. But . . ." *Fuck*, it hurt.

He made a noise like he'd been physically cut, too.

The sound of tearing fabric accompanied it, though. Kessian screamed and grabbed his leg. I jumped up, eyes wide.

Four diagonal slashes had appeared in the leg of his trousers, and between his fingers, blood welled.

Lunaris rattled like an earthquake, cabinets vibrating, as the wraith materialized out of the ether like ink dripped into water.

It had its claws around Kessian's hip, its head bent over him. I couldn't banish it with my talisman, I couldn't teleport us elsewhere with Kessian in its grip, and I didn't know how it could appear like this with no warning from Lunaris or without breaking my wards, so I lashed out with the only weapon I had left—my fists.

I wasn't a trained fighter, but I'd read enough books to know not to tuck my thumb in my fist or I'd break it, and I had enough anger in me to numb the fear of fighting something so intangible. I put my fist through the shadowy void of its face. The dark absorbed me, thick and viscous, but through it I struck something more solid.

Once, twice, again. Kessian rolled free from under us. The next strike of my fist sent the antlered head careening into the wall behind it.

While it was stunned, I backed up, grasping Kessian around the waist to support him as we made our way through the narrow hall. The wraith recovered quickly, moving like a spider through the door.

"We have to lure it to the trap." I scooped his cane up from where it had fallen to the floor. "Can you run?"

His hand came away from his leg stained red. "I'm not proud. If you can carry me . . ."

I stumbled with him down the steps before scooping him up and running across the green. Never had I been so glad Lunaris incorporated a personal gym in her revolving door of rooms for me. Kessian wasn't big, nor was he light, and though I'd parked as close as Lunaris could get to the hut, it didn't feel close enough with the screech of the wraith gaining on us and my gait staggered while I adapted to Kessian's weight in my arms. Looking over my shoulder, he went pale.

"Almost there," I said.

The hut was in sight, but a thought occurred to me as I sped toward it. The sigil inside occupied the entire floor. If we ran in hoping to lure the wraith in with us, we would be trapped in there with it.

I had to hope we could squeeze into a corner and that once we were confined, it couldn't harm us.

The ground vibrated with the weight of the wraith galloping behind me. My lungs burned. I put on a burst of speed when I felt a breath of cold on my neck and Kessian hid his face in my shoulder.

We reached the hut. The back-left corner was the largest outside the sigil, but still not large enough with Kessian in my arms. I dropped his legs. A cold wind touched my back as I crowded him into the corner. I braced for the sting of claws raking my back.

Blinding light filled the hut with an electric explosion. Blue sparks hit the wall above Kessian's head. He looked past my shoulder, eyes wide, chest rising and falling rapidly.

"It worked," he whispered.

Slowly, carefully, I craned my neck to look over my shoulder.

Shadows filled the confines of the sigil. They roiled and curled against the invisible prison, prompting a punishing burst of sparks. The darkness recoiled as if shocked.

At the center of it all was a figure darker than the shadows, its head held low so its antlers didn't puncture the ceiling, its focus solely upon us.

Kessian's hands squeezed my arms. "How do we get past it?"

"Break down the wall?"

The wraith tilted its head like it was listening.

Kessian looked at the scant few inches of ground between the circumference of the sigil and the wall of the hut. Experimentally, he reached with one arm, hand flat against the wall. The wraith's focus followed his movements.

"Quickly. Like putting your hand through a candle flame," he said.

The second he moved, the wraith lunged, throwing itself at the perimeter of its prison like a rabid animal. Kessian recoiled back into the corner for safety. I caged him in, one hand to either side of his head.

"Okay. That didn't work. Maybe you should try and talk to it."

I looked at him incredulously. "Talk to it? It's barely human."

"It's a part of you. Maybe a part of us. It's got some connection to all the people who've died. Isn't that how it works with ghosts? You soothe them by making right whatever wrong led to their death in the first place?"

In our position, I'd try anything, but—"You're the one who's good with words."

"They're not my family. And you're a lot better than you think. If I'd died this way, I wouldn't want tact. I'd want honesty. Nobody ever has to worry about you lying to them."

Our argument from the changing room still fizzled between us then, but he meant it as encouragement.

Carefully, tucking myself as far away from the edge of the sigil as I could, I turned to face the creature.

I'd never appreciated its size until now. It towered like a plume of smoke to the ceiling.

"What do you want?"

I didn't expect it to answer. It had never spoken before. Smoke boiled from the place its mouth would be, but the sounds it emitted were not human.

"I'm trying to help," I said. "I'm trying to find the one who poisoned the strid, who killed my grandad. Can you tell me who that is?"

Its smoky breath fumed, and something glowed in the place its heart would be. It gave its head a shake and slammed a claw against the barrier of light. More sparks flew. I jumped and Kessian's hands steadied me.

The wraith seemed frustrated. Well, the feeling was mutual.

"It would be a lot easier to help you if you stopped killing all the people I love. Why do you do it? What purpose could it possibly serve?"

The shadows leapt. For a moment the wraith seemed to split, like two frames of a film overlaid, and the glow at its center magnified, pulsing like a beating heart.

"Keep talking. You're getting through to something," Kessian said.

I hardly needed the encouragement. I'd kept all of this bottled up. Now it poured out of me. "I hated living alone! Because of you, I've had no one for years. I was never the best with people, but I still liked them, and I only got worse at talking to them without practice. I miss my dad. I miss Laurelie. I miss Amelia. Because of you I'll never have them back, and now you won't even give me a single, solitary *fucking* clue how to *fix this* so I can finally come home!"

The shadows rattled and burst apart around something emerging from the glowing hole in the wraith's chest.

It was a hand, dripping with umbral ichor and grasping toward us. It was—

It was human.

The wraith flickered again, and this time the two frames were markedly different. The wraith in one, a human figure in the other, tearing free of the wraith's body like its ribs were a cage.

Heedless of the danger, I reached out and grasped the hand. The wraith screeched and reared its head, sparks flying from around the sigil.

I kept pulling, but I needed more room for leverage. "Kessian! Can you sneak past it now?"

Kessian waved an arm through the sigil, but the wraith was too occupied in my tug-o-war with it. He limped as quickly as his injured leg allowed, holding on to the wall for support.

From the doorway, he said, "Now you."

Holding on to the arm protruding from the wraith's chest, I swung my weight to the right, around the sigil, until I was halfway out the door.

My grip almost slipped, but I reeled back, put a foot against the doorjamb, and pulled.

The wooden shed creaked ominously, then the figure trapped in the wraith burst free in a pool of liquid shadow, which melted and fried in the sigil like bacon fat. The figure was a girl judging by its shape. I dragged her the rest of the way out of the hut to safety. She raised her head, the darkness bleeding away from her face, soaking into the earth and revealing her. I recognized her face.

It was Amelia.

CHAPTER 26

We pulled her a safe distance from the shed, where the wraith wailed and threw itself at the boundary of the sigil like a thing possessed.

Amelia, coughing and shivering, backpedaled in the grass until I managed to grab her under the arms and get her to her feet, searching her for any sign of injury. She was soaked to the skin, still wearing the baggy shorts and button-up she'd had on the day she died, now stained with silt.

Shivering, she grasped my shoulders and looked between Kessian and me, then the wraith, which had gone eerily still, staring at Amelia like she was a lost meal.

"You're okay," I said. "You're safe."

Once the words were out, the relief hit me. It took her legs out from under her, because she collapsed into my arms with a sob, hugging me so tight the water soaked through both our clothes.

"Let's get you inside," Kessian said. "Warm you up."

With lightning reflexes I didn't think she'd have the capacity for in her current state, she grabbed Kessian's wrist. His face went white like it hurt, and in a moment of self-reflection, Amelia softened her grip.

"I have things to tell you. Things I saw, knew."

A terrible hope arose. "The others. Laurelie, Dad, everyone the wraith ever took. Can they be brought back, too?"

She shook her head. "Not themselves anymore. You know how caterpillars become goop in the cocoon before they become a butterfly?"

"Yeah," I said.

"No!?" said Kessian.

"It's like, the longer you're in there, the less you're . . . well, *you*. The more you're *everyone*. I—I'm Amelia, but for a little while I felt like Laurelie, but mostly the strid." She shook her head. "But that's not what I need to tell you."

"There'll be time," I said.

"No! I'm already forgetting."

Kessian said, "Tell us inside."

"It wants to go home," she said as we helped her up the stairs into Lunaris. "I—*It* is a people and a place, but it's lost its identity."

My familiar had laid out warm towels and fresh clothes. Amelia had to be convinced to change. I pushed her through the door to my bedroom. She kept babbling as I closed it to give her privacy.

"Someone poisoned it. I should know who, but his face is a monstrous blur. It didn't want to remember. It didn't want to think of him."

"So it's a man?" I said.

"I think so? The strid. It's sick, and taking people makes it feel a little better, but also makes it sicker, but it can't stop."

"I'm listening," I called to her from the kitchen while pulling tithes out of the first-aid kit under my sink.

"It took me to this place. Somewhere in the water. It looked like . . . I don't know how to describe it, and the picture's not as clear anymore. Was it ever? It's like a dream I'm trying not to forget. And I have to tell you. It feels important."

"Keep going," I said. "Maybe talking about it will jog your memory."

Kessian pulled his trousers down so I could run a healing spell over the slash marks left on his leg. They closed, leaving behind pink scars.

"Grandad's house was there. We—I kept visiting it. Something about time. Something about the clocks . . ."

The door burst open. Kessian hurriedly pulled his torn trousers back up. Amelia, drowning in the T-shirt and pajama bottoms I'd loaned her, came out, rubbing her head and grimacing as she tried to remember the rest.

"Take me to Grandad's house."

"Your family will want to know you're okay," Kessian said.

"This can't wait! I'm afraid I'll forget it all. Please."

I grabbed my keys. Lunaris had fired up the engine before I'd crawled into the driver's seat.

We pulled up outside Grandad's house ten minutes later. It still had the stench of smoke to it and a blackened smear fanning up from the burnt-out window. I'd barely parked before Amelia was clambering out the door, rushing up and lifting a plant pot for the spare key.

"Clocks. Clocks. Something about time," she kept saying as she fit the key in the lock and pushed inside.

The smoky smell hit us harder as we entered. Amelia walked up to the grandfather clock, running a hand along the glass. "No, no, not that one."

She walked a lap through the living room, dining room, and kitchen. The clocks were countless. If she required a specific one, I wouldn't know where to begin. She went up the stairs at a harried pace. I took my time in case Kessian needed my help, but he doggedly clung to the railing and used his cane.

The door to Grandad's study was open. I held out a hand to protest Amelia going in, in case the floor was no longer stable, but she'd stopped just outside.

The interior had been remade in shades of black and gray. There were the hulking impressions of what had once been a desk and bookshelves, but most of the chair had been reduced to charcoal. Whatever books or notes were kept there were only ash.

Amelia pointed to the metal brackets where a shelf had once been. "There were clocks there with little Post-It notes beneath, and they all had names. One for your dad, one for Laurelie, one for you."

"What were they for?" I asked.

"Tools for keeping time," she said.

"I know that, but—"

"They don't work. Not here."

"Not anymore," Kessian remarked, looking at the piles of ash on the floor.

"No, I mean Dad's and Laurelie's were stopped at 3:16 and 12:00, but yours, Tal? It still ticked."

I was trying to follow. "So . . . mine worked?"

"Not here. They don't work unless they're underwater."

"That . . . is normally the opposite of true," Kessian murmured, but neither of us dared interrupt her. She'd grabbed onto a yarn and was following it to some sort of conclusion.

With a faraway look, she regarded the rest of the room. In a sudden frenzy, she went to the desk, and before I could call her back from the danger of a floor that could collapse, she wrenched open a drawer and froze.

I ventured a few tentative feet into the room to see what she'd found. It was hard to discern amongst the ashes, but a pocket watch lay within, sooty and dark. She picked it up, rubbing away the soot to reveal a flash of silver and a mother-of-pearl inlay. It was tarnished with rust, but it was beautiful.

Beautiful and familiar.

"Grandad gave that to me for my sixteenth birthday," I said. "I . . . I lost it. I had it on me the night I went into the strid."

"How could he have found it?" Kessian asked.

I didn't know. Amelia picked it up reverently and opened it. An engraving on the inside lid read:

34-96-13

"That wasn't there before," I said.

"Do those numbers mean anything to you?" Kessian asked.

I shook my head.

Amelia said, "I think it's for you."

"Why? What do I do with them?" I asked.

She screwed up her face in concentration, rubbing her head so hard it looked like it hurt. "I saw everything in there, and now it's like my head's sprung a leak." She dropped her hands and let out a deep sigh. "I can't remember the 'why.' Just that you need this. Someone wanted you to have it."

"Just . . . someone?" I prompted.

Through her exhaustion, she looked a little afraid. "I'm losing sight of everything from in there, but if I remember right, you left it for yourself."

We drove back to the spa. I called Fae, Mum, and Marlowe and told them to come see us at once. They came expecting bad news.

Fae was first to arrive, and when Amelia came out to greet them, they at first screamed like she was a ghost, then immediately burst into tears and crushed their cousin in a hug. By the time Marlowe, Lettie, and Mum drove up, they couldn't see Amelia, she was so enveloped in Fae's arms.

Lettie nearly fell to her knees and wept. Marlowe looked so shell-shocked that it didn't become real until he hugged her. And Mum, she just looked at me open-mouthed.

"You did this? You brought her back?"

"Somehow, yeah."

"And Laurelie? Your father?"

"I . . . I think it's been too long."

Mum's face fell. I'd been about to ask why she didn't mention Grandad when a thought occurred to me. He hadn't been dragged into the strid. The autopsy report claimed he'd died by the wraith's hands, that it gave him heart failure, but the wraith had never done that before. Its methods had always been, far as we knew, drowning. It had never left a body to bury.

Marlowe extricated himself from the tangle of arms around Amelia and clasped my hands. "Thank you. I don't know what else to say, but thank you."

"You don't have to thank me."

"How did you do it?"

"Grandad's trap. It worked."

At this, everyone stopped and stared in the direction of the shed. It was just visible over the stony knoll and through a strand of trees.

"Is it still—?" Marlowe asked.

"I'm going to check. You all can stand back."

"I'm coming with you," Kessian said.

"And me," said Marlowe.

"Well, I'm not," Amelia said, curling into Lettie's protective arms. "I've seen enough of that thing to last a lifetime."

As we set off up the knoll, Mum came with us, too. Blue light still filtered in beams through cracks in the door. I held out a hand.

"Maybe take a step back."

Everyone did. I swung the door open and jumped back a few paces.

The wraith still stood confined, its shoulders hunched. Mum took a step closer. Marlowe said, "Well done, Tal."

The wraith lunged. All of us staggered back at the ferocity of it. I thought for sure it would break through—light seemed a more flimsy barrier than the wooden door had been—but the sigil held fast, and the wraith let out a keening wail of fury and pain as its shadows singed every time it slammed its shoulder against its cage.

"The question is, what do we do with it?" Mum asked.

Kessian and I exchanged a look.

"The answer to that's complicated," I said. "It's trapped, but the sigil won't last indefinitely. Continuously replenishing the tithes is just asking for a fatal mistake. But we don't know how to banish it permanently. Honestly, I don't think it can be except by cleansing the strid. Which, in practical terms, means finding whoever murdered Grandad and lured all those people to their deaths in the first place, and either bringing him to justice or getting him to undo it all."

"And do you have any more information on who did it?" Marlowe asked. "Warwick?"

The wraith continued its assault on its prison with renewed vigor.

"Not yet." Watching the wraith, I couldn't quite let go of that connection between the strange shape of its antlers and the identical statue in Warwick's house. It played over in my mind again and again. How could he have created such an exact replica without having studied the wraith, and when could he have? It only appeared to take someone, and far as I knew, Warwick had never been present during an assault.

Unless . . . Unless the relic wasn't mimicking the wraith, but the other way around.

I recalled the details of that statue. The hollow tines, the holes placed at intervals along two of them, two central holes fusing into one.

The strange flutelike instrument that had been played on the banks of the strid had that exact shape.

"What if he has the murder weapon in his house, right under our noses?" I asked aloud.

Everyone stared at me, uncomprehending. I walked them through my thought process, the shape of the antlers, the flute from the dream, and the statue in Warwick's house.

"He'd have to be a fool to keep it out in the open like that," Marlowe said.

"Or very arrogant," Kessian said. "Which he verifiably is. That presents a new problem, though. Last time we snuck around his house, we got caught, and even if we managed to steal it, that would make it inadmissible as evidence. We'd be the ones on the hook for possessing the murder weapon."

He was right. "We need something that gives the authorities the right to search Foxbury Manor. Something ironclad enough he can't bribe his way out of it."

Mum offered to search through the contracts kept between Warwick and Grandad, if any had survived the fire. Marlowe, meanwhile, would research Warwick's solicitors to see if any of them had dirt they were willing to part with. I didn't think either would provide us with the proof we needed, though, because I had an inclination the proof we needed was already gone.

First, there'd been the fire. Then, when he'd caught us sneaking around, he'd accused us of stealing a contract. We hadn't, but someone had.

Whatever they'd absconded with, I suspected it was what we needed. With Fae and Camilla's wedding tomorrow, the search would have to wait until the day after, but a little crackle of hope went through me as I said goodnight to Kessian without kissing him, but thinking about it.

If Warwick went to prison for what he'd done, maybe Kessian wouldn't have to fear losing his home anymore.

CHAPTER 27

The preparations for Fae's wedding flew by. I spent the morning so occupied by setting out chairs and helping decorate the dining hall of the spa that I hardly thought of the wraith. Imprisoned in the sigil and a warded shed, it no longer posed as much of a threat as my mum, who'd been on a rampage since the florist told her the peonies had to be replaced with dahlias on account of the former having had a rough growing season.

When it came time for the ceremony, I waited near the entrance to the pavilion set up in the spa's gardens alongside Amelia and the other members of the bridal party. I could hear the trickling water of the spring, which set me on edge. Kessian had been tasked with helping Fae get ready, so I hadn't seen him all morning.

My breath caught when he finally appeared.

In the bustle of the morning, I hadn't given thought to what he'd look like dressed up for the occasion. The cream of his suit complemented his hair, tying in with the blues in the pattern of the waistcoat. He wore it so much better than me, with his cane's frost pattern like lace and the gold chain threaded into his plait catching the light. A sheen of powder on his cheeks brought out the shine of his freckles.

In the changing room, I hadn't the time to properly appreciate how gorgeous he was. He spotted me, beamed, and walked over.

"Looking very sharp," he said.

"I—er—thanks. You, er—"

He had me completely tongue-tied.

"Please tell me the cane doesn't make me look like a pimp," he said.

"If it did, I could be your whore," I blurted.

Kessian's jaw dropped. "I'm so glad Fae decided not to get married in a church if you're gonna talk like that."

"Sorry. Seriously, you look—" I cleared my throat. "Right. I'll keep my thoughts to myself."

Kessian didn't reply as we took our places in the bridal party queues. We'd never really finished our conversation before the wraith interrupted, and the muddy valley between friends and almost-lovers awkwardly hung over us. I'd compliment a friend and have a laugh with them, but perhaps offering to be his whore was a step too far.

The harpist struck up a chord, and the wedding guests went quiet. One by one, we filed down the aisle. I tried not to power-walk my way to the front, relieved to take my seat and join everyone else in craning our necks.

Camilla came first, wearing a modest lace gown with a long train and crystal teardrops dripping from her veil. Fae followed.

I'd already seen their dress at the fitting yesterday, but with the harpist's plucked chords and the hushed atmosphere, it struck me how much time had passed, and how little it seemed to matter now, because I couldn't have been happier to see them happy. I didn't know whether their favorite food had changed from mint chocolate chip ice cream to something else. I didn't know if someone else had broken their heart before Camilla came along. When I'd first arrived back in Shearwater, they'd asked me if I even wanted to stay, and I'd said yes, but had so many reservations, because was I returning to the same place, the same people? Everyone had changed and grown.

I hadn't stopped loving them, though, and if I stayed there'd be time to find out about favorite foods and past flames.

I supposed I did want to stay.

Maybe, if everything worked out, I could.

By the time Fae made it to the podium, tears streamed down Camilla's face. Fae had come prepared and pulled tissues from the pockets of their skirt. When it came time to exchange vows, Fae's came in the form of a stack of cards thick as a dictionary and secured with an elastic band. They looked askance at the guests and said, "Don't worry. I won't read them all," and everyone laughed. "This is how many attempts it took for me to write my vows. I wanted them to be perfect. Because you're perfect."

Which set Camilla off crying again.

She started her own vows with, "I knew I'd be emotional marrying the love of my life, but at this point I think we'll all agree I ought to have been sedated."

They were funny, and earnest, and madly in love. It made my heart squeeze painfully. I'd never been to a queer wedding before, and I hadn't expected it to be any different, but it was as if they gave me permission to want this for myself one day. I'd grown so used to the idea it could never happen, that it was only a possibility for people who didn't live life on the run.

As they sealed their vows with a kiss, the warm weight of Kessian's arm pressed into mine, and I allowed myself one more ridiculous, far-fetched delusion. In it, I'd get up early to make him tea the way he liked it. I'd take it to him in bed, where he'd be stealing a few more minutes to doze. Lunaris would soak up the sun streaming in through the window, just a calico cat no longer burdened with being my home and my only friend. Kessian would wake, and maybe the tea would go cold as we got lost in each other, or maybe we'd just cuddle and talk about the day ahead. The first time we talk about marriage it would be a joke about eloping to a beach where we'd write our vows in the sand, commit them to the sea while getting drunk on margaritas, but neither of us would be joking. Not really.

I want to find something with just a shred of plausible permanency. And I can't ask that of you after a week, and you can't promise it to me, either.

The wedding ceremony was beautiful, but it wasn't the only reason I had to hold back tears.

In the intervening hours between canapes and photography sessions, I mingled with the other guests and ate an embarrassing number of smoked salmon blinis.

Marlowe found me plucking a champagne flute off a tray and said, "First or second?"

Third. "What's a wedding without a few refreshments?"

He nodded his agreement. From the ruddy flush of his cheeks, he'd had a few himself. "No leads yet on that lost contract?"

"It would be convenient if someone gave it to Fae as a wedding gift."

"Wouldn't it just?"

"We'll figure it out . . . The wraith's been connected to me so long, and now Kessian's the Keeper, maybe all the pieces are finally coming together."

Marlowe's expression crumpled. "Hold on, now. Kessian's the Keeper?"

"Yeah. Sorry, I thought we'd said."

Marlowe had such a mild-mannered attitude, his sudden intensity threw me off. "That's . . . odd."

"Why?"

"It normally passes down through families. I wondered why your mum and I never felt anything different. I guessed maybe it went to you." He shook his head, expression pitying. "It drove your grandad half mad trying to find a solution to your problem. I wouldn't wish that on Kessian. It shouldn't be his burden."

"Why do you think it should be ours?"

Before he could answer, Amelia grasped my elbow. "Have you seen Kessian lately?"

"No, what's wrong?"

"I was going to say a little toast to you both for saving me, but I can't find him."

Fear swallowed me. My first thought was the wraith. I'd checked it this morning, still sealed within the sigil and a warded shed with no sign of either spell weakening.

I was being paranoid. No one would be mad enough to risk freeing it. I'd check the bathrooms first. Maybe Kessian was having an outfit malfunction.

In the loo, I tentatively called out his name.

An even more tentative "Tal?" answered.

I followed it to a shut stall. "Amelia's looking for you."

"I, er . . ." A deep sigh. "My hand's locked up. Waiting for the painkillers to kick in."

"Can I come in?"

The door clicked open and I closed it behind me. Kessian sat on the lid of the toilet, massaging his wrist.

"I guess I'm not used to walking with a cane. Maybe I'm not doing it right, putting too much pressure on it."

"You should have told me. I think I have healing tithes that could help."

"I don't want to be a burden. And I'm not your responsibility. Especially after I— You should be enjoying the wedding."

"I'd enjoy it more with you." Remembering last night's conversation, I reluctantly added, "As your friend?"

To my surprise, he looked disappointed. "Right. Okay. If you're sure."

"Give me five minutes."

Living out of a camper van had never seemed more convenient than when it only took me two minutes to run out to the field where I'd parked her and retrieve the tithes I'd need. On my way, out of paranoia, I checked the wraith's shed. It was still warded, locked, with the blue light of the sigil glowing under the door and the wraith's low, uneven breaths. Like it didn't need to breathe but remembered living things ought to and only did so to feel normal.

I hurried back to the toilets. Kessian had managed to relocate to a bench outside them. Amelia had found him and given him a flute of sparkling wine, two more in hand.

"I know what kind of injury that is," Amelia joked. "Don't blame it on your cane."

"I brought the tithes," I said, before things devolved from wank jokes to jokes about Kessian and I, who were not engaging in those activities anymore, a fact that I was keen not to ruminate on.

I pressed the magic gently into Kessian's hand, letting it flow up his wrist. His fingers uncurled from their stiff positions a little, brushing my palm as I drew back.

"Better?"

He flexed his hand. "Much. Still a few twinges, but I can walk from the bathroom to my seat in the dining hall."

Amelia handed me the second glass of wine she held. "You know I'm not comfortable with sappy speeches, so let me get this out fast. I wanted to say a small toast. You both saved my life. Not often anyone gets a second chance like that, but I'm grateful. And I'm hoping it means you'll give Shearwater a second chance, too." She didn't specify whether she meant me or Kessian, just held out her glass to chime against ours and finished, "To you both, and to second chances."

Kessian met my gaze for a beat too long as we echoed her.

"I'll see you both on the dance floor later," Amelia said.

"Ah yes, me with my peanut brittle hips," Kessian remarked.

"I'm sure your boyfriend can limber you up and carry you."

"We aren't boyfriends," I said.

"Ah, my mistake." She turned to Kessian. "Your *idiot* will be happy to limber you up and carry you onto the dance floor."

She departed with a sarcastic salute. We made our way to the dining room, not talking about what she'd said.

Dinner and speeches passed by, an entire day devoted to romantic overtures while my own love life drowned. I had done an admirable job of avoiding the ennui for the majority of the day, but as the first dance kicked off, Fae and Camilla besotted with each other and twirling across the floor under fairy lights, it hit me hard.

Nine years of running, nine years of flash fire connections and faster goodbyes, and the one person I'd decided to risk putting down roots for didn't trust that he could do the same with me. And I understood his reasons—people hadn't been a reliable source of shelter in his life, and he needed a home, and he'd only known me such a short time. It still felt like I was the butt of a cosmic joke.

Or perhaps that was the alcohol making me melancholic.

When the song changed and I came back to myself, I found Kessian had been watching me.

"Amelia was right, you know. If you want a dance, you're going to have to carry me."

Before I could ask if he was joking, my mum descended upon the table. She sat straight-backed and crossed her legs at the knee, wineglass balanced upon them and held by the stem.

"Fae's very happy you came," she said. Subtext: *I didn't want you to, but I'm capitulating that it might have been worth it.*

I was not great at reading people, but my mother was a different story. Sixteen years of predicting her moods and what she truly meant with her passive-aggressive comments had made me an expert linguist in her particular tells.

"I'm glad I could."

"Are you both enjoying yourselves?" Small talk to set the groundwork for what she really wanted to say.

"It's a beautiful wedding," Kessian said. "You must be proud to see Fae find someone who makes them so happy." I could read his subtext, too. *Not that you care about all your children's happiness equally.*

She nodded, tapping the stem of her wineglass with one polished nail. A long silence followed, and I couldn't do the awkward pleasantries thing. (I never could, but particularly not tonight.)

"Did you want to say something, Mum?"

She huffed. "Yes, I do."

I waited. Her tapping got faster and faster until finally she spat the words out as if they'd been stuck in her teeth. "I wanted to tell you that . . . I was wrong. I shouldn't have tried to stop you from coming. I shouldn't have sent you away at all." She took a very large sip of her wine before rushing through the rest. "If you hadn't been here, Amelia wouldn't be here, and it would have made Fae very sad for their wedding. Now I can't help but wonder if I hadn't sent you away, if Laurelie, your father—"

"I don't think I'd have been able to save them," I said. "I was sixteen."

"Yes, well, we'll never know now, will we? I just wanted to say that. That I'm *sorry*."

My mother had never apologized to me. It shocked me so much I didn't say anything back until Kessian gave me a nudge under the table.

"It's okay," I said.

All the tension went out of her. Not with relief. She almost looked defeated. "That's all? Just, 'It's okay.' I sometimes wonder if it bothered you at all being sent away, or if you didn't really care for us as your family. Did you even want to be here?"

After the apology, I was unprepared for the hidden knife of her follow-up, and perhaps I'd have seen it as a malicious attempt to hurt me before, but her words echoed Fae's when I'd first arrived, and it brought me up short.

I'd taken too long to formulate a response. Mum was rising from the table.

"He does care," Kessian said. "He cares deeply. He stayed away to protect you, not because he didn't want to be here. He came back to try and fix things. He loves you all. I can see it. You can see it, too, in his actions rather than his words."

I could hardly contain the dam of feeling welling up in me at being understood. He hadn't known me long, but he spoke whatever strange language I did, the kind my family struggled to interpret.

Mum stood agape for a moment.

"It's true," I said. "I'm not good with words but I do—love you. And the whole family."

For a second, she looked genuinely touched and happy. "Love you, too." With a nod to Kessian, she said, "I'd better see you both on the dance floor later—Oh, unless you can't?" She patted her mouth as if to shove the faux-pas back in there and trotted off with a quick, "Come by for Sunday roast sometime!"

"Sorry about that," I murmured.

He hummed. "Honestly, I think I prefer that to people tiptoeing around it. Makes me feel less like the elephant in the room to at least be acknowledged as different, rather than awkwardly pretending we're all the same, or that yoga will fix me. Though tonight I might have to kick off my shoes and stand on someone's feet while he pilots me around the dance floor."

I snorted. "That sounds fun, to be honest."

"Did you want to?"

The song had turned slow. My heart ricocheted around like a stray bullet in my chest. "I'm not very good."

"I didn't ask if you were good, I asked if you wanted to dance."

"With you?"

He bit his lip. "Yes?"

I got up. He'd started babbling. "So long as you don't mind dancing with a guy who's falling apart like a hard taco shell."

I got on my knees and started unlacing his shoes. "Yes. I want to dance with you." I held out my hand for him.

Kessian's eyes glimmered as he took it. Kicking off his shoes, he leaned on me as I led him onto the dance floor.

CHAPTER 28

I felt several pairs of eyes burning the back of my neck as I tentatively held Kessian's waist. He hung his cane on my elbow and, mischief sparkling in his eyes, stood on top of my shoes.

"It's a good thing you're smaller than me," I said.

Laughing, he said, "Tal, this is ridiculous."

"It is a bit, but you seem to be enjoying yourself."

The hand on my shoulder made its way to the back of my neck. "Seems to happen a lot when I'm with you."

I pushed thoughts of last night's conversation aside. If I only got one dance, that would have to be enough. I was used to everything only lasting short term, so it shouldn't hurt when the song ended.

I began to shuffle us in slow circles around the dance floor. The movement forced him to hold on more tightly, but with his feet on mine, he didn't have to put much strain on his hips or wrist.

It also brought us close together. I could smell the spicy fragrance he wore on his neck. This was the closest we'd been physically since we'd been trapped in the shed with the wraith—and though that wasn't too long ago, so much had happened in the intervening time, it felt like an age.

"You know, I used to really hate the athletes in high school, 'cause they were more often than not the ones who'd bully me. Turned me off the big, strong jock types."

"I'm not a jock."

"You clearly work out, or are you just so genetically gifted that picking me up and running for both our lives was only a warmup for you?"

"My arms are still sore. There's just not a lot to do when you live alone. Lunaris made me a home gym. I became a little obsessed with seeing how many push-ups I could do."

I shivered as Kessian ran a hand down my arm, squeezing my bicep. "Well, I have a new appreciation for big, sturdy blokes now that one of them saved my life."

"How's your hip?" I asked, brushing my thumb where the wraith had raked its claws.

"It was busted before the wraith got to it, so no worse for wear." He swallowed. "Thank you. For not leaving me behind."

"I'd never do that."

Very quietly, he said, "I think I know that now."

My chest ached, something larger than his words wrapped up in them, heavy with meaning and making my heart leaden with it. He stared at a spot just over my shoulder, so I could look at him without reservation. The soft fall of his hair in his face, the glint of his freckles, the way his eyes caught the light like sun catchers, the pink mark left by my lips on his neck just visible above his shirt collar. So gorgeous that the ache in my chest worsened for looking at him too long.

While I floundered, Kessian said something so low and under his breath that I couldn't hear over the music. I had to ask him to repeat it.

"I said, if you keep looking at me like that, it's going to go straight to my head."

"Sorry." I looked over his shoulder instead.

A finger touched my jaw and directed me to turn back to him. "I didn't ask you to stop."

"You sort of did. Last night."

"Right."

"The song's stopped."

Kessian looked around to confirm it. A note of tremulous fear edged his voice. "I need to say something. I need to get this out."

I handed him his cane then led him off the dance floor, away from the people watching.

He still didn't have his shoes on as he walked us through the grass, his cane leaving deep imprints in the soft soil as we left the light of the tent behind. He positioned us behind an oak tree, out of sight of the wedding guests.

He turned to face me, feverish and nervous. Were his insides crackling and snapping like microwaved popcorn the way mine were?

"Last night . . . Last night I told you I needed a sure thing, right?"

"Right . . ." I said.

"And that I couldn't ask you to promise me anything, because even with visions from a magic spring, we have no way of knowing the future. There's no guarantee this works out or breaks my heart and leaves me terrified that, while I'm desperate for a place and a person to call home, I'm never going to be good enough for anyone to find their home in me."

"Kessian, you're—"

"Let me finish, let me finish. Before I forget. The thing is, I'm never going to find happily ever after if I'm not willing to take a chance on happy for now. And you make me happy *right now*."

I suppressed my hope, but it burned up my throat. "I do?"

His eyes crinkled with a mix of joy and terror. "Yeah. You do. So . . . fuck the future. You're a story I'd want to see through to the end, even if I knew the ending was tragic."

"O-oh . . ." My hands shook as I reached up to brush a thumb across the stars on his cheeks. "Are you done talking? Wait, that came out wrong. Can I kiss you now?"

He nodded and tipped forward. Our noses bumped, and his lashes fell over his eyes as, my heart like a hummingbird's, I pressed my lips softly to his.

It was a gentle, feathery thing at first. Then his hand, which had been on my chest keeping me at arm's length, fisted in my shirt to pull me close instead. He whimpered and molded himself against me—lips, chest, hips—opening his mouth for more. I tilted my head so we'd fit together better, and he wasn't the only one whimpering anymore.

I spoke, which broke the kiss, and he made a heartbreaking noise like he was afraid I'd stopped altogether.

"What made you change your mind?" I said.

"You. Saving my life and running off to get tithes when paracetamol didn't cut it." He kissed me harder. "Being so damn *reliable* and *level-headed* while I'm acting madder than a shotgun stag do."

He raked his fingers through my hair, nails sending tingles down my spine and straight to my dick. This was getting away from me very quickly. He was all around me. An arm around my shoulders, a tongue licking into my mouth, his hand grabbing a jealous fistful of my arse as his cane thudded to the grass.

I crowded him against the tree and pressed close, wondering if it was possible to climb into his clothes and under his skin the way he'd gotten under mine.

"I want to fuck you again so damn bad," I said into his neck before pulling the collar down to renew the mark I'd left behind.

"Tal! First at a funeral, now a wedding? What will people say?"

"They won't miss us if we're only gone for half an hour."

"You think you can finish me off that quick?"

"I haven't given you head yet."

"Holy—" His nails dug into the nape of my neck as he said, teeth scraping against my cheek, "I love how you're not a big talker until you're horny, then you say things like *that*."

"Lunaris isn't far away."

Breathing hard, Kessian said, "Okay. Okay, I'm going to excuse myself from the party for a second. Stay and mingle for ten minutes so as not to advertise we're off for a quickie. Then come meet me."

I couldn't wait that long. "Five minutes."

He looked incandescent with glee. I knew I was giving him ample fodder with which to take the piss out of me later, and I didn't care.

"At least seven," he said.

I groaned. "Fine." I set him down, picked up his cane, and put it in his hand. He reached up to arrange my hair back into place, then pressed a lingering kiss to my lips before ambling back toward the party.

I stayed there, hidden behind the tree for a moment. I slumped with my back to the bark, the roughness of it grounding me. Though not quite, as I thought about how Kessian might have felt sandwiched between me and the tree trunk. I could still feel the impression of his ribs against mine, like I was soft clay and he'd left his fingerprints in me.

I checked the time on my phone. Two minutes had passed. It felt like an age. I looked toward the tent, but Kessian was nowhere to be seen there. He'd headed straight for Lunaris. I should go mingle and pretend all was the usual. Fetch Kessian's shoes before our rendezvous.

Fae grabbed me first. They'd had a few glasses to drink and the chatter flowed freely. "Thank you sooooo much for staying."

"Of course."

"It's so nice to have my brother back. You know, I wouldn't have to be the only queer one in the family if you stayed forever."

I tried to suppress a grin. "I don't think you need to worry about me staying."

"You *will*?"

"Once I've sorted all this stuff with the wraith—"

They threw their arms around me. I nearly choked on the bony point of their shoulder.

"That makes me so happy!"

"Me too."

"You look it." They smiled and leaned in for a conspiratorial whisper. "I won't be offended if a certain boy played a part in that. I saw you and Kessian dancing earlier. Are you both going to make a bid to catch my bouquet? Then I can plan *your* wedding."

"Slow down."

"You do like him, though, don't you?"

"Yeah . . . Quite a bit, really."

"Well, normally I'd warn you off a boy like that, but he seems to be fonder of you than his past dalliances, so I *guess* he has permission to date you."

"He needs your permission?"

"Of course. Where is he? I'll tell him. Kessian!" they began to shout.

"I'll go find him," I said, patting their shoulder. "Be back in a bit."

Camilla was already pulling them into another dance. I broke away from the crowd. It had been a little longer than ten minutes. I didn't want to leave Kessian hanging, so I broke into a bit of a jog.

Lunaris's door was open. I thought it was in anticipation of my arrival, but as I skipped up the stairs, it was to find the living room empty.

Lunaris flashed her lights red in alarm, and as I took in the shadow-stained steps and scratches on the door, her radio tuned in to three different stations, song lyrics putting together a message.

A retro pop song cried, "Help!"

A rolling bass melody sang, "Run, boy, run."

And finally an acoustic folk tune sung by a woman in a deep contralto, "Your lover likes a little danger, but not this kind."

I tarried only to retrieve my tithe belt, then turned and tripped my way outside. I sprinted up the grassy knoll, heading for the shed, but I knew what I'd find before I got there, confirmed it when I saw the door creaking open in the wind with no light shining through the gap, and when I threw it open, it was to find the edge of the sigil smeared through.

Warwick hadn't known this was here. Only my family had, but who among them would dare let it out when my family were the ones it targeted?

A strange, familiar melody came over me. A song I'd only heard once before. It had been hard to hear over the music at the wedding, so loud it carried here, but it echoed in my blood more than in my ears.

A gnarled cord of magic like barbed wire wended around my throat, nestled into the crevices of my spine. It tried to force me to stand ramrod straight and walk, but it couldn't quite worm its way into my brain. Whether because I'd survived its thrall once before or because some other force protected me, I didn't know, but I did know one thing.

The wraith had taken Kessian.

CHAPTER 29

Only a scant few minutes ago, we'd been kissing under a tree. The spring was a stone's throw from the wedding. If he'd been drowned there, people would have heard. People would have seen.

I clung to this thread of hope as I took off running into the woods, following the sound of the music and the strid's gargling laughter.

Had Kessian waited long before the wraith was upon him? The idea that he might have, and that the time I'd taken while speaking to Fae had made me late, along with the thought that I could have prevented this, all of it would haunt me. Would Kessian think I'd set this trap for him?

I should have left with him at once. The notion of what we'd nearly had, cut off before it could bloom—I pushed it from my mind and focused on picking my way through the woods. I had no talisman, no trap waiting nearby, and only whatever tithes my belt, the forest, and my own body provided. If I ran to get help, the wraith would reach the strid before I had time to stop it.

My best recourse was to find the flute player. Interrupt their song. Break the thrall over Kessian. But the music didn't seem to come from any one direction, it came from inside my head. Deep down, I knew it was not the flute player this time. It was the wraith, mimicking the music of its own creation.

So I followed a trail of blackened leaves left by the monster. I crashed through the brush, heading in the direction the song had taken me all those years ago, to the sheer bank where the river narrowed so sharply you could leap from one side to the other.

The air got colder as I caught up. I started to hear things other than the song. Plants withering, crackling underfoot. Movement like a fell breeze, and uneven footsteps interspersed with the thud of a cane. Lungs burning, I ran faster. Then I saw it.

The wraith stalked through the woods, a tall pillar of black ink amongst the trees. The thicket and plants of the forest floor curled away from it as if from a wildfire. It cleared a path, and walking behind it with leaden feet was Kessian.

I sped up, but ahead I could see the bright shimmer of moonlight off the water and hear the its rush getting louder, and I was still a good distance from the shore. The wraith began to whisper. The words were unintelligible at first, if they were words at all. They sounded like the river's flow. As we got closer to the strid, its proximity buzzing against my skin like a live wire, the wraith's whispers and song resolved enough that I understood.

You must walk the branching paths, the tributaries and small veins.

Though I couldn't comprehend the meaning of the words, something in my blood answered the call, waking up.

You must find me where the river runs deep, where the poison made its home in Shearwater.

That frightened me. *Where the river runs deep* did not sound like the sort of place I could go without drowning.

Through gaps in the trees ahead, the river ran blackly through the rocky crags, water thick as blood. Kessian staggered. He tried to dig his heels into the soil, but the wraith grasped his neck and moved him like a puppet.

Fear and adrenaline pushed me, but I already sprinted at my limit. A root moved to trip me. I went down, pine needles in my palms. I pushed up again and kept running.

The wraith reached the river, paused at its edge, then strode across. Instead of sinking into the depths, its feet skimmed the surface, the water frothing against it. It turned to face Kessian, insomuch as a creature with no face could. There, it waited, and Kessian went to it.

It all struck me as familiar. The vision. I'd dreamed this. *We'd* dreamed this, dipping our toes into a future we'd hoped would never come to pass.

Heart in my lungs, I cried out to him, "Kessian!"

He looked over his shoulder and saw me. His face might have brought me immeasurable comfort, if he wasn't already six paces from the edge of the river.

He stumbled a few steps as though the wraith had tugged him forward faster. It inclined its head to him, then abruptly sank below the water's surface like a drop of ink, unfurling then vanishing, the splash leaving one drop suspended in the air for an interminable time before it, too, disappeared in the stream.

"Kessian, stop! Fight it!"

I had no doubt he was. It didn't matter. He reached the river's edge and took another step. Ripples spread out from underfoot and under the point of his cane. One step, then the other.

I prepared to watch him vanish like the wraith had, but he walked across the water until he stood at the center of the stream.

The current will carry you home.

The wraith had Kessian in its thrall. It had won. He stood atop its lair, seconds away from a watery grave, and whatever magic kept him afloat, it had the power to dispel whenever it wished. So why didn't it?

"Kessian! Please fight it."

Kessian turned in a stiff, slow circle to face me. He was fighting. I could see it in the strain of every limb. His throat worked to speak through teeth clenched shut against his will.

I was close. I would reach him in a dozen steps. Eleven. Ten.

Even if I'd had the talisman, I couldn't use it. Banishing the wraith would banish its magic—the only thing keeping Kessian from drowning.

I came right up to the water's edge and held a hand out to him, hardly believing I'd made it this far, though a recollection scratched at the back of my mind. The vision we'd shared in the spring when this all began, I recalled how it ended. We were playing it out exactly.

It didn't change the fact that I would try to save him. "Take my hand. I'll pull you out."

Kessian's eyes seemed to scream a warning, but he reached out for me. His fingers were so cold as they grasped mine. Weakly at first, then strong. I started to pull. There was no relief in his expression, only despair.

A black hand rose up from the water, slinking around Kessian's ankle. It dragged him under in one great pull, and he held onto me so steadfastly that I went down with him.

CHAPTER 30

I braced myself for the frigid cold, the struggle for oxygen, the infectious cut of swirling debris, or the snap of my bones crushed into the rocky banks. The water could trap me in the underground labyrinth of tunnels like a rabbit's warren, carved into the stone by powerful currents. Tunnels I shouldn't know existed, but I did know. I *knew* this place.

This place.

I should be struggling for breath. The icy water still dragged me through the stream, still soaked through me, but I didn't feel the need to breathe.

I opened my eyes.

I was floating down a river in a boat the size of a gondola. My head spun as I took in the world around me, all cast in shades of blue and green. The web-patterned reflections of tropical water flickered over the world around me as if I were at the bottom of the ocean.

Yet I was in a boat on the river, and on the banks of that river were houses, shops, buildings, cobbled together like a coral reef. A whole sunken city.

A shadow in my periphery made me snap my head around, but if the wraith had followed me down here, I couldn't see it. I didn't know where "here" was, but that question mattered less than another.

Kessian. Where was he?

I searched the banks, the windows of the houses, the gardens, and jolted when I recognized one of the buildings—Witches and Stitches. It was sandwiched between two stately homes rather than a pizza chain and a betting shop, but I could see Ella and Rhia through the window.

I prepared to jump out of the gondola and ask them for help or if they'd seen Kessian. The river was too broad for me to make the leap without falling in, so I'd have to swim. Just then, something moved in the water.

Next to my gondola, floating face up, was Kessian.

He looked asleep. Worse, he looked funerary, with his hands crossed on his chest, clutching his cane, his hair floating in a veil around him.

I seized him by the arms and tried to pull him out. The water burned my hands with cold like needles. The moment I pulled Kessian's face above the surface, he gasped awake, dragging in air as if he'd been suffocating. As if that water was different from the water I was already in.

I helped him up into the gondola. It tipped precariously as I dragged him by his belt over the rest of the way. In the bottom of the little boat, he coughed and caught his breath, staring shakily up at me, then around us.

"Tal? What happened? Where are we?"

"I don't know. It looks like we're still in the strid. Were you—? When you were in the water, were you asleep?"

"I don't think so. I felt—" He shuddered. "Nothing. I felt nothing, remembered nothing, until you woke me. It was like I was dead."

My stomach dropped. When I'd touched the water, it felt cold enough to catch your death, though swirling with magic and life. Pulling Kessian from it felt just like pulling Amelia out of the wraith.

He looked out at the town square sprawling across the riverbank, full of houses, shops, and buildings from Shearwater. "This better not be the afterlife." He turned his gaze on me, miserably apologetic. "I tried to resist the wraith. I really did. It wouldn't even let me speak to warn you off."

"It's not like I'd have listened."

"Still. You're here because of me."

"I could say the same to you. This mess has always been mine to deal with, and for nine years, I didn't. We're here now. I'd rather be here than up there, wondering what happened to you."

"How did the wraith escape?"

My mood darkened. "Somebody must have sabotaged the sigil. I'd guess it was Warwick, though I don't know how he'd have found it."

Kessian shivered, looking around at the strange underwater world. "Well, we're here now. Wherever here is."

"Now we need to find a way out."

The boat rounded a bend in the river, willow leaves trailing like a leafy curtain. Ahead, a pontoon came into view with a ghostly figure stood at the end, facing us.

My heart drummed. The figure glowed blue, semitransparent and vaguely humanoid the way a half-assembled mannequin or a ventriloquist's puppet was. Its face changed like a television flicking through channels. Now a youthful woman with dark, narrow eyes. Now a portly maid with her hair styled in ringlets the way they'd only done six centuries ago. Now an old man with a wrinkled face like tree bark.

On and on it went, cycling through faces, overlapping one another like an overexposed photograph.

Briefly, I thought I saw *Kessian's* face, but then it was gone amongst the sea of others.

Kessian said, "What is that?"

I didn't know, but our boat was headed straight for the pontoon. We could either let it dock or jump into the river. Given the half-death it had put Kessian under, the latter wasn't an option.

Our boat glided smoothly into the pontoon, bumping against the rubber tires on its flank. We shied away, crowding ourselves into the back of the boat. The spectral figure stepped aboard at the bow. It moved smoothly and silently. The boat didn't rock an inch before peeling back from the pontoon and continuing its journey, the prow carving a path through the winding river.

The figure stared at us from its flickering, ever-changing face. We stared back, quietly terrified and wary.

Kessian said, "Hello?"

"Greetings to the Keeper and his companion," answered the figure in a hundred voices all speaking at once.

"Creepy," Kessian whispered.

"It addressed you as the Keeper, though. Maybe you should ask it about this place?"

Kessian cleared his throat. "Do you know where we are?"

"You sail the waters of Shearwater's Bloodstream," it answered. "These rivers are its veins, the water its blood. They chart a course through time."

The Bloodstream. It had only been an ominous word found in the trace spell Emery placed on our dreams. He'd said that we needed to come here if we wanted to fix the poisoned strid.

Kessian said, "O . . . kay, but how did we get here? The wraith dragged us into the strid, and now we're here."

"You have slipped into the gap between life and death. If you do not find your way back to the former, then you will fall to the latter."

Those words had the same effect as plunging into the icy waters. "How do we find our way back?"

"That is why I am here. To show you."

"And who are you?"

"The Keepers."

Kessian said, "The Keepers? Plural? So . . . all of them?"

"Yes. The Keepers." It dragged in a long breath, rasping in its chorus of many voices. "We stood vigil over the wild magic of old, a vanguard against the destruction wrought by people with no love in their hearts for nature. Or no love in their hearts at all."

"Not done a stellar job," I muttered. "If you've been watching over it, why not drown someone like Warwick instead of my dad and Laurelie?"

"That is why you are here. To discover the source of the poison and the antidote."

"Why us?" Kessian said.

"All the answers you'll find here."

"But you won't tell us?"

"We do not know. We are memories from Keepers past, present, and future, but our memories are fallible, like dreams, and the future is not fixed. We will only know the whole truth behind Shearwater's malady when you do."

I searched the banks of the river, remembering the flicker of shadow I'd seen. "Can the wraith find us here?"

"Yes."

"How do we stop it? What does it want?"

"To go home."

"Isn't the strid its home?"

The Keepers paused, as if having to think hard on an answer. In the end, they answered with a question. "What is a home?"

It only took a moment to see the difficulty in answering, because a home was less one singular thing than it was a collection of nouns. Home could be the house you lived in, but not all houses were homes. It could mean people—your family, a lover—but these, too, could change or leave or cast you aside. Home could be the city you lived in, or the country, but on such a grand scale, how could we narrow it down to find the wraith's true home?

From his expression, Kessian had drawn the same frustrating conclusion. He said, "How are we supposed to help the wraith go back home if we don't even know who or what it is?"

"That, too, is what you must discover."

As the Keeper spoke, our boat rounded another bend in the river. An all-too-familiar house loomed out of the willows.

37 Culpepper Avenue had always felt like a house with history. It had once been a place fragrant with the smells of Sunday roasts and itching with the ticking of clocks. Over the years the place had sagged under the weight of Grandad's obsession.

In the ethereal reflections of the timestream, the house had taken on all its different aspects. Like the Keepers, its face seemed both welcoming and forbidding.

Our boat sidled up to the bank, bending reeds until we'd nearly run aground in the shallow muck. The Keepers waved their hand, and a gangway composed of the same blueish spectral material as the Keepers themselves appeared.

I crossed it, turning to help Kessian out. "How's your leg?"

"I sort of hoped, since our bodies are floating off in the strid somewhere, that I'd be free of the aches and pains, but no." He took my hand and stepped out with me. "At least the . . . Bloodstream had the decency to magic my cane here along with me."

The Keepers said, "From here, you will find many paths to different times, different trials. You must pass them all if you are to find your own way home."

AN ELIXIR FOR WANDERLUST

The Keepers placed a pocket watch in Kessian's hands. It was identical to the one Amelia had found for us in Grandad's study, except that its image flickered between polished silver and tarnished rust. Kessian flicked it open to reveal the time set to midnight, the second hand ticking forward and back without making any progress.

The Keepers said, "This is a place fit only for spirits and dreamers. While your bodies soak in the strid's blood, your spirits sail this stream, where time flows both ways. You must complete your task before the hour hand reaches midnight, or time will flow against you, and both your bodies will perish in the deep. Just as those who've come before you."

We both looked at the pocket watch, the second hand frozen, tapping the twelve over and over. My heart kept time with it.

The Keepers disembarked on their boat and said, "Farewell, and good luck."

The second hand ticked forward. One, two, three.

We had twelve hours.

CHAPTER 31

The door to 37 Culpepper Avenue squealed inward as we stepped inside.

I didn't know what to expect—the horrific variation where wraiths crawled out of grandfather clocks or the warm memories of times long past.

It was neither. The clocks populating the living room and hall were not so numerous as they'd been in the present day, nor was anything quite so dusty, but it looked . . . normal. I had to remind myself we were still in the strid.

"It would have been nice if the Keepers had given us detailed instructions," Kessian whispered.

I didn't think the Keepers had much more information than we did.

Muffled, agitated voices drifted to us through the ceiling. Exchanging a glance, we both made for the stairs. On the landing, the door to Grandad's study was ajar. Grandad himself sat behind a cluttered desk heaped with notes and books, observed by countless clocks on the wall. Including the three on a shelf Amelia had told us about, labeled with mine, Dad's, and Laurelie's names. In front of the desk, Mum chewed her nails while Marlowe paced.

"I only need to borrow five thousand this time."

Grandad had his head bowed in his hands, elbows propped on his desk. "I told you, I don't have it."

"You've always got a little something squirrelled away, and I can pay it back in a few months. After the growing season, I'll make it back from the cider farm."

"Come on, Dad," Mum said. "It'll be his in less than a year if you don't slow down, anyway. You're killing yourself."

"I'm sorry, but I can't bail you out this time," Edwin said. "I don't have the money."

"But the summer brought in more tourists this year than we've seen in a decade. Surely you haven't spent it all on these damned antique clocks," said Mum.

"They're not valuable. And . . . we won't be able to depend on the spa's income anymore."

"Why not?" asked Marlowe.

"Because I sold it."

A stunned silence filled the room.

Marlowe said, "You're joking."

"I'm not."

"Why?"

"Because it was losing money, and I had more important things to worry about."

"Like what?" Mum said.

I tensed. Eavesdropping on my grandad as if he were still alive set me ill at ease, but so did the direction of the conversation. *He sacrificed all that trying to find a way I could come back.*

"I don't want to burden you with an old man's worries," Edwin said.

"No, fuck that, Dad!" Mum said. "Keeping secrets in the name of some noble martyrdom isn't helping any of us, so what's really going on here? From where I'm standing, you sold off the one asset that could pick us up by our bootstraps. Who did you sell it to, anyway?"

Edwin winced and avoided their eyes.

Marlowe's exasperation turned to true anger. "Not Warwick."

"It was worthless at the time. Losing us money."

"So Warwick buys it up for a few copper coins under the guise of doing you a favor, it miraculously regains its magic, tourists flood back in, and none of that strikes you as suspicious?"

I'd never heard Marlowe raise his voice, but we could have heard him downstairs.

"Of course it does," Edwin hissed. "But what's done is done. Hindsight being what it is, and foresight being outside my control, this is where we've landed. And I hate to disappoint you, I really do, but I honestly did what I thought was best at the time." He gestured around him to the state of his study, a horologist's hoard, gray with dust. "Bail yourself out. You can't expect a clap on the back for failure. I've done the same thing my whole life, and it failed. You tried something different with the cider farm, and it still failed. Unfortunately, the world didn't guarantee our success."

Marlowe's mouth worked around a retort, but voiced none. Hurt stained his features. It didn't matter how old you got, your parents' words still cut deepest, and Marlowe didn't take well to his father calling him a failure, even if he'd included himself in the statement.

He looked like he wanted to make some grand declaration, lips moving, but in the end he turned on his heel to go. Mum marched out with him, but paused to deliver one last rebuke. "Sometimes feels like you care more about the people we lost than the ones still here."

"Have you got any right to say so after sending your surviving son away?"

"We'd all be reunited at the bottom of the strid if I hadn't."

She and Marlowe stormed out. Kessian and I hurried to clear enough room for them, but the landing was small, and I experienced the uncanny sensation of my mum and uncle passing straight through my shoulder.

But not Kessian's.

As Grandad said, "Don't let the door hit you on the way out," Marlowe's shoulder clipped Kessian's. He reeled back, glaring at Grandad with true contempt. "Very mature, Dad."

He'd thought Grandad had cast some spell to literally hit him with the door on his way out. Kessian rubbed his shoulder, mouthing an apology, but how was he to know that would happen? We seemed like ghosts in this memory, unseen and unheard, but not un-felt.

Confusion pinched Grandad's eyebrows together as he watched his son and daughter leave. He rose from his chair, went to the doorway, and searched the landing. For a moment, it felt as though he stared straight at me.

"Hello?" he called.

Kessian whispered, "Can he hear me?"

Grandad didn't react.

"He cannot," said another voice.

The Keepers appeared between us in a curl of blue flame. "Edwin Ashborne never tapped the true potential of his abilities as Keeper. Unlike you, he never swam the strid."

That struck a chord with me. "So you're saying, in order to fully use these abilities to help, he would have had to risk his life by diving into the strid like we've just done?"

"Correct. Dreams bring you closer to the Bloodstream's truths, but in these dreams you are a spectator. In order to become their architect, you must let the blood of the strid flow through you."

"That seems an unfair risk to take," Kessian muttered. "Why did it choose me?"

"Because you chose to make Shearwater your home. Edwin Ashborne's family were no longer fit for the task, fractured and sending their own away as they have. The people of Shearwater benefit from the spring's magic, the Ashbornes most of all, yet a balance between give and take was not struck. They exploited it."

"So it took our lives instead?" I asked.

"No. Those are the actions of the poisoner. Lives are a poor substitute for what the strid truly wants."

"Which is?"

"I've told you. To go home. So poisoned, it cannot. You must heal it."

"How?"

The Keepers gestured into the study, where Grandad had turned back to his wall of clocks. "Some things are easier when demonstrated. Watch, and we will guide you."

They vanished once more, and we turned our attention to the study. Edwin stared at the shelf of clocks. He pinched his mouth between his fingers while he thought. After a moment's hesitation, he spun the hands of the clock labelled with my name.

As he did, the world washed out as if it were a rained-on watercolor. The noise of the strid's current roared in my ears. Briefly, I couldn't breathe, lungs straining.

Then the river released me, and I washed up in the warm, welcoming place I used to call home.

It was my childhood bedroom. I looked around at the posters ordered neatly on the wall, the shelf of my earliest ceramics, wobbly and charming in only the way a child's work could be. My teenage self slept with one leg stuck out from the duvet to keep cool on a summer's night.

Seeing myself in a memory might have been strange, but not as much as seeing the calico cat curled up on my pillow next to me. If Lunaris hadn't transformed yet, that might mean—

My side of the room had mathematical order to it while the opposite overflowed with clothes, books, crafts, a plastic bug tank with something crawling inside. And in the bed was a face I hadn't seen in nine years.

Laurelie was curled up tight, cuddling a crochet egg with a duckling hatching out of it.

"Is that Lunaris?" Kessian whispered.

"Yeah. Always slept by my head so my feet wouldn't get too hot."

"So that's . . . ?"

"My sister."

We looked alike. There'd been other fraternal twins at my high school who looked nothing alike, but Laurelie and I had looked more or less identical until puberty hit.

I missed her so powerfully, the nine years seemed to shrink, leaving me freshly stung by the grief of her passing. She slept right in front of me, but I couldn't escape the knowledge this was just a memory.

A noise pierced the quiet night. Something eerie and unnatural that silenced the song of summer insects, replacing it with a different sort of music. I shuddered at its familiarity.

A few hollow notes whispered through the window, cracked open to let in the night air and dispel the heat, and in response, my younger self blinked awake. He sat up wearily, rubbing the sleep from his eyes, and stood. A frisson of fear made him scrabble a hand over the bedside cabinet for something to hold on to. It clenched around the silver pocket watch, the gift Grandad had given me. Whatever directed him pulled too powerfully. His eyes glazed. The floorboards creaked quietly underfoot as he rose and walked past us into the hallway. Laurelie shifted in her sleep but did not wake to stop him.

Kessian and I followed.

On the landing, another figure from photographs and memories appeared. My father wore only his sleep shorts and walked barefoot down the stairs. The sight of him added to the weight of grief burgeoning within me, as he opened the front door, then waited for his son to sleepwalk over and take his hand.

They walked out into the night, leaving the door ajar.

CHAPTER 32

Kessian and I fell into step behind them, and he let his fingers brush mine in case I wanted comfort. I knew if I accepted it the grief would pour out of me, so I didn't.

"Were you awake for this?" he asked.

"Yes."

"You must have been terrified."

"I had cuts on my feet from the pine needles. The forest was so cold, but Dad's hand was hot and clammy. It all seemed . . . far away. Like it was happening to someone else. And after, it was all hard to remember, but now . . ." I clenched my hand, wishing I'd taken Kessian's comfort after all. "I don't know if I can watch this."

"Maybe we can stop it?"

I blanched. "What?"

"I've been thinking what the Keepers said to us. They said in dreams, we could only be spectators to the past and future, but here we could be their architect."

Remembering what Emery had told us, I said, "Like time travel?"

"Marlowe bumped into me. I can affect the world. Maybe I can stop all this from ever happening. Stop the strid from being poisoned in the first place."

I didn't want to succumb to the hope that he was right. It raised so many questions, like what would become of us after, when history had been rewritten?

As we delved deeper into the forest, the shadows thickened, then seemed to move. They *did* move. Out of the dark, more people appeared. An elderly woman in a nightgown, a man in a security guard uniform come straight from the night shift, a teen girl with her hair wrapped in silk curlers.

The strid hadn't discriminated. Old, young, men, women. It took them all.

All the while, the song grew stronger, louder, and something else occurred to me.

"What if we aren't meant to stop this happening? What if we're supposed to find the identity of the flute player instead?"

Kessian looked contemplative. "Could be . . . but he was on the other side of the river. If we want to stop your dad from drowning, we won't have time to get to the flutist before he flees."

As the crowd around us thickened, the trees grew more sparse. We didn't have long to deliberate. Crossing the river alone was a danger.

We reached the bank of the strid. My heart kicked wildly as the reality set in. I was about to watch my dad and I walk into the river and get swept away. Knowing I survived did nothing to calm me. The urge to grab them by the arms and drag them to safety was overwhelming, but I could not affect this world. Only Kessian could.

We drew closer. Ahead, someone I didn't know reached the edge. They kept walking as if there was no drop, as if they meant to walk across the surface to the other side. Instead, they vanished, sucked under the moment their foot submerged, as if the strid had grasping hands poised to yank the unsuspecting down, down, down.

The flutist's music shrilled in celebration of the first death.

"I don't know if I can watch this, either," Kessian murmured. "Not without trying to stop it."

I said, "I don't think it will help. The Keepers told us history is already written."

But as a second person plunged in, and a third, terror seized me. What if it did go wrong? What if I died this time, and our entire world rewrote itself so I'd never lived past sixteen?

I couldn't control that, but catching a glimpse of the flutist, *that* I could do.

We were ten steps from the shore. Nine. Eight.

Kessian said, "I have to try."

I'd come to the opposite conclusion. I didn't want to relive my worst moments, but finding the one responsible? "I'm going to try and jump the gap. You try and save me and my Dad."

Kessian looked alarmed as I broke away, running for the river's narrowest point.

My young self and my dad were three steps from the edge. Two.

The darkness, the cold. Perhaps the memory made me more aware of the real world, where time suspended Kessian and me in icy repose. Drowning, but slowly. Maybe it was the weight of grief. Or maybe it was just that the rocks were slippery.

I leapt but only got minimal traction. It felt as though the strid had its own gravity, sucking me down. My foot slipped on the rock of the opposite side. Kessian screamed as I slammed down on my chest, pain punching all the air from my lungs. Gasping, I grasped for a handhold to pull myself up.

Memories came back to me. Walking inexorably toward the edge. The damp cold of the roaring strid, the sound of a splash—though no one had been ahead of me to make it—and a warm hand on my wrist pulling me to safety before going suddenly slack. Then Dad had pulled me forward, heavier than me and the invisible force trying to draw us back from the banks.

It had all been a panicked blur. How could I have known the ghostly touch had been real?

All those years ago, Kessian had tried, but the shock of seeing me fail to make this jump had loosened his grip. The three of them—my younger self, my father, and Kessian—all went sprawling into the river right as I pulled myself out.

I screamed. The speed at which the strid swallowed them all made the ache in my ribs sharpen to a knife's point. I scrambled up onto the bank and nearly dove in after them, but a stab of clarity stopped me.

Kessian had tried to change the events of history. Instead they'd played out exactly as they had in reality.

I'd always wondered how I'd survived . . .

In that split second, I made a decision and begged the Keepers, fate, the strid, whatever governed the world as I knew it, for it to be the right one.

Rather than dive into the strid after them, I sprinted into the woods. If I was quick, there could still be time to catch sight of the flute player. In my dream, he'd been within sight of the tree line.

I crashed through in that direction, forgetting I was a ghost, invisible and voiceless, unable to connect with people. I couldn't grab the flutist and make him pay, but if I knew who it was, perhaps I could fix all this.

The music abruptly stopped. Ahead, a figure in the trees whipped around.

The darkness was complete. I could not make him out until he cast a spell, and the bright glow of a portal illuminated his face.

It was Marlowe.

I stopped dead, breathing hard.

Not Warwick. Marlowe. My uncle Marlowe.

In the light, his face was waxy with fear, eyes wide, searching the forest for the source of the sound and, seeing nothing, fleeing through the portal. It vanished behind him.

My pulse hammered. Marlowe had given me the talisman to protect me from the wraith. Marlowe had helped us trap it. His own daughter had been taken by it. How could he have been the one to play that song, lure all those people? Why? And how had he come by this flute, which Warwick had on display in Foxbury Manor?

I had to bury the feelings festering within me. There was no use contemplating them here on my own.

I started running again, back the way I'd come, toward the spa and the spring where I'd washed up nine years ago, the mysterious sole survivor. If my theories were right, it wouldn't be a mystery anymore.

As the night air chilled my burning lungs and the forest floor drummed underfoot, a needle of doubt punctured my certainty. Memories from that night flooded back. My father, struggling to surface. Those struggles ceasing abruptly when a rip current drove his head into the rocks, a ribbon of scarlet streaming into the water like a loose scarf. The scream I'd let out, and all that precious air with it. The current had played with my father's limp body like a cat with a toy before it sucked him out of sight, into one of the tunnels pocking the stone walls of the strid's banks.

I didn't know if we could die in these memories, but if that was what became of Kessian, I'd never forgive myself.

I burst out of the woods, Shearwater Spa across the green, lights on as people searched for the two family members missing from their beds. The spring's waters trickled placidly with the bright coin of the full moon reflected on its surface. I pulled up at the shore, watching and waiting.

People had asked how I'd fallen in the strid and washed up in the spring. I had never known, and my memories around that were foggy. There'd been magic like a song sung in a million different voices. A hive of music that, at its crescendo, cracked apart and let me pass through something like a portal. But mostly I remembered being cradled. In my dazed state, I thought it had been Dad, but he was dead already.

In that moment when I'd chased the flutist rather than dive in after Kessian, it had been because I was sure whose arms had held me. Not what, but *who* had saved my life all those years ago.

The longer the spring remained a smooth mirror of the sky, undisturbed, the more I doubted it.

He can't be dead. Please don't be dead. I couldn't bear it. Not you. Not after tonight.

A soft glow appeared in the water. It turned bright blue, swirling out from the center in ripples. A figure broke the surface, hair painted over their face in inky stripes, mouth open to suck in greedy lungfuls of air, dragging something—someone—up with him.

Relief couldn't break through the adrenaline. I surged forward, wading up to my waist to help them to shore. The figure flipped their soaking hair out of their face. I nearly collapsed seeing Kessian, scratched but otherwise unharmed.

The body in his arms was mine, nine years younger. I helped drag him out and lay him on his back. Kessian performed compressions on his chest. Plugged his nose and breathed into his mouth. Compressions again. He—I—looked so painfully frail. Limp, rocking with the motion of each compression, lips blue and hanging open.

Despair might have choked me if not for my certainty that this worked. In a sense, it already had.

On the fourth set of compressions, water spouted like a geyser from his open mouth. He rolled, vomiting up the strid's briny water. It tasted like salt and iron and blood, I remembered.

Kessian sat back on his heels, letting out a sob of relief.

"It was you," I said. "I felt like we'd met before, and we had. You saved my life."

He smiled weakly. "I guess I did."

"How did you survive the strid?"

"I could navigate it, somehow. The Keeper's magic, it was like a purer version of the song sung by the flute. I . . . can't really explain it, but I followed it here."

Footsteps resounded in the night. A light bobbed through the darkness, and as it got closer, I recognized my mother's face in the glow of her lantern. She wore a puffy jacket over her pajamas, eyes red with tears. She must have run here after finding her husband gone and her son's bed empty.

She ran to me—her young son—and threw her arms around him. It only took him a few shaky moments to do the same, sobbing uncontrollably. I'd backed away several paces into the tree line, but I still heard my cracking, teenaged voice say, "Dad's gone. Dad's dead."

My strength to hold the grief at bay failed me. I remembered that hug, the power of my mum's arms to make me feel safe again. I remembered how this was the last time she ever hugged me like that, because soon Laurelie would be taken, too, and I would be blamed.

Kessian said, "Are you . . . ?"

My breath snagged in my throat, the world gone blurry. And like my mum had done years ago, Kessian wound both arms around my ribs so tight they creaked when I breathed.

I didn't reject the comfort this time. I gathered him close and wept into his shoulder, grieving the death of my dad, Laurelie, the love of my mother, the home I'd had to leave behind, and—

Kessian drew back and wiped my tears with his sleeve. "I'm sorry, but I have to ask. Did you find the flute player?"

"Yes," I said. "It was Marlowe."

CHAPTER 33

Kessian's mouth fell open, face wan with shock. "Marlowe! You're sure?"

I wished I wasn't. "I saw his face right before he went through the portal. It was him."

"Oh, Tal . . ." Kessian's thumb brushed at the dampness on my cheek. "Why would he do that?"

I could only guess based on the argument we witnessed in Grandad's study. "An old grudge? I don't know." The pocket watch ticked once, so loud I heard it from within Kessian's pocket. He retrieved it and flicked it open to check how much time we had left. His face went paler than it already had been.

"Three hours have passed? Surely not, that felt like an hour at most."

I checked the watch myself, but Kessian was right. The hour hand pointed to three o'clock.

Kessian swore. "What do we do now?"

Before I could answer, the world washed out, the colors dripping. With the rush of water in my ears, I felt myself swept away, the tide pulling me elsewhere and dumping me outside 37 Culpepper Avenue again.

Landing on my arse, I dusted myself off as I helped Kessian to his feet. He winced, the transition less gentle on his hip.

Beside us, the Keepers reappeared, inclining their head. "You have returned successfully from the first of many trials."

"We found out who the poisoner is," I said, pushing aside my feelings on the subject. "Now if you let us out of here—"

"You have found the poisoner, but not the nature of the poison or its antidote."

I sagged. I'd hoped telling the authorities and bringing him to justice might be enough to soothe the strid, but of course it couldn't be that simple. A bone-deep exhaustion plagued me after the last memory, too fraught with feeling to fully process while still trapped in this alternate reality. The thought of venturing into another didn't thrill me.

"I have a question," Kessian said. "What we're doing, it can't . . . rewrite history, can it?"

"In theory, but in practice this has never come to pass. History is written, and you will be its architects."

"So you're saying we don't have a choice? Whatever happens is destined," I said.

"Whatever *happened*. Not what happens now or later. Some choices you will make because you have already made them, because you are who you are and act in accordance with your nature. But the future is still flexible, not yet written. You have likely seen glimpses in dreams. Things which were so likely to happen that they might as well have been set in stone. But they are *not*. Those stones can still be moved. Or shattered."

So the past was like a pot that had already seen the kiln, but the future? That was still a lump of clay waiting for the wheel.

"Where do we go next?" Kessian asked. "Or *when* should we go?"

An idea had already begun to form in my head as Kessian turned the watch over and over in his hand. An amalgamation of the one from our reality, and it brought up a question.

"Can we take things with us from these memories? As Keeper, Kessian can affect the environment, but can he steal pieces of it?"

The Keepers only inclined their head and gestured to Edwin Ashborne's house, the door of which swung ajar, as if to say, "Why don't you try?"

"What do you want to steal?" Kessian asked.

"Proof of what happened nine years ago. I think I know where we can find it. Or where we already have."

Kessian followed me into the house, up the stairs to grandfather's study. "Where?"

"Foxbury Manor."

Kessian's eyes lit up. "The stolen contract. You think that was us from the future?"

"What else explains its disappearance? Besides, if Warwick owns the flute, he could still have been involved. Marlowe might not have been working alone."

It was also a memory I didn't dread revisiting. I got the sense I would have to relive the worst horrors of my life to better understand this poison the Keepers spoke of, but I didn't relish the thought.

Particularly not Laurelie's death.

"All right. How do we get there?"

"These clocks of Grandad's, particularly the labeled ones, have to have some significance, don't they? Maybe we can use them to control the who and when of which memories we visit."

Mine kept ticking. The other two didn't, their hands frozen in time, perhaps a reflection of their time of death. If we wound the clock back twenty-four hours, would we see the events of their last day alive? It seemed an inefficient method. How many times would we have to wind the clock to show my memories from nine years ago?

"How did Edwin know how to use them if he never entered the Bloodstream before?" Kessian asked while rifling through papers on his desk.

"I think he used them to visit memories in his dreams. Like the ones we shared, though they were random. Controlled by the whims of the strid or your wild magic maybe?"

"Hm. Here." Kessian held out a beaten-up notebook with a broken spine that fell open to a particular page. "Could this be the formula?" He read aloud. "*Spin the hour hand to each number for the year, pausing for three seconds between each. Then turn the hour hand to the number corresponding with the month, minute hand to the day, second hand for the hour, which you tap twice for p.m.*"

I followed his instructions, counting back to the day we'd visited Foxbury Manor. When I got to the hour—two in the afternoon—the by-now-familiar sensation of the world diluting around us washed out the study and replaced it with a conservatory.

Sitting on the settee before us, Warwick was serving me tea. As I reached for the sugar, he said, "That's the salt. I prefer salty tea. Strange, I know," and pushed across the second cup, removing the lid.

He'd put truth serum in it, I remembered.

What I hadn't recalled was Kessian striding forward and slapping the sugar off the table. It shattered on the floor, the lid rolling off behind a plant pot, and my memory sharpened around the moment.

"He spiked it," Kessian said. "Rotten bastard . . ."

I restrained him from knocking anything else over. "He'll just have Lionel replace it anyway."

"This is the one time I can punch him without any consequences."

I looped both arms around his waist and started pulling him from the conservatory. "The consequences would be failing to find that contract because we got sucked into a timeline paradox. Nobody got punched in that room. If the contract proves his involvement, he'll get a steeper punishment than a punch to the face."

He stopped resisting me, grumbling, "It would feel very good to punch him in the face, though."

"You really hate him, don't you?"

Kessian grimaced. "He's been raising my rent without giving me a pay raise at the spa for the past six years, and then he evicted me. He's the most poisonous person in Shearwater. If the wraith had drowned him it would have fixed half the town's problems."

I paused in the foyer. We had to wait until my past self snuck upstairs to unlock the door. "Why do you say that?"

"Hm?"

"That's just a very specific choice in words, 'poisonous person.' Did you mean it like that? That getting rid of him somehow could be the real antidote to this problem?"

"Yes . . . and no." He frowned, walking past me to the display case with the wraith statue inside. Now I'd made the connection, the antlers looked less like antlers than a musical instrument. A strange one, yes, with so many tines, but where they all connected was clearly a mouthpiece, and the holes in each hollow tine would control the note. To have it flagrantly on display . . .

He wasn't the one who'd used it, though. My uncle's saliva could still be on the mouthpiece, his fingerprints on the tines.

"I keep coming back to this idea of home," Kessian said. "When Shearwater chose me, it asked me what I wanted, and I told it I wanted a home. Now all Shearwater wants is to go home, too."

"That still makes no sense to me. How can it? It's a place."

"Wild magic doesn't come from the usual tithes witches use. It comes from less tangible things. Things big as love and small as the feeling of putting your feet up after a hard day's work. I think some wild magic comes from feelings we don't have names for anymore. And I think Shearwater's is like that. It . . . it needs to be a home, and have a home, to make its magic."

I didn't like how it made abstract sense. Abstract problems required subjective solutions. This wasn't math, I couldn't solve for "z" and come up with the same answer as the next person. "Well, that complicates things. Couldn't have just been bitten by a snake and given an antivenom."

Kessian's lip quirked. He held up the watch, which had lost another hour.

On schedule, my past self speed-walked down the hall, turning sharply to go up the stairs. We followed close behind, watching him rendezvous with past Kessian and charm the lock open.

Courtesy of the sheer size of Foxbury Manor, it wasn't difficult to follow them inside without bumping into anything. While they were busy unlocking and rifling through the filing cabinets, we focused on the safe.

"Do you remember the combination?" I asked.

"I thought you did."

"You're the one whose hand was guided through it."

"Yes, I was quite distracted by the ghostly touch of my future self and neglected to write it down."

"Well, we have to know what it is, or this wouldn't have worked in the past."

"Do you know Warwick's birthday?"

I groaned. Our past selves were making their way around the room, getting closer to the side of the desk where the safe was visible.

Kessian tapped his finger against the pocket watch as he tried to recall. I sifted through the memories of the past few days, wondering if we'd ever come across a number combination. The trip to Coill Darragh, speaking to my grandfather's ghost, the autopsy—the past week was a blur.

Our past selves noticed the safe and moved in.

Kessian backed up to give them space, tapping more rapidly. "Shit. It's like they're on the tip of my tongue."

Or at the tip of his fingers. "Kessian. The watch. They were in the watch."

He flicked it open, and there they were on the lid.

34-96-13

He smacked a kiss to my cheek. "You're so smart and beautiful."

Without preamble, he leaned awkwardly over his past self, guiding him by the hand to input the numbers, leaving me in the pleasant daze of being kissed and complimented so casually. We hadn't had the time to talk about the kiss at Fae's wedding, or what should have come after. With our lives on the line, our relationship wasn't a priority, but the graze of Kessian's lips reassured me that what he'd said hadn't been a dream.

"You're a story I'd want to see through to the end, even if I knew the ending was tragic."

I fervently hoped it wouldn't be.

The safe clicked open, the door swinging to reveal the sheafs of papers, including a contract conspicuously covered in runes and sigils.

The sound of Warwick's encroaching familiar distracted our past selves, allowing us the opportunity to take the contract. If they'd been watching would they have seen it vanish into the ether? Or would their minds play a trick and insist it was never there to begin with?

Retreating with our prize, we huddled to read it, but the strid, sensing we'd got what we came for, began to pull us away from the memory. The pocket watch emitted an ominous *TICK TOCK*, the study blurred, and we tumbled out of the study, back into the Bloodstream.

Kessian rubbed his sore hip and glared up at the sky. "I miss beds and soft furnishings and blankets and hot water bottles and baths." He appraised the time on the pocket watch and winced. "Another two hours gone. How is each memory stealing so much time?"

I didn't know, but we didn't have much to spare for sitting and poring over the contract. Kessian gave me half the stack of papers, mostly the ones covered in symbols he couldn't read as a non-witch. It didn't take long to derive a few conclusions.

"It's a magical nondisclosure agreement attached to the temporary loan of the . . . the 'bone flute.' It says here, Marlowe had permission to use it for the specified time frame it was on loan, but under the condition that any adverse effects of its usage would be his sole responsibility."

Kessian snorted. "Adverse effects? It lures people to their deaths. He aided and abetted a murderer."

"Unless Marlowe didn't know what the bone flute did. The contract makes no mention of its effects." It was a paltry hope but felt easier to forgive than malice.

"Maybe." Kessian didn't sound convinced.

"Whatever his reasons, it still brings us no closer to identifying an antidote for the poison. The consequences of this contract hadn't come to pass when it was drafted."

"Keep it safe. We'll need it to prove Marlowe's involvement. For now, where do we go next?"

I dreaded the answer, but there were two mysteries as yet unsolved, and I couldn't conceive of how we'd identify the cure for the poison unless we explored the symptoms.

Unfortunately, the symptoms all seemed to involve the deaths of my family members.

"I think we have to go back to the day my grandad died."

CHAPTER 34

Though Grandad didn't have a clock labeled for himself, it stood to reason his would be the grandfather clock in the front hall, but with the pocket watch cheating us out of an hour here, two hours there, an entirely different problem presented itself.

"I don't know his exact time of death. If we arrive the morning of, but he only died in the evening, we could run out of time before we even see the murder."

Kessian glanced warily at the spiteful pocket watch, ticking away the last hours of our lives. "It seems to skip time faster when we jump between memories. Let's arrive at noon on the day he died. If he's already gone, we skip back twelve hours. If not . . . we wait."

It was as close to an estimated guess as we could get. I nodded in agreement, and we faced down the grandfather clock. The pendulums ticked ominously as we opened the glass face to change the hands.

Kessian said, "Are you ready?"

No. "Let's get it over with."

He input the time and date. *Gong. Gong.* The clock chimed loudly once, twice, thrice . . .

On the twelfth, the hallway metamorphosed. Shelves and new clocks grew from the walls like moss and lichen. The wallpaper yellowed with age. When it had finished, silence fell, except for the incessant ticking and the sound of muttering from the living room.

We entered to find Grandad with a mug of tea in one hand, a newspaper in the other. It was dated nine years ago, the headline covering the shame of Shearwater's high street and its falling fortunes. He had it open to the obituaries.

He was still here like he'd never died.

I jumped as Kessian's fingers threaded through mine. "You all right?"

"Yeah. Yeah, fine. Looks like he's reading up on every death in Shearwater around the time everyone got taken."

"Probably hoping for a clue as to what really happened," Kessian said. "I imagine by now new leads were fairly threadbare."

We observed in silence as he finished the paper, folded it up, then got up with his empty mug to go to the kitchen. We followed, but at once encountered an issue.

It was a small galley kitchen with only enough space for two people to pass each other. The door opened with a view of the refrigerator, but the rest of the space couldn't be seen. If we wanted to keep a close eye on him and how the wraith got to him, we couldn't do so from this vantage.

While I didn't have to fear bumping into anybody, Kessian was another story. A fact made abundantly clear when his hip bumped the kitchen towel hung on a hook off one end of the counter, and it dropped to the floor.

We backed out of the doorway as Grandad turned to appraise it. Anyone else might have assumed they'd brushed it by accident, but he stared out into the hallway with a heavy, scrutinizing eye.

After years of investigating wild magic, wraiths, and a ravenous river, he didn't trust these things were just a trick of the light or a draft.

After a moment of waiting, he seemed satisfied it was nothing to worry over, and returned to his business in the kitchen. He pulled a roasting joint from the fridge, then vanished out of sight.

"We can't see much from here," Kessian said.

"We could hide in the pantry. The doors are slatted enough to see through."

"What if he needs something from in there?"

"He always gathered everything he'd need and laid it out on the countertop before he started cooking. We should be safe."

We stuck our heads through the door. Grandad was collecting all the spices, duck fat, and potatoes he'd need for his roast. Once he'd finished and started greasing the chicken, we snuck by him. While his back was turned, we slipped silently into the pantry.

The inside was cramped and smelled potently of herbs and spices. Kessian leaned his cane against a shelf and, to keep from bumping anything, drew me in close with both arms around my waist.

"Are you sure you're okay?"

Oh. Maybe he wasn't hugging me just to keep us from bumping into things. "Do I seem not okay?"

"You seem like you're only half here. Operating on autopilot."

Our purpose here didn't inspire intimacy, but being read so well made an ember in my chest glow. It reminded me of the moment at the wedding when Mum misread me, and Kessian had played translator, untangling the gnarled knots in nine years of familial tension.

"Grandad used to make us a roast every Sunday. Used to always give me the chicken oysters," I said.

"Must have been hard missing them when you first left."

"Every Sunday, I knew they'd be gathering around his table without me. I wondered who got the oysters instead."

"Are all your memories of him good?"

"Mostly. That first memory, with Mum and Marlowe . . . I've never heard him talk like that."

Kessian leaned his ear against my chest. "Is that what's been bothering you?"

"Part of it." I inhaled the damp smell of Kessian's hair, citrus shampoo mixed with strid water. "I guess I'm trying not to think of what might happen if we fail."

"So let's not fail."

"Trying. We can time travel here, but it still feels like time is working against us."

Kessian warily consulted the pocket watch. He frowned, staring at it. "That can't be right."

My stomach dropped. "How much time have we lost?"

He turned the clock to face me. I struggled to register the total lack of movement. After a long delay, the second hand ticked forward. Once.

I kept watching, and it felt as though minutes passed before the second hand progressed a second further.

"None," Kessian answered. "We've lost almost no time at all. It's like we've entered a pocket dimension where time moves slow rather than fast."

I wondered how that could be, but whatever the reason, relief settled over us both. It was unlikely to be more than a temporary reprieve, but we'd had so little time to breathe. The pantry was a sanctuary by comparison, with the comforting kitchen noises, the smell of spices, and Kessian's hands warming two brands against my ribs. Grandad sipped from a cup of tea he had on the go while chopping vegetables. I could almost forget this was the day he died.

Kessian shifted a little.

"How's your leg?" I asked.

"Sore."

"And . . . how are you otherwise?"

A sad smile played across his lips. "Wishing we'd gone back to Lunaris together."

The wraith might have got us anyway, but . . . "Me too."

We were fortunate the clock had slowed to the extent we didn't have to worry about losing time. Less fortunate that there was no place to sit. I held Kessian to support him, but it wasn't the same as letting him lie down. He didn't complain, but from the way he ground his teeth, he was in pain.

An hour into our wait, when he'd started to look particularly pale, something strange occurred.

The pantry transformed.

Just a shelf. It jutted out farther, the contents shuffling to the side, and a cushion was conjured so Kessian could comfortably sit.

He stared at it for a second. While I passed through most things here like a ghost, he could sit. The cushion held him.

He sighed. "I have never known relief like this."

I stared, intuition prickling.

"Did your grandad have a magic pantry?" he asked.

"No . . . I have a feeling it might be— Never mind. Probably not. Nothing makes sense here."

The sound of glass shattering splintered through the quiet.

Scattered shards of Edwin's teacup lay strewn across the parquet, tea seeping into the cracks. He stood back from the oven, chin quivering.

It was the sort of oven that had an arch of bricks like old cottages often did, with a large range hob and a grated extractor fan in place of the chimney flue. Soot rained down from the flue, disturbed by something rattling inside.

I knew what it would be before it emerged, one smoky limb at a time, crooked like a spider. The wraith melted through the narrow grate, unfolded onto the floor, and rose above my grandfather.

"How did it get here? It follows me. It only followed me, and I was nowhere near Shearwater at the time."

With terrible gravity, Kessian whispered, "But you're here now."

CHAPTER 35

Grandad didn't flee, though he looked frightened enough to. His chin wobbled as he spoke. "I knew this day would come."

The wraith tilted its head, antlers dripping dark ichor, which hissed and evaporated.

"I don't know if you can speak or understand me, but . . . I'm sorry I failed you."

"What's he talking about?" Kessian said.

"I don't know."

The wraith kept tilting its head until it was at the entirely wrong angle.

"Are you too far gone to understand or remember me? I should expect as much. You've been gone so long."

What did that mean? Did he know the wraith— Was it a person?

It's a part of you, Briar had said. *That's how it can get through your wards.*

The wraith took a halting step forward.

Edwin didn't retreat. "I won't fight you. I've been at this long enough to see that some things are a choice, some are preordained, and some seem a peculiar mix of both. But I am old, and I think of my available choices, I've made them all." He huffed dryly. "Some I'm far less proud of than others."

The wraith let out a hungry, screeching noise like a rusted hinge, drifting more boldly toward Grandad. He watched its progress, the tremble of his fingers the only sign he was afraid of his impending death.

"Will you make it quick?" he asked.

Then the wraith did something very, very strange.

It knelt.

Its limbs twitched, and at times it seemed to fight itself, like a barely domesticated beast bending to the yoke of some greater power. It reached out a talon toward Grandad's heart.

He stared at it, his expression turning from confusion to enlightenment. Even something like love.

"I see," he said. "I must pass on the mantle to you, or it will go to him."

"Does he mean Marlowe?" I whispered.

"I'm ready," Grandad said.

The wraith, still jerking like a dog at its leash, bowed its head and gored Grandad through the chest on its antlers. Rather than blood, magic surged from the wound, a great rip current of it. It twined up the wraith's horns, lit its skull from within, made a skeleton glow amongst the smoke. In a brief flash, a scrawny, adolescent figure was silhouetted within.

The magic dissipated as quickly as it came. The wraith stood. Grandad sagged to the floor, gaze unfixed, a distant smile on his face.

He was dead.

I couldn't breathe. Kessian held my hand tightly. The slats of the door painted shadows like the bars of a cage over his face. I must have looked pale or wrecked or something, because he put his arms around me.

"Mum was right," I whispered. "It *was* my fault."

"No, Tal."

"If I hadn't come here—"

"You heard Edwin. He'd been waiting for this day. He probably dreamed it a thousand times."

The wraith still stood over its victim, fingers clenching and unclenching.

Kessian shifted his weight, sore from standing still so long. Something crunched underfoot—a piece of dried pasta, its hard shell cracking apart.

The wraith's head turned sharply toward the pantry.

I froze. Kessian did, too.

The wraith's head tilted with interest, birdlike as it stalked a few steps toward the closed doors. The light through the slats painted Kessian's face in a mask of terror before the wraith's shadow blocked it out.

We had no place to run. We could burst out and try to make a run for it, but the wraith occupied the entire breadth of the kitchen.

It advanced a few more steps. Kessian wound his arms tighter around me. I held him, too, pressing a silent kiss into his hair.

The wraith's shadows flickered, briefly dispersing like a swarm of bees. The flash of a hazel-green eye shone through.

Then the sound came of a key turning in the lock of the front door. It opened, and the sound of voices drifted in. I recognized Lettie's background nattering, Amelia's surly, monosyllabic responses. Then Marlowe's voice saying, "Roast smells lovely."

I nearly burst from the pantry to warn them, but before I could, the wraith's head whipped around as it listened. It lunged for the flue above the oven, clambering into the narrow gaps like a spider.

It hadn't come to kill the entire family. It had only come for Grandad, but why?

Kessian, thinking along the same lines, whispered, "I think . . . I think the wraith took on the mantle of Keeper from him."

"What?"

"The way it lit up. That's what happened when the wraith touched me, in Lunaris when we were fleeing from it for the first time."

I'd never thought the wraith was cognizant enough for that. We'd thought Shearwater had chosen Kessian. If the wraith was an avatar of the strid and those who'd died in it, perhaps we hadn't precisely been wrong. But it made sense now, how Kessian had inherited the mantle when it usually passed through families.

Amelia was saying, "What have you got cooking in here?" Then she entered the kitchen.

Her eyes fell on the body. She fell to her knees, crying, "Grandad?" She touched his neck, searching for a pulse.

Lettie appeared next, shrieked, then Marlowe rushed to see what was the matter.

"He's dead," Amelia sobbed.

As my family broke down, so did I. My ribs seized around my lungs like a vise, making it very hard to breathe. "It wasn't Warwick. It was *me*. It was my fault."

Kessian denied it with a shake of his head and a quiet, "No." His arms squeezed and squeezed, the pressure releasing some of the stress from my body, but my head still hadn't caught up with it all.

I didn't understand what any of this meant. Grandad's ghost told me to find the one who poisoned Shearwater, and the truth behind the wraith. *The true face of the one who killed him.* Those were his words. Marlowe poisoned Shearwater, but if he wasn't the face behind the wraith, who was?

I didn't know, but one last memory, one last death, could hold the answers.

We couldn't leave the confines of the pantry amongst the noises of grief and Lettie announcing they needed to call the rest of the family, the funeral director, and oh, Marlowe, who should be the one to tell Fae, what with the wedding so close?

In all the chaos, I didn't notice the temperature in the pantry dropping until something wet dripped onto my bare arm.

I shuddered, touching it with my fingers. They came back smeared with an inky darkness. The room got quiet, as if the world beyond the little pantry had fallen away. Enough that I heard another drip on the floor.

I didn't want to look up, but I knew what I'd find. I tilted my head back.

The wraith clung to the ceiling, watching.

I let out a yell and grabbed Kessian, intent on fleeing with him, but the wraith descended upon us. Its weight bore us down. I anticipated the hard crack of my body against the parquet, but upon impact, the parquet splashed as though it had been a mirage on the mirror of a lake.

We plunged into deep, dark water.

CHAPTER 36

I still had a hold of Kessian, but the wraith had a hold of us.

In the depths, it was hard to see the creature, but I felt it. The ice of its touch was a needle under the skin, bringing back sharply the first time I'd fallen into the strid's cold waters.

I fought its grip, but it was iron. I tried to kick up for the surface, but the water weighed me down like a lead curtain. I clawed at the wraith, hoping to harm it, hoping to free Kessian.

Instead, my hand grazed the muddy bottom of the spring, or the strid, or wherever we were. Something cold and metal grazed my fingers. Rough, engraved. Thoughtlessly, I grasped onto it. It seemed to be embedded in the ground, and I tried to use it as leverage to pull myself out of the wraith's clutches. Whatever I held, it budged. In the dark, I saw a glimmer of silver and rust, attached to a chain. With another tug, it came free.

It was my pocket watch. It had been here since the day I'd nearly drowned, but the panic of drowning *now* blocked out any speculation as to the grander reason for finding it.

Gripping it in my fist, I lashed out with a punch at the wraith. My arm went through the thick molasses of water and shadow. With a swooping sensation and the rush of water in my ears, I found myself vomited up onto the runner carpet in the hallway of 37 Culpepper Avenue. Kessian tumbled out of the grandfather clock after me, water still spewing from its door. He crawled on his arms, dragging his legs.

I scrambled back, too, whipping my head around in search of the wraith, but it had gone. Kessian sat with his back against the staircase banisters, blinking water from his eyes.

I checked him over for wounds, but apart from red impressions on our arms where the wraith touched us, we were unharmed.

"You're all right?" I said.

"Yeah. Yeah, it didn't hurt me."

I sighed with relief and sat back to appraise the house. "Why did it bring us here? Isn't this where we'd end up if the memory had ended as usual?"

"Maybe not." He pointed through the arch into the living room, which was teeming with clocks. We were further along in time than the Culpepper Avenue of the Bloodstream.

Kessian pulled the spectral pocket watch out and let his head fall back against the banister with a painful knock. "We only have five more hours."

I might have despaired, but something about the entire situation struck me differently from our other encounters with the wraith. I opened my own fist to show him what I'd found at the bottom of the spring.

Kessian's eyes widened. "That's the watch we found in your grandad's study."

"It was at the bottom of the strid. That must have been where the wraith took us. Presumably the watch has been there since the day I nearly drowned." I ran my fingers over the engraved edges, trying to wrap my head around two strange elements to this development.

"I'm going to say something crazy," Kessian said.

"All right . . ."

"Maybe this is the day we're meant to plant the watch, and the wraith brought us to the correct time after ensuring we found the watch in the first place?"

I shuddered. "That makes it sound like the wraith is helping us."

"Maybe it's been trying to? If you think about it, the only way this whole mess gets fixed is if we went into the Bloodstream. It's been trying to lure you in by taking your loved ones."

"Why not just take me?"

"I don't know if it can. It's a part of you. It can get through your wards. Maybe that means it can't enthrall you, either."

It did sound mad, but I'd begun to wonder if the wraith wasn't as malevolent as it seemed. Grandad had spoken to it as if he'd known who the wraith was. He'd transferred the powers of the Keeper to it, and it had given them to Kessian.

Kessian had somehow held on to his cane throughout the whole ordeal. Probably tried to give the wraith a beating with it. He used it now to help himself to his feet and make his way up the stairs.

I followed. Anticipation of what we'd find warred with my desire for a hot fire and dry clothes. In these brief moments of quiet between harrowing memories and near-drownings, I remembered that this had started with a kiss under a tree. The prospect of going home and falling asleep in his arms kept my body moving in spite of a bone-deep need to lie down.

That feeling would be all the more pressing for Kessian, who moved stiffly and slowly up the stairs with an iron grip on the banister and his cane.

No one occupied the study except the dervish of notes and clutter, which had expanded from our last visit. Kessian rooted through a few drawers until he found a letter opener. "Use this to engrave the watch. And maybe try to make it quick. We've lost another hour."

I sat down to carve the combination to Warwick's safe. I'd cursed the ambiguity of this message before, but with time ticking away, I didn't have the hours to spare or the space available in the small watch for anything longer. The fire set in his office would burn away any message I left on paper. The watch would at least survive.

Once finished, I set the rusted pocket watch in the center of Edwin's desk. The moment I did, the world blurred, sucking us back into the Bloodstream once more, back to the version of the house lost in time on the edge of a river. Consulting the watch, its hands seemed to race compared to the sluggish tick of the second hand in the pantry. We had three hours left.

We didn't prevaricate over where to go next. The wraith was at the center of all this, and the first time it had been seen was the night it took Laurelie.

In Edwin's study, we turned the hands of the floral clock to the numbers corresponding with the date of her death. It didn't thrill me to revisit every death in my family like the world's most morbid pilgrimage, but happy memories wouldn't yield answers to our questions.

The office washed away, once again replaced with my teenage bedroom. For a moment, I thought we'd accidentally entered the same memory as the last. I still slept in my bed, one foot kicked out to keep cool, Laurelie curled up around her crocheted egg. Her dark hair puddled around her on the pillow, disconcertingly like blood.

Her eyes opened and stared across at me like she'd never been asleep. Slowly, she rose from her bed and went to the window. Her own familiar, a long-haired tortoiseshell cat named Mari, followed her, its tail like a feather duster held in the air. Laurelie whispered to my sleeping form, "Taliesin?"

I didn't stir. Convinced I was truly asleep, she padded out of the room, turning the door handle so softly it barely creaked.

Unlike my father and I, she moved with determined steps. Her eyes were bright and alert. No music lured her out of her bed. She went willingly.

Kessian and I only lingered long enough to glance out the window to see what had drawn her attention. I let out a soft gasp at the sight.

The spring was alive with dancing lights. Red stars like comets flitted through the mirrored surface, gathering most densely around the shore in a glowing foam. It looked beautiful and deadly, the magic of the strid made bloody by the deaths of all who'd drowned a few days ago.

There was no sign of the wraith.

We descended the stairs after her, following her out into the night. She had slipped on sandals and marched halfway across the lawn already. At the water's edge, she waited.

I wondered if I was meant to do something, like in the other memories. Short of tying her down, I couldn't stop her. I could feel the inflexibility of history. Whatever she was doing, she did it willingly, and if I were to stop her tonight, she would come back to do it the next night, or the next. There was a special type of cruelty in making me watch. The war between doing anything to stop it and the knowledge that I couldn't tore at me.

I was here to cleanse Shearwater of the poison, but I couldn't be cured. The things which had soured me couldn't be undone.

From the pocket of her pajamas, Laurelie retrieved a shining coin, and my whole world twisted. It was old, copper, and bore the face of a centuries-old monarch. The same coin Marlowe had fashioned into a talisman for me.

She clenched it tightly in her fist, held it to her chest, closed her eyes and murmured, "I wish Dad would come back to life."

With determination, she threw the coin into the spring. It broke the mirrored surface with a soft splash, the glowing red light coalescing around the place where it sank like a school of fish to bait.

She waited, and in the silence, it seemed nothing else would happen.

Then the woody song of a flute drifted through the reeds, and Laurelie's hands, clutched to her chest in hope and anticipation, fell languidly to her sides.

Eyes glazed, she sat down in the grass and took off her sandals one by one, placing them neatly aside. Mari yowled fearfully before the music ensnared her, too, and she went placidly quiet.

Laurelie didn't notice. She stood and extended one foot, tapping her toes to the water's surface. The glowing red lights flocked to her, condensing around the place where she took one step, and then another, like a sinister swarm of fireflies.

Both feet planted, she waited, hands hovering like a gymnast on a balance beam. Then she walked forward, each step resulting in an exultation of light from the spring, until she stood in the very center of the pool. Her familiar watched from the shore, tail swishing.

The glowing lights in the pool moved less like fireflies now, more like an angry hive of bees coursing at her feet. The water bubbled. I reflexively grabbed Kessian's sleeve, knowing what happened next.

The spring sucked Laurelie under. Her descent caused barely a ripple, only a singular drop rising into the air after her, scarlet with unnamed magic.

All the lights in the spring went out. Not in flickers or dwindling numbers like matches reaching their ends at different times, but like a flipped switch. It was impossible to see what happened below the black surface.

On the shore, a shadowy magic twisted through Laurelie's familiar, strangling a terrified yowl from her before dragging her into the spring with a splash.

The music stopped. The spring was quiet. Then came the crunch of grass, and Marlowe hesitantly emerged from the trees. In one hand, he held the bone flute, its strange shape and pointed tines making it hard to distinguish as an instrument.

He cast a spell, drawing something from the bottom of the spring. The water rippled and broke as the shiny coin Laurelie had wished upon floated into his hand.

Kessian had a hand over his mouth, watching with horror, but my own feelings had become too big to swallow, the helplessness of watching too much to bear.

I had never been terribly violent in life, though there'd been times when frustration built up so strongly I thought my chest would burst like a rotted pumpkin. It all came out of me, all that pent-up rage, as I stomped across the grass and seized Marlowe by the throat.

Or tried to. I could not. I was no more material here than a mote on the breeze, and my fingers passed through his neck like a specter's.

But he felt something. Goose bumps erupted on his skin, and he shivered violently, stumbling away and rubbing his throat where my hands had passed through. I hadn't withdrawn them, still squeezing like I could tear apart the tragedy of our lives if I tore *him* apart first.

He staggered, and I went with him. Something slithered within me, making me corporeal. Marlowe's eyes bulged. We both felt solid as he clawed at my invisible grip, tried to kick me.

I could hardly hear the water burbling behind me for the blood rushing in my ears, or Kessian's cries to stop, his warnings. No, the thing that stopped me killing my uncle was the darkness crawling up my arms like smoke.

I recoiled, flailing my arms, trying to flick the ichor from them when I saw where it had come from.

In the same spot Laurelie had disappeared, the wraith rose up, wreathed in wet shadows and the aura of death. Tendrils of it curled through the ground and into me like tributaries, like veins. Kessian put an arm around me, trying to lead me away. On the ground, Marlowe choked. He'd dropped the bone flute in the bush during our struggle. It looked like driftwood, a crooked branch.

For just a moment, the shadows condensed transparently around the wraith, and I saw it—her—for who she really was.

Green eyes. A gangly, teenage frame.

Laurelie.

Things that had once been a mystery to me resolved, a picture made clear under the right lens. She could get through my wards because she was my twin. Coill Darragh couldn't keep her out because it had accepted me, and she was family, a part of me.

Lights flickered on in the upper floor of the spa house.

Marlowe whimpered. The wraith uncoiled, straightening its hunched back, its head unfolding from within, sprouting antlers from the fissures in its head, no longer resembling my sister, just the ghostly residue of her rage and mine baptized in the spring's wild magic, where I could only guess at what visions she'd seen.

The rest of this memory I knew. Torches bobbed toward us, and Mum's scream followed. I would throw myself at the wraith, and to both our surprise, it would blanch at the sight of me and retreat, forever embedding the notion that I controlled it, that it followed me, when really it had always been Laurelie, who couldn't kill her twin brother.

CHAPTER 37

The memory spat us out onto the banks of the Bloodstream once more. I stared up at the weblike pattern of watery reflections in place of a sky, trying to summon the strength to move, but the last revelation was one too many.

Where did I go from here? I knew who the wraith was, I knew who the murderer was, and yet I was no closer to cleansing the strid.

"Tal?"

Kessian's face appeared in my vision. This time, he didn't ask if I was okay. His hand hovered like he was searching for which hurts needed soothing most. In the end it laced with mine.

"Tal, we have to go. We don't have much time." He flipped open the watch, wincing. "One hour."

"Where do we go? I don't have any more dead family members to investigate."

"I think we need to try and talk with Laurelie."

"She's not Laurelie anymore. She tried to kill you. She took Amelia."

Kessian rubbed his thumb over my knuckles. "She has a connection to you, though. If she's still in there, you're the only one who can reach her."

"How?"

"Do you still have the talisman Marlowe gave you?"

"No. I left it in Lunaris."

Kessian nodded thoughtfully. "That works."

"It does?"

"If we go back to the day of the wedding, when everyone's busy and the wraith is trapped in the shed, we could go to Lunaris nearby, get the talisman, and see if we can use it to reach Laurelie. It's connected to her death, so it stands to reason it could have the power to bring her back to . . . herself."

To life. That was the hope neither of us dared speak aloud. Amelia had come back, but she'd only been gone a day. Still . . . We returned to the wall of clocks in Grandad's study, to mine, and input the date and time of the wedding. When the world melted away, it dropped us into the pavilion by the spring, where the me of twelve hours ago arranged chairs for the ceremony.

Kessian and I wasted no time in crossing the grass, weaving past the gardens and trees to the place Lunaris was parked. My fingers touched the door handle, and she unlocked for me, as aware of my presence as if I were flesh and blood, not a spirit whisked to her through the stream of time.

Her curtains fluttered in greeting. I wished I could hug her.

"Missed you too."

I went to the bedroom and cast around the bedside cabinet and drawer for the talisman. I'd last used it to banish the wraith when it had snuck up on Kessian in his sleep. It had fallen on the floor, where it had come loose from the earring fastener it had been attached to.

I emerged from the bedroom, holding it up. "I've got it. Let's go."

"One second. Look at this."

I didn't think we had a second, but Kessian showed me the spectral pocket watch. It seemed to have frozen, but after a long moment of watching, the second hand ticked forward once more.

"Remember when the pantry sort of . . . transformed to give me a seat?" Kessian said. "Familiars are creatures of wild magic. Do you think she managed to . . . I don't know, follow us into the time stream to slow things down?"

At the time, I had thought I'd felt her comforting presence, but chalked it up to my emotions and the dream-like atmosphere of the Bloodstream playing tricks on me. But time in the real world did pass more slowly, so if she could have a foot in either one, Kessian's explanation was plausible. I leaned briefly against the wall, gratitude for the both of them briefly overwhelming me. Kessian, who presented me with solutions when I was too exhausted to see another way besides the one that had always worked: running away. Lunaris, who'd remained the most steadfast friend over the course of a long, lonely road. We still had to leave to confront the wraith and speak to Laurelie, but the security of having a contingency offered some relief.

Coin in hand, we went out to the shed with the faint blue glow creeping under its door. We unlocked and opened it, taking a few quick steps back.

The wraith waited within, its hunched form twisted up in the sigil. It registered us, uncoiling but calm. Recalling the ferocity with which it had thrown itself at the prison when we'd shown my family, I wondered if that had been a reaction to Marlowe.

"Laurelie?" I said.

The smoke rippled, a low growl making the timber of the shed shake.

I held up the coin. It felt a bit like waving a red flag in front of a bull. The wraith swayed, watching the coin owlishly, the smoke around it roiling with more fervor.

"Laurelie, if you're in there, please hear me. It's Tal."

The shadows blazed against the sigil, the wraith's figure contorting, and in the flicker of darkness around its face, I thought I saw that hazel eye again. The same color as mine.

A frisson of static and magic issued from Kessian. "Keep talking. I'm going to try something."

He took a step toward it. Fear crept into my voice, but I did as he said and kept talking. I called Laurelie's name, asked if she could hear me, squeezed the coin in my hand.

The shadows boiled like water. Kessian reached into them and tried to part them like a curtain. He'd breached the perimeter of the sigil. I stumbled over my words, torn between demanding to know what the hell he thought he was doing and keeping the wraith's attention on me.

"Try to remember me, Laurelie. I'm your brother."

Kessian's presence seemed to soothe the darkness, not agitate it. The fumes of the wraith's body moved more languidly as Kessian's fingers dragged through the shadows, carving through them, until a face emerged and cried out over the rattling breaths of the wraith.

"Help me!"

A hand burst from the wraith's chest, fingers grasping and webbed in dark ooze. With the coin between our palms, I clasped that hand and pulled.

An elbow jutted out. Then a shoulder. A second hand pried its way out of the wraith's rib cage until finally Laurelie's face emerged, retching up black water.

I braced a foot against the doorframe like I had with Amelia, pulled as hard as I could, but the wraith let out a low wail of warning, and Laurelie was nearly swallowed again. Her throat was a lattice of dark veins.

The wraith wasn't going to let her go. *It's a part of you.*

Between choking gasps, she said, "Lunaris. Lunaris can—"

Shadows throttled her into silence, but I grasped her intent as several things I hadn't understood slotted together like shards of a broken pot.

"Kessian. Get back to Lunaris."

"What?"

"Go to Lunaris, open the door, and get inside. I have an idea."

"Are you sure you want me to leave you with her?"

Reluctantly, I let go of my sister and took two steps back. "Please trust me on this."

Kessian swore as he dropped his hands, releasing the wraith from the magic that bonded Keeper and strid. The shadows grew, brewing like storm clouds, swallowing Laurelie once more.

"Go," I said.

Kessian gave me one worried look, then made his way back to Lunaris as swiftly as his legs and cane could carry him. Lunaris held her door wide for him. He climbed up and turned around, watching me anxiously.

I'd thought whoever had freed the wraith during the wedding had done it to sabotage us, but I'd been wrong.

With the toe of my shoe, I smeared through the lines of the sigil on the floor. The light of the prison died.

I had to turn my back on it to sprint for Lunaris. I could hear the grass and sod tearing up under its feet as the wraith pursued. The music from the wedding played the slow song Kessian and I had danced to while I fled for my life.

Kessian waited in Lunaris's doorway. He held out a hand to pull me through faster. I grasped it, plunging past the threshold and whirling to see if it had worked.

The wraith was right there, reared up in the doorway. It seemed frozen on the other side, but if I watched closely, I could see the very slow, soft ripples of movement in its shadows, the infinitesimal descent of its claws.

Within Lunaris, time moved slowly. If I stepped back out, the wraith could dismember me in a second.

Careful to keep my body within Lunaris's threshold, I reached into the wraith's chest cavity. I still held the coin and felt something stir within. Laurelie's spirit answering the call of a familiar relic.

"Come on, Laurelie," I whispered.

Using my fingers like spades, I dug into the shadows and peeled them back. Where before, they moved and undulated like oil, too slippery to grasp and constantly re-forming, now they felt more like mud and soil. I dragged the shadows clear from one section of Laurelie's face, revealing a cheek smudged with dirt, a closed eye, her mouth. Kessian exerted his own influence, calming the wraith, making it complacent.

I unearthed Laurelie to the shoulders, her arms, her hands—the fingernails black underneath.

Her eyes fluttered open as I pulled her through Lunaris's doorway. "Tal?"

As I clawed away the shadows trapping her elbow, she writhed and managed to pull that hand free. "That's it," she gasped.

With a heave, the rest of her pulled free, and we collapsed backward into the kitchen. The shadows fell away from her.

Most of them.

Everywhere her skin showed, dark veins wormed through her. Her hands and feet looked charred, her hair stained and still dripping. She appeared the same age she'd been on the day she died, still wearing her pajamas, but nine years as the wraith had taken its toll.

"I don't have much time," she said.

CHAPTER 38

The wraith still moved a tiny fraction at a time. Laurelie shut the door on it and turned to face us.

I pulled her farther into the sanctuary Lunaris had made for us, grasping her by the shoulders. It was so strange to see her this way, an aged weariness in her eyes, but she still looked sixteen.

"Are you all right? I mean— Of course you're not. I can't believe I just asked that."

"I'm better than I've been in nine years," she said. "You've given me my mind back, at least temporarily."

"Is there any way to get you away from it permanently?"

"Probably not."

My heart staggered.

"I don't want to give you false hope. I am neither alive nor dead. I am neither myself nor the strid, but something in between." Her voice and the way she spoke changed subtly. Like the Keepers, she spoke with the threads of more than one voice. Her own, and something reedy, watery. "Both of us have changed in this unhappy union."

I felt lost, a mix of disbelief and soul-sucking sadness that she was here, but not herself, and probably not for long.

"I have so many questions."

"Ask and I will answer as much as I know, but be quick."

I scrambled, caught between reuniting with her, hardly recognizing her, and needing answers to cure the strid and escape.

"How did this happen? When you made a wish on this coin, how did you become . . . what you are now?"

"Marlowe gave me the coin. He told me it was a true wishing coin, that the spring's magic had returned, and it might grant my wish if I asked with all my heart." The sweetness of her voice rasped with barely restrained anger. "He lied. The coin had no magic. He'd lured me there so he could use the bone flute. He had not meant to kill the first time. But he did with me."

"Why? What could he possibly gain from killing a teenager?" Kessian asked.

"At the time of my drowning, I did not know, but since merging with the strid, the history of Shearwater is a pool of memories I can drink from. I could tell you how Edwi—Grandad smashed a favorite toy Marlowe played with often because he saw it as a waste of time and a sign his son was too lazy to amount to anything, and perhaps you would sympathize with the boy Marlowe was, but over time he grew spiteful. And greedy. He wanted to be rich. He wanted to be the heir to Shearwater Spa who returned magic to the spring. He wanted to prove his father *wrong*."

"And he was willing to kill his own family for that?" Kessian said, disgusted.

The dark veins spidered up Laurelie's throat, creeping over her jaw. "He was willing to make a bargain with Warwick. The coin he gave me had no more power to grant wishes than a pebble picked off the road, but the bone flute . . . It grants wishes at a terrible cost. Warwick knew what Marlowe wanted, and that he could be used to serve Warwick's interests."

"What did Marlowe wish for?"

"For magic to return to the spring, so he could prove once and for all that he was worthy. And so the wish was granted, but magic was returned by—"

"Tithing the lives of two dozen people," I finished hollowly.

"Once Marlowe realized the bone flute had twisted his wish, he could do nothing about it. The contract he'd signed magically ensured his silence insofar as Warwick's part in the tragedy. He could never speak of the bone flute to anyone. He had gotten his wish but could claim no credit for the magic's return without admitting responsibility for the deaths. Rather than guilt, he felt only bitterness and self-pity.

"So to ensure he would still inherit the spring, he hatched another plan. He would make a second wish, and a third, but these would be straightforward, without room for ambiguity.

"While I wished for my dad back, Marlowe wished for my death by drowning."

Laurelie's voice was barely recognizable. I put a tentative hand on her arm and she blinked, looking down at it as if observing a strange, out-of-body experience. Some of her own voice overpowered the wraith's. "I'm . . . sorry. To speak of it now, I would not think nine years had passed."

In the timestream, past, present, and future overlapped each other. Time healed all wounds, they said, but only if time marched in sequence.

"I don't understand," Kessian said. "You weren't the first in line to inherit. Why kill you?"

"Grandad would never pass the torch to him. He preferred Tal and me, Fae and Amelia. Like so many parents, he did his best to raise his children, love them, but he made mistakes. Played favorites. Lost his patience, lost his temper. His grandchildren were easier to love; he didn't have to fear letting them down because they were not his sole responsibility."

"So Marlowe would have come after the rest of us? Even Amelia?"

Laurelie's mouth twisted. "He might have spared her under the assumption he'd have more control over her, but in that he does not know her well. He would have been the ruin of us all, except the bone flute still twisted his wish, twisted me. I became the wraith to haunt him. I would have dredged him from his bed and drowned him in whatever body of water was deep enough. But he fished that coin out of the spring, hooked it in your ear, and bound me to you instead."

I went cold. "But the coin was meant to banish you. I thought he was protecting me."

"The power you had to banish me was not in any talisman; it was in our bond." Her expression crumpled, some of her leashed fury turned inward. "I never wanted to harm you, but over the years, it became harder and harder to tell where I ended and the strid began, and it was *so angry*. Both of us so angry. It fumed that its magic had been corrupted through those sacrifices, and I—I raged over my stolen life."

I tried to absorb it all, but like an over-sodden sponge, I couldn't hold everything. It leaked out of me. "He murdered you just so he could inherit the spring when it had already been sold to Warwick. He made Warwick richer, and us—"

Poorer wasn't the right word. *Broken*, more like. Words for once failed Kessian, too, who could only squeeze my shoulder.

Laurelie bowed her head. "Now you know the whole story of how he poisoned Shearwater."

I scrubbed the dampness from my eyes, set aside my feelings and all the things I could not change in favor of the one thing I could.

"How is a poison like this cured? What's the antidote?"

Slowly, Laurelie's expression wilted, melancholy dampening her anger. She cast a furtive glance to the door, where the tap of the wraith's claws finally making contact set the hairs on my arms on end.

"Laurelie? What's the antidote?" I said again.

"I poisoned the wild magic with my hatred for my uncle, my desire to go home when I could not, with how much I missed you and Fae and the Shearwater of my childhood. That home, the family I once knew, is gone. Changed. Or perhaps it was always this way, and now I can't unknow the things I was blind to as a child. Either way, I can never go back."

The dark veins crawling up her face spidered into the whites of her eyes as she looked into the ceiling lights. She did not want to answer.

"Unless . . . ?" I prompted.

"Unless you bring my home to me."

"What does that mean?" I said.

"No," Kessian said.

"It does not have to be him," Laurelie said to Kessian. "It could be you."

"What are you talking about?" I looked between them, my intuition quaking at the implication while my mind blocked it out.

The scrape of the wraith's claws, slow and quiet, made Laurelie speak faster.

"Wild magic is a tricky thing, not made from tithes or anything we can touch. Its power depends on the spirit of the feeling or gesture it comes from. For Shearwater, its magic is fueled by . . . by a sense of belonging. When you walk a long road, and your feet are sore, but you come home to a dog wagging its tail and a lover kissing your cheek and saying, "Welcome home," that's where Shearwater gets its magic. To return it to the way it once was, you need to show Shearwater the meaning of home again."

"By dying," Kessian finished. His voice shook. "The strid absorbs one of us, who've finally found our home, and through us the wild magic returns, is that it?"

"No." I shook my head in adamant denial. "No, that can't be how it works. *More* sacrifice?"

"Kessian chose Shearwater to be his home. He has put down roots in the place, loved it so well he hasn't left even when stripped of the four walls that sheltered him," Laurelie said. "You are the Keeper because the strid chose you, too."

"So it should be me," Kessian said.

"No." I'd lost all eloquence and could only repeat it more firmly. "*No!*"

"It need not be Kessian. You've fought this past week too, Tal. Not for Shearwater, but for your family, who was once your home as well. You have tried to repair the fractured relationships inflicted by Marlowe's poisonous influence. And . . ." Laurelie got very quiet. "You are my brother. By joining me, I could go home as well."

"A twisted kind of love if it kills him," Kessian said bitterly.

"I didn't want to trap either of you. Anytime I missed Tal, I'd find myself in the Bloodstream, dipping in and out of memories. Reaching for you, I suppose, in the only way I knew how." Her face fell. "I wish it had not come to this."

"Tell me there's another way," Kessian said. "We can bloody time travel in this place, so we can find a way to leave without one of us dying."

"You are out of time to travel with," Laurelie said.

Kessian consulted the pocket watch. The seconds ticked by slowly thanks to Lunaris, but there were still only fifteen minutes left. Not enough to make another leap through time and do anything of substance. And if we failed, we both drowned.

At least one of us ought to survive.

"I'll do it," I said.

"No you won't," Kessian said.

"This problem followed me around the country for nine years, and because I only now stopped to fix it, you've been dragged in."

"You heard Laurelie. I *chose* this. I've had my time in Shearwater, had my chance to put down roots. You deserve the time, after nine years of isolation."

"Of those nine years, the past week was the best of them."

Color rose to Kessian's cheeks, his steely gaze gone a little too shiny. "There will be more."

"Stop talking about yourself like you're already dead! The Ashbornes created this problem, an Ashborne should be the one to fix it." He started to protest, but I said, "*No.* Not you. Please. My life has been a tragic series of goodbyes, but letting you die is one too many. I can't bear it."

Kessian gazed into my eyes with his shoulders set and his jaw clenched, but as he took in my resolve, he slowly unwound.

Shadow had started to creep beneath the door and into the lock. There came the minuscule click of it turning.

"We do not have much time left to argue," said Laurelie.

"You're sure?" said Kessian.

"I'm sure."

Neither way was fair, but after all, I was very used to saying goodbye, and he was very used to being left behind.

Finally, he relented. "How can I argue? I can't stop you. If I fought you, you'd win."

Relief was not the word for what I felt, but I did feel a little release. I turned back to Laurelie. "What will happen to you?"

"In truth, I do not know. Perhaps I emerge from the spring, as you once did, but I fear I am too changed. I will probably die."

"I don't want to kill you."

"Marlowe killed me. You are setting me free." The shadows under the door reached for her, and her voice shifted once more, dripping with the hollow reediness of the wraith. "Your task is set. In a moment, I will open the door and merge with the wraith again. In the same moment, the Kessian of twelve hours past will be coming here from the wedding. He intends to meet Tal, but will encounter me. I will take him to the strid.

You must go to the spring and swim its waters one last time. I—some version of me—will wait for you there."

I nodded in understanding. "Then I suppose this isn't goodbye."

Laurelie smiled sadly. "Let us say it anyway."

I wrapped her up in a hug. She felt insubstantial, like trying to hold a cloud, cold and watery. We released each other, and she reached for the door.

"Wait," Kessian said.

She turned to him.

"Why did you choose me as Keeper? That was you, wasn't it?"

"It was."

"You didn't know me."

Her expression softened so much she almost looked like the real Laurelie again.

"In the waters of the Bloodstream, you were as known to me as Taliesin. I knew you through him. Your connection shone to both of us—the strid and me—like a North Star. Even while cursed to wander and to be left behind, you found home in each other. Making you Keeper was one thing the strid and I agreed upon. Beyond that, I felt it was right to break the rules of inheritance. Edwin chose to give it to me instead of Marlowe. A great irony, when it was this exact eventuality Marlowe hoped to subvert. It happens often. Someone, in their efforts to avert disaster, instead plays into that design."

Kessian's stony expression hadn't shifted. He nodded, and Laurelie turned back toward the door, where shadows wreathed the cracks.

She opened it and stepped out into the embrace of the wraith, whose smoke slowly engulfed her once more. It was too much like watching her die again, so I closed the door. In a moment, she would take off after the Kessian of twelve hours ago. Once the coast was clear, I would make my way to the spring.

In the warmth of Lunaris's kitchen, things were quiet, a reminder of a once comfortably uncomfortable life. I ran my hand along the counter. She'd always come to my rescue, but it had all caught up to us in the end.

Kessian leaned against the counter. "The two of you have come to my rescue more times than I can count."

"You stood up to my mum, which was far braver," I said. "Consider this returning the favor."

"That's not funny."

"Sorry."

"Don't be sorry either. If this is how things have to be, I have one request."

"What's that?"

He leaned his cane against the counter and stepped into my space. His fingers knotted in the collar of my sodden shirt. "Kiss me like you would have if we'd made it to our rendezvous."

My pulse hammered. "I don't think there's time for the kind of kiss I was going to give you."

"We have thirteen long minutes. I counted the length of a second. Ten minutes in here is more like an hour. Time enough to properly say goodbye."

I spun him until his back was to the counter, lifted him up onto the edge of it, and with both hands on the hinge of his knee to encourage him to wrap his legs around me, leaned in to kiss him like the world was going to end.

Because mine was.

CHAPTER 39

I leaned in and kissed him so hard, he nearly bit me back. My hands went under his clothes, pulling at the fastening. He wasted no time in peeling open the buttons of my shirt while his free hand ran steadily over the front of my trousers, feeling the outline of my stiffening cock. His legs, hooked around mine, drew me in so I was trapped against his mouth, which migrated from my lips, to my neck, lower. He shoved aside my shirt to suck on a nipple.

It was harried and manic, the desperate hunger to devour one last meal before we both starved, but I still asked, "Any more rules I should know about?"

"Pretend like this isn't our last night together."

I nodded feverishly. "Okay." I'd pulled enough buttons open to pull his shirt down over his shoulder. I mouthed over the mark I'd left and traveled lower to make more.

He pulled me back by my hair to kiss me again, working on my belt buckle. "And you? What do you want?"

"To taste you."

He abandoned my belt buckle to undo his own and lifted his arse so I could pull his trousers down. "My hips are too banjaxed to do this standing."

"Bedroom?" I asked.

He got off the counter, shimmied the rest of the way out of his trousers and briefs so they pooled around his ankles, then turned and opened the cupboard to retrieve a glass instead.

"Torturing me for a glass of water?"

"It's important to stay hydrated."

I had a moment to admire him while he poured from the tap. His dress shirt still hung on by a single button, its hem hitched up on one hip, falling over the other, exposing only one curved cheek. He stood with one foot arched, his weight on the other, all long legs under the bottom of that shirt. He looked like a half-opened birthday present.

He caught me staring and looked almost shy. "Well? Are you coming?"

"God, I hope so."

He bit his lip and offered me a sip from the glass. He tipped it to my lips before taking a gulp of his own, then headed for the bedroom.

Lunaris had lit it with candles and a softly glowing lamp. Rose petals were scattered underfoot. Kessian looked even more shy when he turned and lay down on the bed.

He propped himself up on his elbows, one knee bent, shirt open in a wide V. I grabbed some pillows from the bed and tossed them on the floor.

He pulled his plait over his shoulder, untying and combing his fingers through it. "Are you setting up a picnic?"

I grinned. "Yeah."

He cocked his knees apart. I grabbed both ankles, pulled him to the edge of the bed, and kissed a line up his thigh to the place where his body hair got thicker. His breath caught.

"I've never done it like this before," I said.

"It's easy. Lick me like an ice cream, suck me like you'd want to be sucked, and finger me when I'm getting close."

I planned on teasing him just a little more than that, but truly appreciated the direction. I tasted sweat as I licked up the crease of one thigh, then the other. His hips flexed, a frustrated breath escaping between clenched teeth.

"Tal."

We were pretending, but if the world wasn't ending, I would have drawn things out so much longer. Still, I said, "Beg."

He groaned, opening his legs wider. *"Please."*

I'd have asked for more detail if the husky way he said it didn't send a jolt of pleasure southward. I held his thighs apart, nuzzled into his thatch of pubic hair, and licked a long stripe over his pussy.

He flopped back against the pillows with a satisfied sigh as I tongued into him, sweat and musk and his peculiar wild magic invading my senses. I put my arms around him, thumbing the trail of hair from navel to sex while swirling my tongue over his cock and sucking it into my mouth. He thrust shallowly into the suction, making a low keening noise in his throat. I didn't think of the looming deadline, or how the nomenclature of the word "deadline" made my heart speed, or of the way Kessian desperately ground against my mouth like he wanted to expedite the finale so we could, perhaps, have enough time to go again.

We were pretending. I didn't think of those things.

I sucked him down, let him rut against my mouth with his fists in my hair, and I teased him with the tips of my fingers just inside him, never past the first knuckle, never enough to make him feel full. He rocked and tried to take more, and when that didn't work he shouted, "Tal, will you please just fuck me already!"

I sank two fingers in to the knuckle and he cried out, "Curl them. Yes, just like tha—"

His thighs closed around my head as he came. I tried to ease him through it with slow ministrations of my fingers and tongue, but the pleasure must have been sharp as a knife, because he begged me to stop. I did, pulling off him and wiping my mouth with the back of my arm.

He looked down at me, panting and pink-cheeked, eyes hooded and dark. His thighs were red from the scrape of my stubble.

I gulped. "How much longer until you can go again?"

"I don't have a refractory period."

"Then hand me that damn water," I said, half laughing and half shuddering as I climbed over him to take a sip, and he rubbed his palm more firmly against the front of my trousers.

"You still have all your clothes on."

I started on my shirt's few remaining buttons. My hands were shaking.

"Come here," he said.

I moved up the bed, straddling his hips. He sat up, and the only sound was the guttering of a candle and the soft *pick* as he undressed me one button at a time. When he got to the last one, he pulled the shirt down my arms, tossing it aside without taking his eyes off me.

He traced a lazy finger down the midline of my belly hair, and all the muscles in my stomach jumped.

"You can take off the rest." He leaned back on his elbows, kicking one leg up. "I'll watch."

I was a basket of nervous energy. I got off the bed and kicked off my shoes first. Then one sock at a time. I unbuckled my belt, undid the clasp of my trousers. Kessian's eyes tracked my movements, his dagger-sharp smile curving the edges of his mouth.

I hurried up because I wanted to kiss that mouth.

I dragged both trousers and pants off in one go, balling them up and tossing them. My cock bobbed free, still heavy and hard. Kessian made no attempt to disguise where he was looking. I walked over and put one knee up on the bed beside him.

His eyes finally raked up to meet mine, a glint of mischief in his expression. "I didn't say anything at the time, but from that first night we met, I fucking knew it'd be big."

"It's not that big."

"Only men with big cocks say that. They all look big next to mine."

"You know a lot of men with big cocks?"

"I've met a few."

I crawled over him until he lay flat against the bed. "Is it all right if I do my best to make you forget them?"

One of his hands hooked around the back of my neck, drawing me in so he could whisper in my ear, "Yes, please."

Then he lay back, his hair spread out like strokes of paint against the covers, his knees knocked apart to make room for me, and he looked so tender and beautiful, it hit me how unfair it was that I'd never see him this way again.

But we were pretending.

I played with a strand of hair that had fallen past his ear, combing it back with the rest, and he did something that nearly cracked my heart in two. He leaned his temple against my knuckles and nuzzled into my hand, until I was splaying my fingers against his cheek, into his hair, and he looked at me with an invitation in his eyes.

"Should I ask Lunaris to conjure a condom?" I whispered.

"I don't think we'll really need that here," Kessian whispered back.

I didn't know what the rules of the strid were around contraception. If our bodies were technically floating off in a river somewhere, he was probably right, but he certainly felt real with his hot skin against mine.

"You sure?" I said.

"Tal, I know we're pretending, but if this is our last night together, I want you bare."

It felt like my brain was made of ceramic and he'd just smashed it against a paving stone.

"I'm afraid I'm too turned on to speak," I said frankly.

"Don't speak. Kiss me again."

I followed his command and pressed his lips apart with my tongue. I let my knees slide out from under me, my arms making a halo around his head, combing his hair back so I didn't trap it under us. And then there wasn't much space between us.

The tip of my cock kissed the crease of one thigh, leaving a drop of precum on his skin.

His tongue plunged into my mouth, and his hips twitched up, and one of his hands snaked between us, guiding me. I groaned at the feel of his fingers wrapped firmly around me, his bush tickling the tip. He dragged my cock head up his pussy lips to part them. When he had me where he wanted me, he broke the kiss.

"Taliesin," he said. Just that. Just my name.

I sank my weight. His mouth fell open, but no noise came out. Just a tense, drawn-out silence as he let me in. He was so slick and warm. As I finally bottomed out, he did let out a small sound. A low-pitched sigh. I stopped holding my breath and released it all at once, and he kissed me like the noises I made were for him to swallow. I didn't move except to sidle my hips a little from side to side, letting him adjust.

He didn't want to wait. He resisted the restraint of my hands, sidling onto my cock, taking me deeper. I ground my teeth together to quell the spike of heat in my belly.

"I hear it feels even better when you move," he whispered in an echo of our first time.

Again, I let him goad me. I rocked my hips, making the mattress bounce. He stopped teasing and held on to me. I pulled out and snapped back in. That punched a surprised and delighted noise from him, which devolved quickly into panting breaths and plaintive moans.

Pleasure bloomed between us, his body pillowed under mine. I felt like I was being embraced by all of him—his arms, his legs, his cunt. Welcomed in. And it wasn't our first time, nor the second, but it still felt unfair that the third would be the last. We hadn't known each other long, but I didn't feel like a guest in his arms. I felt at home and suddenly understood why the strid would be driven mad by the loss of that feeling.

I rolled my hips deeper, and he buried a noise in my neck.

"Is that . . . good?" I whispered.

A long string of expletives was my answer.

I'd like to think I'd kept it together well until then, but hearing him fall apart and cuss me out for making him feel good, it ratcheted everything up. Made it more intense. I fucked him harder, spinning out and so damn close to losing control. I buried my face in his shoulder to muzzle myself.

It didn't help; it just meant that everything Kessian said was moaned directly into my ear.

"Jesus, Tal, fuck. You're doing good. You feel *so* good."

"Please," I ground out. I didn't even know what I was begging for. "I need to. I'm going to—"

"Me too."

I reached down and thumbed over his cock just as he clenched down around me. I saw stars, or maybe that was just the freckles dusted over his skin. I couldn't hear the noises I made, but I know I made them. I throbbed and emptied myself, and he quivered and rocked through it until we both slumped, sweaty and limp.

My arms and legs were shaking as I tried to rise and get off him, but he pulled me back into his arms and started kissing my lips, my cheeks, my closed eyelids.

"I'm crushing you," I said.

"You're better than any weighted blanket."

The rush slowly ebbed into a quiet awe. The heavy lure of sleep drew me in, but I resisted. I wanted to be with him as long as I could be.

Kessian carded his fingers through my hair, soothing me. "I wish there was time to sleep."

"If there was, I wouldn't want to. I'd miss you."

He looked at me like I'd told him a terrible secret.

He traced my spine with his fingers, and I counted and kissed the stars along his shoulders and collarbones.

"They used to be just normal freckles, until I came to Shearwater," Kessian said.

"They're beautiful. They've always reminded me of stars." I kissed the one that fell right between his clavicles, like the pendant on a necklace. "We should make wishes on yours."

Kessian got really quiet. Then he said, "I wish this night could last forever."

We were supposed to be pretending, but we couldn't pretend anymore.

I'd said this once in a dream. It still hurt the second time. "We made the time we had count."

He managed to hold back tears, but it was a near thing. "Water?"

"Yeah."

He leaned over to get it for me, tipped the glass to my lips like he had before. He'd set the pocket watch open on the bedside amongst empty potion bottles and the sachet of paracetamol I'd given him that night he couldn't sleep for the pain in his leg.

I should have taken him up on round two back then. If I'd known there'd only be three . . .

The exhaustion of the night wore away at my resistance to sleep. My eyelids were so heavy. I kept shaking awake, focusing on the tiniest details of Kessian's face, memorizing it like it was the last time I'd ever see it, because it was.

Kessian noticed. He kissed my temple. His warmth, the soft rise and fall of his chest and steady heartbeat were like a lullaby. Distantly, I thought, no, I have to get up. It's time. When I realized one of the empty potion bottles on the nightstand was the sleep spell I'd given him, it was too late.

I fought it, but I lost.

I woke to Lunaris's horn blaring, my bed empty except for the divot that once held Kessian. The pocket watch still stood open on the nightstand. There was a note inside.

It read, *I'm sorry.*

There were three minutes left until midnight.

CHAPTER 40

I snatched the watch off the bedside table and shot out of bed.

The note was a cracked whip against my sleep-addled mind. The rest of the waking world came back to me in sharp relief. The brightness of a room that had been romantically dimmed. The horn blaring, the curtains flapping open and shut, the bed rattling. Lunaris doing everything in her power to wake me.

It would have worked sooner, but the dregs of the sleep potion had done their job.

Lunaris conjured a fresh pair of jeans. I hopped into them, stuffing the watch into the pocket on my way into the kitchen. The front door was wide open.

I didn't have time for shoes. I ran barefoot out onto the grass.

Across the gardens, fifty meters from me, Kessian approached the banks of the spring. Lights from the wedding pavilion winked off the water, music too distant to be anything but bass, mimicking the heavy thunk of my heart as I screamed, "Kessian!"

I'd already started running. I hadn't played sports since high school, but the past few days had given me a few reasons to practice. My legs ate up the distance. Kessian heard me and looked over his shoulder. His expression was painfully familiar. Stubborn, determined, and in unquestionable pain. The same one he wore when he'd relented about me sacrificing myself. He'd never intended to let me.

"Kessian!" I screamed. "Don't do it!"

He didn't listen. He tossed aside his cane on the grass and took a step to wade in. The tainted wild magic surged up from the depths to meet him, a scarlet tide buoying him across the surface. Each step rippled across a bloodred pool. I was closing the gap but still too far to make it.

"Kessian!"

Kessian limped more quickly.

"Don't!" I screamed myself hoarse. "Kessian, please don't!"

My pleas were cut short by an unearthly, serrated wail like cutlery scraped across ceramic. I nearly lost my footing as I darted a look into the trees.

The woods were dark, but the wraith was darker still, an inky shape crashing through the brush. It reached the shore in three sweeping strides, ungainly and on all fours. There was no trace of Laurelie in its body language. Its form had changed, hulking rather than lithe and eerily graceful.

Kessian reached the center of the spring, the wraith and I converging upon him. I didn't slow.

"Tal, go back!" Kessian yelled.

"Like hell I will!"

The wraith and I reached the shore at the same time, but while I waded in, slowed by sodden jeans and the mucky bottom, the wraith slithered into the water like an eel. It pooled like black blood in the water, streaming toward Kessian with the predatory agility of a shark.

"No," I whispered hoarsely. I was so close.

The blackness gathered under Kessian. He mouthed an apology. Then the wraith pulled him under. He slipped out of sight with barely a ripple.

I dove under after him.

Nothing should have been loud underwater, but the strid was. It raged, the howling gale of something lost that couldn't find its way back to solid ground. I'd heard some variation of its song many times now, but it was nothing compared to this. The water crashed like cymbals, momentous and angry.

I could hardly see through the blackness. The spring seemed expansive, but I didn't think the space we occupied was physical anymore. This was the cut in the world between the Bloodstream and the strid, the spring, the water that made up the blood of Shearwater. I swam into the dark.

At first there was nothing. Then came the winking glimmer of Kessian's stars, distant as real ones, glowing enough to see his wide, terrified eyes and the shape of what held him. The same crimson, corrupted magic that had once swirled around Laurelie twisted around him. Circling him was the wraith, its movements graceful as a shark, more at home in water than on land.

I swam toward them, but a current fought me, held me back. I moved as if through molasses while the wraith consumed Kessian. It wrapped one hand around his throat, sickle-shaped claws far too near his jugular. He instinctively pried at its fingers, then froze. Through the gurgle of water in my ears, I could have sworn something spoke.

Kessian listened, wide-eyed and attentive.

No, I thought. *Whatever it's saying, don't listen.*

I tried to swim harder, but there was no fighting the current. Every muscle in me screamed with exertion while I made no progress forward, forced to watch as Kessian bowed his head, absorbing whatever he'd heard. Briefly, he turned in my direction. His eyes met mine.

No, please don't, I thought desperately.

I could read his lips as he said, "Trust me." Then something else I couldn't decipher.

"No!"

The wraith ducked its head, and the antlers seemed to split apart. The entire wraith did, like it had been unzipped, shadows discarded like old clothes, revealing the shape of Laurelie one layer at a time. She looked pristine, untouched, the same as she did the day she died. Laurelie was set free, but the empty cage now reached for Kessian. The ribs opened like spider legs, holding him like a fly, and its skeletal face bent too close. It didn't have teeth, but its proximity made it look like it would bite.

I fought the current, but I could not move. The water was cold, but everything in me burned.

The wraith said something, and Kessian tipped closer as if enthralled. He nodded, and the wraith leaned forward like it really would bite him. Instead, the shadows crawled up Kessian's face, pried his jaw open, and poured down his throat like the wraith was forcing him to drink poison.

Bubbles foamed from my mouth as I screamed.

The strid threw me out onto the shores of the spring, as if depositing me out of a bad dream into the waking world. Or the opposite.

Because Laurelie was coughing up water on the grass beside me, and Kessian was gone.

CHAPTER 41

I rounded on the spring, wading in. "Give him back." The words clawed their way up my throat. "Give him back!"

But the water didn't stir. No one else crawled out of it. Despair threatened to drown me more readily than the strid ever had. I couldn't lose Kessian. Memories of him blazed through me in a grieving wildfire. How he'd made me laugh when we first met, the steady way he'd listened to me ramble, that quiet night spent at my pottery wheel.

I couldn't accept that we'd never spend another night like that. I'd only barely accepted my own death by sacrifice, I couldn't accept Kessian's.

Laurelie coughed up a lungful of strid water. My heart warred between disbelief that she was here, doubting my reality, hoping she was, and grief that Kessian had been traded for her.

She could have answers. The strid had spoken to him, said something. Maybe she knew.

"Laurelie? Are you . . . Is this real? What happened?"

She clutched her head, pulling aqueous weeds from her hair and blinking around in confusion.

"Did he trade places with you? Is he still— Can we go back?"

She didn't respond, staring past me at the house. I turned to see torchlight flushing through the gardens like hounds. Voices filtered closer, some I recognized. Fae's was among them.

Oh God. What could I say to them?

I lost him. I tried to hold on, but the strid stole him away. I traded my lover for my sister.

The image came back to me. Those bilious liquid shadows forcing his mouth open and spiriting down his throat like a plague of insects fleeing the light.

I refused to believe he was gone. If Laurelie was here beside me, we could get Kessian back somehow.

"Laurelie, listen," I said.

But she was getting up and running toward the torches. Their glare fell upon her. I shielded my eyes from it.

Someone said, "It can't be."

Then one of the torches dropped from the hand of the person holding it, and Fae marched out of the glare and threw their arms around their lost sister.

"Are you— Is it really you?"

"My God. How is she alive?"

And someone else said, "Where's Kessian? Where's Tal?"

"I'm right here," I said, but they didn't hear, and I stopped expecting them to.

Something about this wasn't right. It tugged at the corners of my exhausted instincts.

I reached into my pocket for the watch. My fingers brushed metal. It was still there, still flickering between the new and the rusted, tarnished images of itself. I opened it and could hardly make sense of what I saw.

There were four hours left.

But . . . that shouldn't be the case. There'd only been minutes left before.

If the Bloodstream had somehow given me more time, I wouldn't waste more questioning it. I had to get Kessian back. I racked my brains for what could have caused this sudden skip backward, how it was possible.

My fingers ran over the cool, semitransparent surface of the pocket watch in my fist. It had counted down the final hours of our lives. Sometimes it had run fast.

What if it hadn't been skipping ahead? What if . . . What if I—this future version of myself—had skipped back, and used up that time in another memory. One my past self hadn't lived yet?

It twisted my brain, thinking of time like this. As squiggles and loops rather than a straight line. But as I connected the dots, it started to make sense.

There was one way to test if time travel still worked, but I did not want to waste the precious time I had. I needed to pick the right moment. To fix this. For good.

Though, if history was fixed... But I had to try. I picked at the seams of all the events leading up to now, trying to pull out the stuffing. What was I missing? What thread could I follow that would convince the strid to give up Kessian?

I'd once asked the wraith, "What do you want?"

To go home.

But where was home? Grandad had alienated his own children in favor of his grandkids. My mum resented me and pushed me out to preserve the rest of the family. Marlowe had broken us for the sake of an inheritance and his own pride. The houses we lived in were haunted, the very waters flowing through Shearwater were drenched in blood, and the rest of it belonged to Warwick.

Everyone in this town clung so hard to each other and the past that when they'd been pulled apart, their claws tore great rifts in their futures.

It struck me then. We'd explored all the mysterious deaths in the strid. All but two.

When we'd examined the death glow left by the wraith on my grandfather's body, there'd been two names amongst the others. Mine and Kessian's, yet neither of us had died. Neither of us had merged with the wraith.

Yet.

As I heard Laurelie burst into tears, I touched the dial on the side of the spectral watch and turned it back, uncertain it would work until the wedding melted away, replaced by Lunaris's kitchen.

Through a gap in the bedroom door, I could see Kessian and I wrapped around each other, making the bed creak.

I'd lived this moment, but I still felt as though I'd intruded as I quietly stepped outside and closed the door to give them—us—privacy.

Now I'd confirmed I could go back in time, I knew the event I needed to circumvent would come in only a few minutes, and as if sensing my resolve, the Keepers appeared before me.

"You understand what you must do?"

"I think so."

"Then come with us."

They led me away from Lunaris, to the spring where it all began, ended, began again in an endless loop. I stood at the edge with just my toes in the water.

"A word of caution: Resentment is contagious, and the wraith has many years of it."

"So do I."

"Yes. And you must let go of it and convince it to do the same."

"I will." I had to. I wasn't losing anyone else.

"Time has a tricky way of making the foulest memories far stickier than the ones that make us smile. If we can impart any wisdom, it is to be most at home in yourself, so you do not give in to that sick tide."

"I will be." But my heart beat a little faster. Did I know how?

"Then go," said the Keepers.

While we'd spoken, the glassy surface of the spring rippled. The tines of each antler emerged first, the wraith's head just above water, elongated like a horse's skull. It stared at me. It waited.

I took a step closer, though my instincts railed against it. It had attacked me so many times, it was more unnerving to see it still. As I got closer, it twitched its head like an animal chafing against its chains, water softly splashing, but it didn't lunge or give chase, so I pushed forward until I floated before it, treading water and summoning words, though I didn't know if it understood me.

"I'm here to cleanse the poison."

The water rippled with a vibration. It beat against me like it was blood throbbing through vessels. A heartbeat. Its song was still filled with all the fury from before, but I was more attuned to its pain. Perhaps because I hurt, too, fearing for Kessian and what would become of us if I failed.

The wraith circled me, its shadows leaving ink trails in the water. I tried not to flinch as it swept behind me.

In my ears, the strid sang, *Come home, come home, please come home.*

My home wasn't just a place, but Shearwater had indelibly carved its initials into me, and I tried to let it in. Tried to sympathize with the wild magic that fed off of ephemeral, ever-changing things like *belonging* and *family* and *acceptance*.

The wraith sensed my willingness to help like a wasp seeking out a crevice in the wall in which to make a hive. I tried not to flinch as its claws wound around my throat, tilting my head back.

It blotted out the stars in the sky before it split apart. The shadows swarmed over me, into my nose and mouth, blotting out my vision. I felt myself sucked underwater, engulfed inside the wraith, my consciousness melting with its own.

In that cavernous nothing, there was only the rabbiting of my heart and the strange, breathless expanse of the water around me.

Then came a torrent of memory. Not my own, but the strid's. Countless people dipping their toes in its waters, hoping to steal a glimpse of the future. Staying for an hour or a weekend, departing, the strid never knowing if that future came to pass. The endless cycle of faces, so few of which it ever saw again. So few who were familiar. So few who cared enough to wonder if the magic spring wasn't exhausted, lonely, and lost.

It hated them. It hated how they squatted in homes that were otherwise empty through fall and winter. It hated how they treated its magic like a novelty, a trick. Where were the ones who said a prayer to the wild? Where had the family gone, who'd lived here six generations? Seven? And of the ones who stayed, how many had happy stories to tell? So many splintered because all the flats were for bed-and-breakfasts. Families hung drawn and quartered until Shearwater was less a home than a hotel. Everyone it loved had left or no longer loved it back. All those people it could no longer see. People like me. They'd gone far from here, where the strid's waters couldn't reach, couldn't see.

It had gone blind. The power of time and memories was only so marvelous when you got to see how the stories ended.

The viciousness of its resentment sucked me under, tumbling me in the undertow. I recognized these feelings, this desire to keep someone in a cage for fear they'll fly away. I'd hesitated to bare my heart to Kessian for fear he'd break it. Kessian had pushed me away for fear I'd leave.

I tried to call out to the strid, press back with my own memories.

People change, people leave, but sometimes they come back. I came back. If you cling too tightly, you'll choke the life out of them, and their loved ones will grow to hate you, and the ones who depend upon you for their livelihoods no longer can. Some of what's happened isn't because the world is ever-changing and unfair, it's because you frightened people too much for them to find a home in you.

I didn't know if it was my blood pounding in my ears or the strid's. I waited in that vast nothing for some answer, some indication the strid understood what I meant. A part of me hoped I'd gotten through to it, but I was in the past, and I knew what the future held.

Without warning, the strid lashed out at me with its own rebuttal of memories. Dad's skull opened against the rock wall of the strid. He'd worked so hard most days, there weren't enough memories of us together to overshadow that one. Laurelie wishing him back to life and drowning in Marlowe's greed. Traveling from one town to another with an open road and an empty heart. Kessian kissing me one last time and not knowing it was goodbye. That moment he turned his back on me to walk into the spring carved my heart open.

My own resentment bubbled up. The strid demanded to know with righteous fury, *How was my desperate refusal to say goodbye to Kessian any different from the strid clinging to its residents?*

The song in my ears fumed. My argument fell on deaf ears. What did I know? When I was just the same.

The briny water boiled in my lungs, turned my veins to tributaries. I tasted smoke and salt and silt. Shadows condensed and clothed me as an ache in my head reached such a peak, I thought it was splitting open like a seed sprouting. My fingers lengthened into claws. My knuckles popped. When I exhaled, instead of bubbles, a stream of ink weaved through the water.

I struggled, swam toward a reflection of light rippling on the surface, but when I moved I felt like a passenger.

I emerged on the banks of the spring once more, but I was not myself. Shadows pooled around my feet. Antlers weighed heavy on my skull.

I was the wraith.

CHAPTER 42

My limbs were corded and dripping ichor. The shadows licked around me like flames. I looked down at myself and did not recognize what I saw. I'd come into this prepared. If I was right about how everything ended, then I had to become this to make that ending happy.

But as I turned and beheld my reflection in the spring's glossy pool, my stomach roiled.

That wasn't *me*.

The strid echoed that sentiment in its own, susurrous language. I glimpsed images of the spring in its full power, when fireflies danced in the reeds and the water lit with glowing nebulas of magic. Blue, not crimson. Back when it had been loved, not used and abandoned.

Those feelings burrowed like termites in my mind. The strid eroded the barrier between us. Ate holes in my brain. Making us more and more alike, trying to make me forget.

But the sight of my reflection reminded me.

That wasn't me.

That wasn't my face.

Was this how Kessian once felt whenever he looked in the mirror?

Kessian.

That's why I'd come here. That's why I looked like this. I needed to purify the strid so Kessian and I could go home.

Home. You are home.

I resisted that thought. It wasn't mine, either.

I needed to find my way back to the Bloodstream, back to the memory where we'd been separated.

Which of us had been separated? The strid from Laurelie? Me from Kessian? Both? My memories and the strid's threatened to emulsify. I had to keep them separate. Oil and water.

The Bloodstream, I reminded myself. Kessian. I had to get back to Kessian.

Before, I'd needed to twist the hands of the clocks at 37 Culpepper Avenue to dip in and out of time, but as I tried to remember how, the strid pulled on my bones like a fell wind, dragging me another way, as though I'd slipped on an icy patch in my mind. I found myself skidding—not toward Culpepper Avenue, but back into the waters of the spring.

I dove into the deep, into the mulch, the bedrock, squeezing through crevasses into the underground tributaries, the veins of the strid. I could swim upstream against the current now, because I *was* the strid. I had a map of the cartography and knew every turn, every tunnel. I used it to slip between the cracks of this world into the Bloodstream.

It was like being plunged into a matrix of memories, none of them my own. Everything the strid knew and had borne witness to. All the things that hadn't come to pass, but could. All the things currently happening.

(My mum is screaming on the phone to police while Camilla puts her arms around Fae, ushering them into the kitchen, where Amelia butters toast for them.)

These weren't the memories I needed. There was a specific one.

The strid's instincts and mine warred with each other. It wanted to keep everyone here. I wanted to set Kessian free. When one memory caught me like a riptide, I couldn't tell whether it was the one I or the strid had aimed for until it dumped me into the conservatory at Foxbury Manor, where instead of making me tea, Warwick served a younger Uncle Marlowe, who held the bone flute in his hands with quiet awe and some suspicion.

"If it grants wishes like you claim, why haven't you used it?"

"Who's to say I haven't already? Look at how I live. What more could I possibly wish for?"

Liar, trickster, murderer by proxy, hissed the strid, while I railed against it. This was the wrong place, the wrong time. I had already taken the contract from the safe, and there was nothing else to glean.

The memory threw me from its back like a bucking horse. I landed back in the waters, both familiar and alien. A part of me and not. It was difficult to remember why that was, or what I'd been doing here. The water whispered *stay, stay, stay*, but I didn't want to. I resented the thing that kept me here, that had stolen something from me.

Someone.

Through the erosion of my self, I conjured Kessian's face. The memories of him didn't arrive fuzzily or in rapid bursts. They absorbed me, gluey and sticking to my heart.

Before I could narrow down the memory I needed to arrive in, the world resolved around me, and I was in a bedroom.

Two people slept on either side of the bed, with a gap between them of only a half foot, but it could have been a gulf.

Kessian was curled up on his side, facing Tal. *Me*, I tried to remind myself. *That's me.*

Mine now.

Had that been my thought or the strid's? The possessive sentiment rotted through the already spongy barrier between us. I found myself clambering through the fabric of the Bloodstream and the real world, slipping into the bed with Kessian. A combination of missing him and muscle memory had me putting my arms around him, as the figure across the bed stiffened.

Me. That's me, I reminded myself.

Kessian's hair smelled like oranges, and he was so warm, and the water was so cold. I could take him right now. Take him into the Bloodstream so we'd never be apart.

Then Tal—*I* punched the wraith, which was also me. I fell back, screeching, and another part of me, a different part (Laurelie? Is that Laurelie?) saw her brother's face and raised fists. She recoiled, and like a collared dog we were pulled back into the Bloodstream from whence we'd come.

Shearwater's memories flooded me again, but this time I clung hard to the one of Kessian warm in my arms. That sensation still lingered through the cloak of shadows. I'd held him like that on the night I needed to get back to.

Please, take me there, to that time, to that place.

The world righted itself once more, countless memories becoming one.

I hovered like a ghost on the ceiling of Tal's bedroom. *My* bedroom.

Relief clutched my heart in its fist. Kessian had just given me the glass of water with the dregs of a sleep draft in it. I saw the magic sprinkle like sand in my eyes. They drooped shut. I slumped into the pillow. Kessian let out a soft noise of despair as he kissed my forehead for what he thought would be the last time and whispered, "Forgive me."

Don't go, I wanted to scream, but I consoled myself that I'd found the right memory. I'd come to the right time.

As Kessian wrote a note, Lunaris began to blare her horn. Kessian hissed at her to be quiet, but she slammed doors instead. He hurried to get dressed. He grabbed his cane and headed for the front door. She tried to lock him inside, but he slid a knife up the crack to unbolt the door.

He looked down the hall toward me. A tear glistened like a falling star amongst the freckles of his cheeks. It took visible effort for him to turn and go.

Lunaris redoubled her efforts to wake me. It would not be long now that she would.

Before we'd first met, he'd been a ghost who fished me out of a river and saved my life.

Now I crept from Lunaris's roof into the woods and waited, a ghost hell-bent on saving him in return.

Moments later, my past self came racing out the front door. The sound of my own voice was always alien in videos and answering machine messages, but even more so now when I could hear my own heart breaking.

As one version of me pelted across the lawn toward Kessian, the other skulked out of the shadows. Through the trees, I kept Kessian in my sights, and the madman chasing after him barefoot.

Then I gave chase, too.

It was strange, remembering their terror. I'd lived it. Now, I experienced the eerie calm of carrying out the past like an actor playing his part, knowing where it led but not how it ended. Trusting that I would find a way to make things right when I got there.

I ran through the trees, up to the bank of the spring and slipped into the water, where Kessian waited for me on the surface.

The moment I submerged, my mind started to bleed. It hemorrhaged into the water, sucked out by the all-consuming strid and its corrupted magic. My desire to *save* became a compulsion to *possess*. I tried to curb it, but the instincts tore through. I dragged Kessian under.

Rescue, I reminded myself. He wasn't an object, a piece of decoration to trick people into thinking you'd made your house a home.

I could hear my own muffled voice screaming underwater. I released Kessian's ankle. I had him now. Mine. The waters embraced and held him up. He floated in the murk, eyes wide and terrified as I circled in.

Take, take, mine, can't leave, can't go, can't let him be taken.

I reached out, wrapping a claw around Kessian's neck. Yes. If we took him here and now, he could never leave. Not Shearwater, not me.

Those aren't my thoughts. This isn't me.

I tried to shake the strid's jealous refrain from my head. Kessian's fingers were digging through the shadows at my wrists, trying to pry my claw from his neck, and he looked—

Horrified. Scared for his life.

And resigned.

He was doing this to spare me. So that *I* could live. Because he cared for me.

A few memories parted the endless deluge of them. Kessian comforting me in a claustrophobic changing room. Revealing his secrets one by one. Leaving marks on each other's lives like a door the color of baked cherries, clay fingerprints on skin, a love bite from all the times I'd kissed his neck.

I didn't need to possess him. These moments were enough.

The strid's memories had felt like hail stones pitted against my own, but now they softened. The strid paused, and my mind felt like my own.

My hand around Kessian's throat transformed into an apologetic caress. I tipped my head forward and fought to speak.

"It's me. It's Tal."

Kessian's gaze was a eulogy of terror, hurt, yearning and, just below the surface, hope.

"I went back in time. It was me stealing the hours from us. I took Laurelie's place, but I can't purify the strid on my own. It keeps taking me over. It twists my feelings. Makes them selfish, and I'm too selfish to stop it."

Kessian looked prepared to protest.

I rushed to say the rest. I could feel the strid trying to reassert itself. "I think we have to purify it together."

I tried to say more, but the strid stole my voice, choked me silent. I feared for a moment I hadn't said enough to convince him, but then Kessian nodded, turned to his right, and mouthed the words. "Trust me." And then, "This isn't goodbye."

I don't know why I'd been afraid. I knew he would agree because he already had. In the moment, it didn't feel that way. It felt like trying to catch a pebble in a riptide.

Kessian surrendered to me. I tried to be delicate, but the strid was rattling its way to the surface. I leaned in to kiss him, but my claws pulled his mouth open.

The wraith, Kessian, and I melted into one. A few memories pricked to the surface, ones I'd lived from the other side. Kessian's memories.

Now it was my foot on the pedal of the pottery wheel with big hands leaving clay marks on my skin, a body bracketing mine, warm against my back.

Then I was lying sweaty in bed while soft lips and a rough mustache kissed my knuckles, and my heart beat so fast and my head spun from how good it felt to be wanted like this, devoured by hazel green eyes, my body not a peculiarity but a source of pleasure for us both. And he said to me, "I'm done with running away. You're worth the risk."

"The risk of what?" I said.

He said, "A broken heart."

And mine, which had been pounding so, so fast, froze, as a tidal wave of recollection swept me under. Mum making me chili for dinner (my favorite) to soften the blow of breaking the news she was selling our council house so she could travel the world with a backpack, but without me. Miriam holding my hand telling me she was proud I'd found myself, but she couldn't love who I'd become. Dom filling up his car and driving off without saying goodbye after asking for one last lay like I was a toy he was close to retiring.

I looked into those hazel green eyes and thought, *Oh no. This is going to hurt.*

The wrongness of it shook me out of the memories. *I* was Tal. And I didn't know what the future held, but I hadn't left him yet, and I didn't intend to anytime soon.

I was here, now, trying to get him back.

I wanted to reach out for him, but he was a part of me, and I, him. We weren't separate. And we weren't alone.

The strid had gone eerily quiet, its own memories a background murmur, as though it had slipped into ours, watching the film of our lives through two separate cameras.

Then the strid started to speak. Not in words, but in images. It showed me a family fetching buckets of water from the spring. Bathing in the waters in the summer while an elderly woman took her shoes off and sat on the banks to dip her feet in. (She loved summer best because the smell of the apple orchards reminded her of her first love, who picked the perfect apple for her before every date.) It showed me a curious child picking up stones and washing them in the water to examine how they sparkled and what colors they revealed. (He had a friend he shared his collection with.) It showed me a man getting down on one knee to propose to the woman his parents didn't want him to marry. (He'd loved her ever since witnessing her cheer and entertain a stranger's crying child on the bus because she could tell the child's mother needed a break.)

It was a flood of memories that weren't mine or Kessian's. They belonged to Shearwater, and these memories grew more and more sparse as time wore on, as people visited the spring less, or only came because they wanted something from it. It wasn't that the photographs they took to show their friends were all vapid or meaningless. It wasn't that the people of before didn't have their share of misery. (The couple who'd gotten engaged had struggled to conceive, the woman who loved summer had lost the lover who gave her apples to a heart attack, and the little boy with his rock collection got bullied relentlessly in school.) It wasn't that people didn't laugh or play or fall in love anymore. It was just that they did so for a day, maybe a season, maybe a year, and then they left. And the strid never saw them again.

It had loved them all, however briefly, but it had never learned how to say goodbye.

I thought about kissing the stars on Kessian's skin and wishing we had more time. How "goodbye" had been the universal conclusion to all my one-night stands and passing fancies, all his long-term love affairs. How one momentous goodbye from my only family had made me afraid of any more, afraid to let Kessian in, and he the same with me. We'd nearly driven each other away.

I didn't know how to convey that to the strid. As usual, I fought for the right words. I despaired that I might fail for lack of eloquence when a soft voice touched my mind, soothing me and the strid both.

Kessian said, *I understand. I miss Tal like you miss everyone. But nothing stays the same forever. Time doesn't stop passing just because we found a moment so good we want to make it eternal. We have to make our own hearts a home if we have any hope of someone choosing to stay. I am in a constant state of renovation; the brick and mortar I thought I was made of was actually thatch and cob. There are rooms I've never explored, doors I've never opened, and I might find things in there that force me to knock down walls, or which aren't fit for the people who once found shelter with me. And I'm no better at letting them go. I'm not. But nobody calls a pair of shackles their home.*

So let them go. If we're good and a little lucky, they might come back.

Let go, the strid repeated. Where its song always sounded like white water, now it had the quiet murmur of a brook. Contemplative and a little afraid.

I had to say something, too. If Kessian could teach it to let go, I could teach it how to stay, or at least how not to run.

I spent years moving from place to place, never putting down roots. Every person I'd meet, I had to wonder what might have been. I'd invent a whole life for myself with a boy I spotted reading my favorite book at a café. I'd watch groups at the pub who'd known each other since they were in nappies and ask myself who I'd be if I'd never left Shearwater. I resented every day you kept me from attending events where I might have met my new best friend. I had Lunaris, and I had myself. And then I had Kessian. There were a thousand and one different Tals I could have been before him, but I'm this one now. And I choose him.

Making a home isn't about everything staying the same. You grow, and things change, and you get to know people for an hour or a lifetime, but the one constant is you. The real you.

And we know this isn't you.

The strid weakly resisted the sentiment, but where before its own memories had chipped away at mine, I could now sense ours had turned the tide. In the spring, we were a creature of shadow and time, but the shadows were slowly filtering away. Wrung out of us like dirt from a rag.

The strid's resistance faltered. It flowed through our memories—the ones Kessian and I had made together.

Let go, it repeated. *Not running away.*

As the last bit of oily poison was drawn out of us, I felt myself split, until I was singular instead of plural. For one petrifying moment, I thought I'd lost Kessian. I couldn't sense his thoughts, couldn't dive into his memories, but then I opened my eyes.

We were underwater. Really underwater. Kessian floated in front of me, eyes fluttering open, and unlike the unreality of the timestream, we were in our bodies. Our *real* bodies. And we couldn't breathe.

I grabbed him by the hand and kicked. We broke the surface together, coughing and dragging in each breath. Morning light glistened off the ripples of the pool, no longer mirror black, but the phosphorescent blue of life and magic.

We swam for shore and collapsed on our backs, squinting into the sun.

I needed a way to tell if this was a dream, a memory, the Bloodstream, or neither.

"Say something to make this real," I said. "Something to prove I'm not dreaming."

He rolled over, brow scrunched in thought, but his expression quickly changed as he looked across the garden toward the house, to the sound of voices coming nearer. I sat up, too.

My family hurried up the cobbled path to the spring. They looked sleepless, red-nosed and puffy-eyed, all of them, except Marlowe, who was not in their number.

At the front of their band was Laurelie.

It should have made everything less real. I couldn't bring myself to believe the strid had released so many of us, but I remembered crawling up onto the banks and watching her reunite with the family she hadn't seen in nine years.

Kessian said, "It's not a dream. We're home."

EPILOGUE

With the last of my cooking pans packed up, Lunaris's kitchen looked unnervingly empty, nothing like the place I'd called home for the past nine years.

I carried the last crate of my things out and set it on the porch of 37 Culpepper Avenue. It had taken all morning to move all my things from Lunaris inside, but there were advantages to Lunaris, and one was not having to hire a moving van.

My cousin and siblings had come to help me pack. I'd insisted Kessian rest because his back had been paining him lately. I knew he wouldn't want to sit around while we all worked, but he hadn't arrived yet, and I didn't want to go through with the next bit without him.

Fae came out of the house, dusting their hands. "Heard from him yet?"

I'd been checking my phone for the dozenth time. "I'm sure he'll be along shortly."

"You're terrified he's not going to show, aren't you?"

They didn't have to say it out loud.

Two weeks ago, when the deed to 37 Culpepper Avenue had finally transferred to my name officially, I'd asked Kessian if he wanted to move in. I'd emphasized that he didn't have to. I understood his need for independence, and his fear that living together would would once again uproot him if our relationship took a turn. But we'd been together a year now. Living so close by, we spent most of our time together anyway.

And the new house was big and empty, except for all the ghosts and history and spiders that had moved in while it remained unoccupied. It would be good to fill it with somebody I loved instead.

He had gone very quiet and hadn't answered.

I was not freaking out about this at all.

"You're freaking out, aren't you?" Fae said.

"No. It's just a big deal, moving in, staying for good. I'd want him here even if he decided not to move in together yet."

"Just call and ask for an ETA."

"Or I could have a quiet breakdown."

"Who's breaking down? I hope it's not Lunaris, after she carted all your stuff and everything."

Laurelie appeared in the doorway.

She'd surfaced from the strid nine years younger than me, an anomaly that would no doubt ensure we forever won any game of "two truths and a lie" we played. In spite of her long absence and our sudden gap in age, we fell easily into conversation with each other, which made it seem as though love was another sort of time travel, connecting us across all the years we'd spent apart.

"Tal's afraid Kessian's ghosted him."

Laurelie raised her eyebrows. "I'll show him a ghost. Want me to drown him in the spring again? For old time's sake."

"No!"

As if to rescue me from my siblings, the garbled motor of Kessian's beat-up Volvo announced his arrival. He parked up and started messing about with something in the passenger seat before getting out, awkwardly trying to balance whatever he was carrying with his cane hooked on his elbow.

I rushed over to help, only registering what he carried when I got closer.

It was his delphinium, taken from his garden, the root ball carefully wrapped in newspaper.

"Sorry I'm late. I thought I should bring a housewarming present, but then I wasn't sure because it seemed weird to bring a housewarming gift when it's going to be my house, too, but then I figured *we're* sort of weird, and if I wanted to move the delphiniums today's good weather for it, so— Why are you looking at me like that?"

"Your house?"

He shifted nervously. "Well . . . *our* house?"

I pulled him into a kiss. Trying to crush him, but not the plant, in a hug was a difficult achievement, but I managed. Over his shoulder I saw the Golf had boxes stuffed in the back seats, too. "You're really moving in?"

"Yes! Did you think I'd say no?"

"Well, yeah. You didn't say anything, just did that quiet pensive thing that you do when you're working something out."

"Oh . . . I was trying to work out where I'd plant the hydrangeas. Your garden gets a lot of sun, and they need shade."

I kissed him again, a little longer so he knew how in love I was.

An *Eugh* of disgust issued behind us.

"You know I saw him snort a gumdrop out his nose when he was five?" said Laurelie.

"You've never shown me that trick," Kessian said.

"And I never will. It wasn't on purpose."

"Shoving the gumdrop up there in the first place was," said Laurelie.

"I brought drinks!" Fae declared, appearing with flutes of sparkling wine sandwiched between their hands and elbows. They paused before giving one to Laurelie. "Aren't you technically underage?"

"I was a thousands-year-old river."

Amelia snatched a glass for her. "If anyone deserves to get wankered, it's you, babes. I was in that pond-scum skin suit for twenty-four hours, and I felt like I needed to be exfoliated with steel wool."

"I would have given her the drink," Fae pouted.

"All right, all right," I declared. "I think it's time."

A breeze of magic whispered on the air, making the fall leaves smell crisper. We all turned to Lunaris, from whom the magic emanated.

I stepped up to her and raised my glass. "A toast to Lunaris. My best and oldest friend. You gave me a home all these years. Now it's my turn."

Everyone echoed my toast. "To Lunaris."

I took a drink and tipped some of the wine out over her bonnet. It fizzled, droplets frying in the aura of her magic. Glimmering, golden smoke rose in plumes, enveloping her in a slowly shrinking twister. My heart tapped a rhythm to the sound of a tune she played on her radio for the last time, one I'd sung to on many road trips.

The smoke seemed to eat away at the camper van, becoming a single pillar, until that, too, dissipated in a sudden breeze, and in place of my house on wheels, a calico cat with crooked whiskers burst from it and tried to run toward me, though she moved the way animals did with booties on their feet.

"Oh, oh no. It's so strange having legs after all this time. Wheels are far more straightforward."

Fae awwed while everyone else laughed. I picked Lunaris up and the sheer familiarity of the way she smelled when I kissed her fuzzy head catapulted me into nostalgia. It was strange to be reunited when we'd never really been separated in the first place. She'd always been there, but I'd still missed her.

In the way of all cats, she put a paw on my face to push it away. "That's enough affection. Put me down now. I must search the premises and ensure there are no vermin."

I set her down and she sprang off into the house, pausing only briefly to weave around Kessian's ankles. "This one is not vermin. I give him permission to stay."

We could hear her claws clattering as she hunted spiders.

"What did she say?" Kessian asked.

"She's given you her stamp of approval, though I think she made that fairly obvious when she was a camper van."

We all took our drinks inside to start the chore of cleaning the house and unpacking. I marveled at how much dust could accumulate in a year.

It had taken all that time for Warwick to meet a meager justice. Legal proceedings being slow as they were, he had plenty of time and money to wrangle himself a lesser sentence despite his collusion in a mass murder and his possession of a dangerous artifact.

While the judicial system might have failed the people of Shearwater, those people had long memories, and Foxbury Manor now had a for-sale sign at the end of its drive, as did Shearwater Spa.

There was a silver lining. The contract he'd drawn up transferring ownership of 37 Culpepper Avenue had been officially voided, along with several others of questionable legality. Those legal costs had postponed his building plans for the caravan park where Kessian lived.

Marlowe had not been released on bail, and there was little doubt in the mind of the prosecuting barrister that he would get a life sentence for what he'd done. He'd tried to run. It had been particularly hard on Amelia, who hadn't spoken to him since, and the rest of us had done the same in solidarity, but as time passed, the scars he'd left had begun to fade. Not completely, never completely, but enough that there were days we did not think about the monster he'd made of our home in Shearwater.

After a pizza party, more cleaning and unpacking, and a round of drinks in the garden, my family left us to settle in.

Kessian was still re-planting his garden when dusk fell. I helped him with the last seedlings despite my aversion to dirt under my nails, and when the primroses were all lining the front flower bed, he finally stopped and sat back to rub a knot in his spine and say, "I think I'm going to regret trying to get it all done in one day tomorrow."

I slipped an arm around his waist. "The bathtub in this place is huge. I could run it for you."

"Is it big enough for two?"

"We can find out."

His eyes flashed bright blue. The magic of the strid had never quite left him, and it was particularly vibrant now. "Lead the way."

"First, I have a gift for you, too."

"A massage with a happy ending?"

"No. Well—Yes, *ahem*. If you wanted, that too, but I was referring to something else."

Dusting my hands on my jeans, I helped him up off the grass. He winced, spine popping as he stretched. He followed me into the house, where I picked up a tin of paint from the cupboard under the stairs.

"I think my arms will snap off like toothpicks if I try to get painting done after all that gardening."

"You don't have to do it, but look." I showed him the color label. *Baked cherry.* "I figured we could paint our bedroom door with it. Maybe a different color for every room in the house?"

His smile melted into something more secretive and fond, and he didn't have words, but he linked our pinkies together and ducked his head into my shoulder.

He made us drinks while I ran the bath, conjuring a few rose petals and lighting a candle. Kessian and my combined possessions could not begin to fill the house, but he'd had enough suncatchers to put one in every window. The study still needed renovations from the fire, and after clearing nearly everything out, we'd discovered even more clocks in the loft. I'd kept a few reminders of Grandad, but I was ready to call the place my own rather than linger in the past. In the year to come, I wondered what colors we'd paint each room, what kind of art would go on the walls, how many hobbies Kessian could collect in the room I'd set aside for his crafts. Would I open a ceramics shop, maybe next to Witches and Stitches?

I found that I didn't know for certain what the future held, but for the first time in a long time, I liked dreaming of it.

Kessian came in with our drinks on a tray balanced on one arm. I took it from him and set it on the windowsill.

"How romantic," he said of the rose petals.

I started undoing the buttons of his shirt. "It's our first night living together."

"We practically lived together already."

"Yes, but now it's official."

He looked at me with a queer vulnerability, fingers hooked in the belt loops of my jeans. His shrugged out of his shirt. I peppered one shoulder with a kiss while sliding off his trousers. While he climbed into the water, I shed all my clothes and got in behind him. He took my arms, looping them around his shoulders like a scarf, leaned back and let out the longest, most contented sigh.

I trickled water over his chest, leaving a trail of goose bumps. I kissed his nape and kneaded the knot in his shoulder with my thumb. I'd sink my hand below the rose petals later. For now, I wanted to scrub out every weary line of tension in his muscles.

"Did you really think I was going to say no?" he murmured.

"Mm?"

"To moving in together. Did you think I wasn't coming today?"

I hesitated. "I knew it was a big step. I wouldn't have blamed you if you needed time."

"When I arrived today, you looked . . ."

"Stressed?"

"Up a notch from stressed. Freaked out."

I sighed, drawing swirls in the fine, damp hairs at the nape of his neck. "I didn't want to scare you off."

"Scared is the last thing I am right now." He tilted his head back so he could look at me. "Maybe if we'd met six years ago when it had all been fresh, I'd have second-guessed moving in with anyone. But after knowing you, I doubt it. I meant what I said at Fae's wedding back then. I'd want to know how this story goes regardless of how it ends, because every day with you has been worth it. This is the safest I've ever felt."

He kissed me, slow and blooming into something more. His tongue danced with mine, the water whispering against the lip of the tub as he shifted to get a better angle, and when his legs spread as wide as the bath would allow, I followed my impulse from earlier. It wasn't long before we were getting water and rose petals on the floor. When he'd finished, he turned, took me in hand, and the glide of his tongue against mine made me see stars behind my eyelids.

There was something awkwardly endearing about watching him get out of the bath after that with his legs shaking.

"Should we upgrade your cane to a walker?"

"Shut up. You made me cum so hard I've got jelly legs."

I helped him dry off. Really, it was just an excuse to keep touching him. By the time we'd navigated around all the boxes we had yet to unpack and collapsed into bed, the house had settled into its night sounds—creaks and bumps and peculiar hissing in the eaves.

But no ticking clocks.

Lunaris appeared as we were drifting off to sleep to tell me proudly, "I have dispatched no less than two dozen spiders."

"Thank you. It wouldn't be home without your dedication."

"Or without me."

"That's what I meant."

"And him," she added, looking at Kessian tucked against my side. "Some days I worried you would run forever."

I looked at the man in my arms, counted the stars on his cheeks, and felt no need to make any wishes at all.

"I think I'm here to stay."

ACKNOWLEDGMENTS

No two books of mine have ever been written the same way. I tend to outline most of my stories, but this one resisted my attempts, and in the end I wrote it one way, and then rewrote it another, and then rewrote it again. It was nothing like the other two Rune Tithe books, except that I still had all the same friends, family, and colleagues fighting in my corner, and in many ways I think they're a part of the reason I keep finishing things.

I first want to thank Monica Bacatello Guerra for reading both versions of this book and gently telling me that the one I'd abandoned and hadn't finished yet was better. (You were right.)

I also want to thank my incredible agent, Ellen, who was the one to suggest Taliesin's magic caravan should be his familiar. What an ingenious way to free me from having to write double the number of characters every time witches appear on the page.

I would not have been able to write the passive aggressive family funeral with the same textural realism that it has without the help of Cait. That makes it sound like she's an expert in passive aggression. No, she's just Irish and funerals are a whole thing.

Thank you Mary Ann for being an early reader, working out time travel paradoxes, and reassuring me that even my pantsed novels somehow work out.

This book was written rapid fire so unfortunately the rest of my acknowledgements will follow suit. To my entire publishing team at Podium, who didn't tut at me when I decided to rewrite this book (again). In particular, my editors Melissa Frain, Crystal Wang, and Felix Chau Bradley for polishing *Wanderlust* until it shone. Thank you Laura Vorhees, Stephanie Beard, and Taylor Bryon for all your hard work behind the scenes.

Thank you to all my writer friends for the craft chats and sanity check-ins, in particular Astra, Avrah, August, Cee, Sio, Mary Ann, Monica, Niamh, Erin, and Steve.

Thanks also to my friends who let me have a life outside my made-up worlds. (Or sometimes give me a different world to take a holiday in.) Cait, Fen, Sam, Becca, the Vien Con crew, Aiden, Isaac, Steph, Kat, Elliot, Alexis, Natalie, Manuela, Helen, Jonny, Helenx2, and Will, you're all so cool. What are you doing with me, huh?

Big thanks to my family for supporting me in all the ways that you do: Mom, Dad, Marney, Shannon, Jenna, Duncan, Ben, and the littles, Burke and Maeve. Love you so much.

Thanks also to the booksellers out there who are championing my book while I still have to Google, "What is marketing?" But particularly Katie Steele and Book Lovers Bookshop, who hosted my first author event and have probably (definitely) sold more copies than I have. Thanks also go to Faecrate for the special edition, which is gorgeous!

Lastly, thank you, dear reader, for picking up my books, for reading them, for spending your valuable time with my characters and my words. Much love.

ABOUT THE AUTHOR

Alistair Reeves is a romantasy author whose stories feature messy queers and morally gray characters. His influences range from video games to Chinese danmei, and when he's not writing, he can be found playing *Dungeons & Dragons* or tending to his frankly absurd collection of succulents. Born in Canada, Reeves now lives in England, indulging his addictions to hot beverages and rainy weather.

FOR A GOOD TIME
follow us on our socials

 podiumentertainment.com

 @podiumentertainment

 /podiumentertainment

 @podium_ent

 @podiumentertainment